MW01657219

IN SERVICE OF HIS MASTER

Balbir Singh Ragi

Publisher: Warwick Group International | Vacaville, CA
ISBN: 978-0-9991117-1-0
Card Catalogue Number: 2017909748
Title: In Service of His Master | Balbir Singh Ragi
Digital distribution | Warwick Group International, 2017
Paperback | Warwick Group International, 2017

DEDICATION

Dedicated to my dear wife Parminder, who has given me unconditional love and encouraged me and sees the best in me. It was with her continuous support and encouragement that I am able to complete this book.

My children Amrit, Aman and Omar and their spouses Gurrinder, Rajwinder and Sonia who have given Parminder and I a life full of happiness and Joy.

To our three Grandsons who are the source of my inspiration, my eldest, Daya, who only sees the best in everyone, and taught me that everything, is possible. My Jai, the one with the twinkle in his eyes, he has taught me how to laugh from my heart. My Fateh Baaz, my joy, who's hugs gives me comfort and make everything in life come together.

INTRODUCTION

It was the start of a brand new decade, the fifties. The Second World War had finished just barely five years earlier. Indian independence was new and the wounds of the partition for most of the Sikhs were still raw on their memories. Many of them had lost their homes and land and picked up what they had and loaded it on a bullock cart few years earlier and had moved to the east side of Punjab while the Muslims moved west. If there is one tragedy, if there are levels of tragedies that one can ever define, then this would have been one that rates at the top of the pages of history.

The Mountbatten Plan set into play the division of India and Punjab. With a stroke of a pen, an Englishman by the name of Sir Cyril Radcliffe drew the line that forever not only divided the great land of Punjab but also the hearts of its people, people that once sat under the banyan tree deep into the moonlit night and laughed and sang ballads of Mirza and Heer. (Legendary lovers of Punjab).

People who laughed together, shared in each other's' festivities and were protectors of each other's' honors had become enemies of each other. The mob rule took over the centuries-old relationships went to hell. Mob rule ensued. People that lived in harmony for centuries were out for each other's blood.

Once landowners and Jagirdars (Lords) now became gypsies loading all they had on a bullock cart and had to move east into an unknown future. Sir Cyril Radcliff seeing the mayhem that the lines he drew caused refused the compensation offered to him, a small solace to his mind for the countless death and destruction his pen had caused.

Over the course of next several years as lands were allocated people settled into their new villages, where lands allocated to them. There was a general distrust between the new arrivals and the old villagers. Those that had gone from the Doab (land between river Beas and Sutlej is referred to as Doab and people from this area who bought land in west Punjab were referred to as Bariae or from the Baar.

People who were from the west and moved to the east after partition were generally seen as outsiders, often referred to as Panhgheer meaning refugees. Or lahoriye, from the Lahore district.

As these people started to settle in, India started to move towards a republic, the mistreatment and the promises made by Nehru, Gandhi and other Congress members were already starting to take shape. The language issue of how Punjabi was not be counted as a language but a dialect, Sikh not being an individual quam (race or Community) and the Hindu marriage act which included Sikhs to name a few.

As Indian Concept of the new freedom under Nehru was taking shape, it was in India where Sikhs were not going to feel the glow of freedom or get political freedoms as equal participants of the independence. Even though their numbers in the fight for the independence be it on the gallows, in front of a firing line, cannons, jails or the loss of land and limb at the hands of mobs was no less than the Hindu Majority.

Sikhs would suffer and be humiliated as the hand of time would turn and the coming years would bear witness to the events of Punjab being split further into three, Punjabi language once again suffering defeat, the attack on Harmander Sahib (Golden Temple.) The riots of 84 would leave Sikhs wondering where they belong.

CHAPTER ONE

Migration of the Sikhs

Because of the amount of land to each Jat Sikhs in the Doaba was not sufficient. Their pioneer spirit taught them always to look at life as an adventure. The migration started at the end of the nineteenth century to places like east Africa to build the railway systems and to Canada to work in the lumber mills around Vancouver and Vancouver Island to places like Victoria and Port Albany.

The people from the village of Paldi built a town near Nainmo on Vancouver Island Canada that they named after their ancestral village Paldi. This still exists today, although it has fallen on bad times due to changes in Lumber mill relocations and people moving to bigger cities.

Some of these people slipped across the border into United States from Canada into Washington and Oregon states to work in the lumber industry, on the railroad lines as they were being extended.

Some of them moved further along into California into towns like Yuba City where the current council comprises of two Sikh council members, Kashmir Gill and Tej Mann.

The number one peach producer of the world or the "peach king" of the world as he is referred to is one Didar Singh Bains. Bains heirs from Nanagal in the district of Hoshiarpur in Punjab. Bains is married to Santi. Santi is the daughter of Preetam Singh Poonia of Jeendowal (village near Banga in the district of Bhagat Singh Nagar in Punjab). Poonia was married to Divan Singh' daughter, Divan Singh's wife belonged to a French-Mexican family. Divan Singh moved to the U.S. from Khairan village (near Banga, district Bhagat

Singh Nagar in Punjab) in the early part of the Twentieth century.

Divan Singh purchased land in Arizona, an arid and dry state. He started cotton farming and devised a system to irrigate his land. He is mentioned in the Arizona state schoolbooks as Divan Singh the man who gave water to the desert.

As Sikhs grew in prosperity in the first part of twentieth century, they began to farm the land and also take up causes. Some of the Sikhs worked on the Holt family farms around Stockton California (you will know the Holt family from the Caterpillar equipment that is used around the world for moving dirt and in buildings). During the weekend, they would come to Stockton; Stockton back then was a party town a port town.

This is where they worked and partied and later created the Khalsa Divan Society, in which Sant, Teja Singh who had a big hand in along with opening the doors of the first Gurdwara (Sikh Temple) in 1929.

This Gurdwara is made most historic because of the association it has with the Gadhar Movement, (Indian Independence movement by US Indians). Most Gurdwara members were supporters of the Gadhar movement; Lala Hardyal who was a professor of Indian Philosophy at Stanford was part of this movement. The Gadhari Babas as they are referred to now (Revolutionary fathers) also acquired a building located at 5 Wood Street in San Francisco California, this is where they would meet and it was the official headquarters of the organization. They would print revolutionary magazine from here called Gadhar Goonj (revolutionary voice) and mailed it around the world. This building is now under the control of the Indian Consulate of San Francisco and is pretty much an empty relic and is not frequented by the US Sikhs.

When I arrived in California, I met with Kesar Singh Dhillon, who lived in Oakland California, on the other side to the bay from San Francisco, him and Makhan Singh in

Stockton were the only two surviving members of the Gadhar movement. Kesar Singh Dhillon had the original printing press that the Gadhars used to print their newspaper *"The Gadhar Goonj"* in his basement. He urged me to take what I could. I told him that I would come back once I had settled in and take it from him for safeguard. Unfortunately before I could get to it, he passed away and a fire engulfed most of the documents. The Printing Press did survive, and some members of the Sikh Youth group retrieve it, it is displayed in the museum for the Gadhri Baba in the Stockton Gurdwara.

The second Gurdwara opened in the town of El Centro near the border of Mexico and U. S. Most of the people that lived in El Centro grew watermelons and melons. Indians could not buy land in the US until 1948. So they married local girls of Mexican heritage in order to buy land and put it on their names and once a male offspring was born they would swap the title to the child's name.

You will find in El Centro people with Punjabi last Jat names like Sangha, Dhillon, Bains, Gill. These people pay homage to both of their ethnicities Sikhism and Catholicism.

Most of them practice Catholicism; according to the Priest at the Gurdwara on special event they will attend the El Centro Gurdwara. However, with the passage of time, this is becoming less and less. The Gurdwara is now managed by the newer arrival Sikhs who have moved into El Centro, which comprise of doctors and other professionals. The past mayor of El Centro was a man by the name of Dave Dhillon. He was very proud of his heritage and was honored by most California Sikhs as the being the first mayor of Sikh descent.

It was this area that the first ever Asian Member of Congress Dr. Dulip Singh Saund was elected. Dr. Saund's brother who held a high position with the Indian Railway system also visited the Coventry Gurdwara.

CHAPTER TWO

The world of Technology and A Sikh named Narinder Singh Kapany

The world as we know would really not exist if it were not for one Sikh, that Sikh is Narinder Singh Kapany.

The advances in medical surgery and diagnostics or the advances in telecommunications, networking or storage would never have been possible had it not been for the discovery of how to bend light. Narinder Singh Kapany as a PhD student in London's Imperial College discovered how to bend light using fiber Optics in the earlier part of the fifties.

Kapany's lineage dates back to his family that managed the Patna Sahib Gurdwara in the early eighteen hundreds. It was his paternal great-great-grandfather who commissioned two Janam Sakhis (biography) of Guru Nanak founder of Sikhism, one of which is now on permanent display at the Asian Art Museum in San Francisco California USA.

His Grandfather Sardar Nagina Singh was a session judge in Maharaja Bhupinder Singh of Patiala's State. His father Sardar Sundar Singh was in the Royal Air Force during the First World War. His mother's parents were from Moga, their estate comprised of several villages, included the village of Sodhiwala, named after his mother's side of the family Sodhi's

Kapany was born in Moga at his maternal parent's home and raised in Dehra Dun where the family moved.

He attended Dehra Dun College. This is associated with Agra University. He showed great promise as a young lad in physics and thus majored in Mathematics, Physics, and chemistry. He told me that the idea of light had always intrigued him. While in his physics class, one of the professors stated to the class “light can only travel in straight lines, it can’t be bent.”

He said he disagreed with him and said so, to which the Professor replied, “Kapany, it’s impossible.”

So it was that the idea of how to bend light became his mission and his life’s goal.

He went straight from being an undergraduate student to being accepted by one of the most prestigious engineering colleges throughout the world, the Imperial college of science and technology of London into a PhD program. It was here that he evolved his thesis and demonstrated the use of optical fibers to the Royal Society. The Royal Society was so impressed that they offered him a full scholarship to do his research.

While studying he met his wife Satinder, a fellow student at the University of London, they were married at the Shepherd’s Bush Gurdwara in London

Once he had developed his thesis and had enough work under his belt, he was ready to deliver his findings. At a meeting, held in Florence Italy, he said,

“I was a bit nervous. I had forty-two foils (these were used as slides are today), and I was allotted ten minutes to present my foils.”

Kapany said, “I was only on my first slide when the chairperson told him that your ten minutes were up. “But by then he had the convened audience pretty well intrigued, that they asked the chairperson to let him finish his presentation.

By the time, he completed his presentation, he was the center of attention, and an American professor quickly got hold of him and asked to meet with him over lunch. The Professor was the director for the Institute of Optics, University of Rochester, , New York, Professor asked him to move to the US.

Kapany told the professor that U.S was not in his future plans, he wanted to move back to India and start a factory, but the professor convinced him that he could do a lot more for himself and the world by being in the U.S.

Upon completion of his PhD Kapany did move to the US and continued teaching and research at the University of Rochester for two years, later moved to work with IIT Research Institute in Chicago and Produced a large number of new patents to his name.

He was in New York to meet a family friend, Maharaja Yadvindra Singh of Patiala (son of Maharaja Bhupinder Singh) who was on one of his United Nations visits. While having lunch someone from the back table shouted, "your highness, there was one of you, now there are two of you, the world better watch out."It was Krishna Menon, who was the head of the Indian delegation to United Nation as well as being the Defense Minister of India. Menon asked Kapany to come and see him the following day at his hotel. Kapany met with Menon and Menon told him that he return home and help rebuild India, which was in need of technical skills of his caliber. Krishna Menon always referred to Kapany as "Chicago Singh"

Kapany went back to India to meet and discuss his options with Krishna Menon. Menon arranged for Kapany to meet with the Indian Prime Minister Nehru. He relayed his meeting with Nehru to me.

He told me, "Balbir, if we can put aside for a minute what Nehru did to the Sikhs and just look at him as a man. He was a brilliant mind, a great thinker who held you in his awe."

Nehru pulled out a thick file and said, "Kapany this is you. Young man, we have been tracking you and we want you to come home and help us build the modern India."

He said that Nehru wrote a note to the chairman of the Union Public Services Commission to give Kapany a letter of appointment.

Later, that week, he met with Menon again who had invited all the heads of other organizations of which one would be the one he would be replacing. Menon inquired if the letter of appointment was ready?

To which man replied, "Sir it's in the signature loop."

Menon asked what was the hold up to which the person replied, “Sir it’s the salary it is highest of anyone, and it is a bit unusual for such a young person.”

Kapany said it was Menon’s question, which alarmed him.

Menon asked the man, “Is it because that he is young? Or that he is a Sikh?”

Kapany immediately said, “Sir among us scientist religion does not play a role.”

To this day, Kapany said that one question had stuck with him.

The letter of appointment was supposed to arrive in thirty days, but it took nine months, by that time he had invented much more and was fully engrossed in his work and had decided to move to California where the Silicon Valley was just starting to evolve, and he became a serial entrepreneur.

The deep-rooted love for his Sikh religion and ethnicity never left him. He started The Sikh foundation in the year 1967, perhaps the second Sikh Organization in the USA.

On one of his trips to visit his dear friend Pritam Singh Poonia of Yuba City (of Jindowal Village, Didar Singh Bain’s father law) Poonia brought up the idea of building a Gurdwara in Yuba City. Poonia informed him that there were two factions in Yuba City between the Sikhs, and they can’t agree on anything so nothing gets done. Poonia requested Kapany to mediate; both parties were called to a meeting and allowed to air their differences.

Kapany said he asked them simple questions, “Your differences are with each other not with your Guru?”

They all agreed that this was so. He further asked them to think of their children and their children and would they think that Catholics or Jews would be without a place of worship?

He informed them to remember their history saying, “Where ever the Sikhs have gone, they have built a place of their Guru along with their own home, will you not?”

He offered to donate toward this Gurdwara in the amount of five thousand dollars (tidy sum of money in the early sixties). Once he gave the first amount the money started to pour in from everyone and all the rich farmers from both side of table. Few years later, the third Gurdwara in USA was erected in Yuba City.

He is an avid collector of Sikh art and Antiquities. His house has one of the finest collections of Sikh art and books that I have seen. He knows the history of each piece to the minor detail. He has been instrumental in establishing three Sikh Study Chairs at University of California at Santa Barbara, Riverside, and Santa Cruz. I have worked with him in establishing Punjabi classes at University of California at Berkeley and also University of San Jose California. He continues to promote symposiums at Universities so that Sikhism will have its place in academia along with other major religions of the world.

Kapany has been instrumental in promoting international displays of Sikh Artifacts of which one of them was the Maharaja Ranjit Singh's throne in museums around the world from San Francisco, Washington DC, New York USA to London UK and Toronto Canada.

The world owes a debt of gratitude to this Sikh with a jolly demeanor and a haughty laugh, who maintains a state of Chardi Kala (an exalted state of mind) at all times. Without his determination to prove to his professor that yes you can bend light the world as we know it would not exist.

He reminds me of the old Banyan tree in the villages of Punjab under whose shade people sit but forget that the Banyan tree gives shade without asking for anything in return. Just content that people are happy.

At his advanced age, he is in his office every morning, and he is there until the end of the day working for the Sikhs in some way or another, an email or letter or a phone call on behalf of the Sikhs. He has a bust of Maharaja Ranjit Singh (Sikh Maharaja) in front of his desk and on his back wall; he has an original painting of KAR SEVA (congregational service of cleaning the holy tank of the Golden temple at Amritsar) His computer sits on the credenza facing his desk.

He told me you with a jolly laugh, “Balbir, I am the luckiest man alive, truly blessed, truly blessed, when I face my desk, I look at my Maharaja and when I face my computer, I face my Guru, who can ask for more?”

Each day he does the bidding of his guru a gift that he got from his lineage from his ancestors.

CHAPTER THREE

History of more Gurdwaras in California

Yuba City Gurdwara at Terra Buena Road Opened in 1969, the split faction from Didar Singh and Poonia side would open their own Gurdwara on Boug Road in 1979.

El Sobrante and Fremont cities would be where the next two Gurdwara would be opened. I arrived in San Francisco in 1972, we were involved with a handful of other Sikhs who founded the Fremont Gurdwara committee in 1976 and in three years we had opened the doors to the Fremont Gurdwara. We would go to Stockton for Gurpurbs and it was on Guru Nanak's Gurpurub in Stockton that I urged the San Francisco Sangat to work toward opening a Gurdwara in the San Francisco Bay Area.

Sikhs are the most prominent agriculturist in California. The numbers speak for themselves. 95% of all the peaches, 60% prunes and 20% almond and walnuts grown in Yuba City are grown by Sikhs. In the southern part of the state in Bakersfield and Fresno, 20% of all the grapes are grown by Sikhs.

It is well worth noting that 70% of all the Almonds grown throughout the world come from California. So the contribution of the Sikhs to world food is a formidable force.

The Sikh community of the San Francisco Bay Area was starting to grow; most of the early students who came to study in US were starting to gather in the area due to the availability of professional jobs, the educational system and also the weather.

Most of the earlier arrivals were engineers or small businessmen; Parminder my wife was the initial Sikh

Registered Nurse to join a major hospital health system. Gurpartap Basrai a pharmacist was already in Fremont, and he was instrumental in bringing Anmol Singh Mahal to Fremont. Gurpartap (Gary as he is commonly referred to, is from the village of Mehli near Phagwara. Anmol Singh Mahal was the first Sikh doctor to open his practice in Fremont. His family belongs to Mahal Gehlan his father went to Banga High school with my papajee he went on to become a doctor and moved to Dehli. Anmol opened his medical practice in Fremont California in 1978 and two years later my Younger brother Kashmira Singh opened his practice, and it opened the doors for many more other Sikh doctors to move into the area and open their practices.

As high-tech industry was picking up steam in the Bay Area, what was later to be called the Silicon Valley, I had established myself in the Bay Area and started working as an executive for a multinational hi-tech corporation, I was the youngest executive in the corporation, I moved from engineering very quickly into management and into the an executive role.

Sikhs from all walks of life were taking up position in every field, from teachers to truckers. It was a sight to see the occasional truck with some line from a Punjabi song written on the side of the truck. One would feel the sense of pride. It is simply the norm to see trucks that will read Doab trucking to Malava (areas of Punjab) trucking. Some of them are named after their favorite Sant (evangelist preachers).

Silicon Valley has rewarded most of the Sikhs well, some of us that have been in it for a while and made it our home. Ajaib Singh Bahdare who migrated from Gravsend UK is one of the stars of the Silicon Valley. Ajaib was co-founder of a company called Cerent, which was sold to Cico System in the late nineties for over 7 billion dollars. I saw one time how much the queen of England's net worth was, and I mused to Ajaib that he was richer than the queen of England.

CHAPTER FOUR

The Growth of the Diaspora in other parts of the world

Sikhs, mainly from the Doab area went to Fiji, others were going to Canada or USA. Fiji being a British colony had sugar plantations and lumber industry. The English being English, needing low to no paying help got around the slave trade by creating what was commonly referred to as “Grirmit” which actually meant an "Agreement”. What the English did was devised a method whereby, they went to the poorest part of India, mostly the state of Bihar and part of Uttera Pradesh area and signed up people on an indentured agreement and then shipped them off to the Island wherever the labor was required. Even today if you are to visit most of the Caribbean islands and also places such as the British Guyana and Fiji you will find descendants of these people living and practicing the religion of their forefathers both Hindus and Muslim.

Idea was that at the end of the agreement these people would be paid some sum of money along with their fare back and would be allowed to return to their homeland or be allowed to stay in the country as free man and women. The English knew that once the people were there after the certain lapse in time they would marry, create a home and not want to return. For the large part, this is exactly what took place.

The Sikhs, however, did not go to Fiji under such a plan they went as free men. For most of them, Fiji was only a stopping point to their destination, which was either New Zealand, Australia, or to Canada or USA.

Only a handful of them made it, majority of them either stayed or married, some also married local Hindu girls others came back to India and married and returned. Others like my Father, Papajee who spent time there but later would move to New Zealand and back to India afterward to Britain.

The First Gurdwara in Fiji was built even before the one in USA. The Fijian Sikhs established their Gurdwara as early as 1922.

One of the early priests (Bhai) of the Suva Gurdwara was Giani Ajaib Singh from our ancestral village Herian. I only have very vague memory of him but what I do remember is that he was a very upstanding Sikh and would never shy away from saying it like it was.

Papajee told me, Giani Jee was a force to be reckoned with, he told me every month there was a day that he would conduct a service for the Sikhs who were in Jail in Fiji. He would make sure that the doors of the jail remained open as long as the Guru Granth Sahib was Parkash (services were in session) in the hall inside the Jail. He told the warden that once the guru is on your premises this is not your place it is the Guru's place.

CHAPTER FIVE

The Sikhs in New Zealand

The initial recorded Sikhs to arrive in New Zealand were two Jat Sikh brothers from Chirak village near Moga in the Malwa area of Punjab. Of the two Bir Singh arrived first, he traveled through Hong Kong to Australia. When his family did not hear from him, they sent the younger brother Phuman Singh to bring him home. Younger brother finally caught up with Bir Singh his older brother in Australia. They decided to go to New Zealand where they settled, according to McLeod married local girls. Between the years 1889 to 1910 there were only a handful of Punjabis, mostly Jat Sikhs from Malwa and Manjha but after 1910 when the opportunity to enter Canada and USA dried up. Doab Jat Sikhs looked towards Fiji and most of them first traveled to Fiji and then to New Zealand. The only requirement to enter New Zealand was that the person had to be able to complete an alien immigrant form in any European language the immigrant chose. Some of the Sikh living in Fiji got tuition and could complete this form and entered New Zealand as legal immigrants. One of them was my Grand Uncle Karam Singh.

Like the Sikhs in USA, the Sikhs in New Zealand also formed an association in1927 to help in the struggle in the Indian Independence movement to which my Grand Uncle Karam Singh is a signatory. His elder brother Watan Singh was active in India at the same time in the Congress party. My grandfather was asked to manage the family affairs.

Papajee were five brothers and a sister. He was number three, younger than him was his sister and then there were two other younger brothers. My Grand Uncle on becoming legal in New Zealand came back to India and adopted my eldest Thaiajee (term used to refer to your father's elder brother) Mangal Singh as his son and took him with him to New Zealand in mid-1920's.

He later asked my grandfather to interrupt the education of my younger thaiajee Sarwan Singh and papajee and drop them off in New Zealand. My grandfather Udham Singh took my thaiajee Sarwan Singh and Papajee and boarded a ship from Colombo Sri Lanka for Fiji. The idea was that they would visit Fiji and when the ship docked in New Zealand, they would get off the ship. Papajee and thaia jee would stay behind and Babajee (term used to refer to paternal grandfather) would board another ships and return to Punjab. Grand Uncle Karam Singh chalked out the plan. One man caught wind of the plan and informed the authorities. Someone informed Granduncle Karam Singh that authorities had been informed. This man told him if your brother and nephews come off the ship they are going to be arrested.

Granduncle Karam Singh was a very smart and cunning individual. He knew how to handle just about any situation. When the ship docked he dressed himself up took off his pagh (turban) and put on a hat and went on the ship. He told my grandfather not to leave the ship. The three of them stayed on the ship and returned to Punjab.

Granduncle Karam Singh considered this as a personal dishonor and was not about to take it likely. He was determined to bring them back to New Zealand, even if it was for a visit. He targeted a job on a judge's farm and befriended the family (we would receive letters from the judge's family all the way to Papajee's passing).

Grand Uncle asked the judge to intervene on his behalf to secure visitor's visas for the three of them, my grandfather, Papajee and Thaiajee. He brought them to New Zealand and called a meeting of the New Zealand Indian Association and stood three of them up and said, “They stand here before you, if the person that did the BHANI (informed) wants to tell anyone, please feel free because they are here on a legal visa.”

Judge asked him to make sure that they returned and not overstay, and they did come back to India.

Papajee would return to Fiji again in the early 30s and would spend time in New Zealand on and off with his uncle and brother, no one would now dare to challenge them as they had befriended the local judge who knew he was there illegally.

The three of them later purchased some cows of their own and would co-milk with the Judge's herd. This meant that they would work the judge's farm and in return, they would be allowed grazing right for their cows on his land.

They eventually purchased a Stud of their own, which is still in the family today. Known as Mt. Cosy Stud, located in the town of Otorohanga on the north island.

They started breeding bloodline Jersey cows and the first one to win an award was a cow by the name of Pretty Primula. The offspring's of this cow now are in some of the best dairies farms around the world.

Some people of note have visited the family stud, among them being Late Surinder Kaur Badal, (wife of the chief minister of Punjab) and the late Khuswant Singh, (a noted Indian journalist) who wrote an article in Illustrated Weekly of his visit.

The first woman to arrive in New Zealand was Daya Kaur, wife of Ganda Singh Khangura, she arrived in 1907. It would not be until 1918 that the next woman would arrive, and that was Fahiman, wife of Hakim Singh of Karnana from the Doab area.

The first Sikh wedding to take place would have to wait until November 26th, 1932, and it was the marriage of the eldest daughter of Phuman Singh Kooner, Kartari of the village Rurki in Jullunder District to Surain Singh Somal of the village Sultanpur in the district Jullunder. Their son Harbail who is a justice of the peace is married to my eldest Thaiajee Mangal Singh's younger daughter Gurjeet Kaur Ragi.

First Gurdwara to be built in New Zealand was in the town of Hamilton, which was central to all the population prior to the arrival of newer immigrants who sort political asylum after 1984. (In June of 1984 Prime Minister Indira Gandhi's forces attacked the Golden temple, aftermath of which was murderous in Punjab for the next two decades, and people left Punjab for other countries in search of political asylum) most of those people that came to New Zealand settled in or around the capital Auckland. There are many gurdwaras in Auckland itself.

Sikhs of New Zealand can now boast of Sikh Member of Parliament. The first Sikh Barrister to be called to the bar was my niece Veena Kaur Ragi.

Sikhs are now in every walk of life in New Zealand, although on my visit there I did notice that the earlier arrivals do not mix well with later arrivals. This is in part that the earlier arrivals are second or third generation and their cultural values and also their Punjabi is from the 20s 30's era. And when you speak with them, you will hear them use words that have long gone from the current Punjabi. It is a walk through the pages of history when you speak with them. Most of these earlier families have white New Zealanders in their families through marriage. They have adopted the European culture but have held onto their roots as well.

On our Parminder (my wife) and my first visit there we felt like that we were walking down the pages of family history.

Growing up, papajee would often tell us stories of his time in New Zealand. One that stuck in my mind particularly was of how he cleared this hill of weeds and made it usable. Kashmir (my younger brother) and I would chuckle and say it's a bit of a stretch of the imagination that a man can clean a hill like that.

When we were in New Zealand my cousin Nirmal, drove us around and said, "Let me show you something."

He drove us to this hill near town and said, "See that hill, well it used to be full of weeds and your dad cleaned it single handed." I had to call Kashmir and let him know that it was really true, papajee had cleared the hill of weeds, and we had just visited the hill. When we went into, town everyone still remembered him as the man who cleaned the hill. I felt very proud that day. Kashmir was astonished when I told him that the legend was really true.

CHAPTER SIX

Sikhs in South America

Not much research has been done on the Sikhs in South America. Most of the Sikhs arrived here around the turn of the twentieth century. Many of them came to Panama during the building of the Panama Canal and stayed. Some of them then moved south to Argentina. Most of them like the early settlers to USA never made it back to Punjab. They married local women and settled in their perspective chosen countries.

One of them was my maternal granduncle, who left a wife and a son and migrated to Argentina from Bharomazara Punjab.

Papajee tracked him down and communicated with him through letters, but he seemed more interested in trying to get financial help than with the family. Communication was cut off with him after some initial financial help that was provided to him. There was one Sikh family that lived by the Mosque just off Eagle Street in Coventry UK. The gentleman's name was Munsha Singh. He had gone back to India then came to England was one of the few that left Argentina. He married late in life, and he was a regular at the Coventry Gurdwara. His family moved to the Holbrook area. I ran to his daughter on the bus on one of my visits to Coventry.

George Bawa Singh was the chief Justice of the supreme court of Belize. His father was an immigrant Sikh. George Bawa Singh was born a Sikh but later converted to Christianity.

There is some evidence that there were Sikhs in Cuba also that worked the local sugar plantations, again like the most other Sikhs in South America, it was a way to enter the USA.

Since Cuba is only ninety miles from Florida, these people were hoping to make the boat journey to the shores of Florida and enter USA and make their way from there to California.

Chapter Seven

Sikhs in England

India being a colony of the British Empire, Indians were coming and going from England freely without a need for any visa. After the war and the independence and partition of India as previously mentioned Sikhs were feeling that in order for them to expand the family wealth they needed to look elsewhere than India. With the division of Punjab, the land opportunities became much smaller. Some of the Sikh were looking to Tehrai area in the Uttra Pardesh state of India for land leases but it was a tough proposition. It meant clearing Jungles to get to the land, similar to what has happened in the Amazon, country needed lumber and agricultural land for food.

Papajee (I am referring to my father S. Dharam Singh Ragi. Although most people called my father Dharam Singh but actually that was not his whole name, his complete name. His actual name was Manga Dharam Singh.) I asked Papajee about his full name and why it was unusual? "Why did Dharam had Manga in front of it. As he explained to me was that his mother, my grandmother, said that she named him Manga first because it means to ask for, and his mother always wanted him to ask for faith which was his second name Dharam which meant faith. So he was named Manga Dharam so that his name would remind him to always ask God for faith and thus always to remain in his service. To his last day, he lived up to his name. I say this not because he is my father, but as an objective observer of his life. He served his community only as a sewadar (servant) not as an official (Audhedaar).

He too was also looking at going to Tehrai and participating in acquiring a land lease. He was adept in cutting down jungles from his time in Fiji; he thought that this experience would help him. I asked him how it was that he was going to Terhai and ended up in England? As he relayed the story to me as to how he ended up in England. He said that he was on his way to Terhai and met a man by the name of Karam Singh from our village at the railway station who told him that he was on his way to Dehli to get his passport, and that he was going to go to England as the reconstruction needed the labor force and the entrance into England was a passport and a steamship ticket.

Papajee said that he turned back to the village and discussed this with the family and decided that he needed to send his younger brother who was a wrestler to England first. His brother, he told me had fallen into bad company, and he needed to displace him. So he decided to ship him off to England. The brother would hear nothing of it, unless he promised that he would also join him.

So papajee got a passport for his brother and a steamship ticket and sent him off to Glasgow. He then followed about six months later in 1952 to Glasgow. When he was in a less serious mood, he would tell us of his journey and how some of the other Sikh Passengers who had never left Punjab would have to cope with eating a very different food and the method of eating the food. He would tell us how some of them would try to tackle a small boiled potato and not quite dig their fork and the once they tried to cut the potato. The potato would go flying across the dining room, and they would let out a swear word loud in Punjabi. Or they would say "Dharam Sinha ah dasi kida kattana yaar, eh soot yeaha ne aanda." (Dharam Singh can you show me how to do this, it's not quite working) or how they would grab a handful of the sugar cubes from the dinner table and would be munching them on the deck as if it was candy, while they strolled and talked about their village life or some act of bravery against the British by someone from their village.

Papajee said the journey to Glasgow took about a month. His younger brother was already in Glasgow and where another wrestler from village Mouli by the name of Parkash Singh had moved who my uncle was staying with. Passenger who came on the same ship as my father was Gurdip Singh Gill. He also later moved to Coventry. He is the father of Gurdial Singh (DALO) Shinda Singh and the late Mohinder and Bahadur Singh Gill.

Most of the Sikhs in those days were Hawkers. Work in factories was hard to get for our people. Papajee said he worked, as a hawker for very small time and what he saw was people he was trying to sell to clearly could not afford the stuff he was trying to sell them. There was so much poverty these people barely had enough money to keep food on the table and to sell them stuff they did not need in the first place went against his conscience, and he felt he just could not do it.

He discussed it with his brother and then with Parkash Singh, who said that, "Well, it is not for everyone."

Parkash Singh's family still lives in Glasgow.

Parkash Singh knew someone in Coventry who for ten pounds would get you a job in a factory. So Papajee and his brother caught a train and came to Coventry and paid this man twenty pounds for two jobs in Sterling Metals.

Like Papajee other people started to gather in Coventry in larger numbers around 1952. Most of these people came mainly from two districts, Jullundur, and Hoshiarpur. These two districts have been further split into other districts. Large numbers of these people came alone without their families, with the intent of staying in England for a number of years and then returning to Punjab and increasing their land holding and the dream of a better life in Punjab.

There were few people that had their families very early, one of them was Tara Singh of Didyal village and my in-law's Hazura Singh Barrhowal, to name a few. Some of these people purchased houses as a way of increasing their income. They rented out what amounted to a bed sharing. Where one person would sleep during the day while the other was at work. The day shift person would sleep on it at night when the night shift person was on his shift.

To the credit of these people, they made Punjab an economic powerhouse of India by sending money home to Punjab on a regular basis, by legal means until some Sindhis (people from the state of Sindh now in Pakistan reference here is to Sindhis that moved to India) figured out the Hwara system and then most of the money that went back in the sixties was all through the Hwara.

Coventry being the industrial hub of England saw most of the bombs in the Second World War. The cathedral was destroyed, and many other areas of Coventry stood in ruins. However, it still remained the center of Industrial England in the fifties.

The car industry and all the associated companies were all in Coventry. Triumph, Morris, Massy Ferguson, Dunlop, along with other companies such as Alfred Herbert, GEC and the remainder of the old Coventry industry of weaving, Courtould and the ordinance factory which backed up to our yard at 7 Red Lane. As a child I was always fascinated with what went on behind those walls that had broken glass on top of the walls? What kind of Bombs did they make there? What if one of them went off, our goose would be cooked.

There were lots of bombed out plots of land all over town with broken cars. As kids we would hang out and pretend that we were driving a car. On Guy Fawkes night, November 5th in England is celebrated with the burning of the effigy of Guy Fawkes, who tried to blow up the houses of parliament. Kids let off fireworks also on this night. These vacant lots would all be lit up with bon fires.

Most food items in the early fifties were still given on a ration card. Sikhs wanted butter, and it was rationed, so it was an item that they all protected better than gold in their communal living. All these migrant men learned to make Roti (Punjab flatbread rolled out and baked on a skillet), and Daal Sabzi (curries) Papajee told us it was sort of a shared cook pot and everyone had a turn being the chef of the day.

Most of these people had to cut their hair (Sikhs do not cut their hair, it is one of the five articles of faith) in order to get employment in the foundries and had to fight discrimination through the sixties until the labor laws, and race relation movements came into full swing.

The highest paying jobs in those days were in foundries. Long hair was considered a hazard. Most of these people were attracted to those jobs because of the pay. Furthermore, because someone else they knew worked there, and put in a good word, or developed a system of bribery to the foreman or charge-hand to get other people hired.

Sterling Metal was the highest paying company of the time in Coventry for our people at least, so they all flocked there.

The other popular place was Dunlop, many that Sikhs worked here. Alfred Herbert, a company local to Coventry had some Sikhs. Work was lighter, but it was lower paying also. Some people worked on the building sites. This was also a lower-paying job it served as a placeholder job until a better job in the foundry came along. Mostly, the building laborers were Irish, and Sikhs were not comfortable working with them. As amusing, as it may seem but most Sikhs also had a hierarchy in which they categorized the whites. It went something like this on top of the heap were the English, next came the Scotts and after that the Irish. The poles, Ukrainian, and the Italians did not rate on the scale. It always used to amaze me and Karamjit (Tara Singh Didyal's son) as we would attend and sit in meeting after meeting complaining about race relations and discrimination or Color Bar as it was called back then how our own people had a discriminatory system all worked out yet we didn't like to be discriminated against.

Discrimination was very real. Men's club would not let Sikhs into their club. They were off limits; there were certain Pubs in Coventry (also other towns and cities throughout England) like Red House on Stony Stanton Road that would not allow Sikhs or any person of Color in the pub. There were shops that would not serve Sikh, Indians Jamaicans or people of color. The one that sticks out in my mind was the shop on Stony Stanton Road, not sure if it is still there, but as you came from Eagle Street into Stony Stanton Road, you looked straight at the shop. It was a camera shop. He had a sign in front hanging on his door that read, **"WE ONLY SERVE AN ENGLISHMAN AND HIS LADY."** When I first read the sign, I remember asking Papajee what this was all about. I told him I was just going to walk in there.

He got mad at me he told me, "Why don't you save your energy for bigger causes. Why do you always think of taking every cause?" I wanted to say to him well I am your son. I knew if I did, he was going to give me one of his disapproving look. I just could never bear that look he would give. It was worse than getting hit. It made you feel really stupid. He never laid a hand on us ever, the look was enough, which said I don't approve.

CHAPTER EIGHT

Sikh Businesses in Coventry

There was only one grocery store back then, it was most commonly referred to as "Gejj's Dukaan" (Gejj's shop). This was on Swanswell Road off Stony Stanton Rd right next to the Funeral home. The proprietor was one Gurmej Singh of Shanker Village in Punjab. He was a balding man in his forties and on the heavy side with a potbelly.

I remember he moved at a pretty good speed, for being hefty. This place had everything you could ever imagine, from daals to spices. He had chickens in the back yard for which people would line up on Saturday. Saturday for most Sikhs was one day in the week that was a meat night. Nothing religious, but most of them just made their Chicken on Saturday and went to the pub and come home had a chicken dinner. Guess this was the making of the national dish of England "chicken, Tikka Masala."

By any measure of health standards, Gejj's shop could have been a poster child as to what not to do, but nobody actually paid any mind to it. They got their stuff, shared some stories met some people and stopped and chatted for a while and went on their merry way. By the yardsticks that most of the people were used to back in Punjab, it probably looked like a nice and tidy place.

He was reasonable with his rates, which was pretty commendable considering being the only game in town, he could have charged any rate, and people would have paid. He was one of them, from the same villages, a Sikh, Jat Man, and he felt an affinity to make sure that he made a reasonable profit at the same time served his community. Some of the corporation could have learned a thing or two from old Gej, as he was affectionally referred to.

He later moved his shop to Foleshill Road as it started to become the commercial hub of the community as people started to buy homes around Queen Mary's street area. They purchased their homes in area so they could walk to work to Sterling metals which was close to Queen Mary's Road. Alfred Herbert was on Canal Rd off Cross Road and Dunlop was on Holbrook's lane but still within walking or bus distance of Queen Mary's Road area.

The Wadwani family, who were Sindhi setup their Indian grocery shop on Queen Mary's Road. However, they added a unique feature to the business. They added home delivery. So, where as Gej's shop it was mostly men would go to buy grocery. The Wadwani;s had a van in which they loaded up all the groceries, Flour, other supplies plus vegetables. They would come around mostly on Friday evening when everyone was paid. Employees back then were not paid by check; they were given wages in cash in what was known as a pay packet, change and all. Wadhwani's knew that people were paid and had money to spend. They would come around and knock on the door and take your order and go to the van and fill the order. Get what was due and moved on to the next cluster of streets.

This did give a commercial shock to good old Gej's business. He was a survivor and when Parminder and I left England. He was still in business.

Third grocery shop to open was a bigger store by a young lad from the village Rurka in Punjab, I believe his name was Mohinder, and he apprenticed under the Wadhwani's and later copied their business model and went to the same customers who gave him a chance.

As a teenager, I also worked at the Wadwani's Shop on Queen Mary Street doing bagging as did some of the other young lads as way to learn and earn.

Wadwani family later left Coventry and moved to London

as London was becoming a larger growing market, and the opportunity for expansion was better in London. Most Sindhis follow the Guru Granth Sahib. The Wadwani family came to the Sangrand (Sikh Service on the first of the Sikh calendar are referred to as Sangrand) functions intermittently even though Papajee always welcomed them, and if they missed a Sangrand, he would remind them when they came around on Fridays the date of the next Sangrand. I did think that they felt a little out of place. Some of the Punjabi Sikhs were not very welcoming, to them they Bahia (derogatory remark most Sikhs use for anyone that is a non-Punjabi from India) shopkeeper, how could he be a Sikh? When Papajee tried to explain they would listen out of respect, but you could see they were not buying any of it.

Wadwani's were seen as outsiders and since most of the people that lived in Coventry came from the two districts of Doab, Hoshiarpur and Jullundur everyone else to them was an outsider. Such was the case of one Randhir Singh, who lived in Oliver Street; he later went into business and opened a clothing shop on Harnell Lane east. Randhir Singh was from the Malwa region of Punjab. One of the few, the other one was one Isher Singh, who lived in the Foleshill area. However Randhir Singh was the one that mingled openly and I remember he was always referred to Dhira Malwai (from Malwa).

I remember asking my mother, Beejee one time, why they were referred to as Malwais?

Beejee told me, "That's because they come from that area. They are a bit different than us, you know your sister's mother in law. She is from Malwa."

I was bit a puzzled. What was the difference? They looked the same as me. If Massijee (my sister's mother law) was any measure, then these people were the best. I think this kind of social Darwinism is just in the human makeup that we tend to stick to our familiar environment and reject or view people a little different than us suspiciously.

I still hear the distinction; it still, confuses me and makes me smile. Now I jokingly say, "You're right! I am sure they think the same of us"

We have a family from Muktsar district (in the Malwa region) living close by us here in the USA. Their parents were visiting. The mother asked where we were from in Punjab, and I said Bhagat Singh Nagar, and she said,

"Where is that?"

To which her husband replied, "Oh udar jider de apne puti De sourae nae." (Over yonder where our granddaughter's in-laws are from)

Her reply was, "Oh Asshha pare jai jakae." (Oh ok over there far away).

It's amusing to me how we Punjabis are so feudalistic that we still see ourselves as either as Doabias, Malwais or Majhails.

Now getting back to other businesses owned by a Sikh, there was "Mahane De Kaffee" (Mahan's cafe'). Actually, it was not a café but an Indian restaurant. It used to be on the inner ring road opposite Vine Street on the right-hand side as you came to the city center. The name of the Kaffee, sorry, a restaurant was STANDARD INDIAN restaurant. I am not sure it was named Standard because it held any particular standard, but it was a good name.

I am sure he wanted to convey that it was just not your ordinary place, but of a higher standard. As a child I was fascinated by it, always wanted to go in and take a peek to see what it was like in there. It took years to fulfill that wish. When I was twenty, I went in to have a cup of tea without Papajee knowing about it. If he found out that I went in there he would get really upset that I had taken a wrong path and started eating at HOTELS (restaurants are referred to as Hotels amongst our lot). The humorous thing is if I had gone to a pub and put down ten pints of beer no one would have questioned it. In fact, there would have been a certain sense of pride that I could consume that much beer. However, going to a restaurant was a big taboo amongst the community back then. The idea was; you should never be eating out.

I took Suadagar Singh Nagra, my childhood friend with me. He was always good for adventure.

I could not lie to papajee, so I asked Saudagar, “Hey wonder what that place is like?”

To which Saudager replied, “Why wonder? Let's go and find out”

I thought, "That was the spirit, it's on you now mate.”

So we went in had a cup of tea and couple of samosas and high tailed out of there. By then it belonged to some people from Bangladesh.

I really could not bear the guilt that I put Saudagar up to it; I told him, “Hey, I was kind of trying to keep honest with Papajee.”

He knew though, and said, “Yeh, I knew that’s what you were up to anyway.”

Mahan Singh was from the village Didyal in Hoshiarpur, I met him only once as a child in New Delhi where he was seeing off one relative who traveled with us to England in 1958.

He was a formidable chap or that was my impression of him as a child, Papajee later confirmed that he was a strong personality. He was one of those people that people went to for advice. He was known to be a candid man and at times, brash with his advice, but nevertheless, honest as Papajee relayed it to me.

I remember him as a big-boned man in a double-breasted suit with a shiny scarf and a very deep voice. He must have left an impression on me because every now and then his image appears in my mind when I drift back to my childhood.

He had a son, Baksheesh Singh. He was a communist leaning individual, or a comrade, as they were referred to, pretty much at odds with Papajee's way of thinking. Because of his socialist thinking, he had no affinity for religion and at the same time Papajee absolutely despised communism and socialism. He was a Sikh and a capitalist at heart. To him,

Communists were all just leeches, who preached to others what they did not practice them self. Papajee could never tolerate hypocrisy of any kind. In his mind Communist were hypocrites, who would not part with a penny out of their pockets but just talked a good game.

Another shop to open although at a much later, time was a cloth on Stony Stanton Road as you are going to the city center on the right-hand side just past Leicester Causeway by the paper shop. Sardara Singh Banwait and his wife Vimal Kaur Banwait opened this. Although most people knew her and referred to her by Vimla, it went on to be known as "Vimla de dukan". (Vimla's shop)

Sardara Singh had arrived in England in the late fifties with my wife's maternal Uncle Mehnga Singh Bhatti. They both worked in Alfred Herbert but Mehnga Singh went to work for Sterling Metals for a while, Sardara Singh stayed on at Alfred Herbert. Mehnga Singh was born in the district of Multan, which was now in Pakistan. USA was granted military bases in Pakistan by the treaty between Pakistan and the USA, so Pakistan was granted more visas in the lottery system. Who had a birth certificate that said born in what was now Pakistan qualified to participate in the visa lottery. Under this Mehnga Singh being born in Multan now in Pakistan qualified to apply for the visa lottery. His lottery number came up and he moved and joined his uncle in Live Oak California in 1958 and later purchased land in the neighboring Yuba City California. Sardara Singh quit his job and purchased a van and prior to buying the shop would sell his wares to specified customers from his van. All these customers were non-Sikhs. However, as families started to arrive from Punjab, he saw there was a growing market for cloth from the newly arrived women to sew their garments. He opened his shop and began to import cloth material from Japan and other places.

Soon after Banwait opened his shop, many more shops started to spring up as the population started to grow.

CHAPTER NINE

Entertainment

We arrived in Coventry in March of 1958. Coventry was littered with cinemas, in Holbrook there was the Lyric, in Folshill area there was the Ritz on the outskirts of Coventry on Bedworth road, Regal also on Folshill road by Livingston road, Forum in Stoke, Empire opposite the main General post office, Opera which was a converted opera house near the Belgrade Theater. Going from the city center towards Gosford Park, there was the Gaumont, which later changed its name to Odeon. There was Paris. It had no balcony, the original Odeon. Past the Coventry Technical College going toward Tile Hill area, there was the Plaza and on the inner ring road or as Sikhs referred to it, "naun (9)" number road. (It got its name from the bus that ran along that route number 9,) there was the Palladium. Sikhs had nicknames or code names like this for many places. If they could not pronounce the name or remember the name, someone gave it a nickname or a code. Pubs were famously named. There was "Thamian wala" (one with the pillars) on and three shoes, which was actually three-horse shoe but for ease they dropped the horse what was left just "three shoe."It was on Stoney Stanton Road. Or if the pub had a certain color, it was referred to it by color as the one by King Georges Street was referred to as "Hara pub" (green pub).

Anyway back to the Cinemas. On the number of Nine Road, there was the Palladium. By pool meadow, (the city bus terminal) there was the Alexandria. Kashmir and I saw a film there called Harry Black. It was about man-eating Bengal tiger. It scared the living day lights out of my younger brother Kashmir for years. I still tease him to this day. “Hey Kashmir Sher aagia” (hey Kashmir, watch out there's a tiger), he just smiles and shakes his head. Later, it was a hangout to see all the Italian muscle men movies. It was the dream of all the kids to be Gordon Scott or Steve Reeves the Italian movie matinee idols Steve Reeves played Hercules and Gordon Scott played Tarzan.

In the fifties, Hindi films were shown at the Plaza cinema by Coventry Technical College. They used to show them on Sundays at an ungodly early hour, nine in the morning. Papajee and Beejee went to two films in their entire life. One was Nanak Naam Jahaj (first of its kind with Sikhism as the main theme) and the other was Nanak Dukhia Sab Sansar. (Similar theme to the first movie). Other than that they were not into this Film business. They always allowed Kashmir and I to go with Sohan Chachaji (you will meet him in the following pages). The kids were allowed in free. We had to be up by six thirty to catch two buses to get there. Kashmir and my measure, of a great movie, was if it had sword fighting; it was a good film. Other than that it was of no use to us. There was this chubby actor called Pardeep Kumar, he was every kid's hero back then. Many years later, he came to USA and fell sick, and someone called Kashmir to see a patient, the person told him that it was Pardeep Kumar.

Kashmir told him, "Sir, My brother and I were your fans.”

Kashmir told me that he was a pretty humble man, and was really grateful for Kashmir for taking the time out to see him.

After some time, Plaza cinema was no longer the venue for Indian films, they were moved to the Ritz. The name implies a regal place, with plush everything. It could not have been further than the truth. This cinema was on the Foleshill road going towards Bedworth. Being located on the outskirt of the city it would always show Hollywood films that had already been shown in main theaters, because of second tier movies being shown Ritz lacked an audience for its films, to generate extra cash, the management rented the cinema out to Sikh entrepreneurs who were trying to carve their market.

The time was still 9 AM in the morning. The only thing that changed for us was a walk up Stoney Stanton road, left on St Paul Road, and a bus from Folshill road to the Ritz. There were times that the buses would be to capacity if the film was popular. We would just start to walk until we either got on a bus along the route. Otherwise, we would walk all the way to the Ritz. It was hard on Kashmir, but everyone would cheer him on, and he would keep walking and asking,

"How much more? I'm tired."

The people running the Indian films at Ritz pretty much had a monopoly on the entertainment market for a while. Later, some Pakistani group got together and rented the Palladium cinema on the number nine road, and started to compete for the audience with the Ritz people.

The competition between the two groups was good for the audience. It meant the newer films were now being shown. It's worth mentioning that children at both places were free up to a certain age. So a lot of children never advanced in age because of it for years. They were twelve for about three years.

People wore their Sunday best to go to these films. I sometimes thought the people were better dressed than the actors in the films.

Films were a source of joy and frustration for Kashmir and I. Joy because we enjoyed the films, frustration was that we had to come home and explain what the story was and then tell Papajee what we learned from the story. Afterward, we had to write an essay on it. So films were bittersweet experience. One Sunday, as we were leaving to go to the cinema. Beeji pulled me aside and said, "Balbir, Kashmir is young, but you now have to have your next lesson."

Not knowing what that was I was a bit nervous. So I asked what that was. I was afraid that I was going to be asked to do some skit or something from the movie when I got back home. However was equally bad. She told me that since most of the action in the film was after the interval, she wanted me to bow my head down and listen to the film and only listen and learn.

I asked her, "Beeje what do you want me to learn?"

She replied, "I want you to learn Hindi, but moreover, I want you to imagine the story, I want you to see the faces each scene as they talk and let your imagination go."

Beejee could not read or write. She took the next-best option that was available to her, to have me learn Hindi and also develop my imagination. That's how I learned popular Hindi. Most of the films back then were overlaid with Urdu; I grew fond of the sweetness of Urdu language. I started asking papajee when I heard a word that I did not understand, but it sounded good. He would help me make a sentence with that word.

I can hold a very good conversation in both Urdu and Hindi. I sadly never did find out what happened in the first half of many of the films.

CHAPTER TEN

Professional Sikhs

There were only two that I knew, Roop Chand from Tuttan village in Punjab (back then not all Sikhs had Singh as their last or middle name, there few with the last name Chand) He was an electrical engineer at General Electric Company (GEC) GEC had three major plants in the city. One in the Binly stoke area, where I would serve as apprentice years later, the other being on Helen Street by Mulliner Street. I would break my apprenticeship and end up working at Helen Street for a while adjusting relays (these were electromagnetic switches used in telephone exchanges. I will address my education lapses and career later in the book) the third plant was on Spon Street down town. Roop first worked at Stoke and then later at Spon Street.

He lived at 31 Red Lane Coventry. He came to England with very little education. He came in the late forties. He told me his story how he became an engineer. He said it was winter, and it had been snowing and the following day the snow had iced over, and he slipped and broke his leg, and he was in the hospital for weeks.

In those days, people were in the hospital for a longer period than they are now. Perhaps because the medicine was not so advanced and the recovery took longer. On the other hand, it was lot simpler times, and everything moved much slower. Whatever the reason, he said he was in the hospital for a long period of time, incapable of speaking English and the nurses unable to understand him, and he could not understand the nurses. He told me that one night, he felt lonely, alone, and he said that I quietly cried all night.

He told me, “You know Balbir, all decisions that mean something come after one is done crying and there are no more tears to be shed, then one has to get up and get on with the job.”

I still remember that today. I am often invited to give motivational speeches to organizations. I tell the audience the story of my dear old friend Roop, and it never ceases to inspire people. He said, "at that point, at the end of my tears, I decided that I was going to go to school, learn English, and then get a professional education and work as a professional.

He told me that when he told his friends of his plans they all laughed at him and said, "Hey old dogs don’t learn new tricks.”

They said, "Walyait kam Karan lay ayan jan parraan lay?" (Have you come to a foreign land to work or study?)

He said that his mind was made up that he was going to school. As any person who wants to walk the less-traveled road, he lost some friends; He would always quote an Urdu couplet to me. "Insaan woh haute hain jau zamane ke saath chalte hain, maggar marad woh haute hain jau zamanae ko badal dete hain!" (People are those that walk the path of the world, but men are those that change the path of the world).

Roop said he started from the very beginning, first learning to speak, read and write English. He progressed inch by inch each day. He told me that like most Sikhs, he had a pretty good sense for math, the other part was a bit tough at first, but he never gave up. He told me at times he would come home so late at night that everything would be closed. He would go into his dustbin (garbage can), pick up the old dried-up bread that he threw out the previous day, sprinkled a bit of water on in it to make it a bit soft and moist, put butter on it and ate it with a glass of warm milk and then went to sleep.

Roop said the day he enrolled at Coventry Technical College was the best day of his life. He finally felt that he had arrived at the point where at times he only dreamt of being.

He said, "Balbir, there were times, I would see students go into the college, and I thought how smart they must be. Now I was among them, felt good."

He received an Ordinary National Certificate (ONC) by today's standard this probably seems like so what, for him and in his days that got you a pretty decent technical position.

He started with GEC as a test engineer first working at their Stoke plant and later moving into the Spon Street plant, from where he eventually retired.

He was a bit eccentric of a man, all the time I knew him. He had a Raleigh bicycle. He was always well dressed. He knew where and the best deals were for top of the line clothes in town. Back then Damon shirts were the most expensive, and he would always wear Damon shirt. He wore the best ties and sports jackets.

He would tell me, "Balbir you must always dress the part."

He was the real Indian gora gentleman. (Indian white man). Yes, he was a Sikh. However, he had one bad habit, which he later gave up and that was that he smoked a pipe. I guess that was all in the part of being the Indian white man.

He had a humorous comment about everyone but also would give guidance to everyone. I remember as the new batch of grooms started to arrive from Punjab as betroths to girls in UK. Some of the families ended up getting a spouse for their child from Punjab. Most of the time it would be someone from a distant relative. This served few purposes. Obvious purpose was a spouse for the child, the spouse being a distant relative made the reference checking lot easier. Furthermore, it would help the family of the spouse as he or she could then sponsor his or her family over to the UK. Most of the male spouses were graduates.

People would end up going to old Roop to seek his advice as to what the young lad should do for his future in the UK. His question would always be the same, Kherri degree, "keeti hai,veahah vali jan kam vali?" *("What kind of degree do you have to get married with? Or one that you can actually get a job with?").*

I would be sitting there. I would just giggle when people came; I knew what he was going to say. It would confuse the young lads, and he would proceed to explain,

"Jeh tan degree Punjabi jan political science de hai tan oh veahah vali hay, jeh English jan Mathematics jan chemistry, jan physic, jan engineering hay tan kam vali." (If your degree is in Punjabi or political science, then it has served its purpose...it got you a bride, if it is English, Physics, Chemistry or Engineering then let's talk.)

He helped lots of people this way; I know that it is a bit aunique way, but it was his way of putting people in the right frame of mind as to what their options were. He was always the advisor for me. I would go over and chat with him, especially when Papajee and I would get into a disagreement over Gurdwara issues. He made me see reason, at times he did tell me to stick to my guns.

He would say, "Tun putt tan udha he ahi na aape samju hole sejhe," (you're his son after all he will have to learn to understand sooner or later.)

He was a really a colorful person. He had the best Single Reflex camera, and would take photos at weddings that he attended.

Papajee you would always laugh and say, "For all the years that I have known him he has taken photos, and I have yet to see one, so go ahead and pose because your posing in front of thin air."

He loved to tinker with electronic equipment, and if he could not fix them; he would say, "Ehdee technology nahi mainoo samaj aai, Balbir deki tan." *("I couldn't understand its technology, ask Balbir to take a look?")*

It gave me a lot of insight into how some new technology worked. Suadagar one time had a tape recorder, and he told Suadager to bring it over. I told Saudagar I was not going to touch it if you give to Roop and he couldn't fix it. He gave it to him anyway, about two months later.

He handed him the whole thing torn up back in a box and said, "Balbir nun push la, maino ehdee technology nahi samj aai" (Ask Balbir, I don't understand its technology.)

He never bought a television set. He listened to the radio, and he read the London Times. He ate food on the floor, sat cross-legged laid-out the newspaper on the rug and eat his food, never on the table. I asked him one day why he did that? He told me this was how I was brought up. "Table te beth ke kerra ehda swad beter ho janna"(by sitting at the table the taste is not going to get any better.)

He married late in life, I guess the advice he was giving to other gooms he finally took for himself, or he felt that the need to have a life partner. He went back to India and married Niranjan Kaur, who was somewhat younger than him, but even so, they were very close. They did not have any children of their own. Maybe his lot in life was to be a father figure to other people's children and give sound advice where needed.

In my line of work, which takes me around the globe, I have met many interesting characters in just about every country around the world. I must confess none as colorful as Roop Chand. He was an inspiring man who always gave you clear-hearted advice in a light-hearted way. I am pushing the time clock myself, and I am older than he was when I left England. However, even to this day in situation where I need to reason and look for an answer, I find myself asking, Wonder what Uncle Roop would have thought about this? In most instances, I find myself getting to the answer and coming up with some sarcastic thought that he would have had.

The only other Sikh person who was a professional back in the fifties in Coventry and the very early sixties was Sohan Singh. Sohan Singh belonged to Bharowal village near Banga in Sardar Bhagat Singh Nagar district of Punjab. He was raised in Fiji, and his early education was in Fiji. He went to Delhi University and got his higher education. He is retired now and still lives in Coventry.

He was a schoolteacher who taught at Board secondary modern school, which was located on Broad Street off Stoney Stanton Road. Once the secondary modern school system was abolished, he moved to Sidney Stringer School and taught there before retiring.

Let me get into this school system in those times. There were four types of schools past the primary school. The first there were private schools, and then there were the so-called grammar schools, which were semi-public and private. Then there were the comprehensive schools and lastly there were the secondary modern schools.

The private schools are self-explanatory you pay, and your child gets the schooling of your choice. The grammar schools were, where you either paid or sent your child, or the child was exceptionally bright, and he could go to those schools. The comprehensive school was what the name implies; It allowed a comprehensive education to children of working-class parents who showed promise. The remainder of the children was carted off to the secondary modern schools and four years later they either went to work or an apprenticeship or went to a trade.

It's funny that English looked upon the Indian caste system with such prejudice and disdain and yet the British schools system was set up to keep the class system in place.

There was this test called the Elven Plus at the end of the primary school, and if you passed it; you went to a comprehensive school otherwise you ended up in the secondary modern system.

The pass rate for the eleven plus was low, and only, a handful, of the children from each primary school made it through. The children of immigrant parents faced an even a bigger uphill battle. They were new arrivals to the country, so for most of those kids their fate was sealed. The majority of them ended up in the secondary school system. There was another chance for few children at age thirteen, but that was only for a handful of children, and the rest remained within the secondary school system until they were fifteen. Then they were cast out into the working world.

The chance for children to go to University from the secondary school system was all but a dream. The best they could hope for was Higher National Certificate or City and Guild. I was a victim of this system. I ended up as an apprentice at GEC. It was not until I came to the USA that I could complete my education. I have advanced degrees, and it is ironic that one of them is from a British university. Maybe something inside my just wanted to make a point.

I think the best thing that ever happened was the dissolving of this ghastly system that deprived children of equal education.

Parminder, my wife and I both went to Fredrick Bird Secondary Modern school on Swanswell Street, and the other one was on Broad Street, this is where Sohan chachaji (chacha means the younger brother of your father. He was not papajee's real brother but Kashmir, and I thought of him as such) taught.

There was a film that was made in the sixties called "To Sir with Love," starring Lulu and Sidney Poitier about a bunch of miscreant kids in a secondary modern school, and it was pretty much to the mark. These places were nothing but holding places for four years, If you were smart enough to figure it out. You made something of yourself. Otherwise, the employment counselor at the end of four years came, and either got you some job or an apprenticeship and at the age of fifteen, you were in the world by yourself, in a job or trade in which you were put for life.

I first met Sohan Singh when we arrived in England. He rented a room from Papajee at 7 Red Lane, and he continued to live with us until he married. He then he moved to Roland Avenue in Holbrooks. To the community, he was known as Sohan Master (Sohan the teacher). Kashmir and I always referred to him as Sohan Chachaji, (Sohan uncle) and to this day, he is dear to us. He may not be a blood relative, but he is not any lesser degree dear to us. I remember one time him and Papajee got into a heated discussion, he said, “Nasib Kaur(beejee) is like a mother to me,” Papajee said. So then, “I am like father to you?”to which he replied "no like an elder brother you are going to have to be satisfied with that!”

He is a well-educated and well-rounded individual who has a strong set of opinions and is not shy about letting you know them either. He will deliver them to the audience to the level that they can understand. I have seen him change from being a typical pendu (a term used for a country bumpkin) to a highly sophisticated person.

Growing up, he was a real role model to Kashmir and myself; he was a hero of sorts to both of us. We thought he looked like Pardeep Kumar, the matinee idol of the Indian screen.

Every Sunday, he would say, "Ok boys get ready. We are going to the cinema.”

We would walk with him to the stop to catch the bus to go to the cinema. He dressed very smartly and always walked to school every day. As long as we were in Coventry he never learned to drive.

He read his Manchester Guardian (what now the Guardian) every day, from page to page.

I can tell you when we were young, and we were subjected to arithmetic quizzes by Papajee and I could not figure it out and I got one of those looks from Papajee and a telling off using his usual line, "Jeh na parrhe tan Suawah chukan jogae reh jana tusi" (if you don’t get an education all you will be good for is picking up the foundry ash, referring to, in essence, that all you will be good for is foundry work)

Sohan chahajee, would grab us by the arm and take us into his room, and Papajee never ever challenged him.

Papajee would say, "Sohan ena nu samjah" (Sohan put some sense into them).

Chahaji would say, "Dharam Singh eny parrh jana evei fikar na kar" (Dharm Singh, they will be educated, don't worry).

He is one tough nut. He never stood for any nonsense as a

teacher. All the Sikh children knew that he meant business, and they all feared him. At the same time, there were those that would also test his limits. He was always good at picking nicknames. Teachers could get away with it in those days. Now, it would be politically incorrect. He had one student who stood out. That was Mohinder the mischief; if there was a mischief to be had. Then Mohinder would be the one to figure it out. So he named Moninder, mischief.

He was very good friends with his co- villager Mohinder, from the village of Bahrowal (no, not the Mohinder the mischief). This was Mohinder was the eldest son of Hazura Singh. I am married to Hazura Singh's eldest daughter Parminder. Mohinder was my eldest brother law. He came around to the house a lot. Kashmir and I would say, "Boy he can talk."

Chahcajee married Meher Singh Litter's daughter Surinder, or Shindo, whom Kashmir and I called Bhenjee (older sister). After they got married, I was bit confused as to how to address her, as Chachi (aunt) or still as Bhenjee (elder sister). Just to tease her, I called her Chachi.

She first smacked me on the head and said, "You ever call me chachi again I will pull both of your ears out. I am your Bhenjee and that's 'what you will call me."

I said, "OK Bhenje Chachi."

She sat me down and gave me a real talking to. She squeezed my shoulders hard and said, "Balbir hat da keh nahin" (Balbir quit it or else) you don't argue and win many fights with Bhenjee.

Parmider calls Chachaje Bhajee (elder brother) and Bhenjee as Bhabijee (sister in Law). Sohan and Parminder are from the same village. From this point, he is truly Parminder's Bhajee, Bhenji her Bhabijee (sister in law).

The Sikhs do not marry anyone from their village. The reason for this is that most of the people from the village will have the same last name, or as it is referred to (Gotra). When the villages first came into being it was one family. As the families got bigger over time they were divided up into other family units. Based on where your father and someone else's father were in, the hierarchy would determine how one referred to the offspring of your and the other villagers' offspring, as brothers or sisters, or uncles and aunties.

The Hierarchy was determined from the inception of the original family, and it remained the same. You notched accordingly. If you were uncle and nephew at the beginning, then your next generation would be uncle and nephew accordingly. This is how for generations you know if it is an uncle aunt or brother of sister.

Sikhs also do not marry someone with the same maiden sir name of the mother and both grandmothers. This is to make sure these bloodlines are not mixed. Other considerations where marriage alliance would not be formed would be where the sisters of the groom and his father's sisters are married. Marrying someone from those surnames would be considered (batta) a swap that is not acceptable. Although some of these practices have relaxed over the years but marrying someone from the same village is still not done.

Parminder and my case we kind of all accepted what we called Chahajee and Bhenjee. Parminder went on referring to them as Bhajee and Bhabjee, and I kept on referring to them as Chahajee and Bhenjee.

It wasn't until many years later when they both came and visited us in USA that it came up again. We have always told our children that they are not to refer to people of the family as uncle and aunt but by their proper Sikh, Punjabi titles. Chachajee Chachijee, etc. So when Sohan Chachajee and Shindo Bhenjee first came to visit us. Our younger daughter Aman, she must have been around eight or nine heard me refer to Sohan as Chachajee and Shindoo as Bhenjee and Parminder referred to them as Bhajee and Bhabijee. After they left Aman was sitting there looking confused.

I asked her, “Aman what’s the matter sweetie. You look like your thinking about something?”

“Well dad I am sort of confused. You know the guests who just left, well you called the man Chachajee and the lady

Bhenjee. Mom called him Bhajee and the lady Bhabijee. So I am confused, you know how you have always told us to call people by our Punjabi relationship titles. So what do we call the guy? Babajee (grandfather or granduncle) or Mamajee (mother's brother)? How about the lady do we call her Majee (grandmother, grandaunt) or Mamijee (mother's sister in law), or do I call her Bhoajee (father's sister) since you call her Bhenjee?"

The words out of my mouth were, "Whatever you do, do not call the lady Majee. She will for sure think I put you up to it."

I must say I was dumbfounded. For once my only way out was, "Sweetie it's a bit complicated. Just call them Uncle and Auntie."

Aman still remembers it to this day and teases me, "Dad you never could explain what I call your Chachajee and your Bhenjee and Mom's Bhajee Bhabijee."

Chahajee continues to enjoy his retired life and reading his guardian. He enjoys his privacy. The last time I met him was a few years back, each time I go to Coventry the schedule has been such that I have been in and out in almost matter of hours. I need to make time and go and visit Chahajee next time I visit Coventry.

CHAPTER ELEVEN

Coming to England

I remember very clearly that Beejee, Kashmir and I returned from visiting my sister in her village Thala, near the town of Phillaur in Punjab. When we got home, there was a letter, and someone said it was a Rah Daari (visa) that Papajee had sent for us to move to England. I remember being confused and not understanding what this meant. So I asked my mother, she explained that Papajee has requested that we move to England.

I think she was a bit confused because she had thought that he would return to Punjab, and we would make a life in Punjab. Instead, Papajee decided that we move to England. She was not happy but decided that to honor and obey was the order of the day.

End of February one morning the Tonga (horse carriage) arrived, and I remember all the members of the family standing outside the gates of our house, in a line solemn and sad to see us off. My majee, Papajee's mother and my vadi Bebe and shoti Bebe (vadi means older shoti younger, were Papajee's aunts. They were wives of Papajee's eldest uncle, his thaiajee)

His eldest uncle was married two times; I guess it was some kind of a status of sorts. Not that I agree with it, but this was how it was in those days. All I can say is that my Majee and both of my bebejee's gave us more love than I could ever imagine.

While they stood outside the gates, lot of thoughts ran through my mind. I will not get to swing on those huge gates again. I will never be able to swing on the swing on the pipal tree just outside our gates.

Our family house was quite large. It had an outer wall extending from the main house, and it encompassed the Havili (the outer house, mostly where the men sat). There was a well that was half on the outside and the other half on the inside of the grounds of the Haveli. The wall ran on top of the well. People on the outside could not see people on the inside, but they could pull water from the outside. From the inside, you could not see who was on the outside. This way, the people of the household could maintain their privacy.

The house was very large; locally it was nicknamed Shota Lal Quila, (junior Red Fort reference to the main fort in Delhi of the Mughal times) because of its size. The other side of the house opened up into an outer Berra (court yard.) There was also a Berra (courtyard) inside the house. This is where the family would gather in the evenings. It was a place full of laughter and joy.

Outside Berra would be where all the women folks of the Ragi homes would gather to spin cotton with their Chrakhas, (spinning wheel). The sound of all those spinning wheels spinning in total harmony is still clear in my head. Like an old song that you hear one time, and it stays with you for the rest of your life. On a hot day, all the Manja's (cots) would be out in the outer Berra, and someone would tell a long Baat (story.) All the children would listen in silence with mouths wide open as if they were watching an oral film.

Our surname or Gothra is actually Khun Khun but in the village and in the surrounding villages, we were known as Ragi. Not sure how we got that nickname, but it is almost a surname now. Most of us use it as a surname. I remember asking my Babajee (grandfather) how the name came about. He said he could not remember, but he said the legend has it, that one of the ancestors was going to the market with his crops, and he stopped where there was a singer singing. Back in those days the singers would be narrating a story, and apparently he was misquoting, and the old man called him out.

Upset over being called out, the singer said, "Oh we have a great Ragi here!"

Since then the name Ragi, stuck. Not sure how accurate the story is, but it was the folklore as it was told to me. It sounded as good as any other I thought.

I get asked a lot why I am called Ragi, so I end up repeating the story as my Babajee explained it to me.

There are five houses or families of Ragi's , and even they have nicknames. Sikhs are really good at nicknames, as I mentioned earlier. Each village had nicknames for different households, it was almost an address system. If someone came to the village they would say I want to go to and repeat the nickname and people would direct them to their home. I have heard some pretty funny ones over the years from different villages. Such as Baddkhanae, (the biters), probably someone was rude in the family, thus the name. Bolle (the deaf), either they spoke loud as a family, so it was deemed, they are stone deaf and that is why they speak loud. Or, more than one person was deaf in the family. Other names, which come to mind, are Divane (lunatics), Milkan (the Americans). On it went. People did not mind, it was accepted. That was how they were known in the village.

Even in our family, as I mentioned there are five houses of Ragis, They all had a nickname; one of the Ragi families was on the darker side. They were referred to as Kalae Ragi (dark Ragi). Another was on a lighter side. They were referred to as Gorae (fair Ragi) and our family had people in all parts around the world, and people were coming and going, and we were referred to as Jahajee Ragi (airplane or traveling Ragi).

Our house was full of joy, there were always the usual squabbles of children fighting and the mothers getting into the blame game and Majee having to mediate but nothing that in the end did not end up in laughter.

That day as we were getting into the Tonga that was parked under the Pipal tree, I touched my Majee's and both of my Bebejee's feet and hugged my aunts and cousins and my sister and my nephew. I knew that I would never see some of these people ever again. My good-bye would be my last for good many of them. Kashmir was my shoti Bebejee's favorite. She hugged him, and he seemed lost in her. She was a large woman, a true malwain Jatti, (from the Jat clans of Malwa) who nobody would dare challenge.

At our village there was daka one time (armed robbery) one of the armed men climbed to the rooftop and put a challenge to the village, saying,

"If there is a man among you out there speak up now and come and challenge us now. Otherwise don't sit with your women folks after we leave and say if I was here I would have taken them on."

My shoti Bebejee went onto the rooftop and said, "Put adamian de tan tun shad mahin nib de an tere naal"." (*Son don't worry about the men folk. I will be over to deal with you myself.*)

She marched down there with a double barrel in hand. By the time she got there they ran off. She did not stand for any nonsense from anyone. She was hard and a strong-willed lady and ruled the household with an iron fist. Kashmir was her soft spot. That day she did not appear to be the same iron lady. Tears were pouring over here large face, her chunni (headcloth) soaking from wiping away her tears.

Majee stood in complete silence, looking out into open space, dazed as if part of her life was going to end forever. It was as if she was thinking that this was the start of how she would see her family disappear from her world one by one, and we were the start of this exodus. How much truth there was in the emotion that she had in her eyes. Her story was going to become the story of many more grandmothers of Punjab, every majee, in every village in Punjab. They would all see their world being taken from them one family at a time, how village after village would be emptied by families moving abroad. If you go to any village of Punjab more so in the Doab, the villages has a lot of houses that are empty and locked up, because the families have moved aboard and the old folks have died.

I could see that there was some divine thought had overtaken my Majee. It was as if she was not there, oh, she stood there all right, but her soul was in the future, her future and the future of other grandmothers like her, and it was passing by her and saying to her "take a good look the Punjab that you once knew. It will disappear."

Majee's ancestral village was KhatKar Kalan Punjab, and she belonged to the Dosaangh gothra, and her family house was opposite the Sandhu house of Kishan Singh Sandhu, Bhagat Singh's father. Bhagat Singh was a freedom fighter. He was hanged at the age of 24 years of age in 1931. He remains an inspirational leader to all of India. Majee would often sit down and talk about the Sandhu family.

She would get melancholy and say, "Ke khataia, bichare sari umar desh lai larr de rahe aur desh vaasia neh vand paun lagia ne pishan morr keh ve na dekhea". (What did they gain? Bhagat Singh's family spent all their lives in the service of the country and people of the country when dividing the country didn't even look back.)

She had witnessed the coming and going of refugees after the partition of Punjab in 1947. She had seen these tongas like these take people with whom she had shared childhood and girl gossip to the railway station to be moved to the other side of the border. She saw the same tongas bring people from the west side to the border to villages on the east side to the border as new refugees. She had a fear of these tongas. When they came they took someone, someone dear, as they were going to do this day.

All the boys who went to primary school with me had gathered. They were all speechless. It's hard to explain at that tender age of nine. What you're feeling. Most of the kids did not even hug me good-bye. They stood there with their head bent down. It felt like we were the ones being sentenced, having to leave home, not knowing where and what we were going to. There was sadness that filled the air.

I saw Bhuja Soniar (goldsmith) running and shouting,

"Oh Balbir, Oh Balbir, sano shad chalian yaar." (Hey Balbir Hey Balbir you're leaving us my friend.)

Bhuja was a man in his fifties, with a white fuzz beard. I would wander through the village and end up at his shop. I would just be amazed at watching him working at his craft. He would let me sit and watch him; he would always be nervous about being told off by Shoti bebejee. Shoti bebejee practiced class system to the hilt. To her, it was not proper for our family members to associate with someone like Bhuja.

He would always say, "Balbir betha beshak reh par Nand kaur nu nah dasi nahi meri jaan to pauara peh jaana." (Balbir by all means stay, but don't tell Nand Kaur (Shoti Bebejee) or my life will be a mess.)

I went to see my pal Bhuja anyway. He was my friend. Bhuja sang Heer (Punjab lover epic) under his breath as he worked. I would always say, "Thaia jee uchi gao." (Uncle, sing louder) He would say, "Na Balle koy bura manvega." (No Balle, his pet name for me, someone will mind.)

He sang Heer so sweet that it seemed to carry you away. I love Heer to this day. I at times sit and listen to Heer, and it takes me to those childhood days at my pal Bhuja's workshop. When I close my eyes, I see him singing to me from beyond.

He wanted to hug me but stopped short when he saw shoti Bebejee. Shoti bebejee relented but was not polite.

She called out to him, "Mar pare mill lae, menu pata teri hutti te benda see." (Go on damn it, hug him then, I know he sat at your shop.)

Bhuja hugged me with all his might while he wailed out, "Oh Balle sanu bhul na jain Waliat jake." (Balle don't forget us when you get to the England Waliat, means foreign, but it is commonly used to mean England also.)

The tonga was loaded with our suitcases along with the three of us. My Chahajee and his friend from Glasgow who both had arrived in Punjab few months earlier were going to take us to New Delhi to see us off. I sometimes go back to that moment and see us loaded on a single tonga, a suitcase full of some of our belongings. Kashmir's and my young life, and our mother's whole life loaded on a tonga in a couple of suitcases.

Beejee's prize possessions, which took a lifetime to accumulate all left behind, her embroideries that she made with such love with her hands, and all the other little things that she had collected over the years. The women folks with whom she had come so close, who would come by in their hour of need and ask her for money, and without hesitation, Beejee would lend them a hand. Never asking when it would be paid back, but paid back it was every time. Possessions until today that in the mind had the word "mine" attached to them would now be going to be someone else in the family. I often wonder that this is what the people coming from the west side and those going over the west side of Punjab must have felt like at partition time. When they had to load up their whole generations worth of belongings on a single Bullock cart or a tonga and move, not knowing what tomorrow would bring.

Human beings are funny creatures. We put labels on things, mine, theirs, when there is nothing in this world that is truly ours, it is all-temporary. We fight over the smallest things, and in a few years, we see the folly of our actions. Then we sit in silence and sigh a deep sigh and feel a bit ashamed of ourselves, thinking, what was so important, that I tried to fight over that and chuckle at ourselves and move on to repeat it all over again.

The Tonga weaved through the dirt roads with passerby's looking, and waving us good-bye and some just stared as the horse slowly pulled the weight of all those in the Tonga. We finally reached Aur, a small town that was being occupied slowly after the partition. Prior to partition, Aur was predominantly a Muslim town. It was a place of one of the worst bloodbaths and butchering of Muslims during the partition riots. The charge on the Muslims was led by a sant (Holy man) from a near village of Mahal. How a man of God could lead such an attack on people because of their faith is out of any line of comprehension for me to understand.

We were to catch one of the few buses that ran infrequently from Aur to Phillaur, from where we would board a night train for New Delhi. Beejee's Nanake (her mother's maiden village) was Mahal. Her maternal uncle (mamma jee) Ujjagar Singh came to meet us here. He was commonly referred to as Bhura because of his red hair. He came on horseback. He always had a shotgun swung over his shoulder whenever I saw him.

He was very formal in his speech; as far back as I could remember he never addressed anyone just by his or her first name. He would say that if you half address a person, then you are making that person think less of him or herself. He always referred to himself as, we, or (Ashin). He hugged Kashmir and I and picked both of us up at the same time.

I remember him saying, "Chote sardar jeo Watan na bhulnan." (Young sirs don't forget your land) and then put his hand on my mother's head and said, "Bibi Nasib Kaur sukhi vass Waahguru tera suhai hove." (Dear Nasib Kaur be happy may God keep you.)

The departure to England was a traumatic experience. I remember every word that anyone said along the way to this day.

We arrived in Phillaur early afternoon and went to the station and purchased tickets for New Delhi. We boarded the four O'clock night train. I had never been on a train before this in my short eight and half years on this earth, this was to be my many firsts on a long journey to England.

As we got boarded the train, the whistle blew, it alarmed Kashmir, and he jumped into Beejee's lap, and she held him tight. The train pulled out of the station and slowly the steam built, and it gained speed going over the River Sutlej and towards New Delhi. I could see the sun setting in the west over the fields, and slowly the sky turning red, the color as the sun. People returning home, with their bullocks running fast to reach home after a hard day's work hungry like

Ironworkers of England running to a pub to wash down the soot in his throat with beer.

Other people with fodder tied in a cloth and loaded on top of their heads, going home so they could feed the buffalos and milk them. This life of which I was a part of and it was a part of me. I was seeing it from the frame of a railway cart window, which would be for the last time. It had already started to appear as if I was watching a film, it started to seem as if it was not part of my life anymore. It started to seem as if it was another life that I was watching. I remember feeling scared inside, asking myself, how am I going to make new friends? When would I see my friend Shinda, Chaman, Pali, Rughbir, my sister, her children or my cousins Kesar, Rana, Shindo, and Bhajan? Will I be able to speak the language of these new people? My head was exploding with all sorts of thoughts and questions. I kept most of them to myself. I just looked out of the window of the rail cart and saw the sun finally setting. The choir of the bird's evening song fell silent and as nature did every day, and I had never noticed it before because I was too busy playing with my friends and cousins or teasing my cousins. Today, none of them were there, just the acts of nature that were unfolding before my eyes. For the first time, I saw the majesty of nature. I saw the sunset. I heard the choir of the birds, and I felt February's cold breeze of the evening hit my little body as I looked out with my head laid over the window frame. I hear people say that the best time to visit Punjab is in February the weather is just-right temperature. When I hear this, I am reminded of the train ride from Punjab to New Delhi.

As the sun set, the moon came out, God's two faithful servants commissioned to appear at the exact time as one goes to sleep, the other one clocks in for his shift. All the fields seemed calm in the moonlit night. It was, though they were asleep, at rest.

I watched this wonder as the train snaked through the landscape and the joints of the rails making click di click noise. The occasional whistle going off, as if the sound of technology was declaring its supremacy over the centuries' old traditions that was the village Punjab. Beejee asked me to go to sleep and rest. However, my mind could not rest. It had to switch off from thoughts to rest, but every time I looked out through the rail cart window, there was something else to observe.

As the train pulled into station after station along the route to New Delhi, I saw the familiar sound of the hawkers hawking tea and biscuits or maroonda (puff wheat or rice and caramelized sugar treat). My chachajee asked if we wanted some Maroonda, we said no. We were brought up very strict that way, we were told by Beejee.

She told us, "You did not ask for things from others, and you never accepted when someone offered to buy you something."

I remember asking Beejee, "Are these people only allowed to sell when the train stops?"

I thought these were the same hawkers that remained on the train and when the train stopped they got off and started selling their good to the train passengers.

Beejee smiled and said, "Silly, they just sound identical. They are different people. The ones at the last station are back there at that station waiting for the next train."

We traveled all through the night, into the early hours of the morning when I started to see lights everywhere. I was in and out of sleep a few times but was determined to be awake when we reached New Delhi. Everyone was asleep. I wanted to awaken someone and ask if this was New Delhi with all the lights. I remember one of my Khatri (the warrior caste of the Hindu caste system) friends telling me who had been to New Delhi to visit his relatives that there were lots of lights at night in New Delhi.

As the train pulled into the New Delhi station, everyone started to awaken, and you could hear the clamor on the platform and the hustles of the coolies with heavy loads on their heads to get passengers loaded on those that were leaving and loading off those that were arriving.

We got off the train and caught a taxi from the railway station to the house of my chachaji's and his friends, a friend from Glasgow's home. This was a Kapoor family who had a house that appeared to be in the newer part of New Delhi. Not quite sure where it was but at that time it was newly built. We got there in the early hours of the morning. I know because I could hear Japjee Sahib (morning prayer of the Sikhs) over the loudspeakers in the background,

"Beejee ethe be Gurdwara hai ga?" (They have a Gurdwara here also?) I asked Beejee "Han Balbir jethe be du Sikh hon gae othe Gurdwara jaroor hove ga, sade vaste eh jaroori hai apne Guru da Ghar banouna." (Well, of course, they do, wherever there are two Sikhs, there will be a Gurdwara Balbir, it is important for us Sikhs to build the house of our guru.)Beejee replied hugging and kissing my face. Little did I know at that time that years later we as a family would be greatly involved in building a Gurdwara.

The Kapoor family welcomed us with open arms. They prepared breakfast for us. We were tired but were also hungry. I wanted something to eat but would not ask for it as I mentioned Beejee would never approve of that kind of behavior. I was so glad to see food. I wanted to dig in and eat, but I used restraint and waited until the family served me and then only when Beejee started to eat did Kashmir, and I start.

We were tired, after taking a bath; we went to sleep and did not awake until about four in the evening, all ready for the tea. There was another family from Punjab also on their way to England that was staying with them. We always had cups and saucers and teapots and cutlery at our house in our village Herian. Beejee already taught Kashmir and I how to drink tea the correct way and how to hold forks and knives in the appropriate manner. Since our family been had been on the move, the western manners were part of our upbringing. Further, my maternal great-grandfather, my Beejee's grandfather was a world war one decorated soldier from his time in France. Beejee from childhood was trained in western manners. When tea was put out, Beejee took her cup of tea; Kashmir and I were given a glass of milk each. Once the biscuits were passed around, we took one each, but this other family's two children, boy, and girl took a handful while our hosts surprisingly looked on. To add insult to injury the lady took her tea and poured it into the saucer and started sipping it with large slurps. I think the first slurp shocked our hosts. Kashmir and I wanted to laugh, but we knew we would get a real thrashing from Beejee if we did that. So we waited until we were done then Kashmir, Beejee and I went out had had a bellyful laugh.

I remember Beejee saying, men tan suchian ona vicharyan to tan gush pe janan jad os jananin ne soota maria," (*Oh I thought the poor people were going to go into shock when she took the first slurp).*

That evening one of the Kapoor daughter's took Beejee, Kashmir and me to Sis Ganj Gurdwara in old Delhi (place of martyrdom of the ninth guru). It was such an experience for us. The place was majestic.

I remember the next time I would return to India, and this Gurdwara would be after the death of Beejee in 1981.

Beejee died in August of 1981, and I returned to India in December of 1981 to see my maternal grandparents, Beejee's parents, and attend my nephew's (my sister's son) wedding. I wanted to visit the Taj Mahal. So again we boarded a train from Phillaur to Agra to visit the Taj Mahal. My brother in Law's grandnephew accompanied me to Agra. He was about eighteen years old at the time. He is about six feet tall with a well-built physique.

We arrived at Agra around two in the morning and started looking for a place to stay. We first knocked on this one small hotel or an inn of some sort; a man came down the stairs and when he saw Lally (my brother in law's grand nephew) he just went right up the stairs. The stray dogs were barking, I must say I felt a bit foolish, being in a foreign place, in an unknown town and not having a place already secured to spend the night. It felt like a real adventure, though. Lally found a restaurant, and he woke the person sleeping on a chair by the front door of the restaurant. Lally kicked the chair from underneath of the man and woke him up and asked the man to open the door. We slept in a room on top of the restaurant.

Lally's words to me were, "Mamaji in the morning if you're scratching because of the bedbugs don't blame me."

Luckily, that did not happen, but the experience has made for a pleasant memory in my mind.

We woke up around 8 O'clock AM, took a bath and had breakfast and went to see the Taj Mahal. It was Friday, the Muslim Sabbath or Jumma as it is referred to in the Muslim world. The site was quite well attended. We walked through it with a guide. He told us the story of how Shah Jahan built the Taj to honor his wife Mumtaz. It was amusing to me how he was misquoting historical dates.

We stayed for about one and a half hours and came to Delhi and went to Sis Ganj Gurdwara. It was about the same time of the day that I had been there the last time; my mother and brother were not with me this time. We went in and sat down and started listening to keertan (hymns that are sung from the Guru Granth Sahib, the eternal Guru of the Sikhs).

Lally tapped my shoulder and said, "Mamaji, shall we go?"

I remember saying, "But we just got here."

He smiled and did not say anything but put his watch that I had given him and tapped it as if to say to take a look at the time. When I looked over at his watch, I saw that four hours had passed by. I had been listening to Keertan in meditation for four hours.

Standing on the steps of the Gurdwara, what Lally said to me will stay with me for the rest of my days.

He said, "Mamaji Taj Mahal bee Kabar see eh be kabar hay, othe tusi kahle see challenen nu ethe tusi uthnen ny tear nehi see, bass faraq eh he hai oh apne lay marne walia de kabar see eh kissi `lay marene walyea de kabr hay."` (Uncle, when you were at the Taj Mahal you were in a hurry to leave, here, you wanted to stay longer. In a way, both places are eternal resting places of someone. The only difference is the Taj is for people that died not for anyone else, and it glorifies the self. And Sis Ganj is the resting place of someone who died for others, and it glorifies the sacrifice.)

CHAPTER TWELVE

Airplane journey

In 1958 when we came to the Sis Ganj Gurdwara, Mr. Kapoor's daughter, walked with us through the tight streets of the bazaars. She insisted that Kashmir, and I buy something or have something to eat.

When we refused she commented to Beejee, "Aunty barri Tameez diti hai aap en dono ku." (Aunty you have taught a lot of manners to both.)

Beejee simply said, "Agar hun sikh jao ge te ah sari umar teek rehan ge." (If they learn now they will be better for it for the rest of their lives.)

The next day we woke early and had a light breakfast, and took off to the airport. New Delhi Airport (Palam) was very small back then. I am not sure if there were many international flights coming into the airport. I can still remember walking across the tarmac, Kashmir, Beejee and I saw a plane for the first time in our lives. We got in line to board, when my chachajee waved to me from the door leading out to the tarmac. I started running backward towards him thinking that he was calling me back. He was actually waving goodbye. It was the first time I had ever seen anyone saying goodbye by waving one hand. I was used to people folding both hands and bowing their head. When he saw me running towards him, he started to laugh and then waved his hand to me to go back towards the plane.

We were boarding an Indian Airline flight (India's short-run domestic airline), and it was to take us as far as Karachi, where we were to board a KLM (Royal Dutch Airlines) flight, which was to take us to London. Little did we know that it was not going to be that simple.

As the propellers of the plane started to propel with speed, Kashmir and me, both put our hands over our ears, it was a new sound for us, a constant grinding noise reminded me of the flour grinding machine in our village Herian that the mistry (craftsmen) family operated.

Once we were airborne, a tall slender airplane captain came out of the cockpit. He cut a fine figure with his nicely groomed beard and his sharply tied turban. He saw Kashmir and I and walked right over to us and asked us in Punjabi, `"Betajee England ja rahe ho?"` (Children going to England?)

Both of us nodded, to which Beejee asked us to answer not to nod, as it were, impolite.

We were both were fascinated looking out the window as the plane went over the Himalayas, seeing the snow-capped peaks was a real splendor of nature that I can still remember this day.

There was another lady with a little baby girl on our flight headed to England, in discussions with the lady, Beejee discovered that the lady's name was Avtar Kaur, and they were also headed to Coventry, and Mahan Singh had dropped them off at the airport. We asked Beejee if we could play with the baby, Avtar Kaur let us pick up the little baby girl. For the two of us, it was a distraction from the uncertainty that we were feeling from the unknown that lay ahead.

We arrived in Karachi. I know that Beejee and Avtar Kaur were both very nervous; this was a Muslim country, a country of enemies. A decade ago, these people lived next to each other for centuries and shared everything, and now they were scared of each other. Politicians can turn saints into sinners, and in this case politician for their own design certainly did just that.

I found these people in Karachi to be very accommodating

and polite, but we were told not to be trusting of them. We stayed quiet and just followed Beeji into the room that was provided for us. Avtar Kaur, her daughter and we were stuck here for over a week. About the fourth day, Avtar Kaur and her daughter were put on a plane to England, but we could not get a seat. While she was there she was good company for Beejee, and the baby was good company for us. We would pick her up and play with her. What else could we do other than the books, which Beejee picked up, for us to read, there were no television or radios in the rooms. Once Avtar Kaur left, we felt alone, stuck in a foreign unfriendly country. After a lot of asking around and talking with a lot of people about our plight, Beejee got us on a KLM flight.

Plane next landed in Cairo in the evening, first time I ever saw a palm tree. They looked very beautiful. We asked Beejee if we were going to have to spend more nights here, and she was scared and didn't know the answers. She told us to be quiet and just finish our milk. We finished our milk while the plane was being refueled. All the passengers got up and started back towards the plane. We moved right along with them not knowing if we were going to be allowed on. We breathed a sigh of relief when no one asked us to get off and the plane, we sat in our seats holding hands until the plane took off. It stopped in Lebanon next to pick up some passengers, but we did not get off here. At every stop, it was an education. We were seeing different types of people, type; we had not ever laid eyes on before.

Once we got to Rome, we were taken off and shown to a room, and it was again a fear as to not knowing where in the world we were and when we were going to be able to get back on a plane to get to England. We were also wondering what if Papajee would be in London when we landed. What if he grew tired of waiting and had left and gone back to wherever it was that he lived? I had memorized the name of the city that we needed to go to, but not the address. Beejee had it in a diary that she had brought from Banga and had someone write Papajee's address and also the address of her nephew who lived in the town of Slough. We had no idea if Slough was closer to the airport or Coventry was. A few years later when we visited Beejee's nephew, we found out that he lived very close to the airport.

That night in Rome was difficult, I remember the long corridors of the hotel, we could not sleep. We were tired, but we were more worried as to what was going to become of us. Beejee never let on that she was worried, but I could read my mother quite well. I knew she was worried and trying to figure out how she was going to get us on a plane again.

The next day we went to the lobby and started watching planes landing, a plane from India landed and on it was this tiny little Hindu gentleman, and along with him was a very tall Sardar (Sikh Gentleman who has uncut hair and wore a turban) in his forties. They both saw us sitting in the lobby and came over and asked us if they could help. Beejee explained that we got there yesterday and don't know when we could get on the plane again.

Sadarjee asked the Hindu gentlemen to stay with us while he checked why we were stuck here, and if he could get us on the same flight as them since they were also on a KLM flight. Kashmir was tired and was fussing a lot. Beejiee tried to console him, but he had his eye set on some toy that Beejee was not buying for him. A bizarre and at the same time a funny thing happened next. The Hindu gentleman pulled out a green chilli pepper from his bag and waved it in front of Kashmir. Beejee asked him why he was carrying a bag full of green chilli peppers. Was it to ward off evil spirit on his journey?

"Oh no," replied the gentleman. "I heard you can't get chili peppers in England, so I loaded up my bag."

Beejee asked him if he was just going for few weeks, and he was taking his stash of chili peppers with him for that time.

To which he replied, "Oh no, I am immigrating there."

Which made Beejee smile, and she said, "Bhaji jad eh muk jao geian fer ke karon ge?" (Brother, what are you going to do when you run out?)

The Poor man had not thought that far, and was just dumbstruck by the question. He was saved by the return of the Sardarji, who asked where our luggage was because he had made the arrangement to get us to board the same plane as them. We gave him our luggage, and he took us to the counter and checked in our luggage and made sure that we were seated comfortably, and he sat few rows behind us.

After leaving Rome, we arrived in Paris; it must have been about four in the evening when we landed in Paris. While the plane was taxiing we saw snow falling. We had seen snow coming over the Himalayas going from New Delhi to Karachi, but this would be our first time to see snowflakes. Both Kashmir and I were fascinated by it. As we came out of the plane, I stuck my tongue out to have the snow land on my tongue. As soon as Beejee saw that she yanked on my sleeve and told me to put my tongue back in my mouth. The cold snowflakes reminded me of the ice vendor who used to sell ice shavings with colored flavoring on it in the village. We again had tea at the airport. I often wonder either there were more profit margins in the flights in those days that they could give this tea and service. Alternatively, currently they are just not making enough margins, and they are cutting back so much on the services.

Once we left Paris, Sardarji told us, "Now it would be a short journey to London, and you will meet your father."

Beejee asked him that, since we had been so late in getting to London if papajee had gone home would he be kind enough to arrange a taxi for us and Papajee would compensate him.

He told Beejee not to worry, usually, the taxi drivers would collect on the other side, but in case they don't he said he would pay it and will give us his address, and Papajee could mail him the money for the taxi. (He was a returning immigrant.)

He told us, "Either way, please don't worry. I will make sure that you arrive at your new home safe."

I often think of this Sardarji's generosity, and it makes me pause and take note of the spirit of humanity that is given to us Sikhs at the need of the hour it comes out in a full measure.

I remember reading an article sometimes back in an Indian magazine written by a Hindu author. He wrote that when he was young, his father told him, if he was ever in a place where did not know anyone, to find Pathan or a Sikh, and you will always get hospitality. He said that he set out to test his father's advice. He first went to Germany, Switzerland, and England. He wrote that in every case, wherever he went and rang up a Sikh or a Pathan, he got help. He recites one incident that particularly stands out in my mind. He said he called this one Singh in Germany, and the man picked up the phone, and he told the man that he was stuck and was from India and had no place to stay and no money to eat.

He said that man told him, "I work the evening shift, and I am going to leave for work soon and there is only my wife and my baby home, please tell me where you are and I will come and see you, and we can take care of you."

He said, he came and took me to a hotel that he paid for the night and his wife had packed Punjabi dinner. In the morning, he came straight from his shift and picked me up, the writer writes, and took me home and gave me breakfast. That is where I told him who I was. The Sikh simply said, "Pehlan he dass dene se, koi farak nahin se pena eh te sada dharam hai dusro de madat karna." *(Why did you not just say that? It would not have made any difference to my actions. This is a part of our faith to help our fellow man.)*

The face of that Sardarji who helped us in Rome to London is still fresh on my mind as it was when I first met him. His generosity towards a frightened woman and two bewildered children cannot ever be measured.

At last, the plane was landing in London. We looked out of the window and saw London that we heard so much about for the first time. I must say it was not what I had imagined. It looked grey and green at the same time, that drizzle, which is all too common part to the English weather could be seen from the plane falling on the buildings, trying to wash away the soot that gathered on them from centuries of abuse by the smoke-filled chimneys of the factories, but to no avail.

There was an excitement of something brand new; children tend to forget everything even if it is for a moment when something new comes along. For me, this was something exciting, I wanted to observe everything, and I tried to get a panoramic view of the city as the plane approached the airport.

Once we had landed we were bought to the receiving area where Immigration and the customs was in a one big room, crowded with new immigrants pushing each other, it was a total mess. England was open for Commonwealth countries so there were people from everywhere in this room, but mostly from India and Pakistan.

I remember Kashmir saying to Beejee "Appan Delhi aagay, hun chalo ghar nu chaliae?" *(Are we at Delhi and we can go home now?)*

He thought because most people looked like us that we were back in Delhi. Beejee told him that we were in London now and we will go to our new home. He asked where that was, and she told him that she was not sure but that your Papajee will take us there.

It was my duty to remember the ribbon color and look for the suitcases and then read the tag that I had written in Punjabi to make sure that we got our suitcases. I pointed them out to Sardarji, which ones were our suitcases, and he pulled them out and had us give the man the tag to retrieve the suitcase.

I heard someone in a tired husky voice calling our "Balbir, Balbir," when Beejee saw Papajee, she turned to both of us and said, "Putt thuhade Papajee." (Boys, that's your Papajee.)

I was two years old when Papaji left for England; Kashmir was born a month after he left for England. Papajee was seeing Kashmir for the first time.

Sardarji saw us to the door, and handed us over to Papajee and folded his hands and looked over at Beejee and said, "Lo bibi ek veer da faraz poora hogya." *(Dear sister now a brother has fulfilled his duty.)*

Papaji thanked Sardarji and asked him for his address, which he did not give. I suppose he thought we would be beholding to him, which he did not want. I can say that I am so thankful to that Stranger Sadarji for all his generosity, thoughts of which have not left my mind.

It is true, that we create heaven or hell on this earth with our actions. When we leave this earth, we then live in people's memories. If we are thought of with fondness that person is in heaven. I know if there is a heaven out there somewhere that Sardarji is there.

It was Saturday March 1st, 1958 when we landed in England. Papaji got us into a taxi to the nearest underground train station. Going down those deep escalators for the first time was scary for the three of us. So Papajee held Kashmir's hand, and Beejee asked me to hold hers hand I said no. I was fine. She grabbed my hand. I think it was for herself than me, so I held her hand down the escalators.

Once we were in the underground train Papajee pulled out some chocolate and gave it to the both of us. Kashmir being cautious did not put it mouth, I on the other hand, have always was ready to try anything new, so I took a bite, and as soon as I did I wanted to spit it out. It tasted bitter. Beejee saw what I was about to do, and she shook her head slightly as to say, "Don't you even dare."

So I swallowed it and my mouth had this terrible taste for the rest of the journey.

Papaje had brought these scarves and also woolen caps so that we would be warm on the journey to Coventry. I remember the caps were woolen with pom poms on them.

Beejee looked at them and said to Papajee, "Scarves are fine, but you are not going to put those girl caps on the boys."

He told her it got cold, but she held her ground. They had a feminine look to them in her opinion, and they were not going over the heads of her boys.

It was early morning on Sunday when we got to Coventry, and we took the taxi and reached what was to be our home, 7, Red Lane Coventry England. We stayed at this house until we left England for the USA in 1972. It was a terrace house with a front room to one side of a corridor that led to the family room and the kitchen. It was a three-bedroom house with a cellar. The cellar was a new experience for Kashmir and I. I would always tell Kashmir that ghosts lived there, and they will take you if you go down there, and I would hide stuff from him in the stairs of the cellar that I did not want him to have.

The following day in the afternoon, we started to have a steady stream of well wishers come to the house to welcome us to England. Among the first was my cousin Harbhajan and her husband Dilbagh Singh. He brought us bunch of toys. The stream of well-wishers continued almost for a month with locals coming by for the first few weeks and then from other towns that knew that Papajee decided to move his family to England. It was sort of a mixed feeling for most of these people who were single, well not exactly single, and only single in England. Most of their families were still back in Punjab. They were happy to see a unification of a family. However, they could also see their dream of going back to Punjab, acquiring land and reuniting with their families slipping away.

Every time a family came, it started the dialog in their mind. What shall I do about my family? Next time you met someone they would say, "O bey oh da be tabar agya hai." *(Oh so and so's family also just came.)* The earlier arrivals would trot over to that person's house to welcome the new arrivals. Tide was turning from going back to more and more families arriving in England.

The community was very tightly knit, also it was going through a metamorphose of sorts from these people being carefree single men to becoming overnight family men again.

Then there was the difficult task for these families of getting to know their spouses. Most of them came from a joint family background where the seniors members within the family made all the decisions, that now fell on them as a couple to do.

Papajee worked the night shift, so Monday morning our training started as to how to maneuver our way around to operating the gas stove. I know Beejee was totally petrified of the stove, thinking that if the gas was somehow left on it could kill us. She asked me to learn how to turn it off. Every time she would cook and turn the gas off, she would ask me to come and check to make sure it was turned off.

I remember how lonely the three of us felt that night and many more nights following, all alone at night in this new cold place with fog that seemed to roll in every night about the same time as an unwanted guest. I suppose because of all the smokestack industry that was in the city back then and mixed with the weather, the fog seemed just very thick.

The streetlights at that time were still gas-lit. A man on a bicycle would come along and light the street lamps every evening. Kashmir and I would sit in the bedroom facing the street and watch him every night. It seemed like something out of Dickens's novel when I look back on it.

I know that for the first week, all three of us would cry ourselves to bed. We missed my sister, nephews and all the other relatives and friends.

The following weekend we went to the city center, the building that housed the market to which Punjabi's referred to as the "gol Market" (round market) because its round shape was not built yet. There were just stands, with lights and hawkers hawking their goods. My first impression was that it was like it was in Banga back in Punjab (a small town near our village). It was how hawkers would call out in Banga. However, this was not Banga, and we were not in Punjab. It was a different place. The cold chill of March was hitting our faces. Kashmir and I were watching people talking away, old ladies standing and having a chat, children giggling. We were hearing new sounds, different voice tones, seeing unfamiliar gestures. It was all very fascinating, at the same time; we felt out of place.

Papajee took us to boy's clothiers, and he purchased all new clothes for the both of us. Suits with shorts, instead of trousers, socks, shoes, ties, sweaters. He bought us three pairs of each. He also bought us suspenders to match. I asked him, why it was that we were getting these suits with this knickers? He told me that we would not wear trousers until we went to secondary school (high school). He said it was not proper to wear trousers for young boys. They must wear the age-appropriate attire, and those are shorts. I looked at Beejee, she gave an agreeable nod, as to say stop arguing and accept it. So I decided to take a different approach.

I said, "Par knicker vech tan thand lagani." *(But it's going to be cold with wearing the shorts.)*

Papajee looked at me and said, "Ape tand lagon hat janni hai." (You will get use to it!) I knew there were no options left.

Once we came home, he wanted to teach us how to tie a tie. Beejee told him that we both knew how to tie a tie. He was very pleased with that. To him, to be proper was always the rule of the game.

"Ek knot wai? Oh show off Windsor knot nahin oh tan unparraha ate shorte log jina kol khandan nahin hai of ban de ne. Khandani log single knot ban de ne." *(I hope you mean the single knot, not that show-off Windsor knot, that is for low class uneducated people. People of class tie the single knot*). Thank God, it was the single knot that we were taught to tie otherwise God knows how he would feel.

He asked us to dress, and then he told us to make sure our shoes were polished at all times, and shirt buttons were never ever to be undone. Socks should always be pulled to the knees and folded over to the correct line without a crease in them. We both knew that the carefree days of Herain and Punjab had come to an end, and we are now being turned into proper Brits.

There were still people coming by to see us and welcome us all weekend long. Beejee was kept busy making cups of tea which Kashmir, and I kept serving. The cheek kissing and pulling and stroking the hair on the head went on all weekend.

"Kidan Boy England kidan laga." *(Hello boy, how do you like England?.)*

I thought that welcome phrase was some kind of a code word.

Everyone that came said the same phrase to us, I remember going into the kitchen and saying to Beejee "Gal vich fatti pa pa lenni aa ke menu England Changa nehy laga." *(I am going to put a slate around my neck that says I don't like England.)*

Beejee said, "Chup koz akal kar." (*Hush, mind your manners.)*

The following Monday Papajee took Kashmir and I to Stanton Primary school in Red Lane and enrolled us in school. We began to make friends with both Punjabi Sikh children and also some of the English children in our respective classes. I remember one English kid, in particular, that I became good friends with. His name was Edward. He lived in Freemen Street. Edward was a tall and lanky kid. He would constantly talk with me as if I understood everything he was saying. When, in reality, I had no clue what he was saying. I guess my smiles and head shaking; he took for meaning that we were having a two-way conversation. Slowly and steadily we started to pick up words here and there, at home, Papajee would only talk with us in English.

There were two other Punjabi Sikh kids in the class that I was assigned to, one was a girl from Oliver Street, I believe her name was Balbir also, (Sikhs can have a similar name for either sex), and the other was Surjeet Singh Bagga. Although Bagga is a surname name for Punjabi's, but in Surjeet's case, it was a nickname given to him by his family because of his commonly referred to, had been in England a bit longer than light skin (bagga means light). Balbir, or Beero, as she was Surjeet had, and I was the latest arrival. I was sat next to Surjeet. He was a very caring kid. We became good friends.

When the teacher would say something I would whisper to Surjeet, "Eh ke kendi hai?" (What is she saying?) Most of the times he could figure out and whisper back to me what the teacher was saying. Other times he would turn to Beero to ask. Somehow those two never saw eye to eye, and she would just give him a look, and not bother telling us what the teacher was saying. Once in a while she would whisper to me but leave Surjeet out, and I would whisper to Surjeet when she was looking away.

Surjeet had an older brother Gurmail. He was commonly known as Gello, and they lived in Cobden Street, but when their father lost his job, they moved to Swansea in Wales, where they had some family. They both moved back to Coventry many years afterward. I saw Surjeet few times after they had moved to Coventry. However, like all relationships, it was now a distant friendship that had run its course. It was polite hello, how are you? I still remember him fondly as a warm and a caring individual. I heard that his brother and he had opened some kind of a machine shop, and they were doing well.

As for Beero, I never saw her after primary school; I know that she was married at a fairly young age as was the case for most girls of the first-generation immigrants. Once the girls were out of the secondary school, their fate was pretty much sealed. Find a suitor to get a marriage proposal, and they were married off. Sad when I look back as to how many good talented girls who could have made it through the education system and gone on to become something, sadly, were never given the chance.

Joginder Singh Sodhi a speaker from London on one of his visits to Coventry with his wife Surinder Kaur (will talk about them later in the Gurdwara section), the subject got onto to education.

Joginder Singh asked Papajee about his views on

education for girls.

Papajee told him, "Munden Kurrian da koi farak nahin hona chahi da, har ek bache nun parrane da mauka dena chahi da hai." *(There should be no difference if it is boy or a girl, every child should have chance at education.)*

Joginder Singh asked him if he would be fine with it if he took on the subject the following day at the service. Papajee told him that he had his blessing.

Joginder Singh was a prolific speaker. Words flowed like poetry when he spoke. He commanded the attention of his listeners. He mesmerized his audience. I learnt a lot from talking with him as to how to make public speeches.

The following day he took the subject on and spoke for a good hour on the subject; he addressed the fears that parents of girls had.

He said, "Mainu pata ke bhana bannya janda han, kurrian de parr kar azaad sauch ho jandi hai, atae mundian naal milan lag pehndian han. Apaane rasam revaz bhul jandian han. Par main push da han Sahiban kehrri University de parri see? Heer pass kehrri degree see? Ena nu appne rasam aur revaz atae Sikhi jevan bare samjaou aur parr ne devo. Shoti umre viah na karro." (I know and I hear this as an excuse that girls that get into education become free thinkers and turn bad and start mixing with boys and lose their traditional values. So tell me then which university did Sahiban go to and which degree did Heer have? (Sahiban adHeer are lovers who defied tradtion and dared to fall in love) A person that is taught values will stay with those values. Teach them the values of Sikhi. Then let them go to school. Stop marrying them of so young.)

Sadly, it all fell on deaf ears, and some even complained to Papajij, saying, "Eh kaun hunda sano kehan vala." (Who was he to tell them what to do?)

Joginder Singh dared to challenge the status quo. Papajee defended Joginder Singh's view and endorsed them.

Papajee was always in the camp that girls should get an equal education. When the time came in Herian for a school, he persuaded the people from Herian not to build a boys school, but a girl's school. The school is now a community college. Villagers from Herian living across the globe gave money to buy buses to make commuting to the school more convenient for the girls attending from neighboring villages. All the girls are picked up free of charge and dropped off at the end of the day at their respective villages.

I asked him one time, "Why a girl's school, why not a boy's School?"

He said, "Balbir, when you educate a girl, you light the lamp of education many times. When you educate a boy it is one lamp. When these girls go to another village, and if they marry into an uneducated family, they are going to be the light of education into that family. The next generation will be educated. I want to make sure the coming generation is educated."

Pretty soon as all children do, Kashmir and I settled in and made new friends and the old ones in the village slowly started to become distant memories.

Papajee bought us books that we would have to read and then copy sentences from the book. Look for grammar and understand what a comma was used for what a stop meant. So as we read and we came to a comma, we would say out loud. A comma means a short pause. And then when we got to a Full Stop (period) we would say a full stop means the end of a sentence and took a long pause to think about the sentence. This way, we began to learn to read and write English and participate in the school.

When I was in Punjab, one of the teachers would teach us Bhangra and Malwai Giddha, (Punjabi Folk dances). I was asked to do most of the Malwai Gidda lami boli, (Boli is akin to an Irish limerick). The teacher had been on Bhangra teams. He loved to get a whole bunch of the children after school together and teach us. I was quite good at it. Here in England one of the classes at school was a western dance class, and it was one that I used to hate. I just could not understand the moves. It felt like I had grown a third leg. Thank God after Primary that went away, and I did not have to embarrass myself again.

Our time began to be taken up with the new friends. As more families started to arrive, all the kids would get together and welcome the newer kids and show them the ropes, so they did not feel alone. Everyone knew the feeling of that first arrival loneliness when you didn't know anyone, and everything is different from the smell to the sound.

It amazes me how we seem to hold on to something as our permanent reality. Thinking things will never change. It will always remain the same. All that I now hold before me is my truth, and these people that I know as friends will forever remain my friends. When, in fact, none of it is real. When it is all a matter of that moment in time and as the time moves, people move and change, our reality changes along with it. Those that we may have loved once now seem as strangers, people we thought we knew, no longer seem like the same people. Their reality changed. Our reality changed. We moved on; they moved on and then when we meet we meet as strangers. The only thing that is real is that we need to let go and move on. However, we hold on and hang on. We try to freeze time in our mind. We see people the way they were when we left them, but they are different. Time has carved them into another person. Life's constant hammer has forged them into a different shape. Our experience has changed us, less trusting more watchful, not so carefree.

We are different, even though we want to say to the other person, "Do you remember when we did this or that?"

Inside, though, we smile, look back and may see the folly of the moment, or it all seems hollow and then when you leave the other person, suddenly you part as strangers.

CHAPTER THIRTEEN

Shaeed Udham Singh, Coventry and Indian workers Association.

Udham Singh came to England from Punjab with a specific task in mind, and that was to avenge the deaths of innocent lives that were taken at the point of a gun in Jillianwala bagh (Park) in Amritsar on April 13th 1919 when Brigadier General Reginald Dyer opened fire on a peaceful gathering with the full blessing of the then Lieutenant governor of Punjab Sir Michael O'Dwyer.

In his letter to the Secretary of war office dated 3rd, 1920, General Dyer says the following concerning his action on April 13th 1919.

He states, "I fired and continue to fire until the crowd dispersed, and I consider this the least amount of firing, which would produce the necessary moral and widespread effect. It was my duty to produce if I was to justify my action. If more troops had been at hand, the casualties would have been greater in proportion. It was no longer a question of merely dispersing the crowd, but one of producing a sufficient moral effect from a military point of view not only on those who were present but more especially throughout Punjab. There could be no question of undue severity."

Dyer admits in his letter to the secretary of war that what his intentions were, he wanted to make sure that whole of Punjab was taught a lesson so that it would be morally wounded and could not rise against the British. Dyer

mentions in his letter that, O'Dwyer was of the similar opinion.
O'Dwyer who was the Lieutenant Governor of Punjab at the time stated:

"I have no hesitation in saying that General Dyer's action that day was the decisive factor in crushing the rebellion, the seriousness of which is only now being realized."

Elected congress government of India some sixty-five years later in 1984 to justify the attack in Amritsar less than a half-mile away on Harminder Sahib (Golden Temple.) Used very similar tactics and reasoning as Dyer did on that fateful day of April 13th 1919. They too wanted to teach not Punjab but the Sikhs a lesson, and they too gave similar reasons. Had they not stormed the Golden Temple, Punjab was on a verge of a rebellion.

Winston Churchill in speaking for the censure of Dyer made the following points to the House of Commons, "Commander had to confine himself to limited and definite objective, that is to say, a crowd doing something they ought not to do. Dyer had gone beyond this and had thereby laid himself open to a 'frightfulness'. What I mean by frightfulness, the inflicting of great slaughter or massacre upon a particular crowd of people, with the intention of terrorizing not merely the crowd, but the whole district or country."

Dyer also had his supporters, the one that stands out is Rudyard Kipling, who not only supported Dyer and the attack but bestowed upon him an uncrowned title of a "man who saved India." This from a man who lived among the Indians, and was a newspaperman in Lahore. When Dyer was refused a pension, Kipling and his band of merry Englishmen raised a tidy sum of twenty-six thousand pounds for the Butcher of Jallianwala Bagh.

Dyer and O'Dwyer and other like-minded believed that India belonged to the empire, and only the Sahib (same for the British, by the Indians, a name, they admired for themselves) could rule it.

In his article that appeared in the Globe on January 21st 1921, Dyer states, "India does not want self-government. She does not understand it."

He further goes on to say, "Under self-government. India would commit suicide: but our politicians would be guilty of the murder as associates in crime."

Udham Singh's original mission in England was to assassinate Dyer. However, Dyer died on July 24th, 1927 of series of strokes.

Nigel Collet in his book The Butcher of Amritsar writes, "Dyer's last words on his deathbeds were 'so many people who knew the condition of Amritsar say I did right—but so many others say I did wrong. I only want to die and know from my Maker, whether I did right or wrong.'" (p424)

Udham Singh wanted to avenge the lives of all those people that died on that day, 13th April 1919. His mentor was Bhagat Singh. The Indian independence fighter who was hung along with two of his collogues for their role in the bomb blast in the assembly for which they were convicted. The star witness for the crown was the late Khuswant Singh's (a prominent Indian journalist.) father Sobha Singh. Udham Singh wanted to follow in Bhagat Singh's footsteps to let it be known that the Indians were not going to take such atrocities lying down. He was going to avenge the death of the innocent, not in India but in England.

I had the good fortune to speak with some of the people who were in Coventry when Udham Singh was alive. One of these people that knew him was Prem Singh Khalsa. He painted a picture of Udham Singh of a man on a mission. He told me that he was a very jolly chap, lively. Coventry was one of his favorite places. Khalsa said that he was a really smooth talker; he spoke English well and could persuade anyone to do anything. He said that most of us would be at work, and he pretty much had keys to everyone's house, and people gave it to him willingly. Even if they did not, it made no difference to him, he would pry a window open or pick a lock just as easily. He would show up and find whichever pot had curry he liked and made a couple of rotis (chappati) eat and be on his merry way. He said when we got home we would know oh Bawa (his pet name meaning carefree) must have come around.

Khalsa said that he was not only a quick study of people, but he was very much mechanically inclined. He would hot wire a car and take to where he wanted to go and just dump it and move on.

One thing that Khalsa said that struck me was that every month Bawa would go to Maharaja Duleep Singh's grave (last Maharaja of the Sikhs who was deposed in 1849 and brought to England and converted to Christianity) and leave flowers there. He said that he would go into a deep silence when we talked about Maharaja Duleep Singh and his mother Rani Jindan and what happened to the Sikh Raj. He would go deep inside himself and give a big sigh; Khalsa said that he had always remembered that sigh. There was so such sadness in his sigh. He said it felt as if the man was weeping on the inside. Khalsa would go on to tell me that Bawa marched to a different drummer, and we all knew it. We would tell him don't do anything rash, but he would just smile.

Khalsa's last meeting with Bawa was in 1939 when he came to see Khalsa before Khalsa boarded a ship back to Punjab to visit his family. He said Bawa had something on his mind, and he wanted to get it out. He was full of energy and wanted to share something.

Khalsa said, "I could feel that this was going to be our last meeting. Every body movement that Bawa was making was speaking louder than his silence."

"Bawa what is it? You seem agitated. I will see you on my return." So Khalsa said I asked

It was then Khalsa said that he finally broke his silence and said, "Prem Singh, I am sure you will be back, but we will not meet again. I am going to kill the king."

Khalsa said I was frightened for Bawa, but I also knew there was no point if not the king it was going to be someone else that he was on a mission to avenge Jallian wala Bagh Massacre and Dyer were already dead.

Khlasa said, I told him to not to talk of such things. He said I was a bit nervous about the conversation. He would not have been surprised if Bawa was not under surveillance. Khalsa said so he stopped the conversation and started to talk in general about other things until he boarded the ship. Khalsa said that was the last, he would see Bawa. When Khalsa talked about Bawa Udham Singh, you could see the melancholy look on his face as if two friends that parted and never met again.

Udham Singh picked his mark, and maybe he already had his mark picked out, but he was just trying to see where Khalsa's emotions were if he suggested the King.

On March 13th 1940, Udham Singh entered Caxton Hall in London where Sir Percy Sykes gave a lecture on Afghanistan. Seated in the back row on the platform was Sir Michael O'Dwyer, as the meeting came to an end. O'Dwyer, Lord Leamington, and Sir Louis Dane all moved forward to the front of the platform. Udham Singh moved to the front and fired the first two shots and mortally wounded and killed O'Dwyer. With the remainder bullets, he hit Lord Zetland and Sir Luis Dane. They both escaped with just minor injuries.

The death of the innocent was finally avenged in the capital of the imperialism London, by a man determined to give voice to those that were killed. Following in his mentor Bhagat Singh's footsteps once again told every Indian sitting around the world that we will not still idly by and accept the imperial rule and injustices meted out. We are ready to fight as equals and are not inferior to the English in any way.

March 14th, 1940 every newspaper in England had the similar headlines, of the assassination of O'Dwyer at the hands of an Indian. They referred to him as a mad man. Papers in India carried the news. Khalsa told me that he first heard the news spread in his village of the assassination, and said he knew who did it without even hearing the name. He said that he got a newspaper and confirmed indeed Bawa was the one who carried out the assassination. He told me that Punjab had a different glow that day. It felt as if heavy fog, which had been over Punjab had been lifted. People once again felt that Punjab was the land of the proud and the land of honor. When that is challenged then sons of Punjab will always rise to take revenge as Bawa did.

Khalsa told me that he was a bit sad as he knew what the outcome for Bawa was going to be for this act, but he also knew that this was his destiny, and he had fulfilled his destiny like Bhagat Singh before him.

Udham Singh's case came before judge Sir. Cyril Atkinson in the central criminal court Old Bailey. The trial ran until June of 1940 when on June 5th, 1940, Sir Cyril Atkinson passed out the death sentence to Udham Singh. Udham Singh was hung on 31st, July, 1940 at 9AM and so ended the life of another man of destiny on this earth. Like his mentor, Bhagat Singh, he had marched into the golden pages of history alongside those that my dear friend Roop Chand would speak of, "Log woh hote hain jo zamane ke saat chalte hain, mard woh hote hain jo Zamane ko badal dete hain." (People are those who walk the path of the world, but brave hearts are those who change the path of the world.)

So it was, a man born into obscurity, in an ordinary Punjabi Sikh family did the extraordinary, and wiped the shame of defeat and helplessness off the face of Punjab. He completed his task and became Shaheed Udham Singh. (Martyr Udham Singh)

CHAPTER FOURTEEN

Indian Workers Association also known as Hindostani Mazdur Sabha

Udham Singh in early part of 1937 along with other Punjabi's of Coventry created the Indian workers Association or Majdur Sabha. He realized that the Indians, mainly Punjabi's who were mostly Sikh at that point in time from Doab area of Punjab were coming into England. Since Coventry was an industrial hub of its time, most of them were either settling in Coventry or in the West Midlands at large. He saw that these people were now starting to move away from the peddling, hawking type of business and taking jobs in factories. He felt it necessary to form an organization that could represent the Indians and their welfare with the local government, trade unions and also company management.

Later, it would integrate into its charter the need to fight towards independence of India, similar to the Gadhar movement of USA. However, unlike the Gadhar Movement whose main charter was the independence of India. Primary charter of the Indian Worker's Association was to represent the welfare of the Indians living in England. Thereby most of the Punjabi's referred to it as Mazdur Sabha (Labor Association). After the initial formation in Coventry, other branches around the country opened up, in 1941 branches in Birmingham and Bradford opened up, then Wolverhampton and New Castle-on-tyne the following year in 1942. A Muslim gentleman by the name of Akbar Ali Khan who initially lived in Coventry moved to East London in 1944 and opened a branch there. Slowly and steadily there were branches in every part of England wherever there were

Punjabi's.

India house (department that administered the affairs for the crown concerning India) kept a close eye on the activities of the main organizers, especially after the execution of Udham Singh. They became extremely interested in the activities and movement of those involved in the Association.

Even though the organization became national and had branches in every major city, it was, however, fairly well insular. Until around 1945, it was a moderately dormant organization. The rebuilding of England plans after the end of the Second World War was starting to be put in place. India moved towards its Independence in 1947. The new influx of Punjabi labor into England gave rise to Indian Workers Association, and it once again started to gain momentum.

In 1958, a coordination committee put forth the idea that a national body should be established, all the London and neighboring branches, including Southall, Birmingham, Wolverhampton, Leamington Spa all became part of this central body in 1959.

One Rajmal Singh led Coventry Indian Worker's Association at that time. Coventry branch initially did join the national body. Papajee cautioned Rajmal not to walk in blindly. He asked him to make sure that he had fair representation on the new body and that the direction of the national body was the representation of the welfare of the Indian workers. Papajee was nervous about the rising influence of the leftist people that were moving into the association and exerting their will. People like Pundit Vishnu Dutt of Kharak Kalan were all the old guards but as newer immigrants started to come the association began to change. The leftist voice started to become louder and eventually in 1964. Rajmal left the national body and decided to have just a local branch that represented the welfare of the Indian people of Coventry. Those that split from Rajmal and remained with the national body were mostly the leftist leaning people. The local branch of the National body elected one Sardara Singh as its new president.

Rajmal Singh was born in the Fiji islands. Papajee knew him and his family in Fiji and knew Rajmal since he was a young boy growing up in Fiji. Rajmal was a stocky man, with a very deep voice. He did not speak Punjabi well. He spoke a mix of Punjabi and Hindi, a Fijian Hindoostani. He worked at Alfred Herbert and was a single man when I met him. He later went to India and did marry.

Being born in Fiji, he was educated in English schools so his English was fluent, which naturally made him a good choice be the leader of the Association since a large amount of the members did not speak English, even if they did it was broken at best. He was a caring man with a deep commitment to his community. He was not shy to let his opinions be known in any meeting with the local English population. He stood his ground as an equal, and he took on many tasks, which resulted in people of Coventry of all colors living as equals.

People sometimes forget what some of these early pioneers did, Sikhs, are not very good at documenting our history and events. Unfortunately, we leave it to others and then complain when they don't do us justice.

Some of the issues that Rajmal took up were an entry into pubs and clubs for people of color, and also employment on the corporation buses for people of color.

On Stoney Stanton road, there was a pub called The Red House, they had a policy that Indians or people of color were not allowed in. Working men's clubs had a similar policy that they too would not allow Indians or people of color into the clubs. Rajmal fought hard against this apartheid, and did not stop until Indians and people of color were allowed into these places as equals. On the surface, one could say why is this important? But it meant you were a second-class citizen. The rights under the law for every member of the British Commonwealth (union of those independent countries that were at one time part of the British Empire) were not yours as an equal other than those the Englishman sought fit to grant to you. It was in its own right apartheid which Rajmal help abolish. Later, after a long fought struggle of which I became a part of, the government that looked at these matters and resolved them created a race relation board at the national and local level.

The other notable thing that Punjabi's owe Rajmal a debt of gratitude for is that before he took up with the city council the issue, bus drivers, and bus conductors (in those days, buses had two employees per bus, one who drove the bus, and the conductor who cut the tickets) were all white. Indians and people of color were not allowed employment on the buses. Rajmal took the city council and the Coventry bus Corporation to task. He argued if we are to pay general property tax and the same fare on the buses as an Englishman, then we ought to be allowed to participate in the employment and have equal representation on the buses. This type of movements caught on in other cities led by other local community activists that resulted in people being allowed to work on the buses in all the cities across the country.

Rajmal was a nationalist Indian, which was a bit odd since he was from Fiji Island; my early recollection of the Indian workers association activities was which mostly revolved around Indian Independence day meeting and also the Republic day meetings. On these meetings, it did not matter who the high commissioner (term used for Ambassador of Commonwealth countries) was in London. He always showed up for the meetings and gave a speech. I remember Rajmal would be beaming at these meetings.

Most of these meetings were held in the upstairs hall of a secondary modern school known as Wheatly School. I believe it's gone now, and Sydney Stringer is in its place. It was right behind the Alexandria cinema.

If that was not available, then they were held in the upstairs hall of Stanton Bridge school on Red Lane. Some of the notable people that I remember that came were the late Vijay Lakshmi. Pundit (Nehru's sister) the late Krishnan Menon, he went on to become the defense minister of India,

Additionally, Kewal Singh who was the high commissioner of India was some of the High Commissioners that I remember coming.

Beejee sewed us tricolor scarfs (Indian flag is referred to as Tauranga, or tricolor because of its green white and saffron colors.) On August 15th the independence day of India, we would be dressed in our finest. I would wear the scarfs around my neck. Papajee would have a tri-color coat pocket-handkerchief that he would wear to the meetings.

Someone from Birmingham would be there to sing some patriotic songs and people would give them money and feel really proud of being Indians. Men only attended these meetings. Women would always be left at home. Kashmir, I few other children who would be present, Tara Singh Heer Karamjeet Singh's father may bring him once in a while but in general there were very few if any children there.

Papajee always made sure that I went. Even if I didn't want to go, I had no choice, it was required that I go, so I went and felt that it was my duty. Papajee wanted to expose us to the community and community work. He always had a plan, there was a vision. He at no time did anything on a whim. It was always well calculated and thought out. He had this habit and it never changed to his last day on this earth. He would leave the house, and close the door. He would stand there for a moment in the doorway, and look right and then left and right again, and stand for a moment and then start his journey. I asked him later in life why he did that?

He told me, "Zindagi vich har kadam suoch ke rakhna chahi da hai. Har kadam phela sauch lehna chahi da hai main kherra kadam puttan lagan han, es taran insaan nu pata hai kai mera maksad ke hai." (Always think and calculate your options in life and journey before you start to take a step and that way you are aware and alert of your task and your planned vision.)

It was not until later I understood why he took me to all those meetings. He had a role that he wanted me to play, and he was preparing me for it.

In 1962 when the Indo-China war broke out there was a fundraiser at the Wheatly school and there was a lot of money collected. Papajee asked me to speak. Rajmal was quite pleased to see me on the stage. I was pretty frightened. The stage was full of people who could speak with big words and here was little old me. It was a frightening experience, but up on the stage I went. I had a small prepared speech, but I soon found myself ad libbing, and I remember getting caught up in the moment and not wanting to be out done by anyone. I went for the Juggular. I remember these words to this day.

"AAJ DESH LAY EKK JATT THE PUTT FAQIR HOGIA BHAR DEO MERI JHOLLY." (For the sake of the country a Jatt's son has turned to begging fill up my bag.)

Once I said that the pounds started to pour in. I was hugged by a lot of people after that speech. It was my first major speech. After the meeting, people came and hugged me. My cheeks were sore from being squeezed by just about everyone there.

Rajmal walked up to me and put his hand out and shook my hand and said, "Balbir Singh well done!"

I was very pleased to hear that from Rajmal. He then turned to Papaji and said, "Dharam Singh jee "Yeh ek din Parliament me jaiga." *(He will be in the parliament one day.)*

On the way home Papajee said nothing. I thought that he would be happy, but he said nothing. When we got home, he sat me down and said what was on his mind. Beejee was also sitting there, Kashmir was not in the house. Papajee said, "Balbir look, never apply the word Faqir again to a Jatt. I don't want the word faqir ever to be in your vocabulary not even for what you did to raise that amount of money.

"We are Sikhs and we are never Faqirs. Our head only bows to Guru Granth Sahib no one else, Faqir's head bows and bows."

Never use words in life for expediency, because it will make you compromise life's principles. I never want my sons to bow to anyone but the Guru.

As usual, he recited an Urdu couplet, "**SAR TU JHUK TA HAI SAB KA KHAIN NA KHAIN, SAWAL EH UTH TA HAI KAHAN JHUKAE GA TERE SAR? SHETHAN KE DHAR JAN** "KHUDA KE GHAR? MAGAR PHARAK HAI JHUKNE MEN, KHUDA KE GHAR JHUKA SAR FAKHAR SE UTAYEA JAI GA, SHETAAN KHE DAR JHUKA SAR BAAR BAAR JHUKYA JAI GA." (All heads ultimately bow somewhere, so where will your head bow, at the devil's door or at God's house? The difference is the head that bows to God will rise in dignity, but one that bows to the devil will bow again and again.)

He left to go somewhere, then Beejee took over, and I got a very long lesson on why Jatt and Sikhs should never ever use those words. She told me that we are a race of honorable people, and we create our own destiny with the grace of Waheguru (God), and that is the only place where your head should bow, nowhere else. I have not forgotten those words. They have guided me over the years, even times of despair. I still go to the Gurdwara and bow and sit and ask for guidance.

Beejee told me that as you move through your life never ever to use the word faqir, erase it from your mind, and chose your words by which you can hold your head up high. Words are who you are; choose them carefully, not for any expediency of politics, or for short-term gain. When you speak, people must know that a man of honor and dignity has spoken. When you leave after speaking people must be left with something to ponder that will make their lives better. If you do this, then your spoken words have a meaning otherwise, they are meaningless. She said to remember, your Babajee is Sardar Udham Singh, and your Nanajee is S ardar Bhagat Singh. (Those are the names of my paternal and maternal grandfathers respectively.) They are also the names of those brave hearts who gave their lives fighting for freedom, not begging for it.

I have always tried my level best from that day to do the right thing. It has meant going against the grain with friends and organization at times, but I have remembered that lesson and have never used the word Faqir again in any context in my language.

Chapter Fifteen

Smethwick Gurdwara opening ceremony and Rajmal

After the first Gurdwara in Shepherd's Bush, the next one to open was in Smethwick on 31st July 1961, it was a church that was purchased and converted into a Gurdwara. Smethwick was where most Sikhs lived, later they spanned out into other areas like west Bromwich Handsworth. Initially, most of the population was in or around Smethwick and the Sangat (congregation) had been holding services known as Sangrand (service held at the first of the new Sikh calendar), Sangrad divan in a school hall monthly from 1958 until the purchase of the hall. The driving force behind the Smethwick Gurdwara was one man by the name of Boota Singh of Sidhwan in Doab in Punjab. He was a man in his late thirties or early forties. He was a very pragmatic no-nonsense type of a person. His brother used to do Kirtan (singing Hymns from Guru Granth Sahib).

Papajee took us to the opening ceremony and it was really a grand affair. It was the first time that I saw families at a function, as I mentioned earlier, at other functions it was always a male affair and people never took their families to those other functions. However, this was a Gurdwara and whole families were here.

On the bus ride home, Papajee said nothing, but I knew something was on his mind. It was always easy to tell when he was processing something in his mind. He would take his right thumbnail and start flicking it against the middle finger nail. You could tell if the processing speed got faster or slower by the speed of the flick.

Beejee saw him flicking, and she looked over at me and

smiled as if to say something is on his mind. I was nervous and started looking back at the day to make sure all my ducks were lined up, and that I did not step out of line, and if I did was there an excuse that I could come up with. I scanned the day and felt safe that I was in a safe territory at least this time. Kashmir never came into the equation. He would never do anything out of place anyway.

Papajee worked nights, and he went about his business all week and nothing was said or heard of his nail flicking until the following Saturday lunchtime.

After we had lunch, he said, "Men thuhade tina naal gal karni chounda han." (I need to talk with the three of you. Meaning Beej, Kashmir and I.) We sat down and knew that this had something do with what was going on in his mind on the bus.

He said, "Mera kheal hai ke Coventry vich be Gurdwara chahi da hai. Hun ethe bauhat tabar han aur ona no appni jaga chahi de hai jithe oh apanni paath puja kar sakan. So men app nu push da ha ke aap mera saath devo ge agar men eh shoro karan?" (I think Coventry needs a Gurdwara. We have a lot of families that are here now, and we need to make sure that we have a place to pray and also a place where people can get a sense of belonging. So I needed to ask all of you if I have your support with me moving ahead in this direction?)

Although I did not understand what all this entailed, it sounded like lot of fun. So I shouted out, "Han sanoo jaroor karan chahi da hai." (Well yes, we should do it.)

That's when Beejee said in a stern voice "Balbir Chup!" (Balbir, quiet.)

Beejee was a very balanced individual and always tried to understand the situation before she made a commitment. To her, there was no turning back once there was a commitment made. So she wanted to know how Papajee was planning to go about this.

She asked him, "Eh sab kedan hove gaa, tusin Mazdur sabah vich hon, Brimigham vali committee ek azad committee hay. Kya tusi Mazdur sabah no shad devo ge? tusi ek navi committee bannavo ge?" (How are you going to do this? You are in the Mazdur Sabha; the Gurdwara committee in Birmingham (even though the Gurdwara in Smethwick it was still referred to as Birmingham) is an independent Parbadhak committee. Are you going to resign and from the Mazdur Sabha and start a new group?)

That was not acceptable to Papajee. He said, No, he did not want to divide the community like that he thought it ought to build it under the umbrella of the Mazdur Sabha (Indian Worker's association).

Beejee asked him if Rajmal and the rest of the members would agree. She knew if Rajmal agreed the rest would come along anyway.

Papajee said, "Mera kheal mainu Rajmal naal gal karin pave ge." (I think I have to speak with Rajmal.)

On Sunday, he went over to Rajmal's place and spoke to him about papajee's plans. When Papajee came home Beejee asked what Rajmal said.

"Oh sunn da te reha par on koi ha na nahin kahy, ena jaroor keha ke eh bauht vada kam hai mainu sauch len deo." (Well, he didn't commit to anything but listen, the only thing he said was let me think about this. It's a big undertaking.)

Few weeks went by but Rajmal never got back with an answer to Papajee. I think in Rajmal's mind that if he kept quite Papajee would get over it, and give up on the idea, and he could move on. Papajee was not one to move on once his mind was made up. Even if he did falter Beejee would not let him move on either, she would not back down like that. Beejee advised Papajee to go talk with Rajmal again. This, time he took me with him, Rajmal's face turned red when he saw Papajee.

It was a Saturday afternoon, and in his usual haughty

laugh and a deep baritone voice said, "Dharam Singh jee Kese aunna hua?" (Dharam Singh jee what is the purpose of your visit?)

That statement was enough to raise Papajee's temperature. However, he kept his calm, but could not resist saying to Rajmal in a very calm voice,

"Rajmal, eh syast hor kisie naal kheli, mere naal nahi, mere tan tun hathan which vada hoian" (Rajmal play that political game with someone else, not with me, you grew up in my arms).

Rajmal knew he could not avoid the subject anymore. He knew the time had come to answer Papajee.

So papajee asked him, "Fer das tehn ke karna, kya mazdur sabha Gurdwara bannayae ge?" (Well, what is it that you want to do? Are you going to allow the Gurdwara to be built under the umbrella of the Mazdur Sabha?)

Rajmal hesitated for a while as if to see if he could wiggle out of it. Papajee was in no mood to walk away without discussing it and reaching a conclusion.

Rajmal's lips were dry. He respected Papajee, but he knew that they were going to be at odds on this. He had that false smile upon his face, and he giggled a bit, he started to speak in a very nervous voice.

"Dehko Dharam Jee je, hum ek satahay sanstha hain, mujhabi sanstha nahain, Gurdwara banana Dharami Kaam hai." (Dharam Singh jee, we are secular organization, Gurdwara requires a religious organization.)

Papajee knew that since Rajmal had avoided him for weeks, his answer came as no surprise to him.

"Rajmal, ek swal hai, kya Muzdur Sabha logan de bhallai waste nahin. Kya es sabaha nu eh nahin dekhna chahi da ke logan de samae de zaroorat kya hai?" (Rajmal I have a question for you, is the Mazdur Sabha not for the benefit of the people? Should it not serve the need of the hour of the people?)

Rajmal knew that there was not going to be an easy way out of this. Rajmal replied to Papajee's question as any politician would. He completely avoided answering the question directly but pointed out another reason for not moving ahead.

He told papajee, "Agar hum Gurdwara banane ke lyea maan jaate hain to Hindu, aur Muslim bhai be kahen ge ke hume be Masjid aur Mandir Chahyae." (If we agree to build a Gurdwara, then Muslim and Hindus will say we need to have a Masjid and a Mandir also.)

Papajee sensed that Rajmal was going to throw every excuse he could at him. Papajee was determined to get to an answer with Rajmal. So Papajee told him, "Rajmal, Musselman ta hunn sade naal rehehe nahin. Rahi gal Hindua dee, thoorre jehe Punditha de ghar ne baki Gujrati tan sade vich rall de he nahin. Pur fer be men teri gal man da. So tan oh ve hissa paun tan aapa Gurdwara, Masjid tan Mandir tin he banna lene." (Rajmal the Muslims have already separated, (*he was referring to the creation of Pakistan.*) About the Hindus, there are few homes of Pundits (*referring to Punjabi Hindus*), and the Gujarati's don't mix with us. Still, if those communities so desire they can join in, and we can build all three, Gurdwara, Masjid and Mandir.)

Rajmal was now speechless. He ran out of excuses, and he came back to his original stance, "We are a secular."

Papajee told him, that unless we have a place that people can point to, a place we can gather at, a place where families can come for not only spiritual strength but also for moral support we will never be looked at as a community.

He told Rajmal, "Rajmal ek gal meri kan khol ke sunn le, jina tak sadi apnni jaga nahi assin bae gahar han Guru de ghar naal he sadi pehchaan bannani hai aur eh ghar bann ke he rahega, par me chaounda han ke eh etfaq de vich banne." (Rajmal listen to one thing very clearly. We have no standing without our house of worship. This will be built, but I would like to build it as a united front.)

Papajee had thrown the gauntlet at Rajmal, Rajmal did not

say a word, but put his head down.

Papajee said to him, "Rajmal kal nu main nu daush na dain ke men juda ho gian ek baar fer sauch le." (Rajmal don't blame me tomorrow that I separated. You had better think this through one more time.)

Rajmal, however, could not get past his belief system, so finally he turned around to Papajee and said, "Dharam Singh jee jeh muj se nhain hoga." (Dharam Singh jeeI cannot do this.)

Rajmal finally admitted that he could not go along with Papajee's plan to build a Gurdwara under the umbrella of Mazdur Sabha.

They stood there in silence for few minutes, and Papajee finally broke the silence and said, "Changa teekh hai phir." (Ok fine then.)

And we came home. I could see papajee was hurt, he was at a crossroad. He loved the Mazdur Sabha, and Rajmal meant a lot to him. They did not always agree on all the issues but there was history from Fiji. Then there was this mutual respect that they shared for each other. He was silent all the way home. I decided to walk few steps behind him; I knew that he was hurt and angry, and I didn't want to become the recipient of his anger, so I just stepped back and followed him home.

Beejee looked over at me, and I lightly shook my head to let her know that it was a no go. She understood and saw the disappointment on Papajee's face. She did not ask him and allowed him the time to sit. He took off his coat and handed it to me. I hung his coat on the coat rack in the corridor leading from the front door to the family room. He sat down and asked Beejee for a glass of water. Beejee brought him a glass of water, and he slowly sipped it. It was as if he was not even thirsty but just needed something in his hand to hold and think his way through.

He finally put out his glass, and I leaned over and took it from him and went to the kitchen to put it away. Beejee worked up the courage to ask him.

"Rajmal kee bolyea?" (What did Rajmal say?)

Papajee grasped his forehead with his right four fingers and his cheek with his thumb and started massaging his forehead gently. Beejee asked him if he had a headache, and if she could massage his head. He lightly shook his head and said, "Nahin." (No.)

He slowly started to talk, "Rajmal bahannen tan key bannayae pur muk de gal eh hay ke oh kehnda ke eh ek secular organization hai es nu dharam naal nehi oh jorr sak da." (Rajmal made a lot of excuses, but the conclusion is that he said that Mazdur Sabha was a secular organization and he cannot mix it with religion.)

Beejee had no clue what secular was, so she asked Papaji, "Eh secular ke cheez hundi hai." (What is this thing called secular?)

"Eh dharam nirpakhta jan duniadari." (It's a word meaning non biasing towards religion, worldly).

Beejee replied back to Papajee by saying, "Esda matlab eh hoya fir har dharam jith eko jehae han, teekh?" (So it means where all religions are treated equal, correct?) "Fir Rajmal no kehna see tan saria nu kaho ke o kam shoro karan. Gurdwara, Mandir, Masjid tene banna lende. Fer oh da secular be poora bach jave ga, naale sare Rab de ghar be bann jaann ge" (You should have told Rajmal to get everyone moving on a Gurdwara, Mandir, and a Masjid. That way he could keep his secularism, and all the people would have their place of worship).

"Eh vi men oh nu keha see par oh fir be nahin manian," (I did suggest that to him also, but he still did not agree) Papajee replied to Beejee's suggestion.

My parents were a team. They challenged each other to bring out the best in each other. They thought alike. Once they put their mind into something. There was nothing that was going to get in their way to make it happen. They discussed everything, openly and constantly shared with Kashmir and I. We were brought up to have a very open and honest relationship in the family, by discussing everything as a family. We were told that way you will not lose any sleep at night.

Beejee threw the challenge to Papajee, "Kena K dum hai, thoadae vich Eh karne de lay." (How much stamina do you have in you to do this?)

"Men teri gal nahin samjeia Nasib Kaur, Mere vich dam hai es lay." (I don't understand what you mean Nasib Kaur; I have the stamina to do this.)

"Dekho jee imthian de gharri hay, rab dekh reha hai ke kalae tusi kharr sako ge? Jerra kadam tusin dil vich lae ke Rajmal kul gai se aur na the jabab melia. Kal nu tan ongal be uth sakdi hai. Aur kay Rajmal narash karan ge. Kya thak ke beth tan na jao ge? Eh swal aj parmatma push reha, mera gahr banoun laga ad vich shad ke bhaj tan na javega." (Look dear husband. This is the hour of your test. God is watching and seeing if you can stand alone, the step that you have embarked upon many fingers will be raised upon you. Many Rajmals will disappoint you. God is saying to you, you are asking me for the boon to build my house. Do you have what it takes to see it to the finish line; you will not quit half way?)

Beejee stood up and had her right hand on her hip and was looking at Papajee straight in the eyes and asking him this.

"Jeh teri haan hai aur saath hai fir men kade pishae nahin hattan ga mere vich dam hai," Papajee replied. (If you agree, and I have your support, then I will never turn back. I have the stamina.)

Beejee replied, "Assi tan ek he han, par ena mundian nu be puch layae." (We are one, but we had better ask these boys.)

Kashmir and I were sitting on the couch listening to both of them. Papajee turned to us and asked Kashmir first, "Kidan boy teek?" (Well boy, Ok?)

Kashmir smiled and shook his head.

Then he turned to me and said, "Balbir tun vada hain, tere te jemevarri bauth peh sak di, teek hain," (Balbir you're the eldest, lot of responsibility is going to fall on your shoulders. Are you fine?) Papajee asked me.

I remember getting up and saying, "Ju marji kahon ge karan ga." (Whatever you say I will do).

I was the eldest. I agreed and had no knowledge or idea what this all meant, all I knew was, that my parents were embarking on a new a journey, and I had to help, and that it was my duty.

The next week there was a lot of talk about how to go about this. Papajee still had it in his mind that if he could somehow make it work through the Mazdur Sabha. He just was not ready to let it go that easy. During the next few weeks, he approached everyone who he had any association within the running of the Mazdhur Sabha to see if they would come to his side. Then they as a joint group would go to Rajmal and get this turned around. He got a lot of politeness and lot of, "we shall see", "let's discuss a bit more." He knew that none of them were ready to embark on this journey.

We had just finished breakfast that Sunday afternoon, and Beejee washed up and put all the dishes away and sat by the fireplace and said to Papajee, "Men thuhano keha see eh raste per pelan kale ho ke turna pena hun jhijik kis gal de?" (I had told you, you will have to walk this path alone first. What is the hesitation?)

Papajee finally came clean with what was really bothering him, why he was pushing Mazdur Sabha.

"Eh Mazdur Sabaha Shaheed Udham Singh De Bannai hai, men oh nu ke jabbab dya ga?" (Shaheed Udham Singh created the Mazdur Sabha what answer will I give him?)

Beejee saw Papajee's anguish, but she was also very strong-willed woman. She told Papajee, "Tusi apnni poori vah la lay he jeh Mazdur Sabha wale nay man de hunn jo sahi oh karoo. Rahi gal Udham Singh dee oh ve Waheguru das deve ga jad jabbab denn that time ayiea." (You have tried your level best if the Mazdur Sabha folks are not willing you do what is right. With regards to Udham Singh, God will give you the answer when the time comes.)

He was having trouble having to resign from the Mazdur Sabha. He thought he was turning his back on Udham Singh and what he had created. However, he also knew that he needed to go his way. His path was chosen for him. I remember Papajee at that moment said something which I did not understand as it was in Farsi. Years later, one day, I asked him. What was it that he said, and he repeated it to me, and I wrote it down?

He said, "GAR TAU KHAI VATAN PUR AZ DILDAAR, KHAANA RA RAU TAEHI KUN AZ AGYAAR." (Let your heart be empty of all others, except God, and other than God let there be no other thought but that of God.)

Once he had reached this state of mind, the following week he went to see Rajmal and gave him his resignation from Mazdur Sabha. Rajmal asked Papajee how he was going to go about this huge project.

Papajee told him, he was sure yet, but knew he had to do this.

He told him the truth, "Rajmal eh aje mainu pata nahin par joh mainu eh keh reha hai ke eh kar rah we oh he dekave ga." (Rajmal that I don't know yet, but he who is telling me to do this will also show me the way.)

Rajmal took Papajee's resignation letter and let out a very deep sigh. It was one of grief, as if he was losing a part of his life. He could not raise his head. His eyes were looking down at the floor. Papajee put his hand on his shoulder and pressed it. They were both silent for good few minutes. Rajmal wanted to hug papajee. Papajee was not one to show emotions that easy. He was formal. He knew that Rajmal wanted to hug him.

He stepped back and said in a very stern voice, "Rajmal seva karin chouder na." (Rajmal serve not command.)

He backed away, and we left.

On the way home, he was silent, and then I asked him a question, "Papajee thuano Dar ne lag da?" (Papajee aren't you afraid?)

He replied to me in the following words, "Balbir Dar har aadmi nu lag da. Par dar ke kade nahin zindgi jeenni. Har vele parmatama de kolo salah leke apnna kam sahi dil naal kar de renna atte sachi gal har vele karini. Fer parmatama aape rah deka deve ga, par bhrosa jarrori hai." (Balbir every person is afraid, but never live life in fear. At all times ask for almighty's guidance in everything that you do. Do your duty with purity of heart. At all times speak the truth, and the Almighty will show you the way.)

We walked home, him in front, I, a few steps behind. He was not the hand holding kind of father. He was Edwardian if anything. He was very formal with us. I think in his mind if he hugged us; it would break the formality and would make us weak. So we had a very formal relationship with him. We would never ever wear jeans, to this day I very rarely wear jeans, it was something that he instilled in me, that formality was always the order of the day.

On the other hand, although Beejee stood for no nonsense and could be far stricter than papajee but she had a softer side to her. She could have a good laugh with both Kashmir and I and tell a joke or two whenever the mood struck her. When Papajee was not around though.

As we got home, Beejee was waiting, and she looked happy and was ready to go. She asked Papajee if it was all done. He nodded his head and sat down. There was air of renewal in our house at 7 Red Lane that day, an air of something new that we were going to start.

It was Saturday, late Saturday morning. We went to town to do our weekly grocery shopping or ration shopping as it was referred to back then by most of our folks. It felt like that we all were light as a feather. The whole world seemed like a fresh morning after a spring rain. Like the entire drudge had been washed clean, and a crisp fresh breeze was in the air.

As always, when Kashmir came to the carousel by the market, he wanted to go on the roundabout. Papajee gave him money and asked me if I wanted to go, I always behaved more matured, as most elder siblings do. Even if I wanted to go on the carousel I was not going to since my kid brother was going on it. How would that feel, me sitting on a roundabout with my kid brother, so I declined. Kashmir is only two years younger than me, but he has always been my kid brother. I have always felt as if I was much older than him then two years.

That whole week in the evening when Papajee woke up to get ready to go to his nightshift job, we would strategize, and talk about our new venture.

He generally woke around five PM in the evening. He came down brushed his teeth and shaved and then sat down to read his Coventry Evening Telegraph. Then he would ask us about our homework, and slowly he would put on his clothes for work. Around seven PM he would leave to walk all the way from Red lane, up Stoney Stanton road though St Paul's Road and on to Folsehill Road and wait there to be picked up by a person who would drive him and others to Sterling Metals in Nuneaton. Some individuals had figured out a service that was needed to cart other people to work. So they had brought vans and would charge people a weekly fee and offer this service of picking people up from strategic spots and taking them to work. It worked really well for all concerned, and people got to work on time plus the cost that these people would charge was reasonable.

Every night after Papaji finished reading his newspaper, we would discuss how we were going to go about our new project, whom we would talk to. Both Beejee and Papajee knew that they would have to approach new people to form a team. These new people would have to have the fire in their belly to see the project to the finish line.

CHAPTER SIXTEEN

Guru Granth Sahib Arrival

The following weekend Papajee wrote a letter to my Phopperji, (his Sister's husband) Sadhu Singh Rai, who worked for the Punjab government in some civil engineering capacity. I am not sure what his official titled was. I remember whenever he visited our village Herian when we were there, he looked smart and always had a smartly tied turban and always wore a tie. He was very polite and kind, he never ever spoke even to us children without saying Jee. (Jee is a gesture of respect added on to someone's name.) He at no time did he failed to ask each of the kids how we they getting on in school. My Majee (Paternal grandmother) would always say Sadhu Singh lives up to his name. He is truly a Sadhu! (Saintly person.)

He was stationed in Amritsar at the time. Papajee wrote to him asking him to send Guru Granth Sahib (The Sikh Holy Scriptures) from Punjab. Papajee wrote to him about his intentions of starting a Gurdwara in Coventry. Phopporjee sent the Guru Granth Sahib and wrote a letter back to Papajee that he had done so and also congratulated him on his decision to take up this task, and wrote,

"Veerajee, Waheguru aap da saath devega." (Dear brother God almighty will aid you.)

There was hidden a message in this simple statement, and it was this. Since Papajee could only read and write Urdu Farsi and English and could not read and write Gurmukhi (Punjabi), he knew that he had to overcome this hurdle and Phopperjee was telling papajee not to let that deter him.

A few weeks later in the Saturday Mail, the parcel arrived.

It was a big parcel wrapped in a white cloth. We all knew what it was. Truth be known, none of us knew how to act around it. It was like some dignitary came to your house, and you did not know how to act and address them. What bigger dignitary was there for Sikhs than the Guru Granth Sahib? Papajee asked us all to bathe. We did not have a bath in the house; no one did in those days. Everyone went to the public baths.

We had attached to the house a coal room that we converted to a bathroom. So we would heat up the water and there was a big bucket in the room into which we would pour the water, the right amount of cold and hot water and bathe. So this is what we did that day one by one. Once we were done, Papajee put a fresh white sheet on the table and started to open the parcel.

Just then Beejee shouted, "Ek minute," (One minute). "Je App nu koj der tehrana pavega." (Dear husband you will have to wait for a while.)

Papajee stopped, and Beejee asked me to put on my coat and go with her. We caught the bus to town, and she went into Owens and Owens (the largest department store in town), and she grabbed some cloth and some quilting padding, and we caught the bus home. I asked her what was all this for. She said just to sit tight and don't ask too many questions.

We were back within the hour. When we came home Papajee asked the same question, to which she replied, "Menu appna kam ker len deo." (Let me do my task.)

She got her sewing machine out and proceeded to sew a fresh couple of padded quilts with the material she brought. Once she was finished, she told both Kashmir and I to go upstairs and remove every bit of stuff that belonged to him and I from the last bedroom that we shared to the middle room. I was shocked, and asked her why.

And she told us, "Oh hon babaji the kamra hai." *(That is going to be Babaji's mean Guru Granth Sahib's room).*

That came as a bit of a shock to us. So both Kashmir and I

went up to pull all our books, toys, and clothes and moved them to the smaller room and put our clothes in the closet in the smaller room.

I still remember Kashmir saying, "Bhaji eh jerra Babaji hay ede naal aapa kate nahi saun sakde? Hor be tan apnne babe naal saunde han." (Brother. Why can't we sleep with the baba? Other people sleep with their baba?) (baba is a word used for paternal grandfather, and it is also a word of veneration for Guru Grant Sahib.

I told him that this was not that kind of Baba and we had to do what Beejee told us to do. Something changed that day in the house for both of us. Not that Beejee and Papajee said anything, but we both started to feel that we needed to behave a little more.

Our voice levels became lower. We both never really did argue much, but after that day it was always easy. When we had a problem, we would go to the room and say,

"Babaji en maino eda keha." (Babaji he said this to me.)

And we would find a solution. Although for the sake of full disclosure, I must say there were more than a few occasions that I did use it to my advantage by saying to Kashmir, you better not tell Beejee or Papajee something or Babajee is going to get mad at you. He bought it hook line and sinker.

Once we had removed our belongings from the room, and Beejee was finished with making the quilts. She went upstairs and cleaned the room and mopped the floors. She then went into the Amour and cleaned it and on one of the shelves, she laid one of the quilts and came downstairs. She asked Papajee to proceed with opening the parcel, once he opened the parcel I saw for the first time in my young life a beautiful book, a marvel I had not seen before. Papajee asked me to get the Gutka (Sikh Prayer book.)

Since I was the only person who could read Punjabi in the house, Papajee said,

"Balbir read the ardas," (Sikh prayer that is recited at the start of anything and also at the end.)

I was nervous, and I told Papajee that I didn't know what to say. So he told me, "you read the Ardas and I will fill in the ceremony for which the ardas is." We all bowed our heads, and I started to read the Ardas from the Gutka. At the point of the reason for the ardas Papajee took over. He gave thanks for the safe arrival of the Guru Granth Sahib and asked for guidance and forgiveness that we would not be able to perform the required duties of Parkash and sukhasan. (Opening ceremony in the morning and the concluding ceremony in the evenings, we did not know how to.)

Once the ardas was complete, Papajee asked me to get a glass of water and walk in front and sprinkle water as I walked in front, he picked the Guru Granth Sahib on his head Kashmir and Beejee followed behind. We went to the room upstairs at the end of the corridor and put the Guru Granth Sahib on the shelf. Beeji put the other quilt on top of the Guru Granth Sahib. We came down stairs and Beejee had made Parishad (holy food or sacrament) Papaji gave it to all of us.

Guru Granth Sahib was now in our midst; there was a new energy in the house. Papajee was on his track, the remorse of leaving the Mazdur Sabha was all gone. He knew that he was set on his new path.

There is a quote by a Persian poet called Sheik Attar of Nishapur, in which he says that, "When the world cuts you and leaves you lying in your own pool of blood by the road. Rise then o man and the road will show you the way."

What he is saying is, when everything that you have ever known leaves you and you stand-alone; then start your journey alone, and on the way you will meet people who will show you to your destination. Papajee reached this point. He had tried all his past companions, and they left him by the roadside with a bagful of excuses and reasons why he should not do this. However, something bigger than all of them inside him was telling him this was the one thing that he must do.

Few doors from us at number 25 Red Lane lived the Atwal family. They belonged to the village of Sidhwan in Doab. This was Nazar Singh, his wife Gurbachan Kaur and their son Balwant. They had three other sons. One lived in Toronto, one lived in Smethwick and one was still in India Pyara Singh who later came and joined them. Pyara was a very jolly person and well-mannered individual. He had a nickname for Kashmir; he would always refer to him as Shahjee (the lord). Nazar Singh and his family were from the same village as Boota Singh the founders of the Smethwick Gurdwara. Papajee asked Nazar Singh to go with him to Smethwick to meet with Boota Singh. Although Papajee knew Boota Singh well, he wanted someone from the village to be there. It is a tradition among us Punjabis that to get someone to commit, it's best to ask him in front of a family member or an elder from the village. Nazar Singh fit the bill.

They both met with Boota Singh the following weekend. Boota Singh was very excited to hear that Papajee had taken this step and said that he and others would help in every way they could to get us going in Coventry.

It was about five-thirty in the evening when Papajee got back from Birmingham. He opened the front door, and his face was beaming with vigor. He didn't smile too often but when he did his face lit up. This was one of those days. He was happy, and the happiness was coming out of his pores.

Beejee had a sense of humor, and said, "Keo jee aaj tan eda kush lag de hun jeve munde da rishta paka keeta hunda." (Dear husband you look so happy like you just betroth your son.)

"Oh bay rab kare odan ve edan he kush hovan ge par aaj tan Boota Singh ne hami bhar ke khush keeta." *(Well, God willing. We will be happy on the betrothal the same way, but today it's Boota Singh saying yes to help. That's making me happy)* Papajee replied.

Beejee made him a cup of tea, and he took his shoes off and as always either Kashmir or I picked up his shoes and put them in the staircase, and he stretched his legs and felt that he had achieved some milestone. He knew that he had found a new ally, someone who had done this and could help him if he needed help.

The next day it was early in the morning, we had just finished breakfast, and there was a knock at the door.

"Balbir dekh kaun hai." (Balbir see who it is.) Beejee said to me.

When I went to the door and when I opened it, there was a lady with a boy about the same age as myself standing in the doorway.

It was Balwant and Gurbchan Kaur, Nazar Singh's wife and son. Although they lived down the street at number twenty-five, I never really knew Balwant that well. He went to Broad Street School, and I went to Fredrick Bird, so we ran into each other, but all that was about to change.

I welcomed them in by saying, "Sat Sri Akal." *(God Is the truth, the Sikh greeting)* and asked them in.

Beejee had met Gurbchan Kaur and had a polite conversation but were never close, but all that was to change also.

Gurbachan Kaur and Balwant came in and sat down, and before Beejee could say anything, Gurbachan Kaur started to speak, "Behn Nasib Kaur, barri bhagan vali eh tun tere ghar guru jee bethe han, main tehenu eh kehn ai han ke ajj tun leke apa bhena ate jo be kam guru da karna aapa maundae naal maunda jorr ke karna." (Sister Nasib Kaur from this day onward we are sisters. Whatever we need to do for the guru we will do it together, shoulder-to-shoulder).

Beejee was overcome with this outpouring of love and support. She turned to Gurbachan Kaur and said, "Gurbachan Kaure aa mere naal." *(Gurbachan Kaur come with me.)*

Beejee held her hand and took her to the room upstairs where the Guru Granth Sahib was, and she opened the Amour door and said, "Babajee asin aj to Bhena, sade

te apna hath rakhi. Ohi karain jo teun bhave."
(Dear lord, we are sisters from this day on, keep your graceful hand over us and only let us do what is your will.)

Funny how strangers become family when God so wishes, it was his will. He was the one that was directing this. Otherwise, Gurbachan Kaur and Nazar Singh lived there for a while, and we had nothing to do with each other. God has his plan, and he makes the team. He is the one that brings people together. They stayed for tea and as she was leaving she again told Beeji that she was to call on her as a sister, and it didn't matter what time or day it was, God's seva (duty) came first.

We were all taken back. We were all changed. We were experiencing the hand of God at work. This was not us doing anything, this was God. He does continue to test you also. He wants to make you stronger, like a good sports coach that rewards, drives, and tests. As soon as you think that you have achieved a record, he again challenges you to break that record. He wants to make sure that your faith is strong enough to withstand any odds. He will continue to forge you; he will continue to make you stronger. After all, it is his name you're representing. As an athlete represents a country, the coach will do anything in his being to make sure that athlete wins. God coaches you in the same way. When you're tired, he will force you to get up and go as Shiek Attar mentioned, he will have people cut you up, the worst kind of cut, the demoralizing type. Saying, it can't be done, who does he think he is, what does he know about this; he can't even read Gurmukhi (Punjabi). Let alone the Guru Granth Sahib. The sword tongue cuts a much deeper blow than any metal sword. Papajee had all these cuts made on him, but he was a determined man of deep faith in God, he knew his destination, and he was on the road.

Papajee drew three circles on a piece of paper, and he asked Kashmir and I to sit with him. He asked us what the three circles meant. Of course, we had no clue what they meant. He explained, the inner circle represents the people who rule people, and they think they have power. These people want to make sure that everything remains the same that is how they keep their power. For them, any change is always a threat. I guess he must have been thinking of the Mazdur Sabha and Rajmal. This group never adds to any progress. The second circle is the group; he explained was the most dangerous. They play both sides against each other and they say they are servants of the people, but they serve no one but themselves, they are self-serving. Most of the times these people complain and want to get into an organization and once in, they add no value other than disruption. The outer ring is the general public, which thinks they have no power, so they never exercise it. However, that is where the true power lies. So you must at all times serve and respect this group. The ordinary people, they are the one the Gurus gave the power to, this is the group once energized will move heaven and earth.

He emphasized, "Boys, remember the word, I said is SERVE, you must always serve this group. You must respect this group, because even in their silence, they know what is going on."

I have not forgotten the lesson of the three circles. When I am teaching new managers, I make sure I make them understand that your true power comes from your employees, if they are not energized no matter how smart you are you will never succeed.

Papajee would give us life lessons and an example from his experience from being around the world which has served us well over our life span. He continued this practice with his grandchildren. I hear all of them when doing something or giving their opinions will often say Babajee one time told me this story. I think it's applicable here and then proceeded to tell the story and make their point. Most of the times it's a story only that specific child was told, and not another, because he felt they needed that specific story in their lives.

CHAPTER SEVENTEEN

The List

Papajee started to work on a list, the list was of those people that were not involved in the Mazdur Sabha and had no affiliation with other organizations. These were the people on the outer ring of the circle, well-meaning people, who went about their lives and had no involvement in anything. These were the people that he wanted to target and energize and get them involved into the Gurdwara.

He wrote down their names, addresses, and their villages in Punjab. He would later explain to me the reasons for writing the name of their villages.

He took that entire week to complete this list. He added, he subtracted, he again added and then subtracted. He sat alone for hours on end in creating this list. He also created the list of people in the middle circle. People he thought would cause trouble; people he thought at some point in time would disrupt the work. It turned out that he was right, that is exactly what happened and people on the middle circle were true to form.

He also created the list of those that were in the very inner circle. These were those that were involved with the Mazdur Sabha. I asked him. Why would he care about adding them since he said that they wanted to maintain status quo? He told me that at some point in time there are some people on this list very inner circle that I will go back to and see if I can get them to join us.

Papajee was a record keeper. He kept a detailed list of everything, but this list was kept very private. I did get to see some of the names on the list in all the circles, but he never shared them with anyone.

Just before his passing, I did bring up with him about the list.

He told me, "Har cheez da waqat hunda tehn hunn us list nu dekh ke ke lena." (There is a moment for everything, what do you want with that list now?)

I think he destroyed the list before his passing. I did not find it among his belongings.

CHAPTER EIGHTEEN

Baba Nand Singh

The following Saturday after we finished our breakfast, Papajee told Beejee that he was going to go see Baba Nand Singh. Beejee did not know who Baba Nand Singh was, but she knew that if Papajee wanted to meet him, it must be for a good reason, so she did not ask.

He looked over at me and said, "Balbir, chal kapre pa apan jaa ay ae." (Balbir, go get, ready, so we can go and see him.)

Back in those days, no one had a phone, it was not like you can announce and get an appointment to see if the person was going to be at home, you just showed up. I did not ask where we were going; I went upstairs to our bedroom and put on my short suit. I tied my tie pulled up my socks to my knees bent them over and made sure there wasn't any wrinkle in them. I looked at myself in the mirror and combed my hair and came down the stairs.

Papajee was ready. He had on his cap and his gabardine overcoat and was standing by the family room door. He gave me a good once look over to make sure that my tie was not crooked, and my socks were folded over correctly, and my suspenders were not twisted. When I passed Papajee's military drill test, he muttered something under his breath, I barely heard it, but I think he said,

"Waheguru laaz Rakhin." (God protect my honor.)

We came out of the front door, and he followed his ritual of standing in the doorway and pausing as he always did. He looked left and then right and left again, and then he proceeded to walk forward towards Stony Stanton Road. Papajee in front, and I was following a few steps behind him. We went up Stony Stanton Road, made a left on Cambridge Street, crossed Harnell lane east onto Bradford Street, which does not exist anymore. Even back then there were only a few houses that were occupied, the remainder were abandoned. We marched along and reached number nine road (Inner ring circle the bus that ran along this route was number nine, so our people renamed it number nine road.) We made a right and crossed the road and headed towards the Palladium cinema. Just before the cinema, we made a left into Wellington Street. This was a cobbled street, and the houses were pretty old. I had walked passed this street many times, and would often stop by and stared at the old church in about the middle of the street and look at the cemetery and wonder how old some of those graves were in the church. I would wonder how those people must have lived and died, and would let my imagination take a flight. I would imagine that I knew some of the people when they were alive. A child's mind as someone said is the world's best cinema.

We stopped at about the third house. Papajee looked over at me, and I was standing there with my hands in my pockets. He looked over and lowered his eyelids, and shook his head. I knew what that meant. I immediately took my hands out of my pockets. He knocked on the door, and a man appeared. Papajee asked him if Nand Singh was home. The man invited us in. The house had no entryway. We entered the room. The curtains were drawn. It was a very tiny room, the man asked us to sit down, and he will ask Nand Singh to come down.

A few minutes later, a tall slender man in his early to mid-sixties entered the room. He had a slightly darker complexion. His beard was nicely tied. He had eyes that looked right through you and read you. He stood erect and proud, but he had a very quiet mannerism. When he entered the room, both of us stood up.

Papajee shook hands with him, and I folded my hands and

said, "Babajee Sat Sri Akal." (Babajee God is True, Sikh greeting.)

He was very pleased to see me fold my hands and say Sat Sri Akal. He was not one of those people who were going to say that he was pleased.

He nodded his head and said, "Huh, Sat Sri Akal," and then asked Papajee, "Boy tera?" (Your boy?)

Papajee nodded his head to say yes. He indicated to both of us to sit, and he sat down, and he asked if we wanted tea. We said no, but that was what everyone said, but you got tea anyway, and you were expected to drink it.

He asked Papajee, "Severe severe kidan aunn hoia?" (What is the reason for this early-morning visit?)

Papajee told him that he was preparing to launch the Gurdwara project, and he needed him to participate. Papajee knew Baba Nand Singh had a reputation for straight talk, and he was not going to be a yes man, and he was going to speak his mind and anytime he saw something was not correct he would not waste a moment in telling people how it was. Plus he also could recite the Guru Granth Sahib. Papajee told him the whole details, how he tried to get Rajmal and Majdur Sabha to participate and head the project, but he had no success, so he decided to embark on the project himself. Babajee listened without saying a word or showing any emotions. He sat there with his piercing eyes looking at Papajee who was telling him the whole details. Once Papajee was done, Babajee spoke he had a deep voice. His words were simple, and his sentences were always short.

He looked Papaji straight in the eyes and said, "Dharam Sihnia Ja ghar nu, aapene niane paal." (Dharam Singh go home and raise your kids).

It was almost as if Papajee expected this was going to be his response, and he was prepared for it. It appeared to me that he knew Babajiee was going to say this, and he was ready for him.

So Papajee fired right back at him and said, "Nand Singh jee, nianiana de tan karke he tan eh kar reh han, jeh eh na keeta tan eh ve Duleep Singh vaang Christians, he banananange!" (Dear Nand Singh, the kids are the reason I want to do this. If we don't do this, then they will end up Christians like Duleep Singh!)

(Referring to the last Maharaja of Punjab Duleep Singh, who was brought to England in the eighteen hundreds after the annexation of Punjab Empire into the British Empire, and he was raised as a Christian by Queen Victoria. Although later in life he returned to Sikhism, but all his children were Christians.)

Papajiee's response hit Babajee hard. He was not expecting this. I saw his eyes shining. They were full of water. He leaned backward on the couch and fought back his tears. He took his right-hand index finger and looked at me and signaled me to come over to him. I looked over at Papajee, he told me to go over. As I moved towards him, he stood up. He held my face with his right hand; his palms were rough from hard work but there was strength in his grasp.

He moved his right hand onto my head and stood there for a moment and said, "Dharam Sihnia men duperon baad aavanga men Kurri Nu melnna, hun Ja." (Dharam Singh I will come overto your house in the afternoon, and I want to meet the girl, (he meant Beejee. He never ever did call Beejee by her name ever. He always referred to her as Kurri, or whenever he addressed her he would always say, "Eh Kurriae," (Hey girl) as if she was his daughter, and they had that relationship)

We left and came home, and once we got home Beejee asked Papajee what he said. Papajee told her that he was coming over in the afternoon, and he wants to meet with you. Beejee asked why he wanted to meet with her.

Papajee told her, he assumed he wants to see if beejee was on board with the project..

Beejee was a very good cook, and she prepared few snacks. Papajee told Beejee not to overdo it or he will think you were you trying to impress him, and he won't be impressed. She did it anyway.

The house was always tidy, but Beejee told us to tidy it up. Like everyone at that time, we all had used furniture, but it was always tidy. It was what all the immigrants could afford, but they were no less proud and kept their houses neat and tidy. Most homes had studio couches that were popular back then. They would be covered with handcrafted sheets from Punjab. This is how all-new immigrants make it first, how they establish themselves. I use to think it was just us Punjabi's that were that way. Then I became friends with an Italian boy named Joe, who lived in Cambridge Street. I went to his house. All they had was a table and few hard wooden chairs, and I felt like we lived in a palace. It's all relative. It's that old Sheik Sadi Story about walking to the mosque in the hot sun in bare feet because he could not afford shoes.

He looks up and says, "Allah look I come to the Mosque in the blazing hot sun in bare feet, please grant me a pair of shoes."

As he went a bit further he saw a man moving on all fours because his legs were not working, so the Shiek looks up at the sky and says, "Allah you know that request I made of you bit earlier, can you please cancel the request." We don't appreciate what we have until we see that it can be worse.

I never ever felt bad about having used furniture after going to Joe's house.

About three O'clock there was a knock at the door. Our front door had two opaque glass windows so you could make out who was out there, and it was Babajee at the door.

I opened the door and said, "Sat Sri Akal" to Babajee.

He muttered, Sat Sri Akal and came through the door and went through the corridor into the family room."

Beejee was sitting on a stool by the fireplace. She always sat there on the stool. It was a low stool, the kind she was used to sitting on back in Punjab. Papajee sat in his armchair. Kashmir was on the couch.

As Babajee walked into the room, everyone stood up, he asked everyone to sit, and he sat down, Beejee got up to go to the kitchen to make tea. Babajee stopped her and told her to sit down.

"Kurre beth men tere naal gal karan ayaea cha peenn nahin." (Girl, sit down, I have come to chat with you, not come to drink tea.)

Beejee sat down, and he started to talk, "Menu eh dass ke eh jerra tera aadmi kehda ke men Gurdwara karra karna tere ke khyal eddeh bare?" (This idea that your man has that he wants to raise a Gurdwara. What is your view on that?)

Beejee shot right back at him with full confidence, "Bhaia ji edae naalo hor ke vadhia ho sakda?" (Respected one, what could be better than that?)

"Eh tera khyal hai ja ehda jor?" (Is that your feeling or his pressure?) Beejee again fired back "Bhaia jee, eh mera khyal hai men choundi han ke Guru Kar banen manu maan hai ke ena ne he kam da uprala keeta hai?" (Respected one, this is my view, I am proud that my husband has taken up this cause.)

But Babajee was not done.

He continued his questioning, "Mainu eh das ke dasan badian de roti bana lavengi, mathae batt tan na pavegi?" (Tell me can you cook for ten people without a frown or complaint) "Dus de shado, sau de kaho ho be kar lavan ge, mere valo aap nu koi shaquat nhai ho vw gee." (I can cook for one hundred let alone ten, you will hear not a word of complaint from me.)

At that point Babajee said to her "chal hun cha pee lenda han" (Ok I will have tea now).

Beejee went into the kitchen, and she had already had the food items separated for the Prashad. It was if she had expected this and was ready for it. She washed her feet, her face, went upstairs and got a fresh chunni, (head scarf) and prepared the sacrament, and we went up stairs to the room where Guru Granth Sahib now resided and Babajee did the Ardass (prayer), he then distributed the Sacrament. We saved some for our neighbors the Atwal family at number twenty-five.

Babajee then turned to Beejee and said, “Lyea hunn kuria cha bana te nale oh pakorre be lae aa.” (OK girl let's have tea now and bring those snacks also.)

He left after tea, but his parting words to us were, “Pata naihn main kenik madat kar sak da, chut Gurmuki maninu hor koz nahin aunda, na men keertan kar sakda par ju be mera oh men tere naal jorreia Dharam Sihan, aaj tu tere mera saat ek jerra guru neh banaia, Eh Kurri ne tan mainu Jitlia.” (Dharam Singh from today on you and I are one and partners the Guru has made. I am not sure what my contribution is going to be, I can only read the scriptures. I do not know how to sing hymns. However, the Guru has joined us, and this girl has won me over.)

Babaji did not know the moral support, the rustic wisdom, and his fearlessness to say it how it was what every organization needs to keep the organization from straying from its path. He was beholding to no man, only to his Guru and God. He told it like it was. His truth was firmly grounded in his faith in his Guru. People like Baba Nand Singh are rare individuals who walk this earth. They enrich us. They are the common folks. Their aspirations are simple truth, and they see the folly of others and call it out. They are the people that politicians and connivers fear. They know their game.

They are the advisor leaders need because they have the guts to call anyone out even if it is embarrassing the person being called out.

Papaji knew Babaji’s character for honesty and straight talk, he knew, with babaji by his side; he would be always good counsel, and know the truth when it needed to be said. To this day when I think of a true Sikh the first picture that comes to my mind is that of Babaji Nand Singh. Unafraid, without malice towards anyone, in constant state of Chardi Kala (constant form of Bliss.) At all times in metal meditative state

Babajee belonged to the village Kukran in Punjab. He had two sons Mohinder and Kewal. Mohinder was a poet, and he went by the name of Saajan. He was the first librarian of the Gurdwara.

That evening after meeting with babajee, we all went over to the Atwal's at number 25 and gave them Parshad (sacrament) and told them that

Babajee had agreed to join. Nazar Singh did say to Papajee, "Barra sakhat hai." (He's real tough.)

Papajee told Nazar Singh, "Nazar Singh ji eh kam be kamzor bandian da nahi sakht badian da he hay." (Nazar Singh ji this is not a task for weak but for the tough.)

Nazar Singh Agreed with Papajee.

CHAPTER NINETEEN

Meeting at the Donkey

That same weekend Papajee went to met with the Pasla wallas'. They lived on Smith Street, two streets down, just around the corner from our house. The head of their household was Bikar Singh; they were a tightly knit family and remain that way even now. Whatever Bikar Singh said was gold. Papajee was always highly regarded by the Pasla Walas'. Even so, the Jats are very feudal, and the due respect to the family head has to be paid. Papajee knew he had their full support, but he still knew he had to pay them a visit. There was a Pub at the end of Smith Street; Smith Street dead-ended into a wall that was a wall to an ordinance factory. In fact our back yard also backed up to the same wall of this ordinance factory. Coventry was bombed so heavily during the Second World War not only because it was the industrial hub of England, but it also had this ordinance factory here.

There was an old bombed out yard in Smith street with a broken car from the forties, and as children, we would go and play for hours in this bombed out yard on the car pretending that we could drive it.

The pub on Smith Street had a grand name, I believe it was called the Golden horse. However, back in those days, the place was a total dive. I mean the rooms were tiny and dark and small so the locals nicknamed it the "The Donkey." This was not a nickname our folks gave it. It was the English that had done the honors on this one.

Papajee went around to the Donkey around eight at night, which was not too early and not too late for Sunday. He timed it to make sure all Bikar Singh's family and other extended family members were all going to be there as that was where they all gather for their beer and to discuss family issues and reminiscence about the old village Pasla back in the Punjab.

Punjabi's may move a half way around the world, but they will always remember to discuss the bullocks they had and the pet names for them and how they ran. They would talk about them, as they were their children. They would talk about all the old folks that would gather under the Banyan tree and play cards or chess, about the village drug addict and his goings on. Everyone was remembered with a certain amount of respect and amusement. They all added to the laughter and solace. A slice of home, with the conversation, was always present in their hearts.

I did not go to the Pub with Papajee since I was under age, but he was back home by nine thirty. He said that they all agreed to support him. He did say that they said he did not need to come to them; it was their duty to come to him. However, he knew that was just polite talk, he had to pay his visit to show recognition.

He also met Bhagat Singh Pehlwan, (wrestler) he was a very close friend of Papajee and would give his right arm for him. A very quiet man, when you think of a wrestler's vision of some loud man's image comes to mind. Bhagat Singh Pehlwan was anything but that. He was a very soft-spoken. He was a gentle giant.

He told Papajee anything you want, you let me know. I guess what he really was saying if there is trouble let me know, and I will be there, and we will take care of it. Papajee was very cautious about this kind of talk. He said that he told him not to think along those lines. I am sure internally Papajee felt a sense of security that people like Bhagat Singh were there.

CHAPTER TWENTY

Visit to the City Car Park

The following weekend Papajee, Beejee Kashmir and I went to as we always did every Saturday like everyone else to buy our weekly groceries. Papajee told Beejee to continue with her shopping while he went to see someone. He asked Beejeeto let me come with him.

We went to the City parking lot and at the booth where we met Tara Singh Didyal. Tara Singh was a stout man with very soft-spoken mannerisms. His son Karamjit and I would become good friends and remain so up until now. Tara Singh was active in the Labor party. It was Tara Singh, who would push both Karamjit and I into local politics, both of us were quite active in all the local elections until I moved to the U.S.

Before Papajee could say anything Tara Singh said, "Dharam Sihan Chnaga hoya tu agia men aunne wala see, befikar reh aasin tere naal han." (Dharam Singh its good you came, I was meaning to come and see you, stay undeterred. We are with you.)

I could see papajee felt humbled, as always, he folded both his hands and looked up and said, "Waheguru." (Lord.)

Tara Singh asked if there was anything specifically he needed to do, Papajee told him not this time that he was just getting people to sign on, and as he gets closer, he will let them know.

We told Beejee to meet us at the Bus stop number 21 in Broadgate (city center of Coventry).

We were done a lot sooner than we thought so we waited for Beejee and Kashmir by the bus stop until she arrived. She was eager to find out how our conversation went. Before

Papajee could say anything, I told her that we did not have to say anything the uncle said he is with Papajee.

Beeje said to me in a stern voice, "Sianian de gal vich nahin boli da." (Don't talk when elders are talking.)

I was a bit deflated by her revoke, but I also know it was right. I never stayed down very long and picked right back up and asked Kashmir if he got a toy. He was really good at manipulating Beejee, either by throwing a guilt trip of some sort if that did not work he would just park himself in front of the shop in the market until he got what he wanted. And this time was no exception. He never spoke much just nodded his head and pulled out of his coat pocket a water pistol enough so I could see it but not enough so that I could grab it.

I said to Beejee, "What about me?"

She gave me a look, and I went quiet and Kashmir gave me one of his smiles and pulled his tongue out at me. Enough that Beejee would not see it. I gave him a thrashing when we got home that day.

CHAPTER TWENTY-ONE

Oliver Street People

After lunch that Saturday afternoon, Papajee went to Oliver Street. Oliver Street was about five streets from where we lived on Red Lane. It had quite a few Sikh Punjabi families that lived on Oliver Street. My cousin and her husband lived there also. Papajee felt that he needed to go see them since she was the maternal daughter of the house, and her husband was a Jawai (son-in-law of the house), Papajee needed to make sure they felt included, counted. Dilbagh Singh, my cousin's husband was a happy-go-lucky kind of person, and he deeply cared about us. However, he was also very honest and was not always politically correct. So when Papajee approached him about the Gurdwara project, he was not one who just signed on. He pointed out to Papajee all the negatives that he saw.

He told him, "EH larrai da ghar hai, pher ehd vich Balbir hunna de parrai rul jaani hai." (This kind of project is going to be a house full of trouble, and Balbir and Kashmir's education is going to suffer.)

Papajee listened to Dilbagh Singh and felt a sense of hurt, but he did not show it since he was a son in law of the family. He was pretty upset when he came home and told Beejiee Beejee would later bring it up with Dilbagh Singh, and he would explain to Papajee just because he pointed out all that was negative with the project, did not mean he did not support it. It is a family project, and I support the family. Jats don't take too kindly to half-hearted support from the family. Papajee was no expectation. He would never again ask

Dilbagh Singh for support. Dilbagh Singh for his part showed very little interest in the Gurdwara either. He was more concerned with our education, and he saw the Gurdwara Project as a real roadblock in the way of our education. Unfortunately, it did affect my education, but Kashmir could stay focused on his and go on to become a doctor.

He also visited the two brothers Ajit and Pargan who lived further down the street from my cousin. Ajit worked with Papajee, and he was very close to him. Pargan Ajit's elder brother both threw their support behind Papajee. As you will see later having Pargan's support was not a blessing but a bit of a curse.

CHAPTER TWENTY-TWO

Man with the curly moustache

The next-day Sunday early morning there was a knock at the front door, I think it was about nine in the morning. I know it was pretty early because Beejee had not even started breakfast. We did not have television back in those days even if you did you were not going to watch it as there was nothing on that early in the morning. Even if there was Papajee would have never let us watch television before the evening anyway. So we sat around and talked while Papajee read the Sunday paper. I would get the paper for him from the paper shop few doors down every Sunday. Once Papajee was done with his paper and his first cup of tea; then we would have our breakfast. He was a bit surprised to hear the knock that early. He asked me to see who was at the door. I opened the door and there he was, Sohan Singh Gaffa, (boss) as he was referred to. Not quite sure how he got that name, maybe he was a foreman or something never did find out. He always appeared to be a man on a mission; perhaps that's how he picked up that nickname along the way. Punjabi's are kind of like the Irish in that respect. They love to give nicknames to people.

There was some poor fellow who they referred to as two chicken. The story goes like this. He used to work a lot of overtime and had grown accustomed to the money from his regular overtime as his ongoing income since the overtime was always available. Then there was a slow down, and his overtime was cut. Poor fellow could not speak English, in trying to explain to his boss that he needed the overtime because he had a wife and two children. He forgot the

English word for Kids to be children and said two chicken instead, and the Punjabi lot named him "two chicken". He was referred to henceforth as two chickens. This was common and mostly taken in stride.

Sohan Singh Gaffa was from Littran village. He was in his early forties or late thirties back then. At that young age to me, anyone over twenty were ready to push daisies and were old. He looked around that, late thirties early forties I mean. He was a man of medium height and was quite well built with a heavy filled in face. He had a moustache that was curled.

He had a real husky deep voice and spoke in a fast rhythmic voice, "Sat Sri Akal, Sat Sri Akal, Dharam Singh hega kede Gaffa ayaea." (God is true, God is True, is Dharam Singh here tell Gaffa is here.)

I told him that Papajee was home and to come on in. Back in those days you were told to always invite people in, no matter what. Otherwise it was considered impolite. So I asked him to step in, Papajee heard his voice and came into the corridor. He asked him to come in; Gaffa shot right passed me and went into the family room. Papajee asked him to sit, but he said I am fine standing, but on Papajee's insistence, he sat. Papajee looked over his glasses as he closed his paper and slowly took off his glasses. He passed me his glasses and the paper and shook hands with Sohan Singh Gaffa and sat.

Before Papajee could even speak and ask him why he came so early on a Sunday. Sohan Singh Gaffa was in full speed. It was if he had put down a whole Starbuck store before he came. Not that we had that back then. Later, I was to find out that he was always that way.

"Dharam Singh baut changi Baut chagi gal jjerra tusin Gurdwara shroo karan lagen ho. Men be seva karni hai jethe laven ga uthe he lagan ga, darana nay darana nay tere naal kharrean ge, Kharran ge." (Dharam Singh it is a great thing, a great thing that you're starting the Gurdwara work, don't have any fears. We are with you all the way, we are with you all the way.)

Papaji replied, "Sohan Singh thuhade varge jawan mere naal khare tan menu kada dar?" (Sohan Singh if I have young people like yourself with me then why would I have any fears?)

I could see this beam of Joy in Papajee. Papajee insisted that he has a cup of tea,

Sohan declined, he said, "Aj ne, aj ne, ajj tan men kuj den ayaian lehn nahin, baut mauke aune han jad men es garh vich cha peeva ga." (Not today, not today. I came to give, not take, let me go; there are many times more when I will drink tea in this house)

And he left; left all of us dumbfounded. Papajee asked Kashmir and I to come and sit near him, and he would give us another lesson. He told both of us, never think that people like Gaffa are serving us. Never let your ego think that if people offer to serve in your cause, it is you who are doing something big. Always remember it is they that are doing something big. It is they who are offering you their help. Never forget the generosity of people. Always make sure you remember who stood with you. At that moment he went upstairs to the back bedroom where Guru Granth Sahib was and sat there for good half an hour and then came down. He would do this to keep himself focused and also to remind himself that he was in service of the Master, Guru, and it was the Guru, who was driving him.

CHAPTER TWENTY-THREE

The Rurka Wala Brothers

The Rurka wala brothers were three brothers. The eldest one was Gurbhachan Singh; the middle one was Sucha Singh, and the younger one was Jhalman Singh. Sucha Singh and Jhalam Singh both lived on Eagle Street at that time. Papajee went to see Sucha Singh the following week, as I remember Papajee telling me that Sucha Singh asked Jhalman Singh to come and meet Papajee Papajee said that they were a bit annoyed with Papajee for coming. He said that they told him it was their duty to come, not his to come to him. First, he was older, and secondly he was doing the Guru's work. They told him the same thing as Sohan Gaffa did; we are with you all the way. Boy were they ever. They stuck with him through thick and thin.

Papajee was so humbled by the outpouring of support that it frightened him. It frightened him that he was being somehow put on a Pedestal, and he was afraid to let these people down. He would spend time with his Guru, just sitting, thinking, and praying that he would do the right thing.

The momentum was building. The anticipation was getting stronger as to how soon he was going to have the first function. Every time we met someone in town or on the way to town they would want to know.

I was at Frederick Bird Secondary School on Swan Lane back then. Even at school, the boys were talking about the Gurdwara that was going to get started. Papajee's three circles were emerging. I could see it in the groups that were starting to form in the schoolyard and the types of comments that I started to hear. The inner-circle group kids would say this is nonsense. He (meaning Papajee was one of us, he can't achieve this. The kids from the middle circle were having their own opinions, why a Gurdwara? Why not a community hall? This should be decided by the community first not, by one man.

The Kids from the outer circle would all show their support with me. There were moments that some of the kids from the inner circle wanted to pick a fight. The Kids were just acting out what they were hearing being said at home. Only thing is that at that age logic, and tempers are both short and fights are easy. I was pretty astute to avoid them, as we were told that we would hear all of what was being said. I did get into a couple though. I could stand my own ground, plus if it really got out of hand, I had Darshan to take care of things. Darshan was big and tall for his age. Darshan was Pargan Singh Oliver Street Wala's son. We had been chums since I came from India. He was at hand and ready for a good scrap. I usually had to reason out of an argument, and he would always get upset that I talked us out of a good fight, and he did not get to thrash someone. He was on the school Rugby team. He was Akin to the high school quarterback, a jock. Schoolwork was never his strong suit. He was just a great rugby player and a good friend.

CHAPTER TWENTY-FOUR

Towards the Big Day

Around Mid May Saturday afternoon Baba Nand Singh came around to the house, we knew that something was on his mind otherwise he would not have bothered. He would have let Papajee carry on and only interfere when he needed to say something.

So he was here to say something, "Kure kithae Dharam Singh?" (Girl where is Dharam Singh?)

Beejee told him that he was upstairs and asked me to call Papajee down. We were never allowed to shout. We would always be told to go and tell the person. So I went upstairs to the back bedroom where Papajee was and told him that Babajee was downstairs.

Papajee came down and greeted Babajee Before Babajee could say anything, Papaje spoke as if anticipating what he was going to say. Papajee told Babaje that he was going to come and see him and ask him what would be a good day to start the first Divan. (The name given to the Sikh congregational gathering.) Babaji's thunder was stolen.

Babajee was never without thunder though, so he told Papajee "Maen theno khen aya see ke panjme Guru Sahib de Shahidi divas aa reha sheven maheine aappa ud shroo karana bass." (I came to tell you that in June it's the martyrdom of the sixth Guru, and we are starting on that day no matter what.)

Papajee was excited to hear his order. It was always taken as a command.

Babajee turned to Beejee and asked her, "Kurrae tiar

hai?" (Girl are you ready?)

Beejee leaned over and touched his feet and said, "Bhaia jee dhan bhaag sadae tiar per tiar han." (Respected one it is blessings upon us. We are ready.)

So that was how the date was set, the first divan of the Guru was to be held on the martyrdom of the Guru who compiled the Guru Granth Sahib and became the first martyr of Sikh religion.

Papajee called a meeting for that Sunday at the house. I was the runner who went to everyone's home to invite them to come to the house on Sunday. I went to the Paslewala's house, Sohan Singh Gaffa's house, Sucha Singh and Nazar Singh's house and also people in Oliver Street. They were all told of when the first Divan would be held. As to which Sunday the first function was going to be held, Papajee said that he would go to town Monday and meet with the authorities and the headmaster of Stanton Bridge School, which was on Red Lane just a few doors from our house and arrange to fix the date for the hall rental and as soon as that was done that Balbir would come by and let everyone know Monday evening and then people can start passing the word along. The time to start was set at 10 Am.

That Monday Papajee got up early and got ready and was about to embark on his new mission, after breakfast as we left for school, he was at the headmaster's office bright and early at Staton Bridge school on Red Lane next to the house.

The school had been rented for Mazdoor Sabha function before so the headmaster knew Papajee and he thought that he had come to talk to him about another Mazdoor Sabha function. Papajee explained to him that he had resigned from the Mazdoor Sabha and wanted to start a Gurdwara. He would be booking the upstairs assembly hall of the school every month for the purposes of Sikh services. The headmaster was only too happy to help when he found out that it was for worship. The school had two assembly halls. One downstairs and one upstairs, and Papajee wanted the top one. I asked him later why he insisted on the one upstairs. He told me that it was mainly for safety reasons for kids; I just did not want it downstairs and have the kids wandering in the playground and someone getting hurt. Upstairs he would have someone stand by the stairs and watch that no kids went out. He was always very detailed. He left nothing to the whim. It had to be planned. He would go into silence and plan things, every last detail.

After he spoke to the headmaster, he met with the custodian Mr. Hancock, he knew that he was the one that he would have to deal with on an ongoing basis for a few years, he needed Mr. Hancock's support. Mr. Hancock was a man of about 60 years. He was the custodian of the School for a very long time. All the teachers and parents alike very well respected him. If Mr. Hancock told you off you better take heed because next the headmaster would hear of it. We all knew Mr. Hancock when we went to the school when we first came from Punjab. He was a very decent man. He was balding and always had a Andy Capp (newspaper cartoon character) (Derby hat) that he wore. The one thing that I remember that was unique about Mr. Hancock was that he had no eyebrows. He would always have them shaved. I would often wonder why he did that. Were they bushy or were they just ugly? Why would he shave them off? Amazing what holds a child's imagination.

Mr. Hancock assured Papajee that he would give him his full support. Papajee did take care of him also because if he ever gave a bad report, we would have to find another place. After every function, Papajee would tip him a ten shilling note. Back in then, there was a ten shilling red note. He made sure it was never in coins. It was always a note. Perception is everything. If he gave him the same amount in coins, it was going to seem less and paltry. However, a note always was something he could take and put in his wallet.

Mr. Hancock would always make sure that if there was something left that was not cleaned he would pick it up, that way there were no complaints. There was one time that some children did some silly stuff and took a bunch of toilet paper and threw it all over the playground. Although Papajee would walk the grounds after the divan, that day I remember it was raining hard, and he did not do it. The paper got wet and was difficult to clean. It annoyed Mr. Hancock so much that he broke down and told the headmaster. There was a knock on the door bright and early Monday morning as we were leaving for school, and it was the headmaster coming to see Papajee. Papajee told the headmaster that he would come by and help clean it up.

Mr. Hancock felt so bad. He turned around to Papajee as Papajee told me later that Mr. Hancock put his hands-on Papajiee's shoulders and said,

"Mr. Singh go home, you have a night shift, I will clean it up. I should have never lost my temper. You tip me and I get overtime, and you are serving your community and for me to do, what I did it is just a sin."

Papajee said he put his hand out and shook Papajee's hand and then tipped his hat to Papajee.

From there on he would just give Papajiee the key to the hall and would say lock up when you are done. I will come by the house in the morning and pick up the key from you. If the divan ran late. It was fine we had the key.

Once the Gurdwara was completed on the opening ceremony, the community honored Mr. Hanock with a clock on the opening day of the new Gurdwara. Mr. Hancock was so happy that his service was recognized in front of all the dignitaries and who's who of the city.

After meeting the headmaster and Mr. Hancock, papajee went downtown to take care of paying and booking the school hall. When he came home, we had come home from school for our lunch. We asked him what date was set for the first Divan. (Congregation) He said it would be June 18th. So there it was, the new date in the history of Coventry, in the History of the Sikhs, a date when the first Divan was to be held in Coventry, June 18th, 1961. A day to commemorate the martyrdom of the Guru Arjan the sixth Guru, who was Martyred by the Mughal Emporer Jahangir.

Jahangir would state in his biography the following, "Guru had opened a shop of falsehood, and it had crossed his mind many times to close this shop?"

Thus he was instrumental in the martyrdom of the Guru. The Guru was the light. It was Jahangir who operated the shop of falsehood, and it was Jahangir's shop that would close a few centuries later with the destruction of the Mughal Empire. The Guru was the sun. Another ray from the Guru's vast illumination was to shed its grace on Coventry.

At lunchtime, Papajee gave me my instructions for how I was to go to deliver the messages. I was to start with Blackberry lane after I got out of school; I went to Blackberry Lane and give the date to Sohan Singh Gaffa first. Blackberry lane was by what was called Morris common. Sohan Singh Gaffa's house was right opposite Morris car factory. I came home and had tea and started on the other leg of the journey.

I walked through Cambridge Street, crossed Harnell lane east, and through Bradford Street on the number nine and then straight to Babajees place, left a message at his place about the date. I proceeded to Eagle Street and left a message at Sucha Singh's house. From there I went along Foleshill road to Holbrook Lane to Tara Singh Didyal's house, coming back on to Foleshill Road to Kewal Singh Bains (Gondgpur's) house. Then through St Paul's road to Stony Stanton Road pass Red House Pub and towards Oliver Street and told everyone living on Oliver Street. When I got home, Papajee was sitting there ready to go to his nightshift.

My feet were aching. My legs had Charlie horses in them. However, I did not complain. I gave Papajee the report, and he just said,

"OK make sure you finish your homework also."

It wasn't as if I expected him to say thank you or excellent job, this was what was expected of me. I was the obedient elder son. I did what was expected of me. Once Papajee left Beejee brought some hot water and put some salt in it and had me soak me my feet. She brought out some mustard oil and asked me to massage it on my calves, which I did. I had my dinner and went to my books to finish my homework. I must say I slept well that night. This was the start of many of these long walks that I would do over the years.

Now the date was approaching fast, you never know what you need until the wedding date is set, as the saying goes. Papajee and Beejee compiled a list of all the items that they would need to buy. Beejee told Papajee that she was going to need more dishes.

He laughed and said, "Sabh tu pheala eh number." (So this is your first item?)

It was important to Beejee to have more dishes because of the number of people would increase that were going to be coming to the house once the functions started. This proved out to be true for every Sangrand (monthly celebration based on the lunar calendar. Beejee would make breakfast Pratha and sabzi (Paratha's are flaky Punjabi bread. Much like a croissant, Sabzi is curried vegetables) for up to fifty people, There were no paper dishes in those days. Even if there were, we had no clue where we would get them. So Beejee bought spoons, more soup plates for Daal curry, more flat plates, more glasses. These dishes would be kept separate and would only be brought out once a month at the time of the function, and they were never mixed with the rest of the family dishes. The purity of these dishes had to be maintained.

Beejee and Gurbachan Kaur from number twenty five got together and made a list of other kitchen items that would be needed. They needed bigger pots to make the Parshad (the holy sacrament), and those pots would be used for only that function. They also put on the list parats' (utensils to hold the sacrament in.) They needed to make a Chaannini (this is tied to the ceiling where the Guru Granth Sahib is seated. Beejee was very good at sewing. This was something she learnt before she came to England. They also needed to buy seating material to put under the Guru Granth Sahib. Beejee bought the material from Owens and Owens and sewed all this by herself. Papajee had to get the Manji Sahib (the seat upon which Guru Granth Sahib is seated). He went to a Sikh Mistry (Carpenter) and tasked him with building the Manji Sahib. It was an old gentleman by the name of Parshotam Singh. He was a lodger at the Atwal house. A saintly old soul, who spoke very little but smiled a lot.

Meanwhile, Beejee and Gurbachan Kaur went on the hunt to find big enough utensils to cook the Parshad and hold it in the Divan.

This proved to be a difficult task as our experience with shops was what was available at retail shops for home use and that was all at the market downtown.

So they kept going from one store to the next looking for the correct utensils. Finally, some storeowner told them about a commercial place that sold restaurant supplies. There they found the utensils they were looking for. They bought them and put a pot each on their heads and had the other in one hand, and they caught the bus and came home. I know this very well because I got into a lot of trouble over this. I was coming home from school, and they were both getting off the bus at Stoney Stanton Road from the town where they had changed from the other bus from where they got the utensils and needless to say, they had gone through hell and back. When I saw both of them coming they reminded me of women back in Punjab coming home after milking the cows with a bucket of milk on top of their heads. They just looked like that, so I started to laugh out right from the belly, and I was bending over with laughter. Needless to say that was about the time the fuse blew. The Usually calm and saintly Gurbuchan Kaur was the first to blow.

"Khasma to Khanian tennu hassa aunda sadi bas hoy pay hai." (You brat, you think this funny. We have just about had it.)

I just kept laughing, by then Beejee put whatever she had on her head or in her hand and put it down and called me over very lovingly, boy was that ever deceitful. When I got close to her, she let me have it, a slap across the cheek; it came so hard that it heated the whole cheek so hot I thought the fires of hell had suddenly landed on my right side of my face. I stopped laughing out loud, but I still wanted to laugh so I was laughing with my eyes. Beejee could see it. So another came from the other hand on the other cheek. That's when couple of the aunties that had come to collect their kids from school who would stop and talk with Beejee intervened and pulled me away and said,

"Bibi Buss" (ma'am enough).

She told me to pick the utensils up and take them in. That day I got no tea; she was very disappointed with me; that was a pretty bad punishment, not getting your tea. Beejee and I had a very close relationship. She could not stay mad at me for long. About five-thirty she came around and asked if I wanted tea, and I told no, the time had passed. She was insistent because she felt guilty for slapping me. Her slaps never bothered me. After that time, every time she would ask me to pull out those utensils, I would start laughing, and she would just shake her head and walk away.

It's funny even today whenever I go to the Gurdwara here in the US in Fremont California. Those utensils remind me of that moment and make me smile and remind me of my mother.

Papajee asked Kashmir and I to clean the shed the following weekend to make space for all the stuff that was going to need storage space. Mainly the next big item to buy was what people were going to sit on.

We needed something where people would sit on the floor. There used be two-second hand shops on Stoney Stanton road by Swanswell Park just past Booth's pharmacy. Those shops also sold army surplus stuff. Following Saturday Papajee went to those stores, and I went with him. He spoke to the owner to see if he had surplus army blankets, and the shop owner said that he did. Papajee asked him how many he had. He said that he had about twenty. Papajee asked him, when could he get more? The shopkeeper asked him how many did he need. Papaji told him that he wanted an even one hundred.

The shopkeeper's eyes were dilated, and he said, "Are you looking to raise an army mate?"

Papajee told him what he needed them for, and he said that he would be able to get the rest by next week. We went the following week to pick them up. We tied them into bundles of 10 each, dragged them to the other side of the road and caught the bus home. (We did this five times both of us carrying a bundle each.) When we got off the bus, Papajee picked one bundle up on his head and told me to put the other on my head. I flatly refused. It was fate's payback, and I was not going to comply. But then I had the fate master my Papajee; he looked at me; I knew I had no choice, and he helped me with the bundle, and it was on my head. On a Saturday morning, a time when everyone was going to town was watching, I was carrying the blankets on my head. Now who was going to laugh at me, then there they were, Nazar Singh and his wife Gurbchan Kaur on their way to town for their weekly shopping.

I tried to see if I could avoid them, but it was of no use. She saw me, as soon as she got close to our house she knocked on the door, and Beejee opened the door there they were both of them, standing, seeing both father and son with these bundles of blankets over our heads.

As soon as I got to the door Gurbachan Kaur took her best shot, "Khasma nu khanian hun aya tekanen aya, sanu hass da see dekheaia." (You brat now you're put in your place for laughing at us.)

I just weaseled into the house through the front door then right to the back door into the shed and dropped the blankets in the shed. Papajee now knew why I was refusing to disobey his order.

Each day, when the sun was out, and it was a warm day. Beejee and Gurbachan Kaur washed the blankets by hand and hung them out to dry on as many lines in the Punjabi houses that there were in the neighborhood. Our English neighbors were wondering what we were up to. The shopkeeper next door to our house asked Papajee if we were going into business selling used blankets. Papajee explained to them what they were for. Once they heard what they were for, they even allowed us to hang them to dry on their lines. It was quite a task washing them manually, wringing them out and drying them on the line. Since there were no washing machines anyone owned, they had to be washed manually and then rung out.

I know that Beejee took a couple of Aspirin every night. Her body would ache from all the washing and wringing. She never once complained about it though, she would always hold her hands tight and take Aspirin. Both Beejee and Gurbachan Kaur washed and folded until the last one was done.

CHAPTER TWENTY-FIVE

The Sound system

Following week on Saturday Papajee asked me to get ready because he needed me to go with him to buy the sound system. He told me that we would need Babajiee also so that he can help us carry it home. We walked to Babajee's house. He was always up early. Papajee wanted to make sure that we caught him before he took off on his chores. When we got to his house, he asked us why we were there.

Diplomacy was not Babajee's strong suit. He was as direct as they come. Papajee told him that he needed to have him go with us to buy the public address system. Terms change over time, what we refer to as the sound system was referred to as the Public address system back then, partially that was all that it did. It amplified the sound of the speaker. When Papajee said Public Address, it confused Babajee, he understood Public Address and system as individual words.

He said looking confused, "Dharam Sihian Public da Address kerre system to lenna? Menu teri gal nahin smaj aai." (Dharam Singh which system are you going to get the address of the public, I did not understand?)

He thought that Papajee was referring to go to some place where we were going to get some addresses of the public. Truth be known I didn't know what the term public address meant either, so I kept quiet.

Had I asked, Papajee was going to say, You don't know what public address system is?

Thanks to Babajee I learnt that day, what a public address system meant. So papajee told Babajee that he was referring to a loudspeaker. That was how I knew it to be.

So Babajee put his hand on Papajee's shoulder and said, "Sidhi jahi gal karia kar eh paririan wali gal mainu kade samaj nahin aunndi." (Talk in simple terms, I can't get this educated staff.)

Papajee smiled, and we went on to buy the Public address system. There was an electronic shop on Far Gosford Street I think near the Inland Revenue offices, so we walked from Babajee's place to the shop to buy the Public address system. Papajee spoke to the sales person and told him what it was for and asked him to show us a system. The man asked some question about the size of the room and also how many and what type of microphones we wanted. There were only two types either it was a small one that stood on the table, or it was the other type that stood on the floor. Papajee opted for the one that he could put on the table. His logic was if there were people sitting on the floor, they could use it along with those that wanted to use a podium, which, in fact, was a table.

When they brought out the loudspeaker Babajee asked Papajee what it was. Papajee told Babajee it was the loud speaker.

Babajee again looked confused and said, "Eh kidan the speaker tan dhur dhroooo jeha hunda jerra manje naal banian hunda eh taan pehli vaar dekhea." (What kind of speaker is this? The one I know is this long and weird-looking device, used to be tied to two cots.)

What Babajee was remembering from his days in Punjab, where, in fact, a cone speaker used on outside events. The rural DJs brought with them on special occasions, such as weddings or other festivities, and they stood up two cots together and tie the cone speaker to them. It would blast out 78 R.P.M. records for miles.

Papajee explained to him that this was the type used for inside in buildings. He was still not buying it. I asked Papajee where was the battery? My own experience was really no different from Babajee. I also remembered the same as

Babajee. Papajee explained to me that there was no need for a battery since we had power. Again in India when we were there, electricity was not available in villages so the DJ's used an amplifier that was powered by a battery that they brought with them. Thus my question on the battery, I agreed as if I understood, but it took a practical demonstration to convince Babjee.

Once we had reached the final agreement, and Babajee was satisfied.

The sales person turned to Babajee and said, "Ok mate?"

Babajee put up his right thumb to give him the OK sign and Papajee paid the salesperson. Babajee tried to give Papajee money, but he would not hear of it.

We each had an item each to carry home from the shop. Babajee and Papajee put a box each on their shoulders, and I carried the microphone home. After much discussion, the public address system or the loudspeaker system as Papajee would amusingly refer to it from that day on was on hand.

CHAPTER TWENTY-SIX

Visit from Mamajee and Chachajee (Maternal Uncle and Paternal uncle)

Both of my maternal uncle (Mamajee) and my paternal uncle (Chachajee) lived in Wolverhampton. Their families had not arrive from India yet. They both worked in a foundry in Wolverhampton area called Qualcast. For the longest time, I thought the name was actually what they use to call it Coal Kaast. When it really was Qual for quality, and cast of course for casting, thus Qualcast. All these Sikhs who worked there would refer to it the only way they knew how, and that was Coal kaast. They both worked there along with a lot of other Sikhs. The work was terribly hard, and it showed on their hands where they grabbed the melting iron bucket with their hands to pour it into the cast. The heat from the handle at times would burn all the way through the gloves they wore to their hands. You could feel the roughness of their hands if they ever touched your face. You would feel like that it was the roughest sand paper that was touching against your face rather than a human hand. The money was good, so these boys were strong, and they had come to UK to make money, so they put up with it.

There was a pub very close to this foundry. Every lunch time the publican would line up pint glasses of Mild beer and these boys would go over, and each have a couple of pints. They left their money on the counter.

When you asked why they drank a couple of pints at lunch, they would tell you, "Suwah thale karne nun." (To wash down the soot.)

They would then eat their lunch and go at it again until the end of the day. Then again, stop over at the pub on their way home.

I went in to see the foundry one time as a college student, to see what it was like in this legendary place. It was scary. It made you realize the human capacity for endurance, what length a person would go to make a living. On one of my trips back to U.K, I asked my cousin to take me by to see Mamajee and Chahajee's Coal Kaast. It was still standing at that time, but like many other foundries had been shut down. I saw the ghost of the sixties there, those times when UK was thriving and things were good, lives were simple.

My Mammajee and Chachajee had pooled their money and purchased a house together. I still remember the address, 31 Bristol Street. Sikhs at that time gave a whole new meaning to time-share. They would pay rent to share a bed. Two people would share the bed. One person who worked nights slept on the bed during the day, and at night the person who worked during the day would take over. During the weekend, mostly, one would be gone to visit a friend in another town or if they both were in town, they would share the bed. Below the bed would be where they would keep their belongings, which would be a suitcase they had brought from Punjab, in it would be their worldly belongings.

Most rooms had at least two beds once in while some would have three. The front (guest sitting room) was also a bedroom. People that could afford to buy homes made extra cash this way by taking in lodgers.

I remember going to 31 Bristol Street every year during our summer holidays. Kashmir and I would spend time with both of them and other close relatives who would be renting from them.

Mammajee and Chachajee would come often to visit us during the weekends, so it was not surprising to see them, they would show up by the afternoon bus around 4 PM. However, today, they were there in the morning around 11 AM. I was home alone; Beejee had gone to town, and

Kashmir was with her. Papajee was out and about getting everything lined up for the first function.

I asked them if they wanted tea, Beejee had taught both Kashmir and I how to make tea and had instructed us to offer tea to guests who came in their absence. They both said they would have a cup. So I made it and they drank their tea and sat for a while, but I could sense that there was something different about them today. Normally, they would have stories to tell, and both had a sarcastic streak about them like most Jats. Today, however, they seemed preoccupied.

Beejee came home around 1 PM, and Papajee soon followed. Beejee became very concerned when she saw them at home that early from their usual time.

She asked both of them, "Kuldev (that was my Maternal uncle) Avtar Sihan (my paternal uncle) Sukh tan hai tusi doven savere savere ay." (Kuldev, Avtar Singh, is everything well you came this early.)

They said that everything was fine, but she was not buying it. She told me in the kitchen that she thought maybe they had a falling out, and they were here to get it sorted out in front of Papajee.

When Papajee arrived, he asked the same question, and they replied that everything was fine.

The other shoe dropped after lunch, they were both edgy, and were looking at each other as to who was going to approach the subject. Papajee was always very good at reading people and body language when he saw people fidgeting about it just got his goat. He wanted people to have the conviction to say what was on their mind and get on with it.

So he asked them, "Ek dooje val deeki jaon ge ke kuj bolon ge be, aval tan menu patta tusin kee kehna." (Are you going to keep looking at each other or are you going to speak up? Although I have an idea what it is that you want to say.)

He had guessed why they had come. They were there to

dissuade him from the path he was on.

Then Chachaji Avtar Singh spoke, "Asin thuhano duhan nun ehi kehn ay han key lehna ena kama bichon niannae shote han kal nu koi ja jandi ho jave fer ke karan ge." (We wanted to say, why would you want to get involved in this work, you have young kids if something happens tomorrow, then what will we do?)

Beejee was furious. She was a very balanced lady, but this got to her. Before Papajee could say anything, she laid into both of them, "Shabaash, ek shota bhra ek shota Devar, ek Bhra, ek sala, shabaash, Ek mere Sardar de Saji bahn ek meri Saji Bahan, Ek mere Sardar de Khabi Bahan ek meri Khabi bahan, Das maan karan tan kada keran? Sadian he Bawan sanon keh rahian han ke Quam Da tan Guru da Kam Shad deo, Vah Merio veero vah." (Well done, my brothers, one my brother the other my brother in law, one my husband's brother other his brother in law. One is my right and left arm, and the other is my husband's right and left arm. If I am to be proud of what is it? That are our right and left arms are telling us to not do the lord's work, not to do community's work. Wonderful, Wonderful.)

Papajee asked Beejee to stop, but she felt betrayed by those that she had raised as her own children, and she was hurt. On their part, they felt a genuine concern, and they felt a fear that public work is never without its own set of issues. Beejee wanted them to support the work not dissuade them from carrying it out.

Others often see people that have a mission in life as walking on the edge of the cliff, and it frightens those that stay on safe ground. They try to persuade them back to the safe road. This was their way of telling Papajee and Beejee the same thing.

Papajee was very calm. I remember he was sitting on a dining table chair. He looked over at both of them, but they could not look up at him; they kept their heads down.

He calmly started to speak, "Doven meri gal suno

changi taran. Men thouano push ke eh kadam nehi chukia. Eh men Parmatama de aasre chuckia, ate eh Nasib Kaur da saat leh ke. Hun jau oh chah ve ga oh hi hove ga, par asi es nu chaodar lay nahin keeta seva karni hai apne Waheguru de. Agar koi galiti ho gai us kolo he maufi manga ge. Madat manga ge tan ve aus kulo. Mera naam Manga Dharam Singh hai. Aaur Dharam he manga ga. Thuano koi ulamba nahin ave ga, je aya keh dena oh saada kuj nahin lag da asin us de kuj nahin lag de." (Both of you listen to me very carefully. I did not take this step by asking you. I took this step with the refuge and grace of my Almighty, and Nasib Kaur at my side. Now what will happen will be his will. I do not want any kind of power. I am in the service of my master. If I make a mistake, I will only ask for Waheguru's forgiveness. My name is Manga meaning ask and second is Dharam faith, I will live up to my name I will only ask for faith, fiath in my Lord and faith that I can carry it through. You will not get any complaints about me. In the event, you do. You have the right to disown me.)

The last word got to both of them; they just broke down and sobbed like babies, usually Papajee was hard on them but today, he was talking to them at a very different level.

Papajee was not good at consoling. He was uncomfortable with seeing outpouring of emotion like this. I only saw him cry one time in my life, and that was when the Golden Temple was attacked in 1984. That day he cried sobbingly.

All he said to both were, "Bus karo hunn gal nun samjho." (Stop now, just try and understand.)

They stayed for a bit longer but that weekend they did not stay the night. They took the early evening bus back to Birmingham and then changed at Birmingham for the bus to Wolverhampton.

I am not sure thing were the same for Beejee again with them. She felt let down by the both of them. Sometimes we see some people as people that support us unquestionably and when they question our motives, we feel that they are questioning our integrity, and we feel let down and betrayed.

CHAPTER TWENTY-SEVEN

The shoe tags

Sikhs don't go bare head or wear shoes in the presence of our everlasting Guru, Guru Granth Sahib. The shoes are left outside with attendants who volunteer to do that task. In order to identify the shoes, there are two tokens with the same number. One is given to the owner for retrieval, and the other one is put with the shoes.

We needed to make a system of tokens. Papajee purchased some small paintbrushes from the stationary shop in town that sold arts and craft supplies along with some black ink. He cut the front half of the brushes and put a tight rubber band around the rest of the bristles so that it would be stiff, and we could make a big enough number that could be easily seen. Then next was to look for boxes to cut the cardboard. Kashmir and I went around to all the shops along Stoney Stanton road asking shopkeepers for boxes. I think if it was not for the two facts, one that most of the shopkeepers knew Papajee and the other that we were always well dressed they would have for sure thought were destitute trying to collect cardboard to sell for pennies. However, that was never on our minds. We knew what we wanted it for, and we knew we had to get them from wherever we can get them.

We brought as much cardboard as we could and piled it in the shed, and then started the real work. We cut the cardboard into two-inch by two-inch squares, and Kashmir started to paint numbers on them in sets of two, starting with one all the way to a total of five hundred. We made five hundred sets. Beejee got a needle and thread and started threading them in backward into a string of 25 in each string, so there was a total of fifty squares in each square. We were concerned how we would identify, which was which set of twenty-five. Papajee thought of an idea that was color-coding them. Inventory in warehouses is color-coded. Every time I go into a warehouse of a factory that I visit and see color-code scheme. I am reminded of those little shoe tags and the color-coding that we developed as a family.

Everything was lining up pretty well, the mistry brought around the Manji Sahib (platform upon which Guru Granth Sahib was to be seated.) He also thought up one other thing that he thought that we would need. He made a large wooden stick that Beeji could use to stir the Sacrament pudding. She was very happy to see it as it was on her list to solve.

CHAPTER TWENTY-EIGHT

Program Line up for the big Day

We were now two weeks to the big day. Papajee needed to solve another major issue, and that was to get star items to attract people to the first function. As with anything-new starting, there are as many reasons why people come, as there are people. He knew some would come out of faith; others out of curiosity, there were those who wanted just to be present when no one showed up, so they could have a good laugh. These were his middle circle folks. Then there those who were loyal to him and his cause. He also knew this was his first program if it did not go off well; there was a real danger that people would lose interest.

So he decided that he needed a Dhadi Jatha (Ballard Singing Group) most of the Sikhs were from rural areas in Punjab, and they grew up hearing Dhadi sing Ballard of valor. This was how history was passed on for centuries by these Ballard singers. Most times with a lot of personal touches that had no basis, in reality, or history, but it made for good listening. So he went to meet with a Dhadi, who lived in Birmingham by the name of Shingara Singh. He was quite famous in those days, and would be a good attraction. Shingara Singh met Papajee and agreed to be present at the first divan function in Coventry with his group. Papajee then met with Boota Singh and asked him if he could spare a couple of Keertan people.

There were no paid professional keertan people from India as there are today it was mostly people that held down a regular job and on Sundays, they would do Keertan, and they were a scarce commodity. Boota Singh was a bit reluctant to give up names, but Papajee was a very a determined individual, and he was not about to leave until he had a resolution to his issue. Finally, Boota Singh said that his brother and he would be present on that day and they would bring with them one other Keertania (Hymn singers.) His brother also could do keertan, so with Boota Singh's brother and one other Keertnia and Shingara Singh would hold down the fort as to speak. Papajee agreed with Boota Singh and the program was now complete.

He now wanted to send the word out to the community that Shingara Singh's Dhadi Jatha would be present on the first divan. This went out into the community, and the expectation started to build. I remember kids at school all talking about a Dhadi jatha coming. How at home their parents were looking forward to coming to see the Dhadi Jatha.Papajee kept going over the list one at a time item by item. He would sit us down every night and go over it and discuss every detail. Finally after a couple of times of this Beejee told Papajee to relax and leave everything now in the hands of God, we had done everything that we could.

The Friday before the first Devan, he asked his foreman at Sterling Metals with whom he had a good relationship that he would like to work days for that Friday. While we were growing up his foreman's wife, every year without fail would bring us gifts on Christmas. It was an amusing event actually. She would always come in for tea. Beejee would make her a cup of tea, and they would have a deep conversation with one another. Beejee speaking in Punjabi and her in English, neither could understand what the other was saying; yet they communicated. She would bring pictures of her kids and grand kids and Beejee would pull out our newer school photos or my sister's kid's photos.

And the foreman's wife would just say, "Mindo's children?"

Beejee would yes, yes and they would both giggle and hug as if they were long lost sisters.

Papajee worked days that Friday and when he got home, he bathed and had early dinner and told Beejee that he wanted to go to Birmingham and meet with Boota Singh and Shingara Singh to make sure everything was on target and wanted to firm up the times. He changed and caught the evening bus to Birmingham; he told us that he would probably catch the last bus back if not earlier after he made sure everything is sorted out.

The last Midland Red bus from Birmingham left Birmingham around ten pm and got to Coventry Pool Meadow station around eleven at night.

Dilbagh Singh my cousin sister's husband would come to visit us every Friday like clockwork; Beejee would always make him something to eat with his tea, and he would sit around for couple of hours and ask us how our school work was going, and he would always tease us about who he thought we would marry. He was a very jolly old well-meaning soul. Even though he had told Papajee not to get involved in the Gurdwara work, and Papajee was a bit disappointed with him. Beejee never ever paid any mind to it.

She would tell Papajee, "Dilbagh Singh de man chit nahin, jo uhde dil vich oh he uhde jaban par." (Dilbagh Singh does not mean any ill will; he just says what is in his heart.)

That Friday Dilbagh Singh came around about six O' Clock in the evening. He asked Beejee where Papajee was? She told him that he had just left for Birmingham to make the final arrangement.

True to form he blurts out, "Mama kehrre kuma vich fas geyea." (What has the maternal uncle got himself into?)

Beejee looked at him, and he knew he was in trouble; he did not say another word. He told Beejee that he was not going to have tea that he was going to go home and come right back with my cousin Harbhajan and stay with us until Papajee came home. Beejee told him that it was not necessary, but he insisted. About an hour later, both were at the door.

Beejee made dinner for everyone, and we ate dinner and sat around, both of us sparring about just about anything and everything. Mostly nonsense; stuff that people talk about when they have time on their hands and nothing to do. Even nonsense becomes an intellectual conversation. Have you ever wondered if we put together all these conversations that go on where people solve every problem in the world from hunger to war to religion? Have you ever wondered if someone said to these countries you are not going to go to war, but all the citizens of the warring countries are going to have to have group meetings and solve their problem and come up with solutions next implement the solutions. If they can't they have to continue to talk even into the centuries. Alternatively, create a video game that they all have to play and afterwards meet online to converse. Perhaps all those that died in wars would not have died. It's a just thought of someone who has time on his hand.

Dilbagh Singh Bhajee and I pretty much kept this going until about eleven o'clock. Kashmir fell asleep and Beejee took him upstairs and put him in bed. Our sights were set on the front door waiting for Papajee to arrive. By about eleven-thirty, he did not arrive. We were starting to get worried. Beejee was worried but tried to keep a strong face. Dilbagh Singh Bhajee said that he would go to Pool Meadow bus station and check to see if Papajee was on the last bus, but Beejee stopped him. She told him what purpose would that serve he will get here once he gets off the bus.

Beejiee did not want Dilbagh Singh Bhajee to go anywhere in the dark. She had her fears, fears that were rooted in my cousin's family past.

Harbhajan was not actually my first or second cousin at all. She was the niece of Papajeei's cousin sister, but our family treated Harbhajan as a daughter nevertheless. Harbhanjan's father were four brothers. One of them was Harbhajan's father. Harbhajan's father lived in Punjab. The other three lived in Fiji. Harbhajan's father went to Calcutta to meet the ship on which one of brother's was arriving from Fiji. While in Calcutta, Harbhajan's father met with some mishap, and no one knows to this day whatever happened to him, he just simply vanished. The tragedy of him vanishing and leaving behind a daughter with no father or mother was something that was always ever-present in our family. So that is how our family adopted Harbhajan. She would come to our village when we were children as if it was her own mother's ancestral village. Her mother had died when Harbhajan was very young. She was treated as a daughter of the house and loved and respected as all the other girls of the house.

Beejee told Dilbagh Singh Bhajee, "Dilbagh Singh kete naihn janna." (Dilbagh Singh you're not going anywhere.)

We sat the night through sleeping off and on. As the sun came up, Beejee asked me to wash my face, and she woke everyone up and she tended to Kashmir. She pulled out a Gutka (Sikh prayer book) from the cupboard, woke Dilbagh Singh Bhajee and Harbhajan Bhenjee (we referred to as Bhenjee meaning sister) and told them to wash their faces and then follow her upstairs. We went into the back room where Guru Granth Sahib was, and she gave the Gutka to Dilbagh Singh Bhajee and told him to recite Japji Sahib (Morning Prayer of the Sikhs). Bhajee recited Japji Sahib, and upon completion, she asked all of us to stand up. She leaned towards the cupboard in which the Guru Granth Sahib was seated, and she opened the door and said the following,

"Whaeguru menu nhain pata mere sar da taj kithe hay. Par oh aap de kam gay see agar koz hogya ta ve koy ulamba nahin jith rakhen ga uthe he reh lavan gee." (Dear Lord I have no idea where my dear husband is. He went on your mission, if something happens to him, I will not utter a word of discontent. I will live where you will ask me to live.)

As soon as she said those words both Harbhajan Bhenjee and Dilbagh Bhaji started crying loudly like children. I was stunned. Kashmir clung to Beejee's legs not knowing what was going on. She bowed in front of the Guru Granth Sahib, closed the door and came downstairs and started to make breakfast.

We all had breakfast in silence, she told Bhajee and Bhenjee to head on home, and she will send me once Papajee comes home. Bhajee would hear none of it. However, she did want him to leave because she knew when Papajee came home Dilbagh Singh Bhajee was going to say what was on his mind, and it was not going to be a pleasant scene. Harbhajan Bhenjee sensed Beejee's intentions and persuaded Bhajee to head home. He reluctantly agreed but only for a few hours and he would be back.

After few hours, around eleven thirty I heard the key twisting in the front door.

I shouted, "Papajee"

By then he had opened the door and the first words out of his mouth were, "What is the ruckus Balbir."

I went silent. He looked like the day he looked the first time I saw him at the airport when we arrived in England, tired, worn out as if the last bit of life had been sucked out of him.

Beejee welcomed him in, and as he sat she looked over at me, and I knew what she wanted me to do, I went over to Papajee and undid his shoelaces and took his shoes off. For the first time, I wanted to touch his feet with my forehead in admiration. We knew he had gone through some tough time in the last twenty-four hours, and the next twenty-four hours were going to be even tougher. Beejee brought hot water for him to soak his feet, but he wanted to wash his face first. He went to the kitchen washed his face, Beejee by then had a cup of tea ready for him. She waited for him to tell us what had happened. She prepared lunch for him. Once he ate lunch and had a moment to get some energy back. He proceeded to tell us what had happened.

He told us that when he got to Birmingham, he went to see Shingara Singh, but he was feeling ill and was not going to be able to make it to the function. So this left a big void in his plans as he had sent the word out to the community that Shingara Singh Dhadi was going to be coming. However,

God and life does have its own plans. He was not one to accept defeat without fighting; he would always tell us that defeat is saying you have nothing else to think. Defeat is not an option, there are always other options, so look at all the options and move onto the next-best option.

He would always say to us, "To say there are no options is to say the universe is finite, and it is not."

He went to the next option. After meeting with Shangara Singh, we went to see Boota Singh and made sure that he was still with the plan. He said that he then caught a train to Euston London, from Euston; he caught the underground to Hounslow and a taxi to one of his friends who lived in Southall. He said that he got to his friend's house about twelve at night. He knocked on the door and his friend was still awake. The household was full of all men whose families had not arrived from Punjab yet. Being a Friday night they were out late at the pubs and had just got home after the last call at eleven at the pubs and were passing the bottle of Scotch around when he got there.

He said he told his friend what had happened and that he wanted to meet with Pritam Singh Dhadi, who also lived within the London area. His friend told him that he would take him around in the morning to meet Pritam Singh. Papajee was never one for delaying anything, and he gave orders. So he told him 'no, he will not.' He will stop the drinking now, and they will go now. His friend told him that it was late. He told his friend if you're up late on Friday chances are he will be. So his friend half drunk drove him over to see Pritam Singh. Pritam Singh knew Papajee quite well and when he saw him; he was surprised and asked him what he was doing there this hour. Papajee explained to Pritam Singh what had happened. Papajee said Pritam Singh was so taken in by the fact that he traveled half the night to come to him to ask him to come he just broke down and embraced papajee. Papjee told me it was really very emotional. He said, "I said to the chap, "Enough, now let's talk business at hand." Pritam

Singh told him that he would move heaven and earth and will be there Sunday morning. He told him that he was out of practice, but he will put his jatha (group) together and will show up.

Papajee's friend dropped him off early at Euston station, and he caught the morning train from Euston to Coventry.

Once he finished telling us the entire ordeal, Beebe finally admitted to him that she was worried. She insisted that he gets few hours of sleep, but he would not hear any of, she convinced him to at try and rest for few hours as he would not get any rest from the evening on. Bhajee Dilbagh Singh showed up just as Papaji went up to lie down, darn good thing too because he was sure to blurt out something that was going to irritate Papajee.

As soon as he walked through the door he shouted, "Mami, Mamaji aage ke nahin." (Auntie has dear uncle arrived or not?)

She put her hand on her lips as to tell him to hush and shook her head that he had arrived. Bhajee Dilgbagh Singh true to form, was not about to let his feelings not be known.

He started, "Bhala Mami eh Mamaji ne ke kam farr lia sari raat waqt paa shadia." (You know auntie. What is this task dear uncle has taken up, kept us worried all night?)

All Beejee said to Bhajee was one word. "Buss" (Enough).

He just stopped in his tracks, sat for a while and left before Papajee got up few hours later.

That even around four o'clock Baba Nand Singh came around to the house, Beejee made him tea, he asked how things were moving along, and if we were ready for tomorrow the big day. If we had any regrets. Beejee smiled and Papajee also laughed when he asked if there were any regrets.

Beejee asked, "Bhaia jee koi shak hai." (Dear respect one. Do you have any suspicion that we have regrets?)

He replied, "Nahin per mera faraz ban da pushna." (No, but it's my duty to ask to ask.)

He stayed late that night, about five O'clock Sohan Singh Gaffa showed up. The door knock it seems always fits a person's personality. Most of the times the people we knew we could guess from the door knock who was at the door. Some had a really loud knock. Others never used the knocker but hit the mail flap as to say sorry to bother you kind of knock. Some hit the doorknocker three or four times. As if to say, hey open this door I have been standing here for five whole seconds. Every knock was different; Kashmir and I use to have a guessing game that we would play as to who would guess the correct person to the knock. On softer moments, Papajee would once in awhile join in.

Gaffa's knock was Bang, louder Bang and then a third louder bang. As soon as you opened the door, there would be an announcement, out nice and loud "Dharam Sinha." (Dharam Singh) and then he would charge in like a true gaffa (boss). This day was no different as he walked through the door and shouted out Papaji's name and walked in and saw Babajee and he said, "Sat Sri Akal" to him. He asked what he needed to do.

To which Babajee in his usual sarcastic manner replied while smiling behind his beard, "Gaffia tenu nee patta tun Gaffa hain." (Hey boss, don't you know. You're the boss.)

Gaffa took it in stride and laughed, Papajee told him to be at the house early on Sunday. Be there no later than nine in the morning.

He sat around a while and then left. Sucha Singh also came and so did lots of other people offering to help. Papaji told all of them to just be early, and he told them one other thing which some of them said was a bit difficult task to adhere to. He told them not to drink on Saturday night. Most of them looked at him a bit dazed.

One of them commented, "Saver tain ta raat valli uttar janni hai." (It will wear off by the morning).

He insisted that they didn't drink. He knew it was really an exercise in futility. Papajee's idea was to try to cause a gentle change, on some it worked; others agreed and went to the pub anyway, but Papajee tried.

Last knock was around ten O'clock it was Milky Singh, Milky was a single man who had been in England for the longest time. He had never married. He had worked as an extra in films at one time in Lahore before the partition and then at London Pinewood studios also when they were making movies based on the British Raj and they needed Indians, so he worked as an extra.

He somehow found his way to Coventry. He was a functioning alcoholic, but a very nice man, did not mean any harm to anyone most people really cared for Milky. He would always have a couple of Stout beer bottles in his side coat pockets. He was crouched over. He walked slowly as if he had hurried all his life and finally had settled on a stride that was more to his inner calling than the stride rest of the world wanted to walk to. He knocked at the door around 10 O'clock on Saturday, and Papaji answered the door.

Papajee was surprised to see him and commented, "Milky, haje tan ghenta hor rendha pub bandh honn wich." (Milky, there is an hour left for the last call at the pubs.)

Milky replied, "Mehn soochia do Ghar jake pe lavan ga, ajj pehalan chal dan nahin tusi saun janna see." (I thought I had better go early, otherwise, you folks would have gone to bed. I have two bottles that I can drink when I get home.)

He took out a crumpled up five-pound note from his coat pocket and gave to Papajee, "Dharam Siniha eh sache Maharaj mure charra dai." (Dharam Singh, please give my respect in front of the true Lord.)

Papajee asked him to come in, but he refused pointed at his mouth that he was drunk. Papajee took his five pounds and went upstairs and put it in the cupboard along with all the other money that people have given

Beejee and Gurbachan Kaur had met earlier and had

decided that they would first make the Parshad and had that ready, and then they would make breakfast for all the out-of-town people who would be coming.

Babajee left around ten thirty after dinner, and by eleven o'clock. Papajee said that we ought to get to bed we had a long day ahead of us in the morning.

It was hard to sleep, felt like a wedding night. Papaji was at peace. I think he felt he had covered everything that needed to be covered, and the fact that people kept coming and offering to help all evening gave him encouragement that things will go well.

CHAPTER TWENTY-NINE

THE BIG DAY

Beejee was up early around four in the morning. She wanted Papajee to sleep a bit longer since he had his ordeal and did not get much sleep, but he was awake. I woke up about the same time. I remember coming downstairs and Beejee had already bathed and was going through the house with incense into all the rooms. She asked me to rest for a while; there was nothing for me to do. There was knock on the door, it was Gurbachan Kaur. Beebe and Gurbachan Kaur started to prepare the Rast (recipe for the Sacrament) and they pulled out the big utensils that they had purchased and started to wash when Gurbachan Kaur stopped and looked over at me. I knew it was payback time; she still had not punished me enough for laughing at them for carrying the dishes on their heads.

She turns to Beejee and said, "Bhenji Balbir nu heh kam deneh." (Sister, let's give this Job to Balbir.)

So there I was washing those big dishes. Once I was done with them she went over and washed them again before they proceeded to making Parshad (Sacrament), but she had felt really good that she had punished me well and proper.

They repeated the process of making the Prashad few times to make enough so it filled the large basins that they had purchased. Once completed they covered it and moved it to the front room where it sat covered away from anything else so as to maintain its purity and holiness.

They then started to cook the food for all the folks that would need to be fed that would be arriving for the occasion from out of town. Papjee wanted to supervise this himself. He wanted to make sure that no stone was left unturned in hospitality. Not that Beejee would anyway, but he wanted to make sure that he saw everything. They cooked for good few hours to have everything ready.

Beejee asked me to wake Kashmir and get him ready, Kashmir was not always easy to wake. He took his sweet time to get up so it was usually an hour before it was time that the process of waking him started.

When Kashmir woke up, he bathed and dressed and as usual took to his books, it did not matter what was happening in the world, he would always gravitate to his books. Even today he is still the same, only now it's the Internet any spare time he has. He is on the Internet reading one thing or another. Both of us were told to read and expand our knowledge at all times.

Beejee was fine with it since it kept him occupied, I bathed but Beejee told me to stay in my Pyjama's and help her in the kitchen. Once she was done she asked me to get ready also. The sun had come up. Papajee went out the front door to the school to see if Mr. Hancok had arrived if not he would go over and fetch him since he lived on Stony Stanton Road just a little to the right of Red Lane.

Mr. Hancock was a very punctual man; he had already opened the gate. Papajee went upstairs to the hall to make sure it was in good order. Even though the hall was clean he went over to the maintenance building, which was by the first house on Red lane in the schoolyard and asked Mr. Hanock to give him a broom. Mr. Hancock told him that the hall is clean. Papajee told him, yes but I want to clean it for my Sangat.

Mr. Hancok smiled and told Papajee, "I know you want to do Seva, well Mr. Singh you can't; you do other seva (service) if the school needs another clean it is my Seva."

Papajee came home with tears in his eyes and he said that MR. Hanock first would not let him sweep and insisted that he needed to do it but what really brought tears to his eyes was the Mr. Hancock took a completely new broom to use to sweep the hall with and told Papajee that the new broom would only be ever used for the purpose of cleaning Sundays before the Divan (services) from this day forwards.

Babajee came around by about eight Am, Papajee told him about Mr. Hancock, Babajee smiled and said, "Dharam Siniah Dharam the naaam he Insanyat hai jis bande ne Insanyat sikh Lay oh de vich har dharam the vasa bann janda hai." (Dharam Singh faith's other name is Humanity, then] man who has learnt humanity has in him all faiths.)

Papajee asked that the front door be left open I put a door stop in the front door and also the door leading from the corridor to the family room and put the other door stop. Papajee wanted to make sure that all were welcomed and felt the prsence of the moment. Indeed, I am not sure what it was, but to this day I feel the cool fresh breeze of that moment. Even to this day, I feel a sense of calmness when I think about that first opening of our door to our house at number 7 Red Lane Coventry on that day on June 18th 1961. There was a different feeling on everyone's face once that door was opened. I think with the opening of the door. Our hearts were also opened and filled by the love of community faith and yes Seva (service).

About eight thirty, there was a slam of a car door outside, I went to look, and I saw a well-dressed Sardar (Turband'd. Sikhs are referred to as Sardar, Sardar means commander or nobility.) with two other Sardars coming out of a small utility van. I ran inside to tell Pappajee, he came out and was filled with Joy and had his arms opened out.

He grabbed the leader and hugged him, "Pritam Singh, wah jee wah tusin tan mera ser par khoon vidah dita." (Pritam Singh you have just made my blood rush with joy.)

Pritam Singh Dhadi kept his word and arrived nice and early and took a big load off Papajee's mind. He brought them in and introduced them to Babajee. They talked about their villages and who they knew in one another's village.

People started to come. Sucha Singh came with his two elder sons Shinda the eldest and younger Mika. Other folks started to show up, and most of them wanted to shake hands with the Dhadi Jatha. Papajee asked Shinda and other young men who had arrived to help with picking up the blankets from the shed and taking them to the Hall and spread them out for people to sit on.

From that day on Shinda became the leader of what Beejee dubbed the "Kambal Paltan" (the blanket Platoon.) Sikhs tend to refer to groups with army reference. "Paltan kdron aai, Fauj kidron aai." (Where has the platoon come from? Alternatively, where has the army come from?)

Beejee went and ironed the Chandni (canopy) that she had made and gave it to Papajee to take and tie it where the Guru Granth Sahib was to be seated. All the blankets were laid out; Chandni was tied on the stage. Kashmir was responsible for the shoe tokens that we had made. He kept them in a very systematic order. Boota Singh had arrived and had gone over to number 25 Red Lane to Nazar Singh's house. He and his brothers came over and asked Papajee if we needed anything, Papajee went over everything with them, and Boota Singh smiled and looked over at Papajee and told him to relax. Papajee was not the relaxing kind of person. He was a very detailed person. He wanted to make sure all the details were covered.

Kashmir handed Boota Singh and his brother the strings of token that we had made of cardboard for the shoe identification.

They took it from Kashmir and told him that we would not needing them. They proceeded to pull books of raffle tickets (This was a book that you could buy at any newspaper shop, basically it was a book from 1-100 segments, and you could also buy in different colors. It had two of the same numbers so you gave one to the person that was buying the raffle and put the other in the barrel in our case in the shoe so when the person presented his number the corresponding would be in the shoes.) from their pockets and said we will be using these. What an idea, we had never thought of it was an ideal ready-made solution.

Kashmir was pouting that his work was in vain. Boota Singh saw that Kashmir was upset, and he moved quickly and handed the raffle tickets to Kashmir and told him that he was responsible for all the shoes along with him. It is amazing what a little encouragement and recognition can do to a child. Kashmir was happy. Boota Singh personally stood with him outside the entrance door helping take care of the shoes that day. I often think of Boota Singh and that seva he took that day. He could have demanded to be recognized as the founding father of Birmingham Gurdwara, but no, he chose to stand with children in the most humble of all places taking shoes of the congregation and teaching kids that being humble is the greatest of all virtues. My brother Kashmir is one of the most gentle, humble souls that I have ever met in my life; there is a brick in his foundation that was put there in part by Boota Singh Jee.

Sikhs take off their shoes in the presence of the Guru as a sign of respect and for cleanliness. We also cover our head in the presence of the Guru. Sikhs should never cut their hair. They must keep them tidy and covered. However, when Sikhs first came to the UK, they worked in harsh and at times unsafe environments like the foundries, and they reluctantly cut their hair. I remember many newly arrivals being taken to the barber shop to get their hair cut. I saw them bring their shorn hair and neatly wrap them up and then put it in their suitcase and put their head in their hands and sob until the tears dried up.

Cutting their hair was a sin that almost all of them felt that they committed. In later years they would rectify by keeping their hair.

Kashmir felt in charge, and Boota Singh was standing there just a few steps behind him letting Kashmir feel that it was his show.

People started to arrive. Most of the men had brought a brand spanking new handkerchief for this occasion, and they had already tied it on their heads. The women were smartly dressed, their first religious and in many ways also a social event. The kids were all sparkling and combed and slicked up with oil that was shining from their hair. Most of the creams and hair stuff that is on the market now, was not there back then. There was Brylcream, but most of our people did not think it really did anything for the roots. It was either mustard oil or better than that, there was a Pharmacy on Stony Stanton Road opposite Broad Street. I think it was called Stevenson's Chemist, and it sold Olive Oil and people would save the empty bottles of Scotch, which, by the way, there were plentiful and take it down to the pharmacy and get a fill of olive oil and use it on the hair. There were plenty of olive oils that day.

There were people lining up from our front door at number seven all the way to the top of the stairs to the hall. People were waiting, laughing, and greeting each other. There were people that we had never even seen before, but there was a build-up of a sense of community in the air.

About 10:30 AM, Babajee said to Papajee, "time hogya hai"

(Its time)

Babaji grabbed Gaffa by the arm and told him to stand by the stairs. He grabbed Sucha Singh's arm and told him to stand by the front door. Babaje made the preparation this way to walk the Guru Granth Sahib to the Hall in the school.

He asked all of us, Papajee, Beejee, Kashmir and I to wash our hands and cover our heads and come to the room upstairs where Guru Granth Sahib was. I told him Kashmir was at the hall he asked me to go get him.

Kashmir was hard to persuade to leave his post, but Boota Singh was quite helpful and told him that he will fill in for him while he was away. Reluctantly, Kashmir agreed.

We all followed Babajee to the room upstairs. He told me to

bring fresh water, I went downstairs and filled a glass and brought it up.

Before I could give it to him, Beejee stopped me and said, "Es de vich nahin jerra men navan leanda jug ude vich." (Not in this in the new jug that I bought in that.)

I went down and got the water in the new jug. Babajee told us, papajee would be carrying the Guru Granth Sahib on his head. Balbir will sprinkle water in the front and he would do the Chaur (this is a Wisk made from Yak's hair; it is waved on the Guru Granth Sahib as a sign of royalty).

To the Sikhs, Guru Granth Sahib is not just a book of Scriptures. It is much more. It is the commandment of the tenth Guru, Guru Gobind Singh that all Sikhs will regard the Guru Granth Sahib as their eternal Guru. For Sikhs Guru Granth Sahib is where they go for guidance and direction. So the Guru has that status of extreme reverence for the Sikhs, and it is treated and respected as the lord. Sikhs will not carry the Guru Granth Sahib in a suitcase or put it under their arm and move about. This would be sacrilegious. The Guru must travel as all royalty does.

When Babajee told Papajee that he would carry the Guru Granth Sahib on his head to the hall Papajee folded his hands and said to Babajee, "Nand Singh mere bhai kesh hai nahin." (Nand Singh my brother I do not have unshorn hair.)

To this day when I think of what Babajee said to Papajee my heart fills up. He did not judge him.

He put both of his hands-on Papajee's shoulders and looked straight into his eyes and said, "Dharam Sinihan, tera safar at e tere emthiaan hun shro hoya, dekh da javin, apanin Guru de tan ohdi Sangad de seva karda gian saaf dil naal tere fal lag de janae at e kesh be uh teno bakshe ga jad oh de meher huni hai." (Dharam Singh your journey and test have just started, as you serve your master and his congregation it will bear fruit and when his grace shines upon you then you will also have Kesh unshorn hair.)

Papajee had gone around to all the neighbors and told them about the function. All the English neighbors came out to the streets with their children to witness the occasion.

Babajee did the ardaas (the invocation prayer; Sikhs start everything and end everything with an ardaas so that everything is carried out with God at your side.) He picked a Romala (tunic used to wrap the Guru Granth Sahib) and put it on top of Papajee's white turban, and Papajee was facing the door. Babajee asked me to start sprinkling the water from the jug in front.) A symbol off cleaning the path for the guru, a sign of the most respect given. Beejee and Kashmir went on their knees with hands folded. Babajee picked up the Chaur (the wisk wand) and started to wave it across from right to left over the Guru Granth Sahib and started reciting loudly SATNAM WAHEGURU (True is the Name of the wonderful lord) he raised his hand to Beejee and Kashmir, and everyone followed to recite along with him. As we came down the stairs, Gaffa fell to his knees and bowed his head. We all joined in the chant of SATNAM WAHEGURU then Sucha Singh standing at the front door followed, as I set foot onto the street, I saw people lined up along the street and the chant started to pick up. The resonance of SATNAM WAHEGURU was giving out vibes, which was just spiritual. People were dropping to their knees.

They were in tears. These were tears of joy. They had waited so long to shed, since they had left their beloved Punjab, their village and the last memory was the respect that they had paid at the village Gurdwara (the Sikh Place of worship). Thinking at that moment when will they ever see their Guru again. Here it was. They were witnessing it right in front of their eyes. These were tears of joy, for a moment, they were at home a place of rest, a place where everything stops and only the resonance of SATNAM WAHEGURU beats in the heart. We sometimes look for eternity as something outside of us. If we just stop the time and make time not mean so much in our life, we will feel the glow of the eternal inside us.

As we moved toward the gate to the school, there were lines

all the way to the building; standing by the maintenance shed on the left-hand side was Mr. Hancock. He had his Andy Capp derby hat on. He reached for his cap but then saw that all the people had their head covered. He pulled his hand back and calmly gave a salute and stood there until we moved passed him.

The stairways were crowded with people waiting as we went up the stairs people followed. Upstairs Shinda and the other boys had laid down the blankets and made the place ready where all were waiting to be first to see the Guru take its seat and wanted to be the first to bow their head before him. However there was not one person that you could say was first but many, who placed their offerings of money and paid their respect in front of the Guru Granth Sahib.

Babajee took the Guru Granth Sahib from Papajee and put it on the platform designed to seat the Guru Granth Sahib by mistry Prashotam Singh. After organizing it Babajee again did the Ardaas and then he took the hukamnama (the loosely translated Hukamnama is a Farsi word meaning the order. Sikhs open the Guru Granth Sahib at a random page and whatever the verse is believed to be the order of the Guru and that is the guiding teaching during that day or whatever function the Hukamnama is being taken for).

Sikhs are not very good at documenting things. Everyone was so caught up in the moment that nobody documented the Hukamnama for that day. Babajee read the Japji Sahib after he took the Hukamnama and the Sangat (congregation was filling the hall, the noise and joy that filled the hall was like flowers in full bloom in some valley in spring and the birds singing their chorus.

Papajee asked that I go home and help Beejee and stay there until she was done feeding the out-of-town people breakfast.

Sikhs have with every Gurdwara a community kitchen, where everyone regardless of religion, color creed or caste can come and eat. Since it was not convenient to have food at the school hall, general Langar was not available until the

Gurdwara was built. The next-best thing was what Papajee came up with; which was to leave the door openof our house on the day of the function. And who ever came and wanted to eat would go over and would be fed.

Mostly out of towners were those that went over to eat as most people from Coventry understood that it was a very grand gesture on the part of Papajee and Beejee but they would not put any undue burden on them. The Langar was always prepared from Papajee's earnings and not from any of the donations towards the Gurdwara. Even if someone did give money Papajee would just add it to the Gurdwara account and deposit it in the account.

It was difficult for me to leave at that point, but as an obedient son that's exactly what I did.

As I came down Mr. Hancock asked, "Where are you going?"

I told him that I had to go home and help my mother finish up so that she could come to the services.

"You're a good lad Balbir." Mr. Hancock commented.

I smiled even though I wanted to be upstairs; his compliment did soften the blow of missing out a bit.

I came home and helped Beejee feed those that were left, Pritam Singh was sitting in the front room with his partners rehearsing, when Papajee came back. He asked me where Pritam Singh was. I told him that he was in the front room. He went into the front room and pulled Pritam Singh out.

He sat him down in the family room and said, "Pritam Singh men aap nun ek gal kheni hay, oh eh ke jo bee paise banan ge oh Guru ghar deh hon ge, asin aap nun juh baajab rate deh deven ge oh aap nun dus pound tan petrol." (Pritam Singh I need to clear something with you. That is that whatever you are given by the congregation will belong to the Gurdwara. We will pay you a reasonable amount for your services. Ten-pounds plus petrol money.)

In Sikh Gurdwaras, to the Kirtan singers (Hymn Singers) people give them donations while they sing and generally that is the mode of payments, and they keep that money. If they do a good job, these donations to them from the Sangat could add up to a tidy sum.

Papajee knew that people will donate generously and he wanted to have a rule moving forward. That would be, the committee would pay all money, which was collected at the divan, was the property of the Gurdwara and anyone who performed Kirtan or sang Ballads. He kept this rule in place all through his service. Even when there were people that wanted to break the rule he would put his foot down and not let them break it.

I think Pritam Singh was taken back a bit at first. It was the first time that in his career as a Dhadi that he had heard this request. However, he respected Papajee and he knew why he was doing this. He knew that Papajee was trying to keep account of every penny and trying to get as much money into the account of the Gurdwara as he could, and he wanted everyone to be a contributor. Some were willing some not so willing. But his rule was the rule and it never changed.

Pritam Singh folded both of his hands and said, "Vade bahi, kee reesan terian, hun meri be sun leh, sanu be petrol deh paise deh day baki kuj nain chahi da, aur meh keh dena hay keh khul ke deyo saare guru de khate vich jaane han." (Dear older brother you are incomparable! Now you listen to me. Don't give us the ten pounds. All I want is money for the petrol. I will also say it at the function. Give openly. It is all going to the Guru's account.)

Papajee took Pritam Singh and his partners with him to the hall. I helped Beejee finish up in the Kitchen, while she put things away I took off my coat and put on her apron and washed all the dishes.

I waited for her to change, and we locked the house and went to the hall, as we were going up the stairs you could hear Babajee singing in Sidhian Dhaarna (a verse sang out in a soulful manner, most attributed to village and rural style of devotional singing).

Beejee smiled and said, “Barri ronuq lagi hoi hai.” (Lot of festivity and joy.)

The line to pay respect to the guru was out the door of the hall all the way down the stairs. I wanted to be up in the hall where the action was, but I was not going to move until Beejee said so.

I looked up at her, and she smiled and said, "Ja" (go).

I went passed everyone and went into the hall to the front and found a spot. People made a bit of space for me because I was my father's son, I suppose.

The hall was full of joy, people that could sing or even those that could not were singing. Every out of tune voice was singing out loud. People wanted to lead with whatever verse they knew.

Finally, it was Pritam Singh's turn to take the microphone. He Stood up along with his partners and gave the Khalsa (the pure ones) Salutation, "Waheguru jee Ka Khalsa Waheguru jee kee Fateh." (The Khalsa belongs to Almighty, and victory be to the Almighty.)

He started by saying that all the donations that you will give will go towards the Guru's account. He then went into his recitation of ballads with regards to the martyrdom of the sixth Guru, Guru Arjan Dev jee in whose memory this first function was being held.

He reminded everyone that it was Guru Arjan who compiled the holy Guru Granth Sahib, which not only contains the works of the Sikh Gurus but also of Muslim saints and of Hindu saints. These Hindu saints were of all castes high and low. Under the Hindu caste system, low caste people were not even allowed to utter the name of God and now they have a permanent and an equal place in the Guru Granth Sahib. He further reminded that it was Guru Arjan Dev ji that built Harminder Sahib (The Golden Temple). Therefore, it was befitting for the Sikh Sangat (congregation) of Coventry had taken the task to build this Gurdwara (Temple) on his martyrdom day. He then went on to congratulate Papajee and wished him the strength to see it through. He did comment that he knew Papajee and if one man who had the fortitude to do it, it was him, but asked the Sangat to help him.

He was supposed to conclude in one hour, but he went on for over hour and half, and the table was so full of pounds notes that he had to keep moving them to the side so he could see over them.

After Pritam Singh finished the final Ardaas was performed, and Parshaad (sacrament) was distributed to the Sangat, and the first function in Coventry had taken place. Commemorating the martyrdom of the sixth guru and a new chapter in Coventry's history was opened on this day of June 18th, 1961.

CHAPTER THIRTY

Days Following

Next day at school I was crowded by other kids who wanted to be friends with me, they wanted to congratulate me; they wanted to know more about what happened behind the scenes. They wanted to know about different people. The kids of the Indian workers association families and also of the second circle that was closer to me in the past shunned me. Groups started to form. I remember telling Papajee what was happening and who was acting how. He told me that I ought not to act any different towards them, as I would have in the past.

He told me, "Balbir mausem badeled de han, ruck badled han, aur waqat baleda hai. Par insaan de zameer nahin badlani chahi de." (Balbir, seasons change. Circumstances change, times change, but man's good character must never change.)

I made sure that I went out of my way to speak to those that shunned me. After a while, most of them came around.

People who could not come to the first function came around to the house and gave money for the fund; most of them apologizing that they were unable to come.

Those missing were the members of the Mazdoor Sabha, they stayed away. I think this hurt Papajee, but he was not a man to hold a grudge. He would let you know how he felt and then move on. He also knew that he had a path that he had carved out, and it was going to clash with them sooner or later.

He kept enhancing his list of people on the third circle,

people that were not before counted. He was now approaching them. He made sure that he was reaching out to all people from all parts of the community.

Sikhs are not supposed to believe in the caste system, but I heard someone tell me one time that he thought culture was stronger than religion, and it is culture, which molds religion into its own form.

I am still not sure if I agree, but the evidence is strong that culture does have a heavy influence on an ongoing basis on religion. You see inside the Sikh Gurdwaras there is never any question of a practice of the caste system. Outside in the normal life in the villages it is as strong as it ever was. Sikhs really are as guilty as the next man for the practice of this taboo. I know this statement may be seen by some of my fellow Sikhs as controversial but truth often is. It needs to stop.

Papajee just felt that Guru Nanak's message of Universal brotherhood had to start with his own people. He needed to make sure that he went to every caste. He even went to some Hindu families and Sindhi families and told them that they were welcomed. His message to them was very clear and simple. This is the house of God; let us all serve him and build it together as brothers and sisters.

CHAPTER THIRTY-ONE

The Sikh from Singapore

Second week after the first function, on Sunday morning, I was chiseling out the putty from the window pane of our front door. Our front door had two long window panels, Saturday night someone had put a brick through the front door window, and it was shattered to bits. This was a common occurrence that most people from India or Pakistan were subjected to. Some hooligan would get drunk on Saturday night and looked for an Indian or Pakistani house and put a brick through it. Most people never even bothered reporting it to the police. Everyone knew it was futile. So we would just repair the damage and wait for the next brick to come through the window. Most of the times it would be kids from the neighborhood. These types of humiliation were common.

Discrimination is death by thousand blows, remarks like, WOGS, PAKIS, BLACKIE, NIGGERS, were all too common during those days, to which people would not respond, in fear of starting a fight, they would just walk on. Or groups would get together and say let's go Paki-bashing and look for some poor soul alone and beat the living daylights out of him. The marks that this type of hatred leaves on you lasts a lifetime. You become less trusting. You see people not as individuals but as a group and you then in a way start to practice similar hate towards a community yourself. Pretty soon if you're not careful, you become like them, the bigots, and you develop your own set of words of hurt, and bigotry comes full circle.

But Kashmir and I were lucky to have Papajee and Beejee

as our parents. They always taught us that you are not what others call you but what you believe in your head and heart. We were always taught to believe in the tenth master's concept of "CHARDI KALA" (STATE OF EXALTED SPIRIT AT ALL TIMES.)

As I was chiseling away the putty with a chisel, so I could put cardboard or some plastic so that we would not be exposed to the wind from outside. I saw Babajee, and he had with him a man who had a turban tied high and neatly in a style that I had not seen before. He appeared to be about medium height and quite stocky.

I called out to Papajee that Babajee was coming, and he has another man with him with a turban.

As Babajee came and I greeted him and the other man with the Sikh greeting of "Sat Sri Akal" (the timeless one (GOD) is the truth). He responded and asked me if Papajee was home not even inquiring what had happened to the door, because he already knew what most people faced and were doing on a Sunday morning was what I was doing.

I told him that Papajee was inside, he went in with the other Sikh, Papajee greeted them and Beejee came in from the kitchen and touched Babajee's feet as a sign of respect for elders.

She had always touched his feet and he would put his hand on her head and say, "Teekh hain kurriae?" (Girl are you fine and well?)

Beejee went into the Kitchen to put the tea on; this was automatic with Sikh families. When a guest comes to your house, you do not ask if they want tea or anything to eat or drink it is just presented. Some people take this to the extreme and almost force-feed you.

I remember on one of my visits back to the UK from USA. I went to visit my first cousin, and they brought tea and spring rolls and Samosas (Indian savory snack), and I had to eat one each just to be polite even though I was not hungry. I went to see the next cousin and the same thing, again I repeated it. By the time I left the second cousins house I was busting at the seams, I loosened my belt and told my cousin who was taking me around that it would be great if he let the third cousin know that we have eaten at two places, and I was full and please don't prepare any more food. He told me that he was not going to be in the bad books by saying so; he said if you feel that way say it yourself. I did say it myself and it is the last time I will do that.

My cousin got huffy and said, "Bloody American. You think you're too good for us?"

Then his wife came from the Kitchen and said, "Bhaji kee gal hoi aasin bakeian nallo ghatt han." (Brother what is this, are we less than the rest of them?)

I had to calm both down while my cousin who accompanied me looked on and was grinning like a Cheshire cat. Needless to say I had spring rolls and Samosas with my tea. To this day whenever I think of that trip and that incidence, my stomach somehow fills up, and I lose my appetite.

Babajee introduced the Sikh gentleman that he had brought over to meet Papajee,

"Dharam Sihan eh Giani Naunihal Singh hai. Eeh Singpore tu hai pehla Bombay tu hai, eh push da see eth Gurdawara hai. Meh keha tain nu mila devan." (Dharam Singh this is Giani Naunihal Singh. He is from Singapore, originally from Bombay. He asked me if there was a Gurdwara here, I thought I would have him meet you.)

The title of Giani is conferred on people who have completed and passed a course in Sikh studies. It is a degree in divinity. However, it is loosely applied to people who can recite and also have good knowledge of Sikh scriptures. Sikhs don't have a clergy. Anyone of us can lead the congregation in prayer, including women. So those that do so most often are generally referred to loosely as Giani's or Bhai. The title Giani should apply only to those people, who have completed the studies, and the others are known as Bhai but both are used and are acceptable.

Naunihal Singh folded his hands and said Sat Sri Akal to

Papajee and went on to introduce himself. He told Papajee that he was originally from Bombay, and then he had moved on to Singapore and had lived there few years and had freshly arrived in Coventry. He told papajee that he wanted to go to the Gurdwara and had asked a Sikh he saw in the street. Where there would be a Gurdwara. He said the man mockingly said to him, "Eth koi Gurdwara tan hai nahin, sada tan Ggurdwara pub he hai." (We don't have any Gurdwaras here. Our Gurdwara is the pub.)

He told Papajee that he was so shocked to hear this. He said then he met Babajee who has brought me to you. Papajee was saddened by what he had heard about the reference of the Pub to the Gurdwara but it was not news to him. He heard people refer to the pub as Gurdwara. He told Naunihal Singh not to pay any mind to that kind of talk. Changing the environment can only change that kind of talk, and that can only be changed once we have a place to worship. Then families can come together to the Gurdwara and people will slowly change.

Naunihal Singh got off his chair and moved towards Papajee's feet to touch them.

But Papajee stopped him saying, "Nahi Giani jee mere pair nahin, tusi tan guru de Sikh, men ek patit, mere pair nahin, mere pair nahi." (No Giani ji, please don't touch my feet. You are a true Sikh of the Guru and I a patit. (Patit is someone who has cut his hair)not my feet. Not my feet, not.)

I remember Papajee repeated it two or three times. He was feeling unworthy because circumstances of the kind of work he was doing in a foundry which had forced him to cut his hair, and he never could reconcile with it. Like many people from that generation suffered the same fate of cutting their hair for the sake of finding employment. They silently carried the shame of it. I actually saw some of my family members break down and cry when they saw photos of themselves when they had hair and how they looked after.

Naunihal Singh was eager to help in any way that he could,

he told Papajee that he was a classically trained musician and a classically trained singer of Kirtan. He said he had been a singer on Singapore's radio singing Kirtan. Papajee was glad to hear this. It was a gaping hole of not having a person to do kirtan, which Naunihal Singh would fill.

It is my personal belief, and I must say for me in life. It has also been my experience that if you ask for something with a clear heart and mind that your request is granted. Provided that you have the faith and patience to wait and let God take over.

There is a Rubaiyat by a mystic Sikh Poet Bhai Vir Singh, he says, "Hovan Quadi pinjare tere da, Pinjra tun nit hath farre, sabh fikrane sayaad nu kusharr rahyae asin charrae." (Let me be enslaved in the cage of your love, all then is left to you, and I will forever be in your embrace.)

But we don't have this kind of faith. We doubt faith, we question it, and we say this is blind faith, but faith is blind. We can't prove God. We can only have faith, and love is also blind, when we fall in true love, it is not because we see and say that we are like-minded now we can fall in love. We play the game of chance. We fall in love. We sink or swim, but we don't care, because love beats inside of us with every heartbeat. It does not ask to be accepted; true love does not have an ego. Love does not ask to be accepted or rejected. It is beyond any such transactions. Faith is the same. It is beyond transactions. It is not now I have been given all this. Therefore, I can have faith. Faith is beyond that, it is the total acceptance and total surrender and only then the game of love and faith begins. If we don't surrender ourselves, we are always going to be the spectator, never in the game.

Faith is Guru Nanak walking the world delivering his message of one God and one humanity. Faith is Siddhartha leaving the kingdom of Nepal as a prince and becoming the enlightened Buddha, Faith is Mohammad, in the mountains waiting for the message. Faith is Christ on the cross. Faith is Moses moving his people to the promise land. Faith is Saint

Pralahad gripping a hot pillar to prove his faith.

It is faith and only faith that shaped the world. If it was not faith, Kapaney would not have bent light. We would not have had fiber optics and the world as we know it would not have existed. If it was not faith, Edison would not have discovered the electric light bulb, and we would be in darkness. Was all their faith not blind, was Kapaney not told by his professor that light could not be bent? It is faith. Nay blind faith, seeing something that the rest doesn't see that moves us from our present state to the next.

Papajee asked Naunhial Singh if he had ever worked with people from the villages, he was taken aback a bit by Papajee's question but Papaji never asked idle questions. He always had his reason and usually was ahead of everyone else in his thinking.

Naunihal Singh replied, "Jee men aap de gal nahin samja." (Sir I don't understand your question?)

Papajee explained to him that most of the people of the community came from villages in Punjab and they were all well-meaning, but diplomacy was not one of their strong suits. He explained people who came from big cities had a real issue with the straightforward approach of the people from the rural areas. Papajee explained he would face these people was he to come on board.

Babajee chimed in, "Giani jee, Dharam Suhn teekh kehnda, jattan da pata nahin kad kee kae denna, enna deh muh vichon jad phul be kirde oh bee kandian vale hunde han." (Gianijee Dharam Singh is saying the truth; you don't know what these Jats (village farmers) are going to say. Even the flowers coming from their mouths have thorns.)

What Papajee and Babajee were saying would prove to be prophetic. Some of the people that already signed on and some other colorful characters who your will meet later would prove out what Papajee and Babajee were saying to Naunihal Singh.

Naunihal Singh was committed. He did not care, and all of

this did not mean much to him. All he was interested in was to help in any way shape or form and Papajee was glad to have him, but he also knew what he was taking on.

After Babajee and Naunihal Singh left Beejee told papajee, "Tusin munde nu ena drownna thori see." (You should not have frightened the lad like that.)

Papajee knew that it was going to be a challenge, "Koi nahi Nasib kaur jadd ehno jattan ne drownana fir tenu he man-nuna pehna." (Ok Nasib Kaur, when the Jats frighten him then it's you who is going to have to console him.)

I lost count the number of times that took place. When the brash language hurt Giani Naunihal's sensitivities and undiplomatic and straight forwardness of the Jat mentality, and Beejee would have to sit him down and explain to him that they meant nothing by it, it's the way of the village folks. If you continue to be sensitive, they will do more of it.

He was a bit of a misfit, Papajee, and Beejee had to protect him from the others who would always come at him and tease him.

CHAPTER THIRTY-TWO

Second Function

The second function that came around the next month in July, all the functions were celebrated on or the Sunday following the Solar Month of the Indian calendar. Although Sikhs don't have any special day of prayer, for us every moment is a moment of prayer, work is a prayer for us, and as I mentioned earlier we start everything with a prayer and end everything with a prayer and that also means every day.

Since the calendar is a solar calendar, the Hindus celebrated this first day of the Solar month by visiting holy places and worshiping Sun God on this day. The Sikhs do not believe in worship of any idol or any other power other than the God. The Sikh Gurus wrote the Baramah "the twelve months" but the difference is in the Baramah it is not the Sun that is the object of adoration. It is God so on the day of the Sangrand the lesson for that month is read as to how a Sikh's relationship with God is to be bonded. It makes reference to the season for the month and the relationship between God, season and man. The ritual of praying to the sun was transformed by the Guru to become a time to reflect on this day how to strengthen the bond between one's self and God. So Sangrand celebration has a special significance for the Sikhs.

On the second function, the hall was completely full but was not overflowing like the first opening function. That is to be expected, there are those that are loyal and there are those that are curious, and the curious ones are always there on any new opening day but then may show up once in a while but otherwise move onto the next curiosity.

Giani Naunihal Singh performed kirtan, but he started out in classical format. Babajee looked over at Giani jee and he understood that he needed to make it in the Dhaarna (free flow) format so that people would appreciate it as that was what they were used to in the villages. He quickly realized what Babajee was trying to say to him, and he changed. He was showered with pounds.

Papajee had forgotten to mention to Giani jee that all the money belonged to the Gurdwara funds, and once he had finished with his Keertan he picked up all the money and kept it. At the end of the function, Papajee went over to him asked him to turn over all the offerings that people had given to him. This was his first pout. He was unfamiliar with this rule and had never had to give money that was given to him while he performed keertan. Papaji explained that he was sorry, it slipped his mind to mention to him, but if he wanted to do seva then he was not to be paid and all the money collected came to the fund and a decided amount was given to people who did keertan but in his case that would not even be the case since he wanted to be part of doing the seva.

Giani jee gave the money but did complain to Beejee that he thought money should have been his. Beejee did not mince words with him. She set him on the right path one time, and that would be the last time as it was with Beejee most of the time.

She told him, "Gianijee seva guru de karni tan pher tyagi bann ke karroena pasian te guru da huq hai kesse hor da nahi." (Gianijee if you want to serve your Guru then serve him selflessly, only the Guru has claim on this money no one else!)

Giani jee may have been taken back by the firmness with which Beejee put the matter to rest. One thing was certain he understood the rule and he never demanded a penny from that moment on that he ever got as his, it all went to the Gurdwara fund.

CHAPTER THIRTY-THREE

The Letter

Following week after the second function papajee received a letter through the mail, it was in Urdu, and it was from someone in Coventry. When he looked at the letter, he had a puzzled look on his face.

Beejee asked who the letter was from, "Prem Singh Khalsa de hai" (It's from Prem Singh Khalsa.)

Beejee had not heard of him before so she asked who he was. Most of the reference always started by what village he was from which sort of gave you an instant association with someone from that village that you might know.

Papajee told Beejee "Pasle da hai, oh pare rehnda kisse naal ghat he milda vart da." (He is from the village Pasla, and he lives at a distance and rarely associates with anyone).

Papajee opened the letter, and it was written in Urdu (Urdu is now the official language of Pakistan but during the British rule, it was the primary language that was taught in British Punjab. The word Urdu is Turkish, meaning army. The language was originally created from Persian and Hindi to make communication between the Persian Mughal ruling officers and their forces easier).

Papajee read the letter, and Khalsa congratulated Papajee on starting the work to build a Gurdwara in Coventry. He wrote that he had a bank account where he had been depositing money he had collected from the services which he had performed and wanted to give Papajee the money to add to the Gurdwara fund. It was not a whole lot of money, but it rightfully belonged in the Gurdwara fund. He further wanted to offer his services and help any way he could toward building the Gurdwara. I think the letter surprised Papajee since he had heard that he remained clear of all his village people and did not mingle with them much.

Papajee was very happy to get this letter as it meant that people sitting on the outer circle were now gaining strength. He was also apprehensive since he did not know Khalsa, and he had heard he did not mix much with the community, how he would fit in. He went to Smith Street and met with Bikar Singh and other Paslawalas. He told them about the letter from Khalsa, but they were not very excited about the proposition of having Khalsa be part of Papajee's team.

They told Papajee that he was a bit of a loner, had some views that were very much out there and was not always conventional. They told Papajee that he had been here in the UK for a very long time, and the people from the village did really not know him that well. They also told him that Prem Singh's father Arjan Singh back in the village was a very respected man who did a lot for the village.

Papajee decided to meet Prem Singh Khalsa and wrote him a letter and told him to come to the house next weekend so that they could talk. Papajee was one for gathering information, but he made up his own mind at the end and was not easily persuaded. Plus when he heard about his father from his villagers, he was more eager to meet him.

He came home and told Beejee, "Paslewaleian de rai Prem Singh vare bhaut ouch nahi, kehnde koj vakhra he hai bhaut milda nahin." (The people from Pasla did not have a high opinion about Prem Singh, they said he is a loner, and he his own set of opinions and did not mix well.)

However, he was not convinced, how could it be, if a man calls up and not even knowing Papajee but yet says I want to offer the funds that I have collected for the Gurdwara fund and offered to help? There are only two reasons that people do that, one they are sincere the other, they are trying to buy their way in. Papajee wanted to find out for himself what Prem Singh Khalsa was all about.

When the following week came around there was a knock at the door, papajee suspected that it was Prem Singh Khalsa. I went to answer the door, and I saw a well-built man in his mid-fifties. He was about five feet ten or eleven inches tall. He had a hat on his head; it was not a cap but a hat, you know one of those hats you see in the movies set in the thirties or forties era. He had a mustache but otherwise clean-shaven, and he had absolutely not a single tooth in his mouth.

My first reaction was this couldn't be him. This can't be Prem Singh Khalsa. He is supposed to be Khalsa. Khalsa as mentioned before was created by the tenth master, by giving them the Five K's: Kesh, unshorn hair, Kanga, comb to keep the hair tidy, Kach, knickerbockers as a sign of readiness to climb on a horse with ease and ease of movement, Karra, a steel bracelet worn on the right hand as a representation of the omnipresence of God in every action, and finally a (Kirpan) a small sword, the thing to note here is that the Punjabi word for a sword is a borrowed word from Farsi which is Talwar, "mean to attack."

However, the tenth master changed the name to "Kirpan," mean to "grant mercy." What a wonderful philosophy he instilled that you have the power to attack, but you must practice mercy you must be the defender of the weak and downtrodden.

Prem Singh Khalsa had only one of these symbols, the Karra on his right hand. He did not look like a Khalsa, so I was puzzled how he could be called a Khalsa. I kept my thoughts to myself and decided to wait and ask later.

"Boy kedan bay, daddy ghar hai?" Khalsa said, (Boy how are you, is your daddy home?) "Sat Sri Akal, hanjee ghar nae aajavo andar." (Sat Sri Akal, yes sir he is home please come in.)

Khalsa came through the corridor to the family room, and Papajee got up to shake hands with him.

Beejee came from the Kitchen and greeted him, then went into the Kitchen to prepare tea.

He did not waste much time, got right to the reason why he was there. He first congratulated Papajee for taking such a bold step, he told papajee that he had been in Coventry since the late thirties and had been a hawker and then started working for Dunlop and had been there ever since. Papajee knew that he would have known Shaheed Udham Singh wanted to ask him. But he did not have to. Khalsa brought it up himself.

"Dharam Singh men Bawe nu changi taran jann da see oh ethe hunda un uchi uchi hassanna see, ke assi appanna ena de ghar apnna adaha jamah leah." (Dharam Singh, I knew Bawa very well (nickname of Shaheed Udham Singh.) If he was around today he would have been laughing out loud that we have established ourselves as independents and equals in their country.)

Papajee told Khalsa how he tried to convince Rajmal Singh to build the Gurdwara and Mandir and Masjid under the umbrella off Mazdoor Sabha, and each community will collectively help the other, and then we can really truly honor the man who started the Mazdoor Sabah and who gave back us our dignity, and he did it for all the communities. Udham Singh changed his name from Udham Singh to Ram Mohammad Singh, Ram for Hindus who were Massacred, Mohammad for the Muslims who were massacred, and Singh for the Sikhs who were massacred at Jallianwala Bagh. He wanted the British to know when he was brought on trial that in avenging the Jallianwala Bagh Massacre, he represented all three communities that lost loved ones in that massacre of 1919 in Amritsar.

We can truly honor the name he took of Ram Mohamad Singh and by doing so we would also carry out one of the most sacred tenets of Sikhism that of respecting all religions. Alas, Rajamal does not have the vision. So I have started this with the grace of God and the help of the community we are off to a good start. Now to have you come and offer up help is a humbling experience for me. Papajee got up and went over and hugged Khalsa. You know sometimes when two people meet, it is not easy to explain but there is a universal connection that is there. This was one of those moments. I could see that was there between these two men. Both appeared to be unemotional and pragmatic men, and they saw each other as such and they connected.

Papajee asked Khalsa about why he had not connected with his own village people and how would he reconnect with the rest of the community. Khalsa was a high school graduate like Papajee, he was a very well-read man. He could hold his own in any discussion with any intellectual; I would say at times he would have fun at the expense of people who saw themselves as intellectuals by acting as a country bumpkin and then taking them to task once he hooked them in.

His explanation to Papajee why he had kept his distance has stayed with me. He explained to papajee that there was a generational gap between him and those from his village. Papajee said how could that be? Some of them are of your age? He was not referring to the age gap. He pointed out that when people leave their place of birth for them time freezes. Customs, rituals, language and values all freeze for that time, and they become a generation of immigrants for that era. When the next wave of immigrants came some years later, they bring with them their own set of values. Language, customs, and rituals which in the community may have changed with people interacting with each other in the village or other outside influences. Such as more education, more external communication, better economic situations all affects the outcome. So this at times creates a generational gap. He went on to explain to Papajee, that in a way papajee by starting the Gurdwara was doing two things one is the creation of a place of worship but at the same time was bringing together all these different time diasporas on a common platform and causing a new culture to be formed here in Coventry for the Sikhs, and he wanted to be part of creating this.

They both talked for hours about their past, even though there was nothing in common in their past except for the fact that both had been out of Punjab for a long time. However, there was something that was very close between the two of them. There was mutual respect. A friendship that would last a lifetime was formed of people whose personalities were worlds apart. Papajee a planner weighed every option reviewed every detail and its impact before he acted or spoke. Khalsa as Papajee would find out, impulsive, shoot from the hip. World be damned. That's how I see the world, and by golly that's how the world should fit kind of person. Kashmir and I would later nickname him the "Volcano". You never knew what he was going to say, Good job Papjee did not have a blood pressure problem, because no pill in the world would cure the blood pressure Khalsa would raise.

When he left I finally got my chance to ask papajee why he was called Khalsa when he did not even look anything like a Khalsa. Papajee explained that his father Arjan Singh in their village of Pasla was a very well known personality, and he was a true Khalsa, and it's become a family name of sorts.

"Par" (But) before I could finish my sentence, Papajee interrupted me, "Balbir men smaj da han, par hun tan eais naam naal he Prem Singh jannian jaanda hai." (Balbir, I understand, but Prem Singh now is known by this name.)

It ended that conversation, and it was never raised again.

CHAPTER THIRTY-FOUR

The Coming Storm (the clash of the three circles)

We had two successful functions, and the word was getting around and more people were showing interests to the point that people would just drop money through our mailbox as their offerings. We would pick up that money and put it besides the Guru Granth Sahib to be added to the donation the coming month to be counted.

At school, the kids from the Mazdoor Sabha started to echo what they were hearing at home. Kids are not the world's best diplomats, and they don't filter much, especially teenagers.

So I heard things like, "You wait, my dad is going to show your dad who is the boss," "This won't last. We will make sure of that."

I told papajee what I was hearing, for the first week he paid no attention to it. But then Dilbagh Singh Bhajee came around as he always did on Friday. Beejee made him his cup of tea, and he told Beejee that he was hearing rumblings that Mazdoor Sabha was gearing up to stir trouble in the coming monthly function.

Beejee took note. Saturday morning when Papajee came home from his night shift, she made him his tea and breakfast and then told him what Dilbagh Singh Bhajee had told us the evening before. He listened and as he would always do, he went quiet. He would do this, if you did not know him, you would think that he was ignoring you, but that was how he processed data.

He looked over at Beejee and said, "Dilbagh Singh nu

Baat da Batangarr banuoun de adat hai." (Dilbagh Singh has a habit of exaggerating what he hears.)

Beejee reminded him that I had heard the same thing at school.

"Chal sauch den hai." (So we will think about it) and went to sleep, but it was on his mind. Usually, he would sleep until about early noon on Saturdays after his night shift, but he probably could not sleep so he got up around ten. He came down and told Beejee that he would go and talk with Kewal Singh.

Kewal Singh Bains was from the village of Gondhpur. He was a fast-talking smooth tongue tall lanky man. He was very fond of Papajee. He was the best politician, if had he stayed in Punjab he would have had a great career as a politician. He was smart and wily as a fox. He would talk fast and get you so confused and by the time he was done with you, you had spilled your guts out to him and didn't even know it.

He had this raspy voice. It had a trusting sound to it; he used it to his advantage all the way. He supported Papajee (later on after the Gurdwara was built, Papajee would pull him in and make him the general secretary, and he would be the spokesperson none would dare to take on. He could turn from sophistication to a country bumpkin in the same sentence and confuse the hell out of you. It's a rare gift. People like Lincoln and Bill Clinton had it and so did Kewal Singh Bains).

Kewal kept his toes in the affairs of Mazdoor Sabha waters and also was very fond of Papajee and what he was doing, so he would quietly lend support. On the outside, he would oppose Papajee. So they had an understanding of sorts. Papajee went to his house to talk with him. As soon as he saw papajee, as papajee would tell us. He would not invite him in so that he would not blow his cover all he said was, "Dilbagh Singh nu men dass ditta, Dilbagh Singh nun men Dass Ditta." (I told Dilbagh Singh, I told Dilbagh Singh)

Person who speaks fast often repeat and Kewal was

famous for repeating a sentence.

Papajee came home and told Beejee what Dilbagh Singh Bhajee was saying was, in fact, true.

Beejee was smiling and told him, "Tusin be bechare Dilbagh Singh te avany var pene ho." (You come down on poor Dilbgah Singh for no reason.)

I knew also that I had some running coming my way.

So he looked over at me, and I just remember saying to him, "What time you want everyone to be here?"

"Panj" (five).

I started off and ran to Blackberry Lane, to Sohan Singh Gaffa's house, next to Charter House Road to Khalsa's place and from there to Babajee's and Giani Naunihal Singh's place. They lived next door to each other, from there to Eagle Street to Sucha Singh's house and told all of them to be at our house 7 Red Lane at five O'clock because Papajee wanted to discuss something important. This route I would repeat many times over the years as I was growing up.

They all started to file in, and all were present and accounted for before five. Indians as a habit all running late and are somewhat proud of it. If you tell them to be at a certain place at a certain time they would ask you is that regular time or Indian time. Indian time is generally an hour later. That was not the case with these men. First, Papajee was very disciplined and would not tolerate it, further, they had a mutual respect that when they were called it was a call to arms, and it was their duty to be there on time.

Papajee apprised them of what was happening, and that he had confirmed it to be true that the Mazdoor Sabha was looking to cause disruption of some nature in the upcoming function, and they needed to figure out what to do. There was both fear and anger, Giani Naunihal Singh was a bit fearful and suggested that we inform the police.

Papajee told him, "Giaini ji eh sade ghar da Mamala hai, aj he police sad lay fir asin fail han." (Giani ji this is our internal affair if we call the police this early in the game, then we have failed.)

Sucha Singh was hot and wanted to take them on. He turned to Giani Naunihal Singh and said, "Bhai ena darr da kyon an, dil farr dil." (Brother why are you so frightened? Hold on to your heart hold on).

Babajee turned around to Papajee and said, "Dharam Sihnia fir kidan karni chahi di hay?" (Dharam Singh what do you think we should do?)

Papajee went into his usual quite zoned outlook and sat there for a few minutes. By now, all of them were used to this, and they knew he was thinking.

He looked over at Babajee and said, "Sab tau phela tan meri benti hay ke kisse ne ve jinna koi jor lave gusse nahin huna, aur haton pai nahin hona, Duji gal eh hai ke appan yaad rakhana ke appan guru da kam karde han har ek de sunenvaste tiar han. Teeji gal eh ke sabh nu das dena keh shaid rola pave aure sabh ne auna pat larra na nahin. Appa una de sunn ke jabab deva ge." (First of all, it is my request that no matter how much you are provoked you will not get angry, or get physical. Second, remember we are doing the work of the Guru and should be open to hearing everyone out. Third alert everyone that this is brewing, and they should come and hear these people out.)

"Shabash Dharam Sinhan, Guru teno bhaag lave menu tere tau eh hi sunan see." (Well done Dharam Singh may the Guru bless you. This was what I needed to hear from you.) Babajee said to Papajee, as he was happy with Papajee's response.

He was testing Papajee to see how he would respond. Whether he would advocate a harsh hand or with logic, calm and reason as this was how in Babajee's mind a true Sikh should act.

Giani Nauhnial Singh was clearly shaken. Sucha Singh turned to Gianiji and said, "Kambhi jaana koi fikar wali gal he nahin." (Stop shaking there's nothing to worry about.)

Khalsa giggled and said, "Sucha Sinahan Giani

vichara sheri addami, eh nu vichare nu ke pata ke pind vich ke hunda." (Sucha Singh, poor Giani is a city slicker. What would he know how we deal with such matters in a village.)

Which finally brought a smile to Giani Naunihal Singh's face.

They all left, and the word started to get out. Kewal Singh passed the word out in his usual manner to people that they should go to the next function. He made sure that he was encouraging the supporters.

On the day of the function, as usual papajee went to the school and met Mr. Hancock and informed him what may happen. Mr. Hancock said if you just point those people out to me; I will make sure they are not allowed on the premises. Papajee told him that he did not want anyone turned away, he wanted to have an open communication with him, and that is why he was letting him know.

Mr. Hanock again turned to Papajee and said, "Mr. Singh if you change your mind let me know, and I will take care of it."

Beejee and Gurbachan Kaur prepared Parshad, and as always they carried the utensil with the Parshad on their heads to the school hall, and I would sprinkle water in front as a symbol of sanctifying the ground. As we approached the school building the Mazdoor Sabha people had already started to gather. Rajmal himself was not there. These were people of the second circle, people who were looking for positions and were the instrument of the inner circle. They looked over at us and did not say anything, not even Sat Sri Akal. Papajee and Beejee taught Kashmir and I to say Sat Sri Akal to everyone. So I said Sat Sri Akal, they replied back, but it was not a heartfelt greeting. They were clearly in a mood for a fight and had been briefed as to what their task was and did not want to be distracted from it.

Beejee, Gurbachan Kaur and I came home and told Papajee that these people had already started to gather and there could be real trouble. Papajee was not a man who was easily shaken. His response to all of us was get on with what you have to do, and we shall deal with everything.

I still remember the words, "Sach te Kharro, Sach te Larro baki Whaeguru te shad deo." (Stand for truth, fight for truth and leave the rest to the almighty.)

As the function started the line in front of the Guru Granth Sahib was out the door down the stairs. The amount of people today was more than the first function. Papajee told Khalsa to do Kirtan and told him to make sure he made no remarks towards anyone and keep doing kirtan. He turned to Giani Nauhnihal Singh and told him no speeches and told him also to keep his comments to the minimum and keep them on topic to the Sikh faith.

The whole function went along fine, but the atmosphere was fully charged up, as the function was winding down Rajmal appeared in the hall. He came front of the Guru Granth Sahib put his donation in front and only slightly bowed his head. I saw Papajee shake his head and close his eyes. Rajmal, with whom he was close and saw him grow up in Fiji and had given him every opportunity to lead, and he missed every opportunity. Now here he was to challenge the Guru Sangat.

I would ask Papajee later why he closed his eyes that day and shook his head. He said, "Balbir I actually felt sorry for Rajmal. I felt that he was a lost soul, I felt how he could have been the person and should have been the person to unite, and here he was now ready to try and tear us apart. I know that he was taking on the Guru not me."

As the function ended and the final Ardas (prayer was taken, and the Hukamnama was (verse from the Guru Granth Sahib) was read. Parshad was being (sacrament pudding) was being prepared. One of Rajmal's men stood up and started to talk.

He started to ask, "Dharam Singh ne eh kehnu push ke shuro keeta? Asin election karwaoni, eh kaun hunda hay moore hoon wala. Mazdoor Sabha de thale sabh eh kam huna hay. Mazdoor Ssabha da es ute haq hai." (Who did Dharam Singh ask before he started this? We want an election, and this should operate under the umbrella of Mazdoor Sabha, and Mazdoor Sabha has governance over this.)

Papajee moved toward the microphone to answer them but was stopped by two people and others came on the stage and stopped him and said that you don't need to answer them, we will. Behind this man others got up and started demanding the same.

That's when a woman stood up and said, "Besharmau koz tan sharam karau, betheri dekh lay thuhadi Mazdoor Sabha, daffa ho jao." (Hey all you shameless ones, have some shame, we have had enough of your Mazdoor Sabha, get lost from here.)

That's when all the women stood up. Rajmal tried to say something he was drowned down with cries of the women shaming them. Culturally men can take anything, but a put down by women. It is the ultimate insult to be put down by women. The reason is in our culture women put up with a lot and when they finally break and put a man down it is that the man had crossed every boundary of decency and that he had to hear it from a woman. The shame of women shouting you down is not easy. These men had that just happened to them, and they started to get quiet. Finally, Kewal Singh got up straightening out his overcoat. He had this overcoat that he wore all year round. Kashmir and I would joke many years later when that detective show with Peter Falk Columbo came out.

"Oh look, that's Uncle Kewal's overcoat."

He went over to Rajmal and told him that it would be better if he left. Rajmal had no idea that Kewal had orchestrated the whole thing against him. Neither did Papajee until many years later when Kewal Singh told him that he had asked some of the women to stand up. Rajmal left with his merry men with his tail between his legs, shamed and was told his place. People from the congregation came one at a time and just gathered around Papajee and women around Beejee and told both that they were behind them all the way and would not allow anyone getting in their way.

Papajee asked Sucha Singh, Giani Naunihal Singh, Babajee, Sohan Singh Gaffa and Prem Singh Khalsa to come to the house after the function. I think they were all a bit overwhelmed by it all.

Papajee told them that we need to make a formal structure, He never intended to have a committee and officers, his original thought was that whoever wanted to volunteers should be allowed to do so, and all decisions should be taken in the Sangat. Beejee would tell him your hearts in the right place but this is not how the world works. I am of the belief that women are much more adept at being state persons than men. They are far more practical than men are. Papajee knew that they needed to form a committee.

He asked Babaji to do Ardas and call out the committee. Babaji did the Ardas and looked over at Khalsa and said, "Tuun Pardhan." (You are President.) Then he looked over at Sohan Singh Gaffa and said, "Tuun Meet Pardhan." (You are the vice President.) He looked over at Giani Naunhial Singh and said "Tuun Sectar." (You are the secretary) and then to Sucha Singh he said, "Tuun Meet Sectar, (you are the vice secretary.) He turned to Papajee and said, "Tere te main sara bhaar paun lagan, tuun Khazanchi." (I am going to burden you with the entire load. I am naming you the treasurer.) He turned to himself and said, "Men unpardah aadmni men tan sirf jethe kahon ge uthe joti jurrh javanga." (I am an uneducated man I will put my head under whichever yoke you put it under)

He then turned over to me and asked me to come over to him. It was one of his rare and I mean rare soft moments, he took me in his arms and said the following to me, "Kaka tera bachpan esk kam vich lag janna, seva raj ke karin Waheguru tenun joh mange ga mele ga eh mera tere naal wadha reha." (Child your childhood will pass through this work now, serve the Lord and the Lord will give you whatever you ask for. This is my promise to you.)

I must say Babajee's words are true. I am truly blessed!

Papajee brought a Gutka (Sikh Prayer book) and put it on top of the coffee table, and asked each one of them to put their hand on the Gutka as they were about to take the oath Beejee spoke up, "Tehro Jee" (husband Stop.) They looked over at her.

She came over and put her hand on top theirs and said, looking over at Babajee, "Eh mere Baap Smaan," (he is like a father to me) then she looked over at Khalsa, Sucha Singh , Sohan Singh gaffa and Giani Naunihal Singh and said, "Tusi mere Bhra." (You are my brothers.) And then she looked at Papajee, "Aur tusin mere sar de sain," (And you my husband). "Men Sabh kam baraber karon ge. Meno Mata Bhago de saun men koi bhajan ne denan, hunn sauch keh saun chukio." (I will work alongside you, and I swear by Mata Bhago (Mata Bhago was a lady in Sikh History when there was a siege laid to the tenth Master's fort, forty of the Sikhs signed a letter disowning the guru and left. When the news reached their villages as to what they had done Mata Bhago gathered all the women folks and welcomed them home with shame. Then she led them back to the guru, and they all died fighting. When the guru went on the battlefield he saw the leader of the group still alive, and the guru asked him what he would want his last wish to be. Mahan Singh the leader asked the guru if he would tear the letter that they had given him disowning him. The tenth master carried the letter with him. He pulled it out of his pocket, and ripped the letter and Mahan Singh breathed his last in the arms of the tenth master. Beejee was referring to the historical lady Mata Bhago who brought Mahan Singh and his men back into battle riding along side them.)

There would be times that some of them would start to lose focus and become petty. She would remind that person of the pact and pull back who would either fall out of favor with one another and wanted to call it quits. She would call them on it, and they never ever questioned her and would fall in line.

No one questioned Babajee's decision, everyone bowed and said, "Sar Mathe." (I humbly accept.)

Babajee told them again and again, "Eh audhe gorian de ne tusi sabh guru de sevadaar ho aur brabar ho." (These positions are western created. You are all in service of your master and are equal.)

Papajee asked everyone to be available to go to the bank in the morning as he wanted to add everyone to the account. Monday morning they all met at Lloyd's bank in the City Center and asked to meet with the bank manager. He again asked everyone to take an oath in front of the Manager that the accounts would be managed in the best interest of the community and will only be used for the Gurdwara activity. He asked the bank manager to add everyone as trustees on the account.

Papajee put a condition that it would need everyone's signature to draw funds from the account. The trustees were for life. He wanted to make sure that once there was a change in management that the community funds would have oversight. If a member died or moved, another would then be added to replace them otherwise they would continue for life, unless they chose to resign which they could not do until the Gurdwara was built to which they had taken an oath.

He put another condition on these men and was that none of these members were allowed to be members or office bearers of any other organization while they served on the Gurdwara committee.

He further advocated that the elections would take place on the Vaisakhi (the day of the first baptism by the tenth master, and it fell then on April 13th now with the creation of the Sikh Calendar it falls on April 14th) following the opening of the Gurdwara. Until then, anyone who would donate ten pounds would automatically become a member of the committee.

His aim was three fold, to collect funds, try and get cross-section of the community involved, and also keep the freeloaders, those that had more opinions but nothing else to offer out.

In the course of next month, he reached out to as many people as he could that were advocating the Gurdwara and asked them to donate ten pounds so that he could have a committee that could build community strength. He went cross sectional from rich to poor, from different caste groups (even though there is no caste system in Sikhism but old habits die hard.) He loaned people money out of pockets that could not pay but wanted to. All paid back within the year. He charged no interest. That was not his way.

The word went out that, "Dharam Singh ne committee bna lay hai," (Dharam Singh has formed a committee).

It was by design that he wanted the word to go out that the committee was formed. He wanted Rajmal and all his people to know there was no stopping the Gurdwara now. People that may have been common folk now mattered. They were part of the formation of the community and the elites such as Rajmal and the Mazdoor Sabha's power base had been shifted to the people of the outer circle.

Papajee had bowed to serve the Sangat (community) but only until the Gurdwara was built, he had every intention of holding election, and he wanted everyone to make their own decision if they wished to contest elections, but he would not.

CHAPTER THIRTY-FIVE

Van's and uncles from Wolverhampton

When the next function came around, Papjee had completed the process of creating a committee and signing up people from the community. The accounts had been set up. In his mind, he had no fear. He had total faith in his Guru and the community. Even if Rajmal and the Mazdoor Sabha tried anything again it would not work. He had the total support of the outer circle. This outer circle rewards honesty and service with total loyalty. Papajee and his compatriot had shown to the people that they were loyal and sincere

My Mamajee (maternal uncle) Kuldev Singh and my Chachajee (paternal Uncle Avtar Singh had heard of what had happened on the prior function. On the day of the function on Sunday morning around eight O'clock, three vans full of people pulled up in front of the house. I was just coming from picking up the key from Mr. Hancock's house when I saw them. I was excited to see them both, and also some of my distant cousins.

Three van loads of them. I could see field hockey sticks, bars and other sticks through the back window of the vans. The Vans were packed with people. Some I knew. They were my cousins or distant cousins from both Papajee's side and also from Beejee's side of the family. There were also villagers from our village and also Beejiees village and some other people.

Both of my uncles had heard of the melee that took place at the last function from someone, as the word spread pretty fast since the community was still small and what had happened was a major incidence. Papajee had never told them anything, but they found out anyway, and they were here in full force to stand behind Papajee and Beejee and fight.

I was always glad to see both of my uncles; all of my cousins and villagers came out of the vans and gave me hugs. I went in and Mamajee Kuldev and Chachaje Avtar both followed me in. As soon as Papajee saw them his face dropped, he knew what this was all about.

Beejee was glad to see them and asked, "Eni severe, severe doven ethe, and sukh tan hay?" (This early in the morning here, is everything Ok?)

Before they could reply, Papajee asked, "Naal kon kon hai?" (Who is with you?)

I remember Kuldev Mamajee replied, "Sare, tin vanen han." (Everyone, three vans full).

Beejee raised her voice and said, "Ve eh ke tusin Dhaarra marea." (What is this foolishness you have done?)

Papajee was furious, and he got up and looked both of them in the face and said, "Dimaag kam kar da keh nahin? Meh tan logan nu jorrene te sar dharr dhe lay hoi ha tusi danda wartana chounde ho. Shach te kharra han sach te he marra ga. Dande de jor naal jag jitia tan ke jitia, men tan pyar aur daleel naal jitna. Es tun phela koi dekh lave murr javo rab da vasta murrjave. Dharre da klanak men nehin launna." (Is your brain working or not? I am putting everything on the line to unite people, and you want to use force. I stand by what is right; I will die with what is right. If one wins the world by force, what kind of victory is that? Win it with love and thought. Before anyone finds out about this, I implore both of you go back. I don't want a black mark on me of a man who creates a mafia.)

He did not even go out to greet the other people. He just wanted them gone. Beejee even refused to give them tea. This tactic was against every principle that both of them stood for.

Both Mamajee Kuldev and Chachajee Avtar went out. I followed them out, they told the others that Papajee and

Beejee were not at all happy at this and they were to go back. None of them ever took it personally they had too much respect for both Papajee and Beejee they just went into the van and drove away back to Wolverhampton.

Even though most of those people in the vans would come and visit us on occasions, but that incidence was never brought up. They knew that if Papajee wanted it this way, it was the only way for them. They knew that he was a man of principle, and it was his courage to stand by his conviction that they all admired and whenever there was anything to be done back home in the village, he was the first person they would ask. I would always laugh and say why do they ask you? You left the village when you were young.

He said, "Balbir du tin cheejan yaad rakhninan, ek, jith ve rahiae, aapna pisha nahin bholna, duji gal roti dasan nuhan de kahanee, teejee gal, kisse da ehsaan kade ve nahin bulnan, chouthi gal jo marji ban jaye yaad rakhna din kadhe vee fir sak de han es karke teri shuruaat kith hoisee tun kaun see kade nahin bholena. Panjve gal eh ke etfaaq vich rab vas da, jad etfaaq tut janda sab kuj tubah hu janda Sheveni gal Waheguru te bharossa rakhna." (Balbir there are few things I want you to always bear in mind. First, never forget your roots, where you were born, second earn what you consume, never look for handouts, three never forget those that helped you in your hour of need, forth always remember your beginning no matter how rich you get. Fifth the most important is that God dwells in unity when unity is broken then all is lost. Finally at all times keep faith in God.)

At the function, Papajee asked Giani Naunihal Singh to inform the Sangat (congregation) of the new committee and also names of those people that had donated ten pounds each, and they were now members of the committee. He told him to let everyone know that the election would be on the first Viasakhi following the opening of the Gurdwara and until then those that wanted to join the committee were more than welcome to, providing they pay the ten pounds and relinquish their membership in any other organization except for their membership any union that they may belong to at work.

There was not one descending voice, the Mazdoor Sabha members would have to resign and pay ten pounds to become members of the committee and they were not prepared to do so they stayed away and accepted their defeat at the hands of the third circle.

CHAPTER THIRTY-SIX

Newsletter

Everything was on track, the organization was now in place to move forward and as few months went by Papajee would make sure that the accounts were given to everyone every month without fail. However, he wanted to do more than that; he wanted to give everyone written accounts also with the following month's program. He wanted to have a leaflet made that gave all the accounts plus gave the program for the coming month. He wanted to make sure that not only the community had transparency of the accounts but also somehow tie them together. A newsletter that would go out every month to the Sangat (congregation) would do this.

We did not have the technology to pump out on a computer back then as we do these days. There was a process in order to get there. First, you needed a stencil, so that someone could type on it, which would make the indents. That would take care of English portion but there were people that could not read English, and they only read Punjabi. So you needed someone to write in Punjabi with a sharp pen that would make the indents and there were those who could not read Punjabi or English and only read Urdu so that was also another language that he had to contend with.

Papajee could not even start until he found someone to do the English portion, which was the major portion.

CHAPTER THIRTY-SEVEN

The British Indian Army Clerk

Papajee told me one day, Balbir we are going to Freeman Street and meet with Bawa Singh. One Sunday morning after breakfast we walked over to Freeman Street, which was about seven streets away from our house at 7 Red Lane. Bawa Singh's house was near the end of Freeman Street. There was a built over the houses entry that went into the backyard of the houses. We went through the entry to the back. I asked Papajiee why we did not knock on the front door. He said, "You will see in a minute."

We went through the kitchen. The Kitchen door was open, kids were in and out and Bawa Singh's wife who was about four feet ten inches and a temper to match was chasing them and telling them off.

"Enia shrarata karde ho meain thoade sar vich kuj marna." (You guys are misbehaving so much I am going to hit you on the head with something.)

Next thing I heard, "Ao' that hurt, that did."

It was one of the kids she caught by the arm running out of the kitchen and let him have a wooden spoon on his head. It was a real pandemonium.

She stopped in her tracks when she saw Papajee and said, "Bhaji sorry, main dekhia nahin, Sat Sri Akal." (Brother sorry I did not see you, Sat Sri Akal.)

Papajee turned to the kids and said, "Dekho vay auntie nu tang na karo." (Look now, don't annoy your aunt.)

It seemed to calm the bunch down; at least until we went through the door, as soon as we did we could hear it all start on the other side again.

Her name was Gurbux Kaur, but she was known as Baksho. See Bawa Singh and Baksho did not have any children of their own, but they loved kids and all the little kids would gather around their house and there was always food that the kids helped themselves to, and they would play there. She was sort of the den mother to all of these kids.

Bawa Singh was so used to them running through the house that the noise never seemed to bother him

What I find amazing to this day is that he could have his head down and be typing away, but yet he could call out a kids name and know exactly what they were up to.

There were lines of chairs in the family room with people sitting there waiting for their turn. Papajee pointed to the entry from the front door that was blocked by chairs. Answering my question why we could not come through the front door. Although I had reached my own conclusion as to why we could not come through the front door. Even if we had knocked on the door no one would hear it with all that was going on. Baksho with the kids and Bawa Singh head down engrossed in his work.

Bawa Singh typed letters, completed forms wrote letters to employers for people asking for an extended leave of absence because they wanted to go home to India. Sometimes he would make up a story that the person's brother was sick, or mother was sick. It was amazing how he could keep it all-straight. I was amazed that he did not kill on paper a mother twice because the person wanted an extended leave excuse again. He had a mental record of what he wrote the last time. He would complete any legal document that people had who could not speak English; he would do this for them free. He did not charge for any of this. I often wonder how much money he could have made if he had, but that was not how these people the early settlers thought. They saw this as their opportunity to serve.

By the window, looking out to the back yard was a dinner table where Bawa Singh sat at his typewriter punching away.

He was a man in his mid-forties had a marine cut very short salt and pepper hair and a tiny Hitler type of a mustache. He kept typing; Papajee and I went and sat down.

Then all of a sudden as if he just woke up, he stands up, bows to Papajee and said, "Ah Dharam Singh ji, ji aya nu Ji Aya nu, welcome, welcome so nice of you to bless my house, and who is this young man? Your son I venture to guess, ji aya nu." (Ah Dharam Singh welcome, welcome and then continues in English)

This is a typical style of speaking, first in Punjabi and then repeating it in English, especially of those people who served in the Indian armed forces under the British. Bawa Singh served in the clerical unit in the British Indian Armed forces.

He was the absent-minded professor type of a personality, lived in a world of his own, had strong opinions, which were never up for debate, so you just agreed, and he was happy that you understood what is correct. He had this favorite term that to this day makes me laugh, and I would use it on my kids when they were younger just to tease them.

He would always give his opinion and then say, "Samjhe, kee samjhe." (Understood, what did you understand?)

Papajee got up to greet him and shake his hand, but he was not going to do that, he bowed in front of Papajee and Papajee went over and hugged him just to break him out of his bow. Papajee was not the hugging type, and I was giggling quietly at what I was witnessing.

Finally, Bawa Singh sat down, and then he called out very lovingly, "Baksho" no answer, then he raised his voice a bit and said, "Baksho, eh Baksho." (Baksho Oh Baksho.) Still no answer so then he sweetened his voice and said again "Baksho".

This time the door from the kitchen to the family room swung open. Every ounce of the four-foot ten-inch lady was in rage and her forehead was wound like a good Swiss watch. "Kee Baksho Baksho lay hai deko men busy ha kee hai?" (What is it with Baksho Baksho can't you see I am busy, what is it?)

He gives here little smile and gently points over to us and says, "Cha please Dharam Singh vaste aur biscuit for the boy." (Tea for Dharam Singh and biscuit for the boy.)

He never got angry. This was their way of communication with each other. They loved each other deeply, and since they had no children, they were a kid to each other.

"Dharam Singh ji Daso ke seva mere jume? Kiddan aun hoya." (Dharam Singh ji so tell me how I can be of service? Tell me your reason for the visit.)

Bawa Singh quickly put his question to Papajee. Papajiee told him that he needed to produce a monthly newsletter so that he could give the accounts from the previous month to the congregation and also give announcements for the upcoming month's function, and that he wanted him to prepare the stencil so it could be copied. Papajee also told him that he needed it not only in English but in Punjabi and also In Urdu.

"Wah Wah Dharam Singh jee eh te bauht he badhia gal hai. Aur eh seva meri rahi." (Wow, wow Dharam Singh jee this is wonderful. This will be my service. I will do this.)

Bawa Singh again got up and bowed. I was wondering if Papajee was going to get up and give him another hug. One hug a year was all that Papa jee gave, and that quota was used up. So when Bawa Singh sat down he asked him if he could write Punjabi also.

Bawa Singh replied, "Dharam Singh ji, Punjabi Urdu Angrezi kahon tan Farsi be lic dian ga." (Dharam Singh Jee, Punjabi, Urdu, if you wish I can write it in Farsi also.)

Papajee smiled and said, "Farsi de jarrorat nahin, English, Punjabi at eh Urdu kafi hai." (No Farsi is not required, just English, Punjabi and Urdu is fine.)

He again called out to Baksho for tea and biscuits, this time he did not need to make the second call. She opened the door and brought a pot of tea with biscuits and gave him a look and fired missiles from both of her eyes at him, but with Bawa Singh, it was water off ducks back.

He just continued to be himself and said "Baksho, thank you very much."

We were to witness this drama of their affection many times over the years and always come home I would call out to beejee in the same manner and make her laugh.

Papajee wrote all the accounts and the upcoming program, and any other information that he needed to send out and sent me over to Bawa Singh's on Sunday was to tell Bawa Singh that it needed to be ready by Tuesday night for me to pick up so that Papajee could drop it off in town on Warwick Row Wednesday where they would run the printing, and it would be ready for pick up on Friday evening. He would get up from his sleep in the middle of the day on Wednesdays, review what Bawa Singh has written and then drop it off in town on Warwick Row, and I would catch the bus straight after school on Friday's and pick the printed matter up and then catch the bus home.

Papajee also had a rubber stamp made with the Sikh emblem, Kashmir and I would stamp the top edge of each paper to make it look official. It would take us a good part of Friday evening to finish stamping five hundred of these papers.

CHAPTER THIRTY-EIGHT

Distribution

The first newsletter was January of 1963. The winter of 1963 was known as the Big Freeze in England, it was one of the coldest winters on record in centuries for the whole of Britain. The temperature dropped so far down that lakes, and rivers started to freeze over. In fact, as far the records went back only one other year was colder, and that was about three hundred years earlier.

That Saturday when we got up, Papajee gave Kashmir and I a list, it was of all the houses on one side of the area of town and said ok boys, please start dropping these off in people's mailboxes.

It had freshly snowed Friday night, but the morning looked clear although you could see the white clouds were full of snow. Beejee wrapped both of us up and put on our overcoats and our scarves and gloves, and then we tried on our Wellington (gum boots that you wore over your shoes so that it protected your shoes and your feet from getting soaked). I suppose they were called Wellington after the Duke of Wellington, not quite sure but that's what they were called. We had outgrown our Wellington from the previous year. So Beejee asked us to put an extra pair of socks which we did, and we moved out on our trek to drop off the newsletters in people's homes.

We started in Cambridge Street going through what is known as the Hillfields area. Our people lived in mainly the inner cities as most immigrants do, it is less expensive and closer to all the amenities, and also they tend to garner strength from each other living closely. For the Sikh immigrants in Coventry this was the Hillfields area and the Foleshill area. This covered a vast amount of the city.

Today we were delivering in the Hillfiled area and Sunday, we were to cover Foleshill area. We moved along following the route that Papajee wanted us to follow; our feet were starting to get cold. We slipped and fell a couple of times. About halfway through the route, it started to snow, first not so much, and then it started to pick up. Kashmir stopped, and I could see tears in his eyes. I knew he was upset and cold, so I went over to him and asked if he wanted to go home? If he did I could drop him off and come back and continue and finish the job. He asked if that was what I wanted to do, I told him no, that would not be what Papajee expects. He would expect me to finish the job, and stay in service of the master.

Not sure at that time what his words meant much, we were just cold, and we were on a task but I do reflect back on it sometimes and see how that shaped us as people, those long walks in the cold freezing weather.

We got done about four in the evening with the route and headed home in the snow, it was starting to get dark, Beejee was waiting at the door, not sure how many times she had come to the door throughout the day to see if we were coming but when she saw us, she came running towards us and fell in the snow and we helped her up.

We came in and she asked both of us to get out of our clothes and strip down to our underpants and get close to the fire.

She gave us a blanket each and wiped our head with a towel, and she got two basins with warm water and some salt and soaked our feet in it and got another basin with warm water and two wet cloths and asked us to wipe down our bodies with the cloth just to get our body temperatures up. She then gave both of us a cup of tomato soup to drink. She brought a fresh set of warm clothes and asked us to put them on and sit in front of the fireplace for a while.

We must have sat there in front of the fire for a good hour, talking to Beejee about our trek before Papajee came. We did not have a television set back then so all you could do was talk, and we talked. Even though Beejee was listening, I could see something was brewing inside her. She was not her usual self; she did not listen and participated as she normally did.

Around five Papajee came home. He asked us if we had delivered all the papers. I went over the list with him and told him that each and every paper was delivered.

All he said was, "Good."

Beejee brought him a cup of tea and gave it to him, as soon as he was done with his tea, she looked over at me and I knew what it meant so I went over to the table and picked up Papajee's dishes and took them to the kitchen.

Beejee then asked Papajee, "Saara din any tanhd vich eh doven ghum de rahae, eh paper post ne keeta ja sakde see?" (The two of them were out there in the cold all day long could you not have mailed these newsletters?)

He went into his zoned outlook and sat there for few minutes and was flicking his right thumbnail into his fingernail, as he would do when he was in deep thinking mode.

He looked over a Beejee and said, "Post men kar sakda han par dau swal mere mur-e kkarre han, jau main iss taun rok de han. Oh eh ke men aus baap nu kee jabab deva jehde dau ena dee umar de he san shayed dau saal shote honge jau eni dini Burj vich behte see. Das kherra jabab deva ge? Ke teri qurbani da eh mul pyia ke asi apne seva dee lorr pay tan appnae asi ghar bithaal lai, das kee jbab deva ge? Dosra saval eh hai ke mazoodri kar ke kuz paise bicha ke he matha teken walian de paise ne, kin ku appa nu bach de ne? un ne he ona no bach de ne, das eh ona dee emanant nu mae kiven la devan jad mere bache eh kam karan de kabal han. agar chani ahin te men sut da paper par eh suto ge tan ek, ekpaper naal mazboot hon ge." (I could have mailed them but there are two questions that stop me.

First, how will I answer that father whose two kids about about their age maybe couple years younger were kept in a cold tower around the same time of the year some three hundred years ago? Tell me what will I say to him? That your children's sacrifice was for naught, that when the need of the hour to serve I kept mine out of the cold. Tell me what we will say to him? (He was referring to the sacrifice of the younger two sons of the tenth master who were about seven and nine, and they were captured by the Mughal Governor of the Sirhind Province along with their paternal grandmother and were kept in a tower in mid-December while the cold wind from the Himalayan mountain range ripped through the open tower that stood high and exposed.) They were finally put to death. That was who Papaji was referring to and the father was the tenth master) Secondly, the people that have made the donation, work labor jobs in factories and out of that meager earnings, they save a little and donate, tell me how much money is left over after we are done with our expenses? They all are in the same boat. This money is their trust in me that I will guard it. How can I just waste it on postage when I have the alternative of my sons who are capable of carrying out the job? If you wish instead of them, I can send it by post, but believe me with every paper they deliver they will become stronger.)

The next day he said nothing, he left the decision to Beejee, Beejee gave both of us breakfast and then asked us to get ready and wear two pairs of socks. She asked Papajee to get the list ready for the other side of the town, the Foleshill area. He got up and got the papers ready and the list and explained to me the route he wanted me to follow. Which was up Stony Stanton Road and through St Paul's Street and to Kewal Singh Bain's house then up along Foleshill road through all the streets and all the way up to the edge of town.

The snow had iced over overnight, but we still went, this time, it was with the blessing of Beejee. She kissed both of us and held us. It was almost as if she was reliving the moment of the tenth master's sons and their grandmother as discussed earlier. She waited at the door until we went around the corner from Red Lane onto Stony Stanton Road. This was a longer route even though we started out around nine thirty in the morning, we still were not back home until around six that day and the next day we had to go to school. It was pretty tiring. I remember it took a lot of calls from Beejee from the bottom of the stairs to get both of up Monday morning. Going in late or being late to school was never an option. The homes that were left for delivery were the streets around our house and those we would do few streets each night after school until it was all done.

CHAPTER THIRTY-NINE

The Only Incidence

Monday evening there was a loud knock at the door, I mean a real load knock. BANG, BANG, I opened the door and there was Baba Nand Singh standing there. He was fuming, as always he had both of his hands in his overcoat. He pulled one hand out. In it, he had a crumpled up paper. I could make out that it was the newsletter.

He looked over at me and said, "Kithe hai tera burra." (Where is your old man?)

He was not one to talk like this, something had clearly got his goat, and he was looking to take it out on someone.

Papajee came down to meet Baba Nand Singh, as soon as Papajee came down the stairs and Babajee saw him; he sprang to his feet and opened up the crumpled up letter and came over to Papajee and said, "Eh kee hai? Orly, eh orly ke hai?" (What is this orly? What is this?)

Papajee looked confused and pointed to him to pass him the paper and asked him in a hand gesture what he was referring to. It was clear that Papajee was not fully awake yet.

Babajee came over and pointed to the bottom of the total and said, "Ah dekh Orly." (See here this Orly.)

Papajee was a bit irritated, but he kept his composure and said, "Nand Singh jee, orly nahin, Only," (Nand Singh not Orly it is Only).

"Han ehda matlab ke Guru da Khazana Orly hai." (Yes, it means that the guru's accounts are only). Babajee said giving dad a stern look.

Babajee took only to mean meager. Someone had read the document to him and literally explained the meaning of only to him, and he thought that only being used was wrong for the accounts of the Guru. Papajee explained to him that it is an accounting way of shutting off a number and being specific and nothing more than that. However, that was not going to satisfy Babajee he wanted to talk to Bawa Singh and wanted Orly or only removed from the end of the figures.

Papajee tried to reason with him, but he was having none of it; he wanted to talk to Bawa Singh. Papajee was trying to avoid these two meeting each other, especially under these circumstances. Babajee was not backing down, so Papajee got ready and left with him to Bawa Singh's house. Bawa Singh worked at Jaguars and came home around five thirty in the evenings.

Both of them left to meet with Bawa Singh while Kashmir and I had a good laugh about Babajee's pronunciation of Only.

Once in awhile, I will still jokingly say to Kashmir, "If Orly we could," affectionately remembering Babajee.

Papajee told us the next day what happened when they met with Bawa Singh. He said first Bawa Singh was calm and tried to explain to Babajee the reason why only is written and when Babajee would not back down Bawa Singh finally got so mad that he called Babajee, "Dhahti Pendu unparrh." (An ignorant uneducated village Billy) to which Babajee called him an "Angrezi Babu" (English brown Clerk.)

There was no stopping them. Finally they ran out of steam, and Papajee said he told Babajee "Deko Nand Singh jee estaran likhna penda hai tusi is cheez nu smajo."(Look, Nand Singh, it has to be written this way try to understand), Papajee said when Babajee realized that Papajee sided with Bawa Singh on this, he backed down but not without his last words. "Tusin likhi jao men apne pepr the ede te shiahi fer deni hai."(You go ahead and write it if you wish. I will ink it over on my letter). Which he did religiously when he got his paper, and he would keep it and show it to Papajee that he did so and hand the paper over to Papajee. It was his way of resolving the issue in his mind. His silent protest that he did not agree with the Guru's account ending with the word, "Only."

CHAPTER FORTY

The Smiley kid from Cobden Street

As we did every month on the day of the function. Sucha Singh's son Shinda would come early along with other teenage boys, and they would go into the shed in the back of our house and pick up the bundles of blankets to lay out on the floor of the hall on the second floor of the school building.

This month when we got to the hall, there was a tall lanky boy standing waiting for us. He was all smiles. His thirty-two teeth were all sparkling and ready to make new friends. We noticed him, but as is the case, anyone new is always invisible to the rest of the club. Here it was no different. We started to lay down blankets and he started to help. He was fresh from Punjab. You could see from his clothes and his socks. The hardwood floor of the hall was freshly polished probably that Friday night. So as he tried to lay one end of the blanket, he slipped back and fell on his buttocks. We all burst out in laughter.

Shinda looked over at us and shouted, "Oye what so funny?"

We stopped and the boy got up looked over at us, and it did not deter him; he just smiled and went at it again. He fell again, Shinda told him to take his socks off. Once he took his socks off he could hold steady. All along he never lost his smile.

After he was done he came over to me and introduced himself and said, "Mera na Saudagar hai auo samanni vali gali vich rehnde han." (My name is Saudagar. We live in that street ahead.)

We talked about which village he was from, He told me that his father's name was Prem Singh and that they were from village Nagra. I had seen his father but did not know him well. Papajee knew him well. We talked until Shinda again gave us orders.

I told Saudagar "Eh boss bahji hai." (He is brother boss.)

Saudagar and I talked a lot after the function was over; he helped with putting the blankets back in the shed. We would see each other in between the function and would wave to each other. Once in a while he would cross the street and come and talk to me.

We did not see each other at school if you could call them that. As far as I am concerned, they were no more than holding tanks to hold you until you turned fifteen, so they could turn you out into the apprenticeship or trainee labor force, and you would provide cheap labor for the next five years, and they may teach you a skill. There were few lucky ones that would go on to higher education but for the rest, the die was cast that you were going to be a blue-collar workers. Saudagar went to Broad Street secondary school, and I went to Fredrick Birds secondary school. On school days we never saw each other, only on the weekend, we would see each other. On the day of the function, he would help with the blankets, and I would ask him to stay and help with counting the collection. Papajee would never touch the money at the end of the function. He would have some other people usually four or five people count the money sort the change into the little bag and then put them in a plastic leather bag that Beejee had sewn. Once random members of the congregation had counted the donations, it was handed to Papajee and when we came home our job was to verify that it was correct.

This process took few hours on Sunday after the function, and once the Gurdwara was built it was every Sunday.

Saudagar would stay and help. Papajee and Beejee grew very fond of him. He started calling them Papajee and Beejee. After a while, he was part of the family. We became best friends with each other and remain so to this day.

However, that's not the whole story about Saudagar and I. We were so good friends people did not know if he was a friend or another son, he was everywhere with us. We did everything together went everywhere together. People would say if there is an example of true friendship there they are. On his wedding day, I was his best man. Although Sikhs don't have one as such, but his dad asked me to take charge. I did everything. Uncle Prem Singh, Saudager's dad trusted me like a son and put me in charge.

Saudagar got married in Walsall, Don Clark the photographer went with us. Don probably would be described as the Sikh Community's photographer. He was at every wedding. He knew all the gossip in the community, his wife; a very dear lady also knew who was who in the community, and they both kept their ear to the ground. Don knew both of us well, and he took a photo of both of us at Sudagar's wedding, and he put it in his studio window, and it stayed there for years.

I would say to him, "When are you going to take the photo down Mr. Clark?"

He would smile and reply, "Hopefully never Balbir."

And then he would smile. It never registered with me what he meant.

Few years went by, the Gurdwara was built then something happened between the two of us, Saudagar and I; I am not even sure what it was, we said something to one another and we fell apart. It's amazing how the same streets where you meet each other and cross over to see one another now took on a different face. Now when we saw one another, we would cross the road to avoid one another. On my wedding day the one person that should have been there was not there, I had ruled him out of my life. We were not friends anymore. I left for the United States in seventy-two, Saudagar and I had not talked for few years. He knew I was going, and I did not make any attempts to make up. I found out that he had a son. It could have been the perfect time to make up, but youth and arrogance go hand in hand and I was arrogant and young.

I stayed away but I knew, deep down, in my heart that he was still my best friend. I remember going by Mr. Clark's studio one day on my way from work as I would often do when I got off the bus. I saw that in the window, he took our photo down.

I said to him, "I see you have taken the photo down."

He looked at me and shook his head and said, "I thought I told you I hope I would never have to, you two have hurt a lot of people. Me included, I am really disappointed in both of you."

I was pretty hard back then, but age teaches a lot, like water shapes a rock, time shapes you and takes the rough edges off you. However, at that age in your late teens and early twenties, you have all the answers.

I just looked at him and said, "Well it's not for life, we all move on." and left.

Whenever I would see Mr. Clark again he would be polite but in his eyes, we had disappointed him.

After Parminder and I got engaged, I found some redemption with Mr. Clark, he and his wife were both were very fond of Parminder.

They sat me down one day and said, "She is a gem young man, and we care a lot for her; you had better take care of her."

I remember smart mouthing and saying, "And are you going to tell her to take care of me also? Make my chapatis and all?"

Mrs. Clark pointed her finger at me and said, "You are a cheeky bugger Balbir."

Parminder and I left for the States to start a new life thinking that I was leaving behind everything that was in my past. I do remember that I packed my copy of the photo that was in the window. Parminder, my wife would ask me who it was in the photo. That she saw the photo in Mr. Clark's studio window for years. I would not talk about it for years, but I missed my friend.

As years rolled by we had our children Amrit, our first daughter was born, then our second daughter Aman and them our son Omar. By then, Papajee and Beejee had also moved to the United States to be with us .

My kids grew up knowing Saudagar, the first time they saw him was in eighty-six on a family visit to England. We were walking along a street. I saw him coming I told my kids and Parminder to cross the street over to the other side.

That's when Aman shouted, "Dad, there's that man, your friend in the picture at home."

She was referring to Saudager. He lowered his head pretending not to have seen us, and we just ignored each other and went about our way.

We were staying with Parminder's cousin in Coventry. That evening Parminder pulled me aside and said, "One of you is going to have to make the first move here. I have never met him but judging from that show earlier in the day both of you are still friends and are too bull headed to own up."

I listened and then just went and sat down and started watching television.

Years rolled by my kids would ask me about Saudagar, but I would say he was the past, but they knew it was not it was the present had always been. Parminder would tell the kids Dad is stubborn, and he has drawn a line and now won't cross it.

It was our eldest daughter's wedding in the early part of ninety-six, and my cousins from England had come to the wedding, and one of my cousin's sons was getting married in May the same year. My cousin insisted that, come hell or high water, I had to be there. I told him I will try, but he told me that was not good enough that I had to show up.

I went to the wedding, and I stayed in Coventry with Parminder's cousin. After the wedding, I stayed on for few extra days typically when I go to weddings in England, I go on Friday from the States and arrive on Saturday and catch the first flight out Monday morning. However, this time, I had some businesses in England and had decided to stay few extra days.

Saudagar had got into his own business and had a clothing manufacturing company; one day as we were going by Saudagar's factory, Parminder's cousin pulled to the curve and stopped the car.

I asked him, "Why were we stopping here? "Eh tere yaar de factory hai." (This is your friend's factory.)

"Fer?" (so)

He looked over at me and smiled and said, "Bhayia edan nahin kari da ja mil lay apnne yaar nu." (Dear brother in law don't act this way go meet your friend.)

I told him, no, and asked him to drive on. He would not take no for an answer. He is the kind of person who keeps gnawing at you until he gets it his way, but I was also stubborn. I told him to move, but he was not going to. He got out of the car and went into the place. When he came out I thought he was going to bring Saudagar with him, it was going to be an awkward moment. He came back alone.

I looked over at him said, "Layian swaad morr dita na khali hatin." (So got the taste of it, turned you back empty handed.)

He laughed and grabbed me by the shoulders and said, "Bhaiya oh ithe nahin see, ah farr ou da card tan ohnu ghar ja ke phone kar lain." (Dear brother in law he was not there, here is his card call him when you get back.)

I told him to keep his card,] I was not interested. He kept it and said nothing of it. I left for London the next day to my meeting and to catch my flight back to the US.

On my return as always when Parminder was putting my clothes away she found at the bottom of the suitcase a stack of cards.

She brought them over to me and said, "So you two finally came to your senses and made up. I see."

I looked over at her confused and asked her what she was talking about. That's when she showed me the stack of cards; her cousin had slipped into my suitcase.

I told her what had happened, and she said, "It is really unfortunate that you two can't sit and sought this out."

I kept quiet. I came back on a Thursday went into work the next day. We were right in the middle of a merger with another company. I tried to put the whole incidence out of my mind and get on with the merger. Somehow I could not get it out of my mind what I had gone through, what would have I said if Saudagar was at his factory and did come out? What would he have said? Or would he even have come out to see me? I went through this for weeks on my commute in the morning and the evening.

Parminder can read me like a book. I suppose when two people are deeply in love there is nothing that the other person does not feel.

She said to me one night as we were sitting watching television, "you know, it's none of my business it's between the two of you, but I know that you're hurting and sometimes the only way to heal the hurt is to risk getting more hurt."I listened to her, and I could not get the conversation out of my mind. Next morning, I took one of the cards that were still sitting on the dresser and put it in my pocket and drove off to work.

I usually went to lunch with a bunch of other people, but that day I told them that I was busy and would not join them.

I took the yellow pad that was sitting on the side of my desk and started to write, I wanted to write it in Punjabi not in English this much I knew, I had to speak to him in Punjabi. English was going to seem formal.

I wrote Saudagar a letter, I had to let my guard down and

risk rejection, risk getting hurt, after such a long-time people change, maybe he had changed, had new friends and old friends don't matter as much. Time had marched on and maybe I was just stuck in my twenties and was missing my youth. After all, it was me who had moved away from Coventry and what if it was just memories that I was yearning for.

I knew though I had to talk to him from my heart.

I wrote to him and told him how I had come to his factory and would not come in and Jeet Parminder's cousin tried to get me to come and see him, I would not, and he went in but you had already left. I wrote to him that I was not even sure if I had any right to connect with him. I wrote that I was not sure why we even stopped speaking to each other, but I know how stubborn I was back then. (Although Parminder would contest the "back then", she would say you put Oxen to shame with your stubbornness.) I may have been the one at fault, and it may have been me that stopped talking with you. If fault needs to be put at someone's doorstep, then let it be mine. I wrote I had left England, but our friendship never ended. My children grew up knowing you, and referring to you as, Dad's childhood buddy whom he does not talk with anymore. I wrote I was not sure that there is anything of our friendship remained with him, but even if there is a ray of it then do call me or write to me and let me know. If our friendship did not carry the test of time, then so be it, but if it did, then call me. It has taken me a quarter of a century to reach this far.

I mailed the letter at the office mail, when I came home once kids went to bed; I told Parminder that I had written Saudagar a letter.

She held my hand and said, "I am so very proud of you, now let it go."

I remember remarking to her, "I am sure nothing will come of it."

She shook her head and said, "Oh ye of little faith, if not you are still ahead, but my heart says that he will contact you."

About a couple of weeks went by, and I had no time to think anything of it as I was really consumed with our pending merger. One day as we were getting ready for work, Parminder is usually up before I am and back then she got up and made lunches for the kids. She always made lunches for the kids in the morning, not the night before, and she made Papajee Breakfast and brought me a cup of tea. I never ate breakfast back in those days even though she would chide me for it. She would bring me a cup of tea in bed I would sit and drink while she got ready for work, and we would chat. It was Tuesday about seven in the morning. When the phone rang, it was not unusual for the phone to ring that early in the morning, most of the times it was someone from the community that had a beef with someone, and they would me call to sound it off. It irked Parminder, but I did not mind I would take the call.

She put the hand on the microphone of the phone and came over to me and said, "I think it's your friend from England. It doesn't sound like any of the usual local suspects."

I asked her to hand me the phone, and it was Saudagar. He asked if this was me.

He said, "Menu teri chithi melli aur mainu tan Zakeen nahin aunda se, eh tun he hain Balbir jin chitthi likhi, koi muzaak ta nahin." (I got your letter. I could not believe it is really you, Balbir. It's not some cruel joke.)

I told him no, it was no cruel joke it was me, I wrote the letter. It just felt at that moment that a gap of a quarter of century just closed. We talked for about ten minutes; I remember telling him that I had to get to the office as we were in the middle of a merger. Parminder shook her head. I told him I would call him later in the day as soon as I got some time. It was how I would tell him when we were growing up and it just came naturally right back. I knew what his reply was going be and it was exactly that. "Changa" (fine).

Parminder was standing there by the sink shaking her head, and I looked over at her and said, "What?" she replied "My dear man, you Ragi's (our family name) are all work, man, after twenty-five years you told him, I will call you back? After twenty-five years, you put the man on hold because of some bloody merger, now I know whose fault it was that you guys fell out of grace, you take him for granted man."

She was right on every count. I did take him for granted. To my family, work comes first, has and always will. That's how Papajee and Beejee brought us up. It felt like Saudagar and I were the same again, me telling him what I will do, him saying "Changa" (fine).

However, Parminder wanted to make sure that I called him back. So I promised her that no matter what I would call him back. At lunch, I called him; he knew I would call him. We talked for a good hour. We tried to fill twenty-five years into one hour before I ran off again.

But his final words to me were before we hung up "Lappi da viah hay." (It's Lappi's wedding.)

I asked him, "Lappi kaun?" (Who is Lappi?)

"Mera Vada munda." (My eldest son.)

I know he had two sons but I did not know what their names were. He knew we had three children but he had no idea what their names were either. We were slowly getting to know each other. So when he told me that it was Lappi's wedding he caught me off guard.

"Kad Viah hay?" (When is the wedding?)

"June," he replied. But I had just got back from England in early part of May from my cousin's son's wedding and tried to tell him that it was going to be difficult to come right back in June and I was in the middle of a merger. But he was persistent and said, "Dekh Balbir jad Lappi da janam hoya ud de aapan russae hoy han hunn uhde viah te tainu aunna penna, naale uh mainoo aakh de ne Taia jee aunn ge viah te dad." (Look Balbir we have fallen out since Lappi was born now you have to be at his wedding, besides they are asking if uncle is coming to the wedding.)

I had no choice, merger of no merger I had to go, I had to find time out of my work schedule and do my over the pond on Friday and back on Monday sourjoun. I told him I would be there I will book my tickets.

June came around most of the merger action had been completed, I could take a breath and was not feeling as I was leaving someting incomplete, the final few items others could do without me, mergers are tricky business you never know one last little item or a sentence can throw things into a spiral. But it looked like we had all the major items under control and I could take couple of days without feeling guilty that I had left in midstream.

I caught the United flight at 1 PM out of San Francisco for London and it landed in London in the late morning. I usually had no language to collect as I went on these trips with a carry on. My cousins would always joke in picking me up that they would cut it close and I would be waiting for them outside.

They would always say, I did take for granted "Bhajee suitcase lake aya karoo nahin asin late ho jande han." (Dear brother bring a suitcase or we are late.)

They would start late thinking that it would take an hour for me to go through collect my lugagage and go through customs. Since I did not have to collect luggage I was always out before they got there.

In Punjabi culture its bad manners to make a guest or an elder wait, so my cousins would time their journey from the Midlands (central England about 100 miles from London is referred to as Midlands).

One of my cousins would step out while the other circled around and when the guest would come out, the one that was there inside the terminal would pick up his bag and when the other came around from circling they would hop in the car and take off to the Midlands. This way they would not have to park, their reason for not parking was to be efficient.

I would always say, "No its not, you're just too cheap to pay for parking." Nevertheless, I would put a kink in their method by not allowing them the time to circle and would arrive and be on the curve before they got there. It would make their face go red with embarrassment, and they would stop at every pub on the way back to the Midlands try and buy me a pint. Even though I did not drink they would try and make it up. Most of the time they were drunk by the time we got to the Midlands and blame me for making them feel bad, so they had to buy me a pint and drink for me.

When I landed I took my carry on and I checked through the immigration and walked towards the exit door. As I was going down the stairs towards the exit doors, I was wondering what would this tall lanky kid that was slipping on a waxed floor when we first met, when he first came from Punjab would look like now after these many years.

I saw him in the crowd he was standing there not anxious in anyway. He had a phone in his hand. He had a short-sleeve Hawaiian type of shirt on that was tucked in, over which hung twenty-five years of fine dining, and his hair was not well-groomed and parted to the side as they were when we were young, but they had thinned out over the years and somehow were more curly now. I saw him and picked him out of the crowd. He saw me. He did not wave nor did I, but he smiled and there it was the full teeth smile that had not changed. When he smiled his eye muscles tighten up and his smile is from ear to ear.

I got close he walked out of the crowd and got hold of my bag and the first thing he said, "Bass ehe hai?" (This is all you have?)

I told him yes that was all I had, no suitcases. I always wondered if they felt embarrassed that they were picking up a guest who could not even afford a suitcase. He asked me how the family was, and I asked him the same. We went towards the car. The ride back to Coventry had no past discussion as to what had happened, just him filling me in about what had changed in the city and with the community and the Gurdwara. We had connected. The twenty-five years had just gone and time was just somehow sewn together.

When I got to his place, his family had arrived, his sister from London, his younger sister who was just learning to crawl when we fell out with each other, his older Sister and younger brother from Liverpool and his youngest brother from Germany and many of his other family members who remembered me were all there in the back yard. I must say at first I was a nervous entering his household after so many years. However, they made me feel like I was the son coming home after so many years, not someone from whom they wanted answers from as to why we broke up. They left that to both of us, and we needed no answers from one another. We just wanted to pick up and move on. I really met Ravinder, Saudager's wife for the first time, and it felt like I had known her all my life.

The kids gave me a dunk pen and inkwell, they said, "Dad told us you like to write, so we got you, this dunk pen and an inkwell."

Saudager gave me a glass plate that reads, "Friend. You bring me the comfort of peace. You help me see the beauty in life."

I have the plate sitting on my desk in my study and the inkwell on my bookshelf in my study.

These two items are amongst the two of my most treasured items. Funny as to what we think of as wealth, we measure it for the most part, by our investment our financial holding, but when it is boiled down, it's not that at all. It's those things that remind us of fond memories or those that remind that we did something decent in our lives.

Saudager pointed to a photograph that was taken at his wedding the same one that was in Mr. Clark's window and pointed to it.

Lappi said, "Thaiaji we grew up with that photo of you and Dad, it seems like we already know you."

I smiled and said to Lappi "Son, cross the pond in

the States you have two sisters and one brother, meaning my children who also grew up with the Photo."

Lappi's wedding was a grand affair, his in laws are from Pasla village, Khalsa's village, and they knew me and knew that I was coming. Saudager asked if I would speak at Lappi's wedding, which I was very happy to do. People from the community came up to me after the wedding and congratulated me for coming to Lappi's wedding.

Most of the folks that knew us as youngsters hugged us and told their kids who were toddlers when we were teenagers, "Ena dohan de yaari Pakki yaari dekhlo veeh pachi saal baad ek duje nu mel han." (These two have a true friendship, seeing each other twenty to twenty-five years later.)

We closed the gap of time in our friendship. We locked out from our mind any misunderstanding of our youth and our friendship survives. We talk at least once on the phone each month.

CHAPTER FORTY-ONE

Ramgaria Incident

Things were moving along well. Papajee had weathered all the storms from Rajmal's Indian workers association and the comrades (people who believed that India should follow the communist doctrine were referred to as Comrades. The term Comrades was meant in a semi-derogatory manner in the community. Papajee was able to unite the community and form a team that he felt he could work with to take the project to completion.

People looked forward to Sangrand Diwan (the ceremony of the new month). Bawa Singh wrote the newsletter every month, every month Babajee would cross out "Only" at the end of the accounts on his paper and in protest hand it over to Papajee without fail and would give Bawa Singh the look of disapproval. Bawa Singh would acknowledge by lifting his face in disgust and saying "Huh".

Papajee would just ignore their little interaction and take Babajee's marked-up newsletter and put it in his pocket. Papajee kept every document. It was just his way. He neatly filed the marked up newsletters Babajee gave him and had them until he came to U.S. that was when he finally was going to throw them out. He asked Babajee if he wanted them. Bawa Singh had moved back to Punjab by then.

Babajee said to Papajee, "Dharam Sian tehn ena cher saamb rekhe?" (Dharam Singh you have saved them all this time?)

Papajee told him yes. But for Babajee it was not the same anymore since Bawa Singh was not there to spar with, so he told Papajee to throw them out.

As it is with life, one thing that we can count on is that life does not remain the same, when we are feeling that its smooth; the almighty just changes the game.

Sangrand divans were now full of joy for most people, where before, in the beginning, Papajee had to go asking and almost begging people to come and do kirtan at the Sangrand function. Now, everything was different. Giani Naunihal Singh still resisted doing Kirtan since Papajee had made the policy that every contribution would come to the general fund. So Naunihal Singh would act as the announcer since he was the general secretary but would resist doing kirtan. I am sure he must have thought of leaving but since he along with all the others had vowed to stay in until the end to Beejee so he could not opt out.

Sikhs who had come from East Africa were now well involved and were doing Kirtan. Most of these Sikhs had started to leave East Africa where they had settled for over a century. As the Independence movement in Kenya and Uganda started picking up steam. Most of these people felt that the British days in Africa were numbered and since they all had British Passports it was like coming home. Most of them felt that they would not get a fair treatment after the independence since they had served the British, and they were not really seen very favorably by the Africans.

Most of these people migrated from the Punjab in the early 1900 hundreds or in the late 1800. Originally, they went there to build the railway lines but later took over other businesses.

Most of these people were carpenters. They had done really well. They had ventured out into other businesses, mainly small businesses and had created a thriving economy in and around Nairobi. However, as the winds of fortune started to change and the African country's independence seemed all but a foregone conclusion the migration to England started to take place. Slowly at first around 1962, but it started to pick up steam in 1963 and after the independence of Kenya at the end of 1963, there were planes full of Indians who were landing at Heathrow Airport daily.

Most of these people settled around London, some moved to parts of the Midlands.

They were devout Sikhs who referred to themselves as Ramgharias. Although Sikh religion does not recognize castes, but cultural aspects of life are hard to remove. Indians will tell you that the British were very good at divide and rule. I generally smile when I hear this because when I see what the British did, it was nothing more than giving each group the recognition that they wanted as a community, and then they controlled and exploited them for their own end. So why blame the British when it is important to Indians to be Marathas, Sikhs and Rajputs. The British created the British Army along these lines, so nobody was fighting for a national cause but for their own identity. This is a bit simplified I will confess, but the baseline thesis is sound.

So who are the Ramgharias? As I mentioned before, the early settlers from Punjab to East Africa were from the carpenter class. They refer to themselves as Ramgharia. Under the feudal Misal system prior to the creation of the Sikh Empire under Ranjit Singh who united all the warlords and formed the Sikh Empire. One of the warlords was Jassa Singh Ramgarh. He was referred to as Jassa Singh Ramgarhia (Ramgarhia meaning from Ramgharh). He happened to be a Sikh from the Carpenter caste. It sounds a bit strange for me to write a Sikh and a caste in the same sentence but unfortunately as I mentioned above people's cultural ties and identities are stronger than their religious ties.

Papajee was happy, finally, everything was on target and going well. The Ramgharia families would do Kirtan and also people from other cities mainly Birmingham started to come and do kirtan. Some of them became regulars every month. Beejee would prepare breakfast and Lunch for them, when they came they came straight to our house, and breakfast would be ready for them. They would eat breakfast and then go to the school hall where the congregation had gathered, and they would perform kirtan.

One of the regular people was a Ramgharia Sikh by the name of Giani Udham Singh, who came from Birmingham. He would perform Kirtan and give a sermon. His sermon would have a theme, ego pride, etc. He would tie some Sikh historical incidence and then sing a shabad (hymn) from the Guru Granth Sahib to illustrate the point.

He was a man in his late fifties about a medium build and height with a flowing white beard; I remember he always wore a white turban. He was very well regarded and was seen as someone of reverence by most people because of his sermons. There is a saying in Punjabi, that under the lamp, it is always dark, meaning that people project outwards but not inwards, as we would find out in the case Giani Udham Singh Ramgaharia.

On one of these occasions, he came to do kirtan at one of the Sangrand divans. He started his Kirtan, at the time when the Sangat was fully gathered. I remember the sermon to this day, as it would be another turning point in the Sikh Community of Coventry. His theme was loyalty, devotion, faith and the final test of this by your Guru and God.

He started by singing a hymn and then started to recite his sermon. His sermon was about Guru Gobind Singh (the tenth master) testing the loyalty of Dalla Choudrey. Dalla was a Jatt of the Sidhu Clan who later was baptized as Dal Singh. Dalla received Guru Gobind Singh at his village of Talwandi Sabho. Being a landlord of some repute, he kept an army of few hundred men, The Guru had been through many battles and had lost all his four sons and his mother and had taken a rest at Talwandi Sabho at Dalla Choudry's invitation. Dalla was a very proud and boastful Jatt, as most Jatts tend to be. He boasted that had the Guru called upon him maybe the outcome of these battles would have been different.

During Guru Gobind Singh's stay at Talwandi Sabho two artisans from Lahore presented the Guru with a muzzle-loading rifle. Giani Udham Singh was reciting this story to demonstrate the difference between loyalty and pride. Guru Gobind Singh upon receiving the rifle loaded the rifle and asked Dalla to ask some of his fine brave men to come forward so the rifle could be tested. Dalla asked his men, but none would volunteer.

Guru then said, "Well Dalla since I have tested the loyalty and devotion of your men now let me test yours, step forward."

Giani Udham Singh is in full emotion of an orator reciting the story. He goes on to tell the story.

Giani Udham Singh goes on to say, "Guru Sahib ne pushia Dallia maaran Goli?" (Guru asked; Dalla shall I fire?)

"Par Dalla chup kharra reha." (But Dalla stood in silence.)

Giani Udham Singh is now really adding emotion into his sermon and repeats again but this time much louder in the true evangelical voice with lots of emotions.

He holds his arms up in the air and said, "Guru sahib ne fer Pushia Dallia Maran Goli?" (Guru Sahib asked again. Dalla shall I fire?)

At that moment, what came next would forever divide the Sikhs between Sikhs and Ramgharia Sikhs.

At that moment when Gian Udham Singh was at its prime and said "Dallia Maaran Golli?" (Dalia, shall I fire the rifle?) Out of the congregation, someone loudly remarked, "Kee dehkda Bhai shadd de." (What you waiting for brother? Pull the trigger.)

As soon as the person from the congregation said that the whole congregation broke out in laughter. Giani Udham Singh was just standing there dumbfounded, unable to complete his sermon and felt humiliated by the foolish comments.

Giani Udham Singh sat down. Giani Naunihal Singh got up and made a public apology to Giani Udham Singh, Khalsa was enjoying it a bit. Papajee was mad and upset, what he had built he was seeing it falling apart.

Babajee was sitting in attendance of Guru Granth Sahib and shouted out, "Oh mundia bukwaas band kar." (Hey Boy stop your nonsense.)

Papajee went over to Giani Udham Singh and apologized. He did not know at that time who had made the comment. Giani Udham Singh was understandably shaken and humiliated. Papajee was trying to calm things down at the same time trying to keep normalcy but there was no normalcy to be had. He asked Giani Naunihal to cut the divan ceremony short. Which Giani Naunihal Singh did so.

As people started to leave Papajee started to investigate who had made the remarks that led to the congregation breaking out in laughter. Someone finally confessed to him who it was. What upset Papajee more was it was one of his ardent supporters. It was one of the Shampur (Village Name) brothers. The eldest brother Pargon had made the comment. Papajee asked Giani Udham Singh for his forgiveness and promised him that he will bring whoever did this to him to Birmingham and have him apologize to him in person or in public or both.

Giani Udham Singh assured Papajee that it was not required and told him that it was a childish prank let us just leave it and left.

Papajee went to Oliver Street just as soon as Giani Udham Singh left to give Pargon a piece of his mind. Pargon's son Darshan went to school with me and told me next day that when Papajee got there his dad Pargon had already slipped out of the house knowing what he had done and what was coming to him from Papajee.

But Papajee was never one to give up that easy, so he sat there late into the night until Pargon finally came home. He had been in the Pub and waited until they closed thinking Papajee would have given up and would have gone home by the time he came home. But he found him sitting in their front room waiting for him.

Darshan told me, "Thayia Jee (older Uncle) really

let Dad have it well and good last night mate, I have never seen him this mad before."

I asked him what did his dad say.

He said he just kept saying, "I am sorry big brother it just kind of seemed the right thing to say when kept asking to fire the rifle."

Papajee told him that he was going to have to apologize to Giani Udham Singh, and he agreed to do whatever Papajee asked of him. I am not sure he understood why, but just to get Papajee whom he respected like an older brother off his back he agreed to everything.

Giani Udham Singh although said nothing to Papajee and said it was all-Ok but inside he was mad and wanted to take his own revenge. The news spread like wildfire, it was the Jats up to their usual ways, being disrespectful. One man's foolish outburst and another's pride would create a divide amongst the whole Sikh Community. Giani Udham Singh after assuring Papjee that everything was fine and to put it behind him went straight to Princess Street, where a Ramgahria Sikh by the name of Santokh Singh lived and he told him what had happened. Santokh Singh quickly gathered other Ramgharia Sikhs; all of a sudden what could have been a very small thing became a slap to the Ramgahria community by the Jats.

Giani Udham Singh who loudly shouted from the pulpit, many time that ego and pride we must let go because it destroys us. Today became the victim of the very same thing that he would preach time and time again to people. Today the Punjabi statement that it is always dark under the lamp came true. He who would give light to others failed to see his own darkness; a foolish comment made by a foolish man became more important than the unity of the community. Giani Udham Singh's ego and pride got in his way; he could not project inwards and recognize that his ego and pride were getting the better of him.

It became the talk of the town. Every factory cafeteria, every school playground, all of the women picking up kids from school...everyone was talking about it. Some with regret other with something to talk about and others even using the term: "What are you waiting for brother, go ahead and fire". That gave fuel to the Ramgharia hurt sentiment. Papajee found out that Giani Udham Singh had gone and had gathered up all the Ramgarhias and that he had gone to Santokh Singh's house in Princess Street. Papajee was not very trusting of Santokh Singh, he saw him as an opportunist, one who would mention the Ramgarhis Gurdwara in Nairobi often. Papajee found out from Giani Naunihal Singh that Giani Udham Singh had gone to Santokh Singh's house, how Giani Naunihal Singh knew is a mystery to this day. The conclusion that we came to was that Giani Udham Singh must have told him when he walked out of our house at 7 Red Lane.

Next-day Papajee went to see Santokh Singh; Santokh Singh was a very civil and polite man but at the same time was also a very shrewd individual. He listened to Papajee; Papajee did his best to convince Santokh Singh not to push this unfortunate incidence further. He tried to reason with him that it was a foolish outburst of one individual and in no way was it directed against a community, or that it was in any way was premeditated. He assured him that he would have Pargon in front of the community accept his mistake and would take any punishment that would be given to him.

The following weeks there were lots of meetings back and forth. However, once the seed of discontent and distrust is planted it's hard to dig it out. Papajee heard everything with calm; he knew that it was no time to answer back. Sentiments were hurt, and he was up against pure emotions, not reason. His agenda was clear, to keep the community from splitting over a silly comment. He also knew he was fighting a losing battle. He knew that Santokh Singh had already convinced the Ramgahia community that the Jats would not treat them as equals Papajee tried his level best. Rest of his team members tried to convince him that it was of no use the Ramgahrias had made up their mind.

I remember Khalsa saying, "Dharam Singh tarkhana ne tan hunn juddae hon te lak ban leaya." (Dharam Singh the carpenters are dead set on splitting from us.)

I think the comment, which finally got Papajee to stop pushing any further was when someone from the Ramgahria community in one of the meetings made a comment that was in away worst than Pargon's comments.

It was, "Thuhano Jatan nu ta ev ve nahi pata ke tevian nun divan's kedar betalan han." (You Jats don't even have the sense to know which side the women should sit in a Diwan.)

That just made him really mad. I remember when they all came back, and they were sitting in our front room Babajee asked Beejee to join.

Sucha Singh and Sohan Singh Gaffa were so mad they gave few swear words and then said to Papajee, "Bade bhai hor kina kuj sonnna hay?" (Big brother how much more do you need to hear?)

About that time Beejee walked into the room and asked what had happened, Khalsa smiled and gave his giggle that he would always do and said, "Bibi Nasib Kaur bay oh kehnde sano appnnian janninan bethal an da be chajj hai nahin." (Respected Nasib Kaur, they said we don't even have the sense to know how to seat our women.)

Beejee would not interfere until she felt she had to, at this moment she felt she had to. She was absolutely insulted by that statement.

Beejee looked at all of them and said, "Ager Pargon kamla see oun kamal kuttia hunn eh mistry Singh ve tan kamal kutt de ne es taran de gal karni aakl mandi nahin, eh un da jabab ha jis nuh hunn thuahnu mann lenna chahi da hai." (If Pargon did a foolish thing, then is the Carpenter Singh's arn't any less foolish by making such statements? They have given their verdict you should accept it now.)

Papajee knew that he had lost the fight, "Eh vandan, Ramgharia flana flana, kisse din Sikhan nu lae bethen geeaan, koi ve ghatt nahin, tusin vee ghatt nhin oh ve ghatt nahin, sochia see ke jorr devan ga sarian nu hunn tan futt hor pae gai. Dobe ge sano kesse din jaroor dobe ge." (These divides, he's Ramgahia etc, etc will one day take the Sikhs down. None of you are any less than the other. I thought I would unite everyone, but the divide is getting bigger. These divides will sink us one day, for sure it will sink us one day.)

Papajee seemed helpless in the situation lines were drawn. Ramghraia's were now going their way. Papajee's team was asking him to accept the situation; his own wife was asking him to let it go. He accepted, but even after he would come up with different thoughts of what he could do but Beejee would tell him to let it go. Pargon would never apologize to Giani Udham Singh. Giani Udham Singh would never come to the Divans anymore.

Years later when the Gurdwara would be built, Giani Udham Singh would move to Coventry and buy a house on Leicester Causeway very close to the Gurdwara. He fell out with the Ramgharia's and would start to attend the Gurdwara that Papajee and his team would build on Harnell Lane West. He and his son Satnam Singh would become regulars at the Gurdwara and do Kirtan.

Even though no one ever forgot the incident many years earlier, but Giani Udham Singh would be treated with the utmost respect and reverence. It was a shame that he could not have heeded his own sermons on Ego and pride and controlled it at that moment. Maybe the outcome would still have been the same, maybe the Ramgharia's would have built a Gurdwara of their own anyway, but it would not have been under such bitter circumstances. Maybe Papajee could have appealed that it was wrong to build Gurdwaras under a name of any community. Maybe he could have convinced them that we are all represented in the Guru Granth Sahib, every caste, high low they all are there in those pages of the Guru Granth Sahib and later when Guru Gobind Singh created the Khalsa he abolished it even further.

Sadly over the years, other communities have followed the Ramgharia model and have started naming Gurdwaras after their castes or community. Now we have the Ravi Das societies. We have Lubhana Sangat Gurdwara. I feel like at times to want to sit them all down and say the British have long gone who is dividing and ruling you now? This kind of divide and division goes against everything that Sikhism stands for. Papajee's statement that it will take us down one-day rings true in my ears to this day when I see the struggles that the Sikhs face in India. They ring true when I see people brandishing swords in the percent of the Akal Takhat. It rings true when I see different people belonging to different groups settling their differences by shouting and forcing the police to walks in with their heads uncovered and shoes on. Sadly it is now happening in the same Gurdwara that wanted to keep people united.

Even though Papajee was upset at Santokh Singh and held him responsible for the creation of the Ramgharia Gurdwara and the divide. He still respected the Gurdwara, I remember on my wedding he took the Baraat bus (wedding guest bus) under Beejee's protest to the Ramgharia Gurdwara and did the Ardas there before we came to the Gurdwara that he had built where our wedding ceremony was to be performed. The Ramgharia committee along with Santokh Singh were standing outside in the parking lot for our arrival out of respect for papajee.

Beejee never did go to the Ramgharia Gurdwara. Even when Kashmir my younger brother got married, which was at the Ramgharia Gurdwara because it was close to the bride's family's house so they held the wedding there. She refused to attend the wedding ceremony. She held firm to her principle that naming a Gurdwara after a community is wrong.

She told Papajee, "They are Ramgharia and want to be known as Ramgharia I am not, I belong to my Guru and I will not go to a Gurdwara that is named after a Community not the Guru."

CHAPTER FORTY-TWO

Fauji Giani (Army Chaplin)

The Ramgharia incident took a lot out of the community, now the Punjabi Sikh community was divided in four ways, those that were the so called secular and comrades in the Indian Workers association (Mazdoor Sabha) with Rajmal and even they were fighting for power one group supporting a national level Indian Workers association another supporting Rajmal. Then there were the people that showed the movie every Sunday who saw their audience dwindling from all of this and then there was the Ramgahria and the rest.

This was taking a toll on the community, the next few Sagrand divans were not much joy. People still came but after all the jokes had settled down reality had set in as to what had taken place. The reality that we the Sikhs of Coventry were a house divided. The people did kirtan but it was not to the level of evangelical level of Giani Udham Singh. People missed Udham Singh; they wanted to feel that life back again that fervor of yesteryears that only he could put forward. Giani Naunial tried but his reluctance showed through and Khalsa did Kirtan but his voice could not carry the day either. There was a need to fill the void.

I know Papaji did ardas one day asking Waheguru (God) to for help. We all stood in the ardas, he asked God to help.

It is said (I firmly believe this) that if you ask for something with full faith, it will be given to you. Next Sangrand as we were taking the blankets into the hall as we did every month to lay them out for people to sit on, we would generally see some new arrival standing at the door.

Most of them had left their families back home. Coming to the services was a way to get a bit of the home village feeling for few moments. We tend to forget that all of our senses need to have their own satisfaction. Like our taste buds, our nose wants to smell home cooked mom's meal. Our eyes want to see something that reminds us of home. Parminder, my wife, for instance, in her soul never really left England, even now if the weather in California is balmy, which is not often she will still say,

"Oh the weather looks and feels like England today."

That vision and feeling which we have stored away that we sensed which gives us a sense of security comes out.

I remember the first time I went back to Punjab, standing in the middle of Chaura Bazaar in Ludhiana and saying to my nephew who was with me "chup, chup sunn." (Silent, silent, listen.)

He gestured with his hand what?

I turned to him and said, "Sare Punjabi he Punjabi sunai dindi hai." (Everywhere you hear Punjabi.)

He looked at me and said, "Mamaji Punjab vich ho Punjabi he sunnai devegee!" (Dear uncle you are in Punjab so you would hear Punjabi.)

The point is our senses long for those things they have stored in their respective memory banks, for me; it was the sound of Punjabi that I remembered from my childhood. For most of the new arrivals, it was longing to hear the same sounds and see familiar people so that for a brief moment you can look at them and take comfort that someone's voice reminded them of their brother and someone's looks reminded them of their sister. So they came early, eager to be part of the Divan (service).

Waiting in the doorway was a man of about forty with a sharp pointed turban, he was of medium height, he had majestic eyes they almost look like they were in a semi-meditative state. The defining part of him though was the mustache, they weren't big but they were curled like the letter "C."

As we saw him standing in the doorway, Saudager commented, "Fauji lagda," (Looks like a military man).

As we approached he smiled and said, "Kidan way barkhurdaruo, seva vich jorre ho?" (How are you young fellas, busy in doing service?)

He followed us up to the hall and started to help lay out the blankets, he asked by name if anyone of us knew Dharam Singh, I told him that he was my father. About then Papajee arrived as he always did to see if the job we had done met with his expectation. It never did. He always would have us move blankets around.

He looked over and said, "AJJ tan barre changi taran kete." (You guys did a good job today.)

Well, we had help from the man with the curly mustache. He took charge from Shinda and told us how to best lay out the blankets.

When he saw Papajee he walked over to him and folded his hands and said the Khalsa greeting, "Waheguru je ka Khalsa, Waheguru jee ke fateh." (Khalsa belongs to God, and victory belongs to God.)

Papajee replied back to him only. I could see Papajee felt something very deeply when he heard those words from the military man. He would later tell me that it made him feel like the Guru's grace was shining on the community that the word Khalsa was now in our midst. Papajee shook the curly mustache Sikh's hand and asked him what his name was and what the name of his village was. These two questions were asked in a very particular way.

They would ask, "Aap da shub naam ke hai aur aap the Daulatkhana kerra hae." (What is your good name, and where is your place of fortune?) (Meaning that the place where the person came from was thriving. It was a way of making the other person feel honored.) To which the person would reply, "Mera nemanne da naam hai--- aur mera gareeb khana hai----" (My humble name is--- and my humble abode is---.)

There was formality and discipline and honor but all that is lost now.

He told Papajee his name was Swaran Singh, and the name of his village. Papajee asked him if he was an army Giani, (meaning army Chaplin) to which he replied affirmatively. Papajee asked if he could do Kirtan. (Sing Hymns) and he replied that he could so. Papajee asked if he would do so today, and he replied that he would be honored.

Giani Swaran Singh did Kirtan in the old Chorus fashion and asked the congregation to join in. There was this resonance in his voice. His voice had this croak to it; however, he could carry a note. He did Kiratn for a good hour. Papajee I knew felt that his prayers were answered. Giani Swaran Singh could cut a good joke. He would become one of the boys, but he was a devout Sikh. From that day in 1963 until his death, he served the Gurdwara and the congregation.

Last time I was in England, and I was walking out of the Gurdwara and I did not see him, and he called from the back, "Balbir Putt, Balbir Putt milke jain." (Balbir my son, Balbir my son, wait and see me.)

I turned around and saw him and wanted to touch his feet, for he was an answer to my father's prayers, He probably never even knew it. As I went to touch feet, he grabbed me and hugged me close to the chest and said, "teri jaga Kaka sade dil vich peran vich nahiin, tun ta said bhai de nishani hain."(Your place is in our heart, not our feet. You are a memory of our dear brother -meaning Papajee.) Giani Swaran Singh served the community until his last day on this earth.

CHAPTER FORTY-THREE

Where is Khalsa?

Papajee had just gotten over the Ramgharia incident and was feeling pretty relaxed, then that dreaded knock at the front door happened again around July of 1963. It was middle of the week, and it was early evening. Papajee was reading the evening Telegraph as he always did every day before he got ready for his night shift, Just then there was a knock at the door it was not a knock we recognized. We all thought that this was a stranger at the door. Our front door had two opaque windows through which you could actually make out the outline of who it was. Most of the time we could guess who it was from the knock or from the outline of those that we knew.

Papajee asked me to answer the door; I opened the door and there was a young teenager about my height and build and about my age perhaps a year or two younger than me. I knew most of the local Indian boys but him; I had not seen before.

He had a worried look on his face; his face looked like it was waiting to hear some really bad news that was going to take away all his security blankets and leave him standing there naked.

Slowly as he composed himself; he started to talk, "Hello my name is Paul, and I am Prem Singh Khalsa's son."

I looked at him and the first thought that came into my mind was, that's odd, why would Khalsa uncle name his son with a Christian name like Paul? Later, I found out that his other son's name was John.

I asked Khalsa Uncle one day, "How come you named your sons John and Paul?"

He always had a smart answer when he knew he was cornered. He told me, "Maybe I was thumbing through the bible at the time."

Paul asked if we had seen his father. I said no, he had not been around. I asked him to come in.

Papajee got up and put his paper on his armchair and took off his glasses and said, "Boy what is this all about your Dad?"

Paul had tears in his eyes, but he was trying to be brave and held his composure.

Papajee asked him again, he said, "Father did not come home yesterday, and we went to Dunlop factory where he works but they said he had not shown up for work either today, so my mum is very worried."

Papajee got worried. He was a bit of a sleuth, and he started questioning Paul to see if there was a quarrel at home.

At this point Beejee stepped in and stopped Papajee and said, "Dekho ji oh kete digge pay hon ge Police nu dasso and bhalan de koshish zari karo." (Look he could be in a ditch somewhere you need to call the police and start a search for him.)

Somehow Papajee knew in his heart that he was not in a ditch after all this was Khalsa who he had come to know all too well.

Kashmir whispered in my ear, "Get ready for the run Phlipadies." (referring to the runner of Marathon.)"

Papajee asked me to run and check with everyone to make sure he was not with anyone of the other founders. He knew that was not going to be the case, but he wanted to rule that out anyway.

He sent Paul home and told him to wait, and he would come in the morning to talk with all of them. I ran to Blackberry lane first to check with Sohan Singh Gaffa, my instructions were to check if he was not there they were to come to 7 Red Lane right away to meet with Papajee. From

Blackberry lane I ran to Catharine street to Giani Naunihal Singh's house and delivered the same message and then to Baba Nand Singh's house on Wellington Street and finally to Eagle street to Sucha Singh's house. Sucha Singh came back with me. Others were there by the time I got there, also the Pasla Walas from Smith Street who were from Khalsa's village were all gathered. Papajee told them of the disappearance of Khalsa and the fear of him being sick or dead somewhere. It was very interesting that not one of them was convinced that was the case. Beejee still wanted them to inform the police; reluctantly they all agreed to do so but also decided that they would start looking for him. There is a Punjabi saying that is often used for unpredictable people when they are not to be found, "Hethe kite hunna appae ajao." (He is around there somewhere he will show up.)

Most of the time they will say that and go about their business until the person does not show up for few days then they may start to look for him. Besides Pasawala a lot were not the kind to get overly concerned with anything that quickly. They were a happy go lucky lot who did not take life that serious.

Next day Papajee and Babajee went to Khalsa's house to speak with his wife and his sons to see if there were any disagreements in the family, but they all said there were none everything was fine. Papajee asked his wife to go and count their suitcases and see if there was any missing. She went and checked and came back and said yes that there was a suitcase missing. Papajee knew he had gone somewhere so they decided they were not going to tell the police. The assumption was that this was a willful act on his part, but all sorts of scenarios started running through Papajee's mind.

He was visibly angry to the point he was sweating. Babajee tried to calm Papajee down, but he could see what was coming, this was going spread like wildfire in the community, and they had no answers to combat this. So he was in damage control mode. As soon as he got home I had just come home for lunch from school he asked me not to come home after school but go and gather everyone to come to 7 Red lane for a meeting in the evening. All the founders got together, and again he called Khalsa's co villagers the Pasla Walas. He told them that he was not dead anywhere but had left home, and God knows where he is gone.

He asked every one of them to divide areas and go to all the local pubs where community members hung out, in particular, those where people that would talk the most hung out and ask them if they had seen Khalsa, that he has come up missing. It was a smart plan on Papajee's part, rather than it coming out that Khalsa was missing let it come from the founders that they were concerned and were looking for him. By doing so they won over the sympathy of the rumormongers for the positive and brought them over to their side. Papajee bought time for himself while he tried to figure out where Khalsa disappeared to.

He took a week off from work to start his detective work. He interviewed people in the city. Slowly, the political rivals started the rumor mills that Khalsa had absconded with the Gurdwara funds. However, no one was willing to believe it. They all knew that the money was in Papajee's control, and it needed all the six of their signatures to withdraw funds. Besides, people had the utmost trust in Papajee that he would never let that happen anyway. Rumors started to swell. Papajee had to do something, so he got his second-tier group these were people like the Shampur brothers; yes Pargon was brought into action. The same person who caused the Ramgharia incidence, along with others. Including the master of all politics and the real spin master Kewal Singh Bains was recruited to counter the rumors and get people calmed down. Kewal Singh would give his right arm for Papajee, he cared for him that much. He assured him that he will calm things down. While these people went into action going around every pub and meeting with people and having a pint of beer with people, and they explained that while no one knew where Khalsa was the funds were safe.

Papajee at the same time continued his work trying to get

to the bottom of where Khalsa could have gone. His search took him to Birmingham; someone told him that there were about four people from Birmingham and one from Coventry who took off for India by car. They crossed the channel into France and were going to drive to India. Back in those days, India was still an extremely closed socialist country that did not allow outside goods into the country. If you brought them into the country, they were heavily taxed. One rule that they had was if you drove a car into India you could use it for your own use and on your departure give it to the family or sell it and there were no taxes, or they were very low. So some adventurous people would take a car and take on passengers and drive to India. It was not something that was that common but there were handful people that took the journey. God knows even to think of it would be foolish in today's world with the condition the world is in now, but back then it was much safer to attempt this journey.

Papajee went and spoke to the family of the driver in Birmingham, they told him that there were five other people besides the driver, but they did not know their names. He was convinced that Khalsa was one of them, but Beejee told him that he was jumping to conclusions. No one would trek half way around the world without telling his or her family. Papajee looked at Beejee and said" asin Khlase de gal karde han sub koj ho sakda." (This is Khalsa we are talking about. Anything is possible.)

About five days passed by in the search but there was no sign of him. The community had been satisfied that the funds were safe but not knowing where Khalsa was still very much was the talk of the town. Papajee was getting ready to notify the police, but he knew also since there was a suitcase missing they were not going to do much because the assumption was that he went of his own free will.

In the afternoon mail there was a letter, it was a different color then the envelope from India and with stamps we had never seen before. I told papajee that there is a letter but does not look like it is from UK or India it's from some other place and there was no sender address on it. He looked at it and shook his head. He would always got up in the afternoon for lunch and then went back to sleep before he got ready for his night shift. He was not a person that woke up very cheerful. He always looked mad and had a serious frown on his face as he woke up. Beejee would always avoid bringing up anything with him until he had time to wash his face and clean up. I caught him as he came down the stairs. I told him about the letter without uttering a word, he wiggled his fingers towards himself indicating let me have it. I gave him the letter, I knew what he wanted next so I handed him his glasses. He would always go to the family room window to read a letter. It was not because there was not enough light in the room, but that was just his way to stand in the natural sunlight to read letters. He opened the letter. I saw it was in Urdu.

He read it and then crushed the letter into his hand and said in English "Bloody irresponsible fool."

He would always turn to English to show his anger. He had a very strong New Zealand accent from his days spent there. Even though Beejee did not understand much English but from the reaction and the fact that he was speaking in English she knew the letter was from Khalsa.

She asked him just to make sure, "Bhaia jee de hai." (Is it from the elder brother?)

And he looked at her and replied, "Main kehi tan janda see oh oos car which gia honna Persia tun jake pi hai." (I kept saying he is gone in that car. He mailed it from Persia. They always referred to Iran as Persia.)

Beejee was dumbfounded at Khalsa's action and just stood silent. Papajee was just raging with anger.

Finally, when Papajee got his composure, he looked over at me and said, "Balbir school tun baad Oh de Ghar das aain ke oh car vich beth India dee sare karan gia." (Balbir after school go and tell his family that he got in a car and is off to tour India.)

He also told me to go and tell all the others to come over to the house the following day. The following day they all gathered, and they were just looking at each other and were too dumbfounded to say anything. Finally, Papajee broke the silence and said we had better let the news out to the community that he is safe and on his way to India. Once the news hit the community it was just a scandal that a man would do this.

By the time the next Sangrand Divan came around he was still in India, but he had sent another letter to Papajee from his village, and it was full of apology. He told Papajee that he did not weigh the fallout of his action but the need for him to have this adventure outweighed everything, and if he told his family, they would not understand it.

When Papajee read the letter to Beejee she turned around to Papajee and said, "Aap vee tan Fiji, New Zealand sano shad kar gay see." (You also went to Fiji and New Zealand leaving us behind.)

Papajee just listened and did not say anything. The coming Sangrand Papajee read portion of his letter to the Sangat (congregation). As with any scandal after a while, people lose interest in it, and they move onto something new. This also went quiet after the letter was read.

He returned to the UK after six weeks in India, he flew back. He always knew how to get around papajee, while Papajee would shout at him, he would sit and twirl his hat in his hand with his head down until papajee was finished and then he would give that giggle from his month that had no teeth and make some off-the-wall remark and Papajee would feel it was of no use, and they would go back to work.

This time was no different, but Khalsa was quite a fox, so he knew he needed to do something to please Papajee because even though he knew that what he had done was not going to be easily forgiven. Or even that he was not going to be easily defended by Papajee against attacks from the others. So he pulled the best maneuver that to this day makes me smile when I think of it.

There was a great need for books from the community in

Punjabi; people were longing to read Punjabi literature. So Khalsa while in India shipped two to three hundred books to his house, and once he got back he went down to the city library and donated the books and asked them to put the books in the library. Then he went down to the local paper, The Evening Telegraph and said that arrangements had been made and there are now Punjabi books in the City library; A first move of its kind in the country.

Papajee read it in the paper and told Beejee what he had done, "Bass hunn sara gussa tanda hu janna, Bhaia jee nun sarian kunjian the pata." (That's it your anger is all cool now, elder brother knows which knobs to turn.)

Once Khalsa had deposited the books at the central library, Saturday morning he came around, and I opened the door and started smiling. He looked at me with his hat in his hand and did his toothless giggle. He raised his eyebrows asking me with his body language if Papajee was home. I reciprocated with indicating with my thumb toward the family room. He walked with his hat in his hand into the family room where Papajee was sitting reading the newspaper as always. Khalsa first looked over at Beejee and greeted her.

He was a master strategist, he said, "Bibi Nasib Kaur Sat Sri Akal Beeji, replied back Sat Sri Akal kad aye?" (Sat Sri Akal, when did you get back?)

Papajee knew his game, so he turned to Beejee and said, "Bass, bass." (Enough, enough.)

Papajee wanted to have his pound of flesh, so Papajee turned to Khalsa said, "Khalsajee koj hosh hai ah bachian valli harkat karan to phelan kuj sochia see jan jo man vich oh kar lai?" (Khalsa Jee do you have any sense of things? Did you think or just did like children what first came into your mind?)

Papajee went at him for good half an hour. You never wanted to be on the receiving end of Papajee's wrath it was really painful, and today it was in top gear. I have to hand to Khalsa jee he just pulled his tent over himself and waited until the storm blew over. Beejee, Kashmir and I went into the front room of the house; we could hear Papajee just blasting Khalsa.

Beejee smiled and just whispered to me, "Faujan ajj pure jor wich ne." (The army is in full force. Punjab idiom when someone is mad.)

Finally, Beejee had to intervene and stop the torture. Then Khalsa spoke and said a quote out of the Sikh Scripture to justify what he did as a call of your soul. That got Papajee started all over again, Beejee had to tell Khalsa to just be quiet.

Once Papajee was done. Beejee said to Khalsa "Bhaia jee tusin keh deo galti ho gai age nain hove gee." (Elder brother, please say you made a mistake, and it won't happen again.)

To which Khalsa replied, "han teek nain hove gee." (Yes, that's right it won't happen again.)

But he did not say the word mistake because, in his mind, he followed his heart.

Papajee was not about let him off the hook that easy, he asked him, "Kee nahin hove gee?" (What won't happen again?)

Khalsa knew he had to use the word mistake, so he blurted it out with his hand folded at papajee, childlike "Galti master Jee, Galti." (Mistake, teacher mistake.)

Khalsa would go on to do and say other things that would frustrate Papajee but none of them matched this. Every time he would do something, Kashmir, and I would say, oh no, the volcano has erupted again.

CHAPTER FORTY-FOUR

Site selection

Papajee always wanted to build a Gurdwara raised from ground up. All other Gurdwaras until then were converted building of another use. The Shepard Bush Gurdwara, the first in U.K. was a house that Maharaja Bhupindra Singh had acquired and converted into a Gurdwara. Birmingham Gurdwara was an old church converted, and Southall was an old dairy process plant that was converted. Even the Ramgharia Gurdwara in Coventry was an old home that they bought and used as a Gurdwara, which was later extended it by adding a hall and other amenities.

Papajee had it in his mind from the very beginning that he wanted the Gurdwara in Coventry to be the first not only in U.K. but Europe to be raised from ground up.

There were many buildings that he was asked to consider, I remember one of them was the Ukrainian hall in Leicester causeway, but he refused to accept, there were other halls that people proposed to him, but he turned them down one by one.

I remember one day one of the Maulvi (Muslim Priest) at the mosque on Eagle Street saying to Papajee that there was the open space on the corner of Eagle Street and Leicester Causeway maybe we ought to look at it for the Gurdwara. He went by to look at it and I was with him. It somehow did not appeal to him. I remember Sucha Singh also came up from below the street where he and his brother Jhalman Singh lived, and they were impressed with the plot. Papajee was not.

Next few months he tasked me with looking at all the bombed out area (these were plots that sat empty where buildings were destroyed in the air raids over Coventry during world war two). I checked out a lot of spaces.

He gave me an area to go around and check. I remember the area was where most of our people were settled, which was mainly Foleshill Road and Hillfield area. I went all over and made note of all the places and showed him the places. In his mind, they all had something that was missing.

One Saturday, we were going downtown like we and everyone else did not Saturdays to buy our groceries or, as the Punjabis would say ration. We would usually catch the bus at the corner of Red Lane and Stony Stanton Road by the three Horseshoe Pub and get off at the city center and go shopping and meet other people in town and have the usual gossip and then catch the bus home.

On this particular day, the buses were coming by full and after few buses went by we decided to walk.

We walked down Stoney Stanton Road towards the town, and as we got close to Cash and Carry warehouse, Papajee told me to cross the road to the other side of the road. I thought maybe he wanted to go and visit one of his old friends Udham Singh commonly he was known just as Udha, he lived in a really old house at 61 Arthur street. However, when I asked him, he said no, just keep walking. I never did ask more than that he would think it impolite for me to do that and would see it as disobedience, so I did as he asked. As we approached Harnell Lane there used to be an old Pub there. If something could describe a hole in the wall pub, then this would be the poster child. The name of this pub was Rose and Woodbine, not sure if it is still there. Punjabis had their take on the name.

They simply referred to it as "Roshan Boodbaan." For the longest time, I thought it belonged to some Punjabi person by the name of Roshan, Roshan is a Punjabi name. It was much later I would be going by and read the faded sign on the building which said, Rose and Woodbine, that is when I would come to know that this was one of those other names that had been bastardized by the Punjabis. Sort of poetic justice, during the empire days, the British had bastardized names around the globe. Mumbai became Bombay, Kolkata to Calcutta and Kher to Cairo.

Roshan Boodbaan had a tragic memory for the Sikhs. A Sikh by the name of Sarwan Singh was killed here in a scuffle between two warring Punjabi Sikh groups. The poor fellow was trying to break up the scuffle, and in the scuffle was struck a fatal blow by an iron rod in the head killing him.

I remember him vaguely. He was a very nice man, and his wife Bhaag Kaur commonly known as Bhaago was one of the gentlest souls I have had the good fortune to know during my life. They lived on Eagle-street; the family saw their share of tragedies. Few years before Sarwan Singh was killed, their eldest son whose name was Balbir was playing by the quarry and slipped in and drowned. Balbir and I would play often, but he was just as naughty as they get. If there were tree to be climbed, he would be on it. If there was a dare to be had he was would be first in line. I still see him making mischief he is still there somewhere in the fogged memory of time.

I remember Papajee coming home one day and telling Beejee, "Bhay Sarwan hunna de naal tan lohrra hoya, Balbir dub gya." (Great misfortune has befallen Sarwan's family. Balbir has drowned to death)

I remember Beejee was just shocked and quickly changed on hearing the news, and they went off to pay their respect to the family. Few years later Sarwan was also killed. In a small community, you know everyone, the perpetrators, and the victims. Papajee also knew who had killed Sarwan and was surprised because he was actually a nice man. Someone who had grievances with someone and wanted to show his might brought them in and the scuffle broke out and an innocent Good Samaritan lost his life.

Papaji would always stop at the door of the pub on the corner and pay his respect to Sarwan. I thought that is why he crossed the road. As we approached the corner of Stony Stanton Rd and Harnell lane West, he stopped there for a moment as he always did today, instead of going straight, he made a right turned right. I said aren't we going to town? He told me we would, but first I want to show you something.

On the right-hand side of Harnell lane right next to the pub there were these old homes that were built on top of a mound. Not sure why they were built off ground like that. You had to go up about fifteen steps to get to the houses. It was always a mystery to me and still is to this day why they were built so high from street level. We walked past these homes and then there was a plot where the city had built homes for the police constables.

Walking past them, there were old homes that were condemned, also one plot. These properties were a mix of leasehold and freehold properties (city property where the city held the title to the land, but the house was on it for ninety-nine years were referred to as leasehold properties) also some freehold land.

We walked past them and stopped by the corner of Leicester Causeway and Harnell lane West.

Papajee said, "Tell me what you see?"

As always, he wanted Kashmir and I to be always diligent observant.

I told him, "I know this place this is 'Five ways'."

I must admit now I only knew that because of the Pub that was on the corner of Leicester Causeway and Harnell lane West that was known as "the Five Ways" and we were standing by it. But it pleased Papajee.

"Shai Balbir, Panj da sade vast ke ehmiat hai." (Correct Balbir, so what is the importance of five for us?)

"Ehmiat the matlab," I replied. (Ehmiat means?)

"Importance, what is the importance of five for us?"

I told him the five rivers of Punjab, panj pyaras (five beloved, the first five Sikh to be baptized were now as Panj pyaras) of the Khalsa.

He told me pointing to the plot and the houses, "Matha Tek eh Gurdwara de jaga hai." (Pay your respect; this is the place for the Gurdwara.)

I did as he asked; I took a handkerchief out from my pocket, covered my head and bowed.

As we stood there, slowly walking in the distant, I saw a man with a hat carrying a rolled-up bag in his hand walking towards us, and it looked like Khalsa.

As he approached I realized it was Khalsa, slowly as he always did and as he approached he asked me, "Kedan Boy jaga pasand ayi?" (Well boy do you like the spot?)

I told him that it was fine. Then they both smiled because there was more to this spot than met the eye. There was a real reason why these two picked this spot, past the fact that it is where five roads met., fact that it was convenient for people coming from Hillsfield and also Folsehill Road area. It had more of significance than that. And these two already knew and had planned on this spot all along.

Khalsa then pointed to one of the condemned houses and said, "Balbir oh ghar disda, os ghar vich ah ke Bawa rehnda hunda see." (Balbir see that house, Bawa used to come and stay in that house.) (Bawa was the nickname of Shaeed Udham Singh.)

I knew then why these two had picked this spot, why this was more than just for convenience. It was also to build a Gurdwara on a spot where Udham Singh stayed who had washed the shame off the face of Punjab by assassinating Sir. Michael O Dwyer who supported the slaughter of innocent people by Brigadier Dyer in 1919, Udham Singh also started the Indian workers Association (Mazdoor Sabha).

Silently both Papajee and Khalsa wanted to honor Udham Singh's memory, and the plot became available, and they took it. Papajee and Khalsa were complete opposites, and yet they were such good friends.

I asked them if they had bought it and they told me no but this would be it, they never told anyone the Udham Singh part.

Next day they had the rest of the team come onto the site, Sucha Singh and his younger brother loved the sight it was convenient for them. Babajee was fine with it, for him, it just did not matter as long as the Gurdwara was built. Sohan Singh Gaffa complained it was too far for him but a good site. Giani Naunihal Singh complained that it was too close to the pub. Papajee told him to reflect on the future when the community grows this pub will not be here the Gurdwara will grow, and the Gurdwara will take all the adjoining land. Where the current parking lot is used to be a street, and a car parts store; The Gurdwara grew as Papajee predicted to Giani Naunihal Singh.

The Site was agreed upon. That Sunday evening we as a family went to look at the site. I must have gone past this site so my times but now it started to take on a completely different meaning, suddenly it started to appeal to the heart.

CHAPTER FORTY-FIVE

Sikhs, Jews, and Catholics

Now that the land had been acquired, it was time to start the building process; Papajee had already started sending out teams to different people's homes to start the fund collection process, and that was going well. He had asked people to give generously, but also knew the limitation of the family needs of the people. After all, these were working-class people trying to settle down and build roots and bring their families from Punjab. At the same time were sending some money-back home to support their extended families back in the old country or pay off the debt that the family may have incurred to get them over to the UK. After all these responsibilities, there was not much money left over. However, to these people, call to give to their faith was strong, to build something for the community of the future and have a place where they could go and hold their faith and feel bit of the home they left behind was equally strong. So these people sacrificed and gave what each and everyone could afford towards the building fund, as it was labeled.

Babajee came one day to see Papajee. He came in and sat down had his cup of tea but was quiet, Beejee knew that something was on his mind, and he would say it in due time, to push him would only irritate him. That was never a good thing to do.

When Papajee came home, he saw Babajee sitting in the family room erect as he always did. Papajee asked him how he was. He nodded his head as if to say I am fine. Papajee sat down waiting for him to say what was on his mind. Papajee was worried that it was going to be another Bawa Singh fiasco.

Babajee finally looked Papajee in the eye and said, "Gumbat Jaroori han." (Domes are a must.)

You could see the look on Papajee's face. It was one of despair as to how am I now going to handle this request without upsetting Babajee.

Papajee was a very pragmatic man and to him the words like "are a must" were almost most like swear words. He had traveled and lived around the world and to him adapting to situations was the way of life.

He chose not to question Babajee's request but to honor it by saying, "Teek hai Nand Singhjee kooshish kararde han." (Nand Singh Jee fine, we shall try.)

Babajee was fine with his answer. However, Papajee now had to go about to try and find a way to honor his request. That weekend he asked me to go to Khalsa's house and have him come by to see him. Khalsa came back with me. He asked me what it was all about, but I said I did not know.

"What mood is your Papajee in?" was his follow-on question.

I assured him that he didn't look mad. I think this gave him some relief.

Papajee told Khalsa what Babajee had requested. Khalsa gave out one of those childish giggles that he did when something amused him and said, "Dharam Singh Gumbata vich Dharam betha?" (Dharam Singh is faith sitting in domes?)

To which Papajee replied visibly irritated with Khalsa, "Dharam tan building vich bee nahin, eh te dil laun dee gal hai oh da dil gumbat naal lag da, sanoo koshsish karni chahi de hay." (Faith does not reside in a building either. It exists where your heart is. His is set on a dome so we need to try.)

Khalsa looked over at Papajee with a look of disagreement but chose not to engage Papajee further who looked visibly irritated at him. Besides he was still on the bad list with Papaji from his India car trip.

So he just said, "Theek" (O.K.)

They looked everywhere to find an architect of an Indian background who could make the domes. It is worth noting that their reach was limited to areas around Coventry and Birmingham where they were unable to find an architect that could do such a design. When they were unsuccessful to find and architect who could design a dome Papajee had to let Babajee know. He feared the wrath of Babajee but surprisingly Babajee understood and accepted. I think he truly felt that he was heard, and his answer was very simple and short.

"Dharam Sihinan aje Waheguru the hukam nahin gumbat wasate jad honna fer ek de tha dau lag jannae." (Dharam Singh it is not yet the will of God that there should be a dome, when it is his will there be two instead of one.)

Papajee and Khalsa in this process had vetted local architects and they settled on Roland Sidwell and associates. Roland Sidwell was a very distinguish looking man who always wore a bow tie and had a well-groomed salt and pepper beard. He asked Papajee and Khalsa if the congregation was fine with the knowledge that a man of the Jewish faith was doing the design of the building. Papajee said that they told him actually it is quite fitting that a man of another faith do the design, because if we together build a house of God, then we may all have ownership in it. Besides for us Sikhs it is the way of our faith. A Muslim Sufi Saint by the name of Sain Mian Mir laid the foundation stone of the Golden Temple, our holiest place. This Temple has four doors one on each direction so that anyone from any direction can come to this house of God from any direction.

So a man of Jewish faith, Roland Sidwell drew the Gurdwara designs. The contractor picked was one recommended by Roland Sidwell, a small local contractor by the name of John O'Neil. Papajee and Khalsa met John O'Neil. When they signed the contract, Khalsa commented to Mr. O'Neil, "well Mr. O'Neil, a Jew is going to design the building, and a Catholic is going to build it. We have done our part for our faith by honoring all faiths." Mr. O'Neil replied and said, "if we could all join together and build our places of worship maybe we may have few wars, and the hate and intolerance that man has in the name of religion may go down. We are not building your church sir. This will also be ours, and I feel blessed to have the opportunity be able to do this."

CHAPTER FORTY-SIX

Laying the Foundation

The plans were completed and accepted by the city planners and were ready for implementation. Mr. O'Neil was signed on as the contractor. September 5th of 1965 was picked for the laying of the foundation stone of the Gurdwara (Sikh Temple.)

There were many discussions as to how this ceremony was to be carried out and who was going to lay the foundation stone.

First proposal put forth was by Giani Naunihal Singh was to have the Head Jathedar from Amritsar (there are five places of high reverence in Sikhism and the head priest of each one those places are referred to as Jathedar and the leader is the one from the seat of Akal Takhat in Amritsar). Khalsa quickly rejected this idea. In his mind and correctly so, Sikhism is an individual journey without a priestly order, and he felt that these people were no different than Brahmins. In principle, he had a very strong point to which both him and Papajee subscribed that Sikhism is a process of self-learning and one must take that journey on their own to reach the destination which is God.

They then looked to Papajee, Babajee asked him, "Dharam Sinhan tehn shroo keeta see tun neh pathar rakh de." (Dharam Singh you are the founder so you lay the foundation.)

Papajee looked at Babajee and I think he was a bit angry at him because he knew more than the others what was behind his request.

"Nand Singh jee hur kini der tusi mera imthian

lende rahon ge. Men sirf ek sevadaar han aur aap sarian to baager kuj be nahin. So eh neh pathar sare he rakan ge." (Nand Singh jee, how long will you continue to test my motives, I am just a sevadaar (Servant) I am nothing without all you all. If we are to lay the foundation stone, then we are all to do it together.)

I think it was only one time in my life that I saw Babajee get soft and feel humbled this was it.

He went over to Papajee and hugged him and said, "Bass maino tere tu eh he umeed see." (There, there this is exactly what I had expected of you.)

Sunday morning September 5th 1965 the weather was overcast with a mild chill in the air, but warmth, of people greeting each other at the site of the Gurdwara warmed up the air.

Their dream was now soon to be realized, the children were happy. Mothers were greeting each other women were coming over to Beejee and holding her hand and congratulating her.

Papajee was very tense, he always would get that way when there was a big occasion, going over everything in his mind to make sure that every last detail was checked off. He scanned the whole place with his eyes once then twice and then came over to me and said to gather up everyone, so we can start.

Khalsa as usual was late, well not quite late just late to Papajees time, which was an hour early than the expected time Papajee went to the site long before anyone else was there, and he had expected Khalsa there at that time also. I told him that there was a lot of time for him to show up.

"The Bloody man runs on his own schedule."

I told him, "Why do you need him here this early anyway?"

But he wanted him there. They were best of friends, and Khalsa knew by going late he was pressing Papajee's buttons, and he enjoyed being yelled at by Papajee. As soon as Khalsa got there Papaji went at him.

"Khalsa jee ah changavehla oun da." (Khalsa jee this is a fine time for you to show up.)

But Khalsa was never one to just let it go so he replied with his giggle, "Je main pela ah janda pher gussae kehde naal hunde men tan Balbir nu bachiaaa." (If I came early who would you have gotten mad at? I was saving poor Balbir.)

Meaning otherwise Papajee would have blown up at me, which was really not far from the truth. Papajee did not respond to Khalsa's retort told him to meet and greet the contractor and the architect and the other guests.

Khalsa bowed to Papajee and said, "Jee hazoor." (Yes my lord.)

These two were complete opposites, but somehow they made it all work.

Giani Naunihal Singh said the invocation prayer, the Ardas, and all of them Papajee, Baba Nand Singh, Prem Singh Khalsa, Sucha Singh Rurka, Sohan Singh Gaffa and Giani Naunihal Singh laid the foundation stone to the sounds of "Jo Bole so nihal, Sat Sri Akal." (He who says the following shall be blessed, and the reply was Sat Sri Akal meaning God is the timeless truth.)

I stood there. Papajee looked over at me, and he was not happy because he saw me standing there in protest. Maybe I could have handled it better, but I was young and to me; it was wrong. It was totally wrong. Saudagar on the way home walked over and grabbed my little finger and twisted it slightly to get my attention. He knew I was upset. He shook his finger at me to try and stop me from doing what I was about ready to.

When we got home Papajee asked me "What is the problem with you Balbir?"

My reply was no less curt, "I think you know what my problem is."

I must admit I was rude in my remark, but I was upset.

His reply was, "So now you will tell me what we ought to do and how we ought to do it?"

By then Beejee had come into the room and told me to be quiet and mind my manners.

I told her, "There is nothing wrong with my manners, but I do have an issue with the foundation stone laying ceremony we witnessed today."

Beejee was pretty upset with me by now and said, "Balbir chup karda ke nahin." (Balbir will you be quiet)

"Nahin, jo galat hai so galat hai daawe tan bhaut karde ke Auratan no poora haq hai ajj thouhada haq kedar chalegia? Tusin ena naalo ghat kam keeta?" (No I will not, what is wrong is wrong and needs to be stated, they make statements that we give equal importance to women did you do any less than any of them?)

I looked over at Beejee I was upset with the fact that they did not ask her to be part of the foundation laying stone ceremony.

Beejee tried to calm the situation by saying, "Mera haq hai maino appne haq lay larrana aunda tun bas kar." (This was my right that got violated. I know how to look after my rights you just let it be.)

Papajee and I did not speak to each other for a couple of weeks other than polite hello, I guess he felt I ruined his moment, but to me all I was doing was following the principle that they had brought me up with which was always to call a spade a spade. However it is hard to swallow when that gets turned around on the teachers.

We finally made up and I apologized to him, but over the years, I still feel to this day that she had a rightful place with the others because of her contribution to be part of those that laid the foundation stone.

I still see that women are not being treated equal, although they were given equal rights, but I still see that they are not given an equal place.

CHAPTER FORTY-SEVEN

Hate and Sound of Breaking Glass

In life we have both good and evil, love and hate, but we forget this and try and make this world fit into our lives a certain way but it is not that way. You know the way we want it to be, good, full of love where the only season is spring; flowers are in full bloom always. We forget that an autumn wind's cold breeze is going to blow all of it away, and everything is going to dry up. Then winter will set in, and we will long for spring, and a new spring will spring, and once again we fill our hearts with joy and hope. This process keeps the human race on a constant treadmill of hope and despair.

Only if we realized that we must face both sides of the coin in life, and that's how life is, but we still try and make meaning out of incidences that happen in our lives' decades later or in some cases even until our dying breath.

Such was the incidence for me that happened after the foundation stone was laid for the Gurdwara, few months after September the building was going up very nicely. The spring of hope was seen everywhere. People would go by on their way to work on their way home from work and check on how the building was progressing. Women would pick up their children from school and take them to the site to show them the future home of their faith. They wanted their children to feel proud of themselves and their community. People would speak to the building crew some in Punjabi and pat them on the back and others in broken English and shook their hands.

Some would take tea and Samosa's (Punjabi savory snack) for the crew. Mr. O'Neal once commented to Papajiee that it these people keep feeding my crew like this, they are going to put on so much weight, and they won't be able to lift the bricks up the ladder to the scaffolding.

The walls went up, and the building started to take shape then the window frames went in, and the windows were put in on Friday. I remember that Saturday going to town with Beejee and Papajee as was the ritual of everyone, and we went by and stopped at the site on our way to town and saw that the windows were in. We met a lot of other people that had also stopped by on their way to town, and they were all happy. Full of hope for the day when it would all be completed, and they could pray at their own place.

They were all full of praise for Papajee and Beejee for their efforts. Papajee and Beejee were never comfortable with praise; they felt it gave a person a false sense of himself or herself. So in a way they shut it out.

They would always catch the other person midway by folding their hands and saying, "Ohda shukar karo banda tan bhulanhaar hai ouhda ke shukar karna." (Praise God. Man is sinners therefore why praise him?)

We stayed there for good hour talking meeting, greeting people and listening to different plans for different things. Papajee would never stop anyone from giving his or her plans and opinions, and he heard a lot. Beejee was not always that receptive she would always try and tell Papajee to try and cut it short, but he would give everyone as much time as they needed to get whatever they wanted out of their system. He felt that everyone had the right to express how things should be.

We went to town and even in town people that we ran into from the community were all talking about how nice the building was looking and how proud they were of the place.

But good and evil share this earth together, for all the goodness in the world all it takes is a handful of hateful people to destroy people's hope and dreams, and that is what happened.

That Sunday early in the morning around 9 AM there was

a knock at the door that early on a Sunday morning a knock on the door rarely was good news. We were all sitting in the sitting room, and Beejee was cooking breakfast. I had just got home from the corner store with the Sunday paper for Papajee and he had just started to read it when the knock at the door happened.

There was a look on his face as he peered over his glasses and asked me to see who it was at the door.

By that time Beejee also opened the kitchen door into the living room and said, "Ene sajjre kaun? Suckh hove." (Who is that this early? Hope all is well.)

I opened the door, and it was one of Mr. O'Neil's men.

"Is yeh dad home?" he said in his thick Irish accent.

I told him yes, by then papajee was staring at the front door, and he asked the young lad to come in.

"What is the matter, why have you come so early on a Sunday morning?" Papajee asked him.

"It's the Temple building Mr. Singh. It's the temple building," the lad repeated.

"Get on with it boy. What about the Temple building what has happened to the temple building?" Papajee asked him trying to get to what was going on.

"They broke all the windows. With a brick, they broke all the windows every bloody last one of them, they did. Mr. O'Neil sent me to fetch yah."

Papajee looked at me and asked me to get dressed. Papajee turned to the lad and asked him if he had a car, and he said he had a van. Beejee gave the lad a cup of tea while we all dressed.

Papajee said that he, Beejee and Kashmir would walk to the site which was about twenty minutes from our house and they would inform Sucha Singh who lived close to the site and I was to go with the lad and collect Gaffa, Giani Naunihal Singh, Khalsa and Babajee and we meet at the site. I went with Mr. O'Neil's man and collected all the other members and brought them to the building site. Mr. O'Neil and his men along with Mr. Sidwell had already arrived. There was glass everywhere the lad was right there was not a single window that was left whole. A group of people had taken their time that night and made sure they sent a message that we don't want you here. I had read of Ku Klux Klan burning crosses and setting fire to Black people's churches in the American South. Because of the American civil rights movement, we saw those images being flashed on television weekly, but that was so far away there was nothing like that in Coventry.

We knew we were not equals here, we knew about the camera shop on Stoney Stanton road that said that we serve only the white man and his lady. We knew that the workingmen's club did not want us; we knew that the Red House pub had signs that we were not welcomed. But we did not feel that the level of hate had its path all the way to the doors of our Temple.

Giani Naunhial Singh was emotional and had tears in his eyes looking at the devastation; he uttered the following, "Ena gorian ne pehlan bande vande hunn ena ne rab vand leya." (These British first divided people, and now they have divided God.)

Papajee looked over at him in pure disgust and went over to him and held him by the shoulders and said, "Giani Jee saoch ke gal karo saoch ke, nafrat nu thuck, eh sadae guru da ghar hay ethe nafrat de koi jaggaa nahy, samane uadar chere jeherra disde neh eh gore nahin?" (Dear Giani think before you speak, spit out the hatred, this is the house of our Guru, there is no room for hate here, besides are these not Brits standing in front of you with a dismayed look on their faces?)

Mr. O'Neil was very upset, all he could muster up was, "There's your bloody neighbors for you."

Papajee tried to console him. Babajee was walking about by himself and came over and looked every one with that piercing look in his eyes.

He loathed despair, he looked everyone up and down and

got really angry and said, "Khabar daar jeh kise neh hanjoo sutia, guru de ghar nu mitan vale mit chuken ne aur mit chuck de rahen ge asin Chardi Kala vich rahen vaali Qaum han, Chardi Kala vich he rahan ge, Hazaar var sheshae taur lehn hazar var lava ge, en Mundyan nu das deh Dharam Sinahan Kal nu he hass de kam te aun aur kam karan mere Guru da ghar banaaa reh ne, os nu kush aue pyar bhare dil nal banonon myzoosi naal nahin mere guru de ghar Khusi aur pyar he hai." (How dare you shed a single tear, this is the house of my guru. People have tried to destroy it before, and they have perished and they will try and destroy it again and again they will perish. We people live in a state of ever bliss and no one will dare destroy that faith of ours. They can break the windows a thousand times, and we shall replace them a thousand times. Dharam Singh tell these boys to come to work with a smile on their face tomorrow for they are building the house of my Guru, and they should build it with a joyful heart not one full of sorrow and hate for in my guru's house, there is only Joy and love.)

Khalsa was quiet, and I was surprised that he had nothing to say, but he would not let me down.

He looked over at Mr. O'Neil and said, "Mr. O'Neil I am sure your insurance policy will cover the damages."

Papajee's mouth was open wide, and I thought if there was a swarm of bees around, they would be going right in there. I think he was so dumbfound that he just could not think of what to say to him. I started to laugh when Beejee pulled me by the arm and made me stop. At such an emotional time that was his remark, although practically speaking it was just the right question to ask.

Mr. O'Neil looked over at Khalsa and said, "You do have a unique perspective on things don't you Mr. Khalsa,"

The news was carried around the world we received letters from places far and wide, from people of all faith. What was disappointing was that we heard nothing from the local city politicians. It was if we did not matter as if we were not relevant, It was this one incidence in my life that started me on the path of thinking what place will I have in this England, what will be the place my children have in this country? I knew that I needed to move to a place where I felt a sense of belonging where when my children were born would feel they belonged. I had decided that I had to leave England.

England suddenly did not feel like home. It was all a false hope, a dream. This was not home. We were trespassers here or at least that was how I felt. I never shared this with anyone really until this day. But this one incidence changed me. I grew up with a big chip on my shoulder and this one act of hate by unknown faces caused me to indict a whole nation. I did not hear my own father's spoken words that day. I heard Giani Naunihal Singh's words. Hate is a cancer, a terrible cancer. It attacks in many ways. It attacked me. The hate of those bricks not only broke the windows of the temple that day, but they broke the windows of my trust, my trust in people, in a nation, in the teaching of my own faith. Hate is wholesome; once it takes root, it spares no one. I think for the first time I must confess that every time that I have been to England from California. I have always had a chip on my shoulder. I have always felt a little better than Britons. My silent protest, but it must end, for the propagation of hate. Fault does not lie in the hater. The fault lies with the hated. It is the hated that must spit out the hate; the hater has struck with the venom. It is victim who decides to keep or spit out the venom. Decades later as I write this I ask for forgiveness of all Britons and spit out the venom for that is the teaching of my faith.

Hate can only win if we give it a place in our hearts and minds otherwise it is powerless.

CHAPTER FORTY-EIGHT

Controversies and Issues

There is an old Urdu Couplet, "Zakeen ke noor se roshan hai raste apne, yeh woh chirag hai jene tofaan bujah na saka." (Our path of life is lit by our faith. It is a lamp that storm of adversity has been unable to extinguish.)

As long as human race has faith it will continue to rise from every storm it faces and build, it will continue to dream, it will continue to have hope, and it will continue to forgive. The human race is not built on hate; it is built on the idea that death does not bring about the end. Humanity survives; that human life is a precious gift and must go on. Life builds for the future. Life may not see what lies around the corner, but journey goes on in faith that tomorrow is worth the efforts today. Faith leads us to continue to put all storms of adversity aside and gives us the strength to push forward.

The wounds of the broken windows had healed. People picked up and started to dream again of the day when they are able to pray in their own place whenever they wanted, instead of a rented hall once a month.

During the months between the incidence of the broken window and the opening day there were few issues and controversies that came and grabbed the attention of the community. Other than the ongoing politically incorrect statements that Khalsa would make and Papajee would have to deal with.

The Comrade group came one day to visit Papajee and suggested that chairs be placed in the main prayer hall instead of carpets for people to sit on rather than the floor as it is the custom. They said that it was the twentieth century, and we were not living in the Punjab but in England, and we should sit on chairs.

Papajee always listened and tried to reason, and if reason failed he then asked others for input but in the end he made a decision. Once he made his decision, there was never any turning back. He always stood in the doorway and paused, looked both ways, but once he started his journey, he never ever looked back. He reasoned with the comrades that this was not our way. He tried to tell them that something's should not be changed. They would hear none of it. He heard them and then he discussed it with Khalsa if there was any reason that we can give why chairs were not the way to proceed.

Khalsa's first reaction was a predicted one "Sadi Marzi." (Because we say so!.)

Papajee then asked Khalsa to come up with a bit more compelling reason. Khalsa explained to Papajee that sitting on the floor had two reasons; one was that it caused everyone to be on the same level. He explained that when you get into the issue of chairs, those can and will become hierarchal, and they will start having a different type of chairs depending on the position of the person. Even if you try and avoid it, sooner or later chairs will represent status. He went on to say that when Emperor Akbar came calling on Guru Amar Das the third master of the Sikhs, the Guru asked that he must first sit and eat langar (community kitchen) with the congregation and then the Guru will grant him an audience. Even though he sat on a throne in his own court and was seen as the almighty and the other entire couturier had seats according to their ranks in his court.

However, in the court of the guru, there was no rank there everyone sat on the floor as equals so did the emperor. Papajee for the first time saw Khalsa give him an answer that he felt good about, and an answer where he did not have to get annoyed at him. Papajee asked him what was the second reason?

He again repeated, "Sadi Marzi." (Because we said so.)

He could not leave it there. He finished it off by saying, "Ena Nastika nu rab nehy samjah sakea ena nu tusi ke samjao ge Dharam Singh?" (These Godless men even God could not reason with how will you reason with them, Dharam Singh?)

Papajee although was a bit annoyed at Khalsa for his last remarks, but he also knew that he was right. There was no reasoning with these people.

Papajee said to Khalsa, "Maybe we ought to write to the Gurdwara Parbhandhak committee in Amritsar." (This is the elected body of Sikh clerics, Vatican of sorts to use the term loosely.)

Khalsa gave that chuckle of his and said to Papajee, "Dharam Singh oh lok Dharam de Vapaary ne Dharami nahain siastdaan han, ona ne siasi gal karni hai." (Dharam Singh those people are merchants of the faith. They are not men of faith they will only give a politically convenient answer.)

Papajee wrote a letter anyway, and exactly what Khalsa had predicted happened, the letter came back stating that if the Guru Granth Sahib was placed at a more elevated level than the chairs, then you may have chairs. Papajee was shocked when he read this. He told Khalsa about the letter, Khalsa chuckled and said I told you so. Papajee was stuck he did not want to use Khalsa's idea of because we said so, he asked me. I told him well you know the hall capacity would be an issue if you put chairs in there. If people sat on the floor it would fit more people in. He liked the idea, and that was what he used with the comrades. They agreed with him and said yes that would be an issue, so I suppose we should stay with sitting on the floor.

Beejee told Babajee what had happened, and he was furious at Papajee and went on a tirade. "Ena bandeian ne dowani ditti nahin sanno salahan dininde firde, tun hare ek de keo sunn da hain?" (These people have not given a penny towards the funds, and yet they give us advice as what to do and you just listen to everyone.)

That was papajee, he gave everyone the chance to speak their mind, and he always listened.

His reply to Babajee was classic, he said, "Nand Singh jee asin Sikh Han aur sanooo har waqat har ekk de sunn lehnni chahi de hai sunnen de naal he zindgi swari jaandi hai." (Nand Singh jee we are Sikhs, we must listen to everyone at all times, only through listening we shall gain knowledge to better ourselves.)

As this chapter ended another controversial chapter opened up, women of the community approached Beeje and said that they would like to contribute to the building in some way. Papajee said that was wonderful. Beejee told him, but you don't understand. We want to raise money and have a portrait of Guru Nanak on the front outer wall.

Papajee on hearing their idea changed his tune, he said, "Jaroori hai?" (Is it necessary?)

To which Beejee replied, "Han jaroori hai." (Yes, it is necessary.)

He knew that he could go against everyone but not the women folks. So he gave his blessings. Women all joined forces and started a collection drive throughout the city. It was something for the first time that was their initiative, their mark on the pages of history that they were going to put on. Papajee knew it was another controversy waiting to happen. Women all donated ten shillings each toward their cause. They saved from their shopping allowances and donated towards this common cause.

Once the money was collected, they hired a stone artist to carve out an inlay of Guru Nanak. Once this was ready to be put into the outer front wall, Mr. O'Neil asked the local newspaper to cover it. They took a photo of the stone and wrote an article, which said something like this;

"New Sikh Temple being built on Harnell Lane West gets the Statue of its God." The reporter did zero research and made it look like the inlay was a God that we were going to worship. If the reporter had done research, they would have known that Sikhs are totally opposed to any form of idol worship. Sikhism is a monotheistic religion that believes in one God that is timeless and formless. As soon as the newspapers were in the hands of the people, there was a line of people at our front door. People were knocking at the door all day long.

Papajee heard everything, from "We have now become idol worshippers, to when you listen to women this is what you get," to some very derogatory remarks as women's brain is in their braid.

He was very upset by all this, but decided to stand his ground; he decided that he was going to support the women's right to participate.

He gathered up the ringleaders of the protest and had a talk with them. He told them that in every community, including ours that nation building can never be achieved without the participation of women, and they had an equal right to put their share into this building, and if it is their wish that it be in the form of this inlay carving of the guru then so be it. The ringleaders pushed hard that it will lead to idol worship, he told them don't doubt or judge the faith of the congregation, with the marker of your fears. The congregation knows the difference of a picture hanging on the wall and an idol god. We are not worshippers of idols, so I urge you not make this an idol for that is not what it is and we will never let it become that. That Inlay of Guru Nanak went on the front wall and is there to this day as a reminder of women's participation in the building of the Temple, and Papajee's stand to protect their right to participate.

CHAPTER FORTY-NINE

The Big Day

As the building came to completion at the end of April and the final finishing touches were being made. The conversation turned to the Opening day and who will perform the opening ceremony. The team decided that the opening will be set for the commemoration of Guru Arjan Dev Ji's martyrdom day as it was on this day that the first ceremony on June 18th 1961 took place. In 1966, this day fell on May 29th according to the lunar calendar, which was the calendar that was followed at that time by the Sikhs. Guru Arjan Dev ji was the sixth master of the Sikhs who compiled the Guru Granth Sahib and also built the Harimandir Sahib (the Golden Temple) so it was only befitting that the day to have the grand opening be on the day of his martyrdom.

Once the date was decided the conversation moved onto who would be asked to perform the opening ceremony. It was papajee who suggested that we ask the Lord Mayor of Coventry to perform the ceremony.

Giani Naunihal Singh said, "Ek esai keven sade Gurdwarae da udghaten kar sak da hai." (How can a Christian be asked to perform the opening ceremony of the Gurdwara.)

Even before anyone could speak, Babajee spoke up, "Chup oh Giani, jeh Harimander de neh sadae Guru Sahib ek Musalmaan Fakir tun rakhwa sakde tan asin ek Esai tun Udghataan karwa nahin sakdae? Sade Dharam de Darwaje har vaaste sada khule ne. Dharam Sinah bas Laat Mayer he karege." (Giani enough! If our respected Guru can have a Muslim Holy man lay the foundation stone of the Harimander Sahib, then why can we not have a Christian perform the opening ceremony? The doors of our faith are open to all. Dharam Singh the Lord Mayor shall perform the opening ceremony.)

Once Babajee had spoken there was no more discussion. That was the final word; no one dared to challenge his authority as the elder.

Papajee proposed that Bawa Singh should be allowed to make the welcome address since he has been writing the newsletter for the past years, it was only befitting that he should be given the honor to welcome the guests on behalf of the community.

Papajee looked over at Babajee, Khalsa let out one of his giggles thinking that Babajee was never going to agree to it since him and Bawa Singh had a long-standing spat about Bawa Singh writing only after the contribution amount and Babajee's complaint that he was limiting the guru's contribution by writing only at the end of the amounts. So Khalsa was sure that Babajee was not going to agree. Babajee was a very wise person; he could put his feeling aside and see what was best.

Further, he would rarely go against Papajee, if he was going to do so he would say, "Fer gal Karan ge." (We will discuss it later) and talk to Papajee and Beejee first and tell them why he disagreed and ironed it out in private.

But he would not disarm Papajee in public. He did not say anything but raised his right arm slightly as to giving his approval. Khalsa bowed his head and started twirling his hat in his hands, as he would always do when he lost a round.

Papajee and the rest gave me the task to design and work with the printers to print the invitation cards. I was honored but at the same time nervous that would I be able to do it. Beejee saw my face and the concerned look that I was displaying, and she took me aside into the kitchen and said with a commanding look on her face, "Bae-fikar ho ke jor la sabah teek hove ga." (Put your effort into it fearlessly, and everything will turn out fine.)

Once I heard that everything changed, fear was gone and the task at hand suddenly took center stage. I met with the printers and wrote what needed to go into the card and got the cards printed.

Papajee called Bawa Singh to the house and told him that he was to give the welcoming address. His eyes looked like they were going to pop out of the sockets.

He was so surprised, he said to Papajee, "Dharam Singh jee eda vada maan, aur oh be mainu." (Dharam Singh jee this great honor and you are bestowing on me?)

Papajee had something else to say though but he waited until Bawa Singh digested what he was being asked to do and while he finished his tea. He would always tip his tea into the saucer and sip it from the saucer with a long sip sound. Papajee's manners were extremely Edwardian English and very proper, and this habit of Bawa Singh was like someone scratching a chalkboard.

He would always comment to us, "Pata nehin any thezeeb hai Bawa Sing vich par ah barri buri aadat hai, bhol ke be karke eh aadat nahin appnonin." (I don't understand it. Bawa Singh is a man of such proper manners and cultured but this habit of his is so bad, please never make the mistake of picking up this habit.)

Bawa Singh and the saucer would become one. This was some sort of a ceremony. It was a love affair between him and the saucer and the tea. Beejee would have to walk into the kitchen or the garden to laugh it off. Not only did she found it funny, she knew how much it offended Papajee. He would have to sit and quietly suffer through it. Once in a while, if she had a quarrel with him, and he would not relent she would say to him.

"Koi gal Bawa Singh to Chaa lai balandi han." (Ok then fine I will invite Bawa Singh for tea.)

It was a sure way for him to see the point through her way.

When Bawa Singh was on his last pour and ready to sip it. Papajee caught him before he could make his legendary sound.

"Bawa Singh ek hor gal be hi, thusin meharbani karke us din kise hinse baad only nahin akhanan." (One more thing Bawa Singh on that day in your speech, please kindly do not use the word only after any figures that you quote.) Bawa Singh's lips were stuck to the saucer as soon as he heard that, he did not sip but his lips were on the saucer, and you could see his head bent into the saucer I thought he was either going to explode, or he was going to suck the saucer in with his lips. Beejee was standing in the kitchen door with a half of a smile on her face. Papajee and I were just looking at Bawa Singh trying to gauge his next move.

Luckily, he neither sucked the saucer into his mouth nor did he explode. He quietly took the saucer out of his mouth and put it on the table and came back to his chair and sat down, folded both of his hands and looked over at Papajee and said, "Dhraram Singh jiee Parrae likhe ho ke Gwaran de man de ho. Teekh hai main na akha ga." (Dharam Singh Jee, an educated man that you are, you still listen to Peasants, Ok I will not say it.)

He was referring to Babajee as a peasant. Although Papajee was relieved when Bawa Singh agreed, but he was not sure that between then and the time of the speech, he would not change his mind. For now, his word was enough to give Papajee comfort to close this chapter and move on the next task at hand.

Papajee and Khalsa went down to the city hall or the council house as it is referred to in the UK and invited Alderman Rogers, who was the Lord Mayor at the time to perform the opening ceremony of the Temple.

Papajee and Khalsa also gave a card to the Lord Mayor for the entire city council inviting them to the opening day. Papajee said that the Lord Mayor was caught by surprise and did not know how to react. He accepted the invitation, and Khalsa went through the protocol with him.

Papajee said, Khalsa was very good and explained the reason behind every protocol. He told the Lord Mayor that you will need to take off your shoes as in the house of the Lord we need to walk in with clean feet and also to cover one's head if you have no covering we shall provide it for you. We cover our heads as a sign of respect of an elder as did Moses on the mount. He explained that if anyone smokes they should leave their cigarettes at home as Sikhs are strictly against the use of tobacco. He told him that there would be someone there to guide you and the rest of the guests that day that duty was assigned to me

After delivering the card to the Lord Mayor, they next went to the Coventry Cathedral where reverend Peter Berry and the Bishop of Coventry, were waiting to receive them. Coventry Cathedral was destroyed during the Second World War, and a new one was build next to the old one. The Queen opened the new Cathedral in 1962. It is a modern architectural marvel, a true piece of art.

Reverend Peter Berry was very close to the Sikh community; he was much loved by everyone, a gentle soul who always met everyone with a smile. He came to our services many times and was always asked to speak. He was always treated with the same respect that any Sikh preacher would be.

He introduced papajee as the founder of the Sikh Temple and also as my father since the Bishop knew me and had met me on a number of occasions during my work with reverend Peter Berry on a number of projects. Peter Berry also introduced Khalsa to the Bishop. Papajee said that Khalsa could not hold back even this time, he had to test.

He said to the Bishop, "Dear Bishop, I would tell you the protocol for the Sikhs but since you are a man of the cloth I assume you already know."

Poor Bishop kept quite if he said yes he would be lying if said no Khalsa would get the last word and would embarrass the poor Bishop.

Papajee said he had to step in and say, "Khalsa jee of

course, he knows."

And asked Khalsa that they should leave before he could do more damage.

Papajee wanted very much to have the founder of the Birmingham Gurdwara Boota Singh come on opening day but he found out that he had since moved Canada. Papajiee was a bit disappointed but life and time waits for no man, and we must accept and move on. He, however, tried to invite as many of those that had been involved over the years to come on the opening day as he could.

The excitement around April of 1966 was picking up; people were buying new suits women were buying new clothes for the children for the big day. Why would they not? This was a historic day for them. A day that comes maybe once in your lifetime if you are lucky when you could say, you were involved in creating history. It was not history that was going to change the direction of the world, it was, never the less a historic moment for the Sikhs of UK, especially of Coventry. Here they were only nineteen years earlier they had just earned a hard-fought independence from Britain, and now they were setting roots and helping in rebuilding the very country that once ruled them. Sikhs had lost their empire to the British, and later their beloved Punjab was split into two. The wound of 1919 Jallianwala Bagh Massacre was fresh in their mind. They were getting ready to raise their Kesari (the Flag of the Sikhs) emblem flag called Nishan Sahib on the very land that once ruled them. On the land whose people when they ruled they had a sign outside their clubs in India that read, **"dogs and Indians not allowed."**

The humiliation of the British Raj was still fresh, so it was not just a place of worship for them, it was a statement of their resolve, strength of their character, and of the faith in their tenth master's message, "Nische kar apni jeet karon." (Victory through determination.)

Beejee sewed the Nissan Sahib that was to be hoisted on the building on the opening day. Beejee learnt to sew much late in life, when we were to come to England, Papajee wrote to Beejee asking her to take sewing lessons, Papajee was a pragmatic man. He knew that there was no one in Coventry who Beejee could turn to sew her Indian clothes, which she would want to wear, so he suggested she learned to sew. Beejee went to the village vocational school and sat with girls who could have been her daughters and learnt to sew. I would tease her when she got home.

"Paarri parr kae aagay?" (Geek is back.)

She would smile and say, "jeh na hatia tan men ek kan te takouni hai" (If you don't stop I am going to put one right across your ears).

She was a fast learner and picked it up very fast.

The day fast approached. People were stopping by after work one after another offering their help on the day of the opening day Papajee assigned Harvdev Singh Dhillon and other young men to make sure that the people were properly managed, as large crowds were to be expected. Papajee was very detailed; he went over every last detail with them.

He invited Khalsa to the house. I remember Kashmir and I joking that this was behave yourself speech. Sure enough, that's what it was.

Papajee told Khalsa, "Khalsa Ji us din tusin chup rahaina meri doven hath ban ke benti hai koi gal badd gatt nahin karni." (Khalsa Ji please control yourself on that day, I implore you with both hands folded. Please do not say anything that is going to be an embarrassment.)

Khalsa looked over at him and said, "Teekh hai." (Ok Fine.)

Papajee was trying to make sure that everyone was under control from Bawa Singh's and Babajee's "only" spat to Khalsa's off-the-cuff remarks that would embarrass Papajee. He could come up with some zingers depending on how the mood struck him. I remember years later he was conducting a wedding ceremony.

At the ceremony, he turns to the bride and groom and said, "Look, you both look educated enough to me, so there is no need for me to give you any instruction about marriage. I am sure you can figure it out. Just make sure you don't go smooching in the streets, do that at home."

Between the utter shock and laughter that broke out among the people in attendance at the ceremony. I don't think anyone heard back of Papajee's head hitting the wall. Papajee went on to nag Khalsa for good few weeks of that outburst.

Finally, Khalsa got tired of it and said, "Ena tan mainu gharwali be nhain jherrak de jina tusin." (Even my wife does not tell me off as much as you.)Papajee finally stopped.

The original kitchen was not large enough to host a langar (community kitchen). On the opening day, the discussion came to what type food and refreshments were to be served to the non-Sikh invited guests. Everyone thought it would be best if sandwiches, tea and pastries were served. I suggested that we cater the event. I thought I had committed a cardinal sin when I said that.

Babajee looked over at me with a stern look and in his deep voice uttered, "Oh mundia hotel da khana asin ne guru ghar bharrana." (Hey boy we are not going to bring restaurant food into the Temple.)

I thought to myself what about the pastries then, but I kept quiet. Back in those days they all were of the belief that eating restaurant food was not a good thing. It was not wholesome, clean, and it was unnecessary spending. One must eat with the family and must eat a home-cooked meal was their way of thinking. In the case that there was something that they could not cook that was fine to buy as a necessity as was the case for pastries.

As May 28th rolled around, we got up early and once again reviewed already twice reviewed items that belonged to the community and was to be handed over to the community to be moved to the Gurdwara (Temple) from our house at number 7 Red Lane Coventry.

Khalsa was the first to arrive around 8:30 in the morning, followed by Babajee, then Sucha Singh with his brother and sons, then came Sohan Singh Gaffa huffing and puffing thinking he was late. Papajee told him to catch his breath. Finally Giani Naunihal Singh came. Also those people that were designated to take inventory and receive the inventory came. These were randomly picked people from the community along with Giani Naunihal Singh and Sucha Singh representative of the committee. Papajee handed them a list itemising the entire inventory and asked them to please count it. However, they unanimously refused to do so they said that would be a violation of trust that they had in our family who had served the community for these years and refused to count the inventory.

It was a very emotional day for all of us. On one hand, we were happy that we had come to the destination upon which we had embarked years back, on the other hand. It also meant that the Guru Granth Sahib was no longer going to be resident in our house. It was moving to the Gurdwara. It was if a senior member of the family was moving and we felt like orphans. Everyone went upstairs to the back bedroom of our house at 7 Red Lane and Giani Naunihal Singh did the ardaas prayer and Papajee put the Guru Granth Sahib on his head and brought it down where Beejee, Kashmir, Saudagar and I were standing with our hands folded. As papajee came down the stairs into the family room he stopped and Beejee got so overwhelmed with emotion that she broke down and started to cry.

I remember what she said to this day, "Pitta jee koi galti ho gay hove tan maaf karni." (Dear father if there was any mistake made please forgive us.)

For the Sikhs Guru Granth Sahib is a living entity the eternal guru. Why would it not be it is the guru, it contains the word of the six gurus and also many saints from around India. After all what is life? It is words spoken and as long as the words survive the person survives. So for Sikhs the uttered divine words of the Guru in Guru Granth Sahib makes the Guru Granth Sahib the eternal guru of the Sikhs as ordained by the tenth Master Guru Gobind Singh.

Papajee slowly moved to the front door and he would always stop and look right and then left and then leave the porch. But today he went straight to the car; I saw tears in his eyes also but he kept his composure. A caravan of cars left for the Gurdwara on Harnell Lane West. People were lined up outside to witness the event. We locked the house and were taken in a car to the Gurdwara. Once we got there Beejee did the oil ceremony in front of the doors. This ceremony is conducted when someone of importance comes to the door, oil is spilled on both side of the doorframe and then the person enters the house. I am not sure what the importance of the ceremony is but one can deduce that oil symbolizes something of value and spilling it is to symbolize the importance of the other person.

Guru Granth Sahib was brought and put in an area created for the housing. They did not install it on the platform that was built for it. It was decided that would be done on Sunday morning.

People had already come to help. Beejee assigned some young women with experience is making western food to work on the process of making the sandwiches, and people got to work in the true spirit of Seva (service), which is the hallmark of the Sikh faith. Everyone wanted to pitch in. There were not enough tasks that could be given to everyone. Beejee created tasks just to make sure everyone felt they were involved.

People were laughing making lighthearted remarks to each other all out of joy, some of the women folks teased me saying, "Balbir tere viaah te be asin eaden kam karana." (Balbir, we are going to pitch in like this on your wedding day also.)

I looked over at them and smiled and said nothing.

The work ended around five but people were not ready to go home, they wanted more of the day; they wanted to stay together and feel the joy and laughter. People that did not know each other got to befriend each other, talking about where they came from in the Punjab and how some distant relative was married into their village. Once finding that out calling each other relatives, somehow stretching to make a tie, a bond.

Sometimes Kashmir and I reminisce about those days and we have a laugh about the sandwiches and say, "Wonder if all those English guest were a bit disappointed with those sandwiches and pastries? What if what they really wanted was curry, and instead they got sandwiches? Oh well, we will never know. They get plenty of curry now."

While Hardev Singh Dhillion was busy figuring out how to control all the shoes next day, I was reminded of the very first day back in June of 1961 when Boota Singh and his brother taught Kashmir how to control shoes using raffle tickets. Giving one number to the person and putting the corresponding number in the shoes. The process had been the same all those years, but they were trying to figure out where to put them. They lined out a spot and assigned people that were going to perform which duty. Papajee double checked and tripled checked the ribbon and scissor and the cushion on which the scissor that was going to be put and presented to the Lord Mayor.

Babajee looked over at me and said, "O mundia tun eh kenchi wala sarana farrna." (Hey Boy you will hold the cushion with the scissors.)

I looked over at Papajee and the others and they all looked and smiled in agreement. What an honor that was for me and it was bestowed on me by Babajee. It meant a lot to me. Gaining the trust and respect of Babajee was no easy task, and I felt humbled when he said that I would stand next to them. I suppose he wanted to make sure that I was an example to other kids. Not sure what his motives were, but I felt very much humbled that I was going to be part of the ceremony.

Slowly around about 8 PM in the evening, people started to head home, asking if there was anything that needed to be done the next day, or if they need to come really early. Beejee picked few people that she needed to help early in the morning. Told the rest to come a bit later and enjoy the ceremony. No one ever questioned Beejee, whatever she said was accepted and those people that were asked to come early knew that whatever time Beejee told them was the time they needed to be there. Beejee told all of them to arrive by seven in the morning so that everything could be put out, and tea could be prepared for the invited guests on time.

We left around 9 PM. Beejee, Papajee Kashmir, Saudagar and I. Saudagar dropped to the back and slowed down. I slowed down to stay back with him. I knew why he did that. He wanted to have a chat with me and set me straight for the next day. He always did that, he was always nervous doing it. He never knew how I was going to react. I could be pretty explosive in those days, and I had very strong opinions, and they were never held back.

So he gave me that full mouth smile and then said, "Kuj kehnna gussa na Karin." (Need to say something, don't get upset.)

I looked over at him with a frown as if I was going to be put in my place.

I replied, "Kee?" (What?)

He looked at me and said, "Kal nu chup da daan bakshin jo marji ho jave, eh Papajee de lay baut ehm din hai apnni vachaar dharaa na tokin." (Please grace us with silence tomorrow, no matter what happens. It is an important day for Papajee; just don't throw your opinions around.)

I got his message loud and clear. I decided that I needed to keep quiet and not repeat what happened on the day of the laying of the foundation stone.

We stayed up until about 11 PM, when Beejee finally told Saudagar to go home; he lived in the next street and told all of us to get to bed that we needed to get up early the next day.

Saudagar asked Beejee what time he should be back in the morning she told him that we needed to leave by 6 Am in the morning. She knew that he was going to be knocking the door at 5:30 Am promptly. We went to bed but it was hard to sleep, I remember tossing and turning looking back over the day and the past years. How this experience had shaped my life and what effect it would have on my life going forward. Finally, I fell asleep when I heard Beejee call out to me to wake up and bathe. Papajee and Beejee had been up for a while, not sure they really went to sleep, or if they did, it was not for very long. There was always a routine that Beejee had to awaken me, and it had three calls to it. First call was "Balle put uth" (Balle is short for my name. Son get up), this call was very loving. I never woke on this call, the second one was "Balbir uth" (Balbir get up) this was the very polite but stern call, this got me tossing and sometimes, depending on when I went to bed got me up. But on most days, it took the third call to get me out of bed, and that third call was a bit louder but an order, Beejee was never really loud, but this call would be louder. "Balbir uth da ke nahin?" (Balbir are you going to get up or not?) That got me moving. However, today she just needed the first call I was up and in the bathroom brushing and bathing. She had laid out clothes for Kashmir and I that they had bought for us to wear for this day. New suits, new shirts and ties for the occasion.

I was coming out of the bathroom when there was a knock at the door, and it was Saudagar promptly there at 5:30 Am all ready to go.

"Ajje teayare nahin hoya?" (Your not ready yet?)

I gave him a frown, and he quickly hushed up. Beejee did comment, "Dekh Saudagar ready vee ho gya." (Look Saudagar is ready already.)

Saudagar looked pleased like the cat that swallowed the canary at Beejee's comment, but I chose to ignore them both.

We were all ready by 6 AM and ready to go to the Gurdwara; Papajee picked up the keys for the Gurdwara and we started the walk to the Gurdwara. We did not have a car, but we really did not need a car to go to the Gurdwara it was all within a walking distance. It was about a mile long walk. We would walk from Red Lane to Stony Stanton Road, over the bridge cross the road onto Leicester Causeway and make a first left from Leicester Causeway to George Street, then by the mosque a right onto Eagle Street by Peter's house left onto Leicester Causeway again and arrive at the Gurdwara. Papajee would stop by and talk with the Muslim people at the Mosque on his way to the Gurdwara and on his way back. They would always treat him with the utmost respect. They knew today it was the grand opening of the Gurdwara, So the mullah met Papajee early in the morning. He said he was hoping to catch us and give us his congratulations. Papajee told him that they were all welcomed, but they did not come. I suppose they wanted us to have this day. Papajee was very liberal in his views when it came to all religions, he would say if we can't respect one and another then we have lost Guru Nanak's message. How would, then would we learn? We are Sikhs, and our purpose is to learn and grow and the only way you do that is if you respect every man and his faith.

When we arrived at the Gurdwara, Beejee's ladies and other people were already waiting at the door. Beejee organized and assigned tasks to all of them, to get all of the tables setup, and mop where it was needed. All the other members of Papajee's team arrived.

Beejee asked one of the ladies to iron the Nishan Sahib (the Sikh Emblem flag) so that it was ready for hoisting. Hardev Dhillion and his boys set themselves up to handle the onslaught of shoes. Kashmir was giving them instruction as how best to handle it as a voice of experience, and they listened to him but they also carried on as they saw fit. Papajee told Giani Naunihal Singh, Babajee and Khalsa to prepare to do the Maharaj Parkash. (This is the initiation of Guru Granth Sahib onto the platform and opens it at random and read the first verse starting at the very top.) This would be considered as the wisdom of the guru and this is what every Sikh is to take and learn and apply in their daily life as they go about their daily business. Papajee was asked to carry the Guru Granth Sahib on his head to the platform and there onto the seat upon which it rests. The ceremony was carried out about 8:30 AM.

Once this ceremony was completed there were a large amount of congregations that had gathered. Papajee asked that Nishan Sahib be raised. A ladder was brought and people climbed onto the roof in such vigor that all safety rules went out the window. It was a small wonder no one fell and not break anything.

Giani Naunihal Singh went onto the rooftop and raised the Nishan Sahib and did the ardaas. There it was, the Nishan of Sikhs fluttering in the wind in the very country that had over hundred years subjugated the Sikhs and robbed them of their empire. Today the descendants of those very Sikhs, Brothers and sisters of Udham Singh had raised the Nishan of the Sikhs in Coventry the very city where Udham Singh first made his mark by starting the Indian workers association. Today the Sikhs made their mark as free men and women.

Time was getting close to 10 AM when the Lord Mayor Alderman Rogers and the other guest were expected was drawing near. Papajee asked us to usher everyone outside so that the ribbon could be put on the door for the Lord Mayor to perform the opening ceremony. The door was not be closed since Guru Granth Sahib Parkash ceremony had been performed (this ceremony is performed at dawn at every Gurdwara around the world after which doors of the Gurdwara are kept open for all).

Papajee asked Giani Naunihal Singh to stay in attendance to the Guru, and the only other person was Beejee left inside, who was to perform the Oil spill and welcome ceremony at the door.

Papajee and the rest of the committee members, Babajee, Sucha Singh, Prem Singh Khalsa, Sohan Singh Gaffa waited by the gates on the Harnell Lane West for the arrival of the Lord Mayor. A saffron ribbon was tied to the door. I was at the door with the cushion with scissors, and Papajee had a gold key (not real gold) to give to the Lord Mayor. People were trying to push to be in front or to be in a photo that would be a part of history.

Bawa Singh turned to Papajee and said, "Dharam Singh jee ena nu akho ke eh ashi taran kharan." (Dharam Singh Jee please ask these people to behave and stand properly.)

Babajee looked over at him and said, "Eh teri sarkari fauj nahn eh guru de fauj hay." (This is not your government army. This is the army of the lord.)

Papajee knew that the two of them were going to end up in a quarrel right there and then. Bawa Singh uttered under his breath "Gawaar" (peasant).

Papajee had to put a stop to their nonsense, so he just said in a stern voice, "Bass" (enough) and they both stopped.

Papajee did request the people gathered to be respectful and not to break the line when entering. It had some effect but not much. Once the Lord Mayor arrived, along with him also were most of the city council member, Peter Berry, the Bishop of Coventry, and the architect Mr. Sidwell the contractor Mr. O'Neil and his staff and other invited guests. The Lord Mayor looked very pleased as he witnessed for the first time the color, pomp and open-heartedness of the Sikhs. Papajee and Khalsa moved forward to greet them shake hands with them and introduced all the other members of the team. The Lord Mayor asked if we should proceed.

Papajee asked Babajee to walk in front, up the stairs with the Lord Mayor behind him. Babajee moved up the stairs with Lord Mayor following, with Papajee and Khalsa on his sides, and Sohan Singh Gaffa and Sucha Singh right behind. I was waiting at the top of the stair by the door with the scissors for the cutting the ribbon and Beejee on the inside with a bottle of oil to spill at each end of the door frame.

As the Lord Mayor cut the ribbon Babajee let out the Jakara (cry of glory), "Jo bole so Nihal." (He who says shall be blessed.)

To the reply came from the congregation of Sat Sri Akal (the God is truth) the whole chant is that he who says and accepts that God is the truth shall be blessed. The chant was repeated no end of time and seemed as if it got louder at each time.

Hardev Singh and his boys were ready to take the shoes from the guests and gave them a token and those that did not have any head covering were given head covering and those that did not know how to tie them were helped. Once this was done then I led them to the tables for tea and sandwiches.

People wanted to get closer, but we tried our best to keep the people at bay but with limited success. Once the guests were all finished with tea, we informed them of the process inside, we told them that we would lead and they would do as we would do.

Once inside an area was saved for these guests to sit, you could see the amazement in their eyes. For the very first time the India that they had heard about from the returning soldiers from the British India army, that splendor of color, majesty was before their very eyes. This was a church of very different kind, for the very first time they were sitting on the floor on the carpet without shoes and with their heads covered.

They must have experienced the moment Moses witnesses God on Mount and was asked to remove his sandals and cover his head as he was in the presence of God. This must have come alive for most of them. I am not sure, but that look of wonderment could be seen in everyone's eyes. Just few years earlier the new Coventry Cathedral had been opened with its modern architecture, and now this. New Sikh Temple raised from ground up in Coventry. First Gurdwara in the whole of Europe to be raised from the ground up. It was indeed a proud moment for Coventry, and that was evident.

Peter Berry commented, "Balbir indeed a wonderful moment in the Glory of God."

People were lining up to enter and pay their homage to Guru Granth Sahib. Papajee asked everyone to move forward as much as they could so that everyone could have a space to sit, but it was of no uses they could have moved forward as much as they could there simply were a lot of people, so it started to pile into the lobby and the even outside. The line in front of Guru Granth Sahib was endless, Papajee finally had to tell Khalsa to announce that everyone, please just be seated and wait to pay their homage after the formal ceremony of welcoming the guests, and the guest had a moment to speak and then the line could continue. People sat wherever they could. Khalsa introduced Bawa Singh to give the welcome speech to the invited guest. He spoke eloquently with pauses that he emphasized as he made his points. He gave in a very brief introduction on the essence of the Sikh Faith. He emphasized heavily on the need to perform service toward mankind. He mentioned the importance of community and also of the brotherhood of man. He mentioned the Gurdwara (temple) was built with donations from the community who gave their hard-earned money even though there was very little left after their weekly expenses, but they all gave as they could and no person was left behind.

He asked that the city council considers the adjacent land that belonged to the city be sold to the Sikhs as the need to build a residence for the Priest was still left to be accomplished.

He then went into how much it cost. I could see Papajee starting to bite his nails; he knew that Babajee and Bawa Singh were going to get into it right there and then if he mentioned the word only after the figures. Papajee was relying on the fact that Bawa Singh had promised him that he would not do it. So he said the cost to build this building has thus far was twelve thousand pounds then he stopped and looked over at Babajee who was looking at him with eyes that were saying you just dare. Bawa Singh just smiled and moved on without saying ONLY. I think that was the second celebration for Papajee the same day.

Papajee presented the Lord Mayor with the key. The Lord Mayor spoke and wished the community well and said that his door would always be open to the community. The Bishop of Coventry spoke and congratulated everyone on this great achievement. Peter Berry spoke and said that he had always been welcomed into the community with open heart and arms, and he felt as if he was member of the community.

The community honored Mr. Hancock the custodian at the Stony Stanton School with a clock for all his help while the services were being conducted at the school.

As the formal ceremony ended the guest were seen out to their cars and bid farewell the ceremony inside continued with the singing of Hymns of joy by different singers who had come from nearby towns and also local people. People could be seen everywhere, people that did not know papajee were asking other people what did he look like I think some of them were surprised that he was a clean-shaven Sikh. Everyone wanted to shake his hand; some old folks held his hand and kissed it. He was not used to this type of attention and was visibly uncomfortable with the attention. He truly believed that it was not his doing, it was the hand of God at play, and he was just the instrument of it. He believed that all he was doing was just being IN SERVICE OF HIS MASTER. The day ended with most people finally leaving around seven in the evening. Those that remained recited the Rehrass and keertan sohila the evening prayer of the Sikhs and retired the Guru Granth Sahib to its abode.

Papajee asked a senior retired member of the community a certain Beant Singh Chitti to volunteer to be the caretaker for the present time.

Beant Singh bid us farewell and closed the door behind us. Papajee looked up at the sky and wiped a tear from his eyes and folded his hands and uttered a Farsi couplet which translated says:

EMPTY YOUR HEART OF EVERYTHING EXCEPT YOUR MASTER (GOD), YOUR THOUGHT SHOULD AT ALL TIMES

GO TO HIM AND HIM ALONE.

This was what Beejee had told him also when he had doubted that he could not read Punjabi to the point he could read Guru Grant Sahib, how was he going to accomplish the task that he was embarking on? Beejee told him to start the journey and let God be your guide. Today they both felt as if they had been guided along with the hand of God while they were in his service.

CHAPTER FIFTY

Epilogue

Papajee kept his promise about having an election so that people could decide who would be the next group of people that would manage the Gurdwara. He had promised on the fourth gathering that when the Gurdwara was built on the first Vaisakhi he would let elections be held. That is exactly what he did. Vaisakhi fell on Thursday April13th in 1967 and the Saturday following April 15th 1967 was set up for a general body meeting, and April 16th was set forth as the day for the election. A list of voters and voter ID cards was prepared, and people were asked that on the day of the general body meeting those that wished to contest the election to give their names or before.

Papajee took all the ledgers and keys and any other belonging to the Gurdwara and placed them in front of the Guru Granth Sahib on the day of the election. The hall was completely full with people, but no names came forward.

Papajee spoke and thanked the Sangat and said that it was an honor that he, the humble servant of the community and his family were given this great task to serve the community. He said the accounts have been checked and audited, all the account books and keys and any other article that he had which belonged to the Gurdwara, were all in the front of the Guru Granth Sahib.

He said, "Guru Granth Sahib along with the Sangat are the rightful owners and whoever you elect to be the new members, I urge you, make sure that they serve the community, they put the welfare of the community before anything else even their family."

He said he had stated at the very beginning that I shall be servants of the community, and once my job was done I will step aside and would never contest any election.

He thanked everyone and said, "I have made a covenant with the Lord, that no member of my family will contest an election. Our task is now complete, and I beg your leave. Any mistakes that my family or I may have made in your service for those I ask your forgiveness. I am so happy that you can never imagine for the opportunity that you gave my family and me to serve you."

"Please move forward and now, grow and expand what has been started here."

He bowed in front of the Guru Granth Sahib, Beejee, Kashmir, Saudagar and I followed. As we reached the door everyone was on their feet and moved towards the door people blocked the door.

With folded hands and said, "Dharam Singh tusi sanoo shad ke nahin ja sakde koi be election nahin chonda." (Dharam Singh you cannot leave us like this. No one wants an election.)

Papaji said, "Eh thuhada haq bann da aur mera waida see." (This is your right, and this is what I had promised.)

They turned and told him that he had fulfilled his promise, and they order him as Sangat to continue. But he told them I have my covenant to consider that I have with my God. Then they told him to walk out of the door and onto the street and ordered us to stand there until you are told to move.

In the Sikh faith if an order has been given to you by the Sangat it is final, you do not challenge it, even the Sikh Gurus would never challenge an order given by the Sangat. We went out to the street and waited, the whole Sangat came out and said your covenant has been fulfilled you have left the premises, and we are now ordering you to come back in and continue to serve this community. There was nothing that he could do but obey.

He was brought into the hall the cries of "Jo bole so

Nihal Sat Sri Akal". The ledgers and all other articles that he had placed in front of Guru Granth Sahib were put on his head, and the Sangat said that you were commanded by the Guru to build this Gurdwara now the Guru's Sangat commands you to serve it. He did say to them that each year he would ask them to hold an election as their right. That is what he did each year and each year no one ever came forward. He continued to serve the Sangat from that day in April of 1967 as he had done from 1961 when first started the project until Beejee and him came to the USA in 1979 to be with us. He served his community for eighteen years.

Beejee died eighteen months after she arrived in the USA, Papajee lived to an old age of 84 and died with all his family at his side.

As he was leaving this earth, I told him, "Papaji we are all fine now, just think of your Sangat in Coventry and leave when you want."

A few moments later he was gone.

At his funeral his Grandsons, my son Omar and Kashmir's son Harman eulogized him. It was something that my son Omar said that summed up his life.

He said, "My Babajee (this term is also used for paternal grandfather) was a great man and many things to many people. To my father and uncle, he was a father, to us kids; he was a friend and grandfather, to a lot of you. He was the naked truth because he told you what you needed to hear not what you wanted to hear. He was very proud of what he had accomplished with his life all the titles he may have been known by, but the title that he was most proud of was Sevadaar (servant). He served his master with his heart and soul. So sleep well great knight, sleep well Sevadaar Manga Dharam Singh you have earned the name of Dharam (faith.)"

Khalsa moved back to India and died in his village of Pasla. Babajee remained in Coventry and lived into old age. I saw him one time after we had moved to USA. Sucha Singh remained in Coventry and lived into an old age and stayed active in the community. Giani Naunihal Singh moved away to London shortly after the Gurdwara was complete and died fairly young shortly thereafter. Sohan Singh Gaffa lived in Coventry then moved to the USA for a short while but moved back to Coventry and lived to an old age.

It is worth noting that they all became Sikhs and none of them ever shaved again, and they all became baptized Khalsas (the Pure).

How fitting that these great souls first purified their souls in the service of their master and then received his holy nectar of Amrit and proudly marched into heaven into the bosom of their lord chanting:

"WAHEGURU JEE KA KHALSA
WAHEGURU JEE KE FATEH"

THE PURE BELONG TO LORD, AND LET VICTORY BE TO THE LORD.

ABOUT THE AUTHOR

BALBIR SINGH RAGI, is a serial high tech entrepreneur in Silicon Valley. Between running various successful tech companies, Balbir is a community member who has been involved with helping to establish the Punjabi language as a part of the curriculum at several Universities in California. Ragi is also one of the founders of the Fremont Gurdwara (sikh temple) in California.

Semi-retired, he spends his time with his family, grandsons, and advising aspiring young entrepreneurs with their companies. Balbir Singh Ragi also writes and lectures on the topic of management. He lives in Northern California with his beloved wife, Parminder.

Dharam Singh Ragi Herian in California Photo Circa 1990
Photo Courtesy Balbir Singh Ragi California USA

Ground laying Ceremony September 5th 1965 left to right Sucha Singh Rurka

Baba Nand Singh Kukran, Dharam Singh Herian, Sohan Singh Gaffa Littran, Prem Singh Khalsa Pasla
Photo courtesy Balbir Singh Ragi California USA

Ground laying Ceremony September 5th 1965 left to right Jhalman Singh Rurka, Giani Naunihal Singh and Tulsa Singh
Photo courtesy Balbir Singh Ragi California USA

Ground laying Ceremony September 5th 1965 Left to right Architect with the bow tie Roland Sidwell, and his partner in the back J, O'Neil the contractor and his daughter and other members of his staff Photo courtesy Balbir Singh Ragi California USA

Ground laying Ceremony September 5th 1965 Ladies and Children of the Sangat
Photo courtesy Balbir Singh Ragi California USA

Ground laying Ceremony September 5th 1965 left to Raja Singh Morawali, Dr. Kashmira Singh Ragi holding the mallet Jhalman Singh Rurka holding Parshad
Photo courtesy Balbir Singh Ragi California USA

Ladies from the Gurdwara , photo taken with Beejee before she left for USA to join her sons 1979.
Courtesy Balbir Singh Ragi California USA

Early Photo of Gurdwara Sahib taken by a Kenyan Photographer sometime in the late 60's
Photo courtesy of Balbir Singh Ragi California USA

Bibi Nasib Kaur and S. Dharam Singh Ragi Herian
Courtesy Dr. Kashmira Singh Ragi California USA